The Great Homecoming

The Great Homecoming

Anna Kim

Translated from the German by Jamie Lee Searle

GRANTA

Granta Publications, 12 Addison Avenue, London W11 4QR
First published in Great Britain by Granta Books, 2020

Originally published in German as *Die Grosse Heimkehr* in 2017 by
Suhrkamp Verlag Berlin.

Extracts from *I Saw the Truth in Korea* by Alan Winnington (People's
Press Printing Society Ltd, 1950) reproduced with the kind permission
of the publisher.

The publication of this translation was supported by a grant from
the Federal Chancellery of the Republic of Austria
(Bundeskanzleramt Österreich).

Federal Chancellery
Republic of Austria

A CIP catalogue record for this book is available from the
British Library.

1 3 5 7 9 10 8 6 4 2

ISBN 978 1 84627 655 2
eISBN 978 1 84627 657 6

Typeset by Avon DataSet Ltd, Bidford on Avon, B50 4JH
Printed by CPI Group (UK) Ltd, Croydon, CR0 4YY

www.granta.com

MIX
Paper from
responsible sources
FSC® C020471

For my father

The Other holds a secret: the secret of what I am.

Jean-Paul Sartre, *Being and Nothingness*

Note on romanization −

For place names and names of known politicians, like Park Chung-hee and Syngman Rhee, I have retained the customary spelling.

− and on the pronunciation of names:

'Ch' is pronounced as the 'ch' in 'cheek'. The only exception is the Japanese word 'Chōsen': here the 'Ch' is pronounced like a 'J'.

The vowel 'ŏ' should be pronounced like the 'a' in 'always'.

The double 'e', like in 'Yunmee', is pronounced as a long 'e'.

1

The thirsty late afternoon light made the pine trees seem greener, lusher, and cast a shadow-play between the walls. This was the light I remembered. I had seen it for the first time many years ago, when it brought the drab façades of the old town to a shimmer; later, the monsoon rain had veiled all colour, transforming the city into a steaming basin, the sky into a lead-grey expanse, and yet the many odours, cooked by the summer heat and infused with damp, were more intense than I had known anywhere else. Today, however, here in the former American missionary quarter in front of the only one-storey house on the street – surrounded like all the other buildings in the neighbourhood by a brown wall that censored the view, part of a labyrinth of which only fragments survive in old Seoul – it smelt mouldy, neither of spices nor of fruits. A rusty drying-rack with wrinkled washing stood on the pavement, and music trickled out from inside the house; the mewling trumpet, the pitter-patter of the piano, the plodding bass, and finally, louder than the accompaniment, Billie Holiday's voice.

I had just decided to wait for the end of the song, to use the stillness between the tracks to knock on the door, when a man's voice pushed through the crack in the window.

'What are you waiting for? Or are you spying on me? If you are, then you're a goddamn awful spy, so I certainly hope you're the translator. Come on in, then, seeing as you're here!'

I didn't catch the last, mumbled words. While I was still

considering whether or not to ask for clarification, the voice barked: 'Come on, what are you waiting for?'

As soon as I stepped inside the house, I found myself in a place that consisted entirely of music, a cavern of noises and sounds. Some time passed before a picture began to develop, the surroundings filling slowly with colour and detail; I made out plants in pots, cushions on the couch, pictures on the walls, figurines and books on dark shelves that swallowed the scant light. I thought there were only a few books at first, but in fact they were everywhere, even stacked on the floor – I was in a library.

Only now did I see the man who was crouched on the floor; my colleagues called him 'the archivist'.

'You look Korean,' he said, staring at me with unsealed eyes. 'Not a bit like a German.'

Yunho Kang studied me from beneath the cover of twilight; I was standing in the spotlight of the window. 'I'm both,' I answered.

'Did I understand correctly that you were adopted by a German couple?'

'Yes.'

'How old were you?'

'I was four.'

'Can you still remember Korea?'

I shook my head.

'How could you, really. Is this your first visit?'

'No, my second.'

'What do you know about your homeland?'

I looked at him, puzzled; he rephrased his question: 'I mean, have you studied Korean history? Or the language?'

'Both,' I answered.

'And you speak English?'

'I lived in London for a while.'

He tapped a cigarette out of its crumpled pack and lit it.

'Were you surprised by my request?'

I hesitated; I don't know why.

I eventually said that I'd been asked to translate a few times already – there was clearly a demand for it. He looked at me for a moment, then nodded slowly. 'You're very tall,' he said, 'and your ears are big too. As big as mandarins.'

He smiled.

'How long have you been working for the Maryknoll order?'

'Two weeks now.'

'What are your duties?'

'I deliver food.'

'To the old and sick?'

'Mainly to the old and sick. Sometimes I help out in the office too.'

'Why do you do it? Couldn't you find any other work?'

'I haven't really started to look yet.'

He nodded again. He asked if I could understand him, or was he speaking too quickly?

'Just about,' I answered.

'*Just about.* Where did you learn Korean?'

'At university.'

'*At university.*'

Yunho repeated my sentences, as though to make sure he had understood me correctly.

A little later, he said: 'You have a Japanese accent.' 'I have a Japanese accent?' I asked; he too had an echo. It was my intonation, he explained. 'I don't sing, I speak,' he said, 'I push the words in front of me. When you speak, you whirl them up, you throw them into the air.'

He took a deep drag.

'Don't worry,' he said, slowly exhaling the smoke. 'It sounds sweet.'

When I answered, I made a conscious effort to neither throw nor whirl. There was a singsong to his voice as well, I said, while I forced mine to make an emergency landing. He looked at me thoughtfully. No one had ever told him that before, he said, it must be his navel laughing; and as if to make sure that no laughter could escape from it, he laid a hand on his stomach.

Yunho was seventy-eight years old, and besides Korean spoke fluent Japanese and a little Chinese. His hair was silvery, wavy, shoulder-length. Because he thought his bald patch was getting bigger, he carefully eyed each and every hair that fell out, inspecting the root before he placed it in the bin; he didn't throw it, but placed it, just as he didn't walk, but strolled, his dark pinstripe trousers flapping around his legs, the contours of his lower abdomen glinting through his white shirt. The trousers, which had been worn thin by too many washes, reached far above his middle, and were pulled up further still by grey braces. Yunho never went out without his cane, gloves, hat and glasses, the latter having belonged to his father, and he didn't really see better with them on, even though he told himself he did.

He used the polite form of address when speaking to me, which I wasn't used to; I knew spoken Korean only from my childhood nanny, Yŏnghee Maria, whom I had always called Young Maria, despite being surprised that an elderly woman, who at the time seemed ancient to me, would refer to herself as young, even though she no longer was; I thought she called herself that because she had never been young.

Young Maria took me under her wing when I was a child,

feeding me Korean sentences and delicacies while she carried out chores around the house. In the evenings she would bring out her ironing board, which was an old pillowcase stuffed with newspapers, and crouch down on the floor with a pile of clean washing next to her. She didn't pass the iron over the clothes in a gliding motion, but instead merely pressed it down; she was afraid of the steam and claimed that the device was snorting with rage. We ironed in the evenings, when Monika and Wolfgang (who I didn't want to call Mother and Father) had gone out, and I lay happily in the yellow kitchen light next to Young Maria on the strangely soft linoleum floor, while she pressed the laundry and told me stories about a time in Korea when the noble young ladies, shrouded in floor-length silk cloaks, their faces concealed beneath their hoods, were permitted to wander in the dusky glow of the gas lanterns. Men wouldn't walk the streets at this hour; only the blind and royal messengers were allowed to mix with the ladies. The blind masseurs would take out their flutes and begin to play, and their sad melodies unfurled through the city; sometimes a window would open and they would be invited inside. The dogs, seduced by the strains of the flutes, struck up a song of their own, punctuated by the rhythmic knocking of the working-class women pounding their laundry with wooden clubs.

She sighed, stroked my hand and said that the sound of the birds crying was much more beautiful, and I called out: 'But Young Maria, birds can't cry!'

Whenever I think of Young Maria, I remember the doll I used to take with me everywhere, to school, to my piano lessons. She slept in the front compartment of my rucksack, and sometimes beside me on the couch; she didn't fit in the pockets of my trousers, and my skirts had none – a major shortcoming which led to their banishment into the Siberia of my wardrobe. One day, when the doll was lying in her usual spot on the floor next to me, Young Maria took off her headscarf and used it to strap the doll to my back. Now I could carry her like a Korean mother carries her baby, she said. In Korea there were no prams, she explained, and the women always had their infants strapped to their backs; much more practical than pushing them around in some little house.

As I galloped across the living room with my new adornment, a thought occurred to me. Had I been carried on my mother's back too? I asked. 'By your mother?' asked Young Maria. 'Yes,' I answered, and pleaded with her to show me.

She looked at me for a long while. In spite of her brown eyes she had a gaze which was bright, I would even say it was cool, alert and hard, but on that day it was dark and soft, framed by short curls. She had treated herself to a perm at the hairdressers, though normally she did it herself, letting me watch while she put in the curlers and sprayed on the white fixing spray, blurting out the most peculiar swear words in the process.

I remember that she sighed loudly, before eventually answering: 'No, Hannaja, no. Your mother didn't get to know you, she parted ways with you immediately after the birth. She left you with the pastor, who introduced you to your German parents.'

She left me with the pastor who introduced me to my German parents.

These were the words that later prompted me to give notice at my job and hand back the keys to my apartment; the words that put me on a plane and brought me to a country where I knew only a single living soul.

After I arrived, I realized that I had forgotten to take any lightweight clothes with me, so I was constantly on the hunt for air conditioning, open windows and doors. I slept through the first few days, disorientated by the time difference; I thought it was evening when it was actually morning, and the light confused me too, behaving differently from what I was accustomed to: like the bright light of spring, even though it was late summer.

Immediately after my arrival in Seoul, I made an attempt to find Young Maria. But her name, Yŏnghee Jang, made it impossible. It was too normal, too *ordinary* – too many people had the same name.

Eventually I set off to the Maryknoll brothers' mission, with a map of the city and a dictionary in my rucksack, in the hope of finding work that could keep my head above water for a while.

'Blue moon,' sang Billie Holiday; and indeed we were on a blue moon, the floor lamp between us cast a bluish shimmer over the low tables and the cushions scattered across the wooden floor, it even tinged blue the smoke rising from the cigarette in the glass ashtray – and Yunho's profile, which, because he avoided my gaze, I was able to study at leisure. After a while, I started to feel that I had before me not a human being, but a photograph, an image of light and shadow inhabited by a voice and a touch of smoke; it seemed fitting for this world, in which I dreamt my way through the days and stayed awake through the nights.

'Hanna,' he said – and from his mouth it sounded like *hana*, the number one in Korean, and in my head I counted on: *dul*, two, *set*, three, *net*, four – 'will you look for your parents?'

I had been waiting for this question; I had hoped to wait in vain.

'Probably. I haven't decided yet.'

He nodded. I should think about it carefully, he said, for it was impossible to know who I might find. Even the people we know best surprise us with their secret lives.

'Secret lives?'

'Yes. Everyone has secrets. Yourself included.'

'And you?'

He held my gaze, but changed the subject.

'Am I right in thinking you're a translator?'

I had resolved to be cautious, so I said: 'From time to time.'

'And what languages do you translate from? English, Korean?'

'From English into German.'

'And from Korean?'

'Less often.'

I reached for a cigarette. It was a year since I had last smoked. 'Why do you ask?'

'I would like you to translate this letter for me.'

'A letter?'

He had received it a few days ago, he said, a letter from America, but he couldn't read it. Yunho laid it on the table; the envelope was snowy white, the address written in block capitals, the handwriting angular. He cleared his throat and mumbled, as if wanting to hide what he was saying, that he believed the letter contained important words, and I was to tell him what they were.

He gave me the envelope, and I opened it and unfolded the piece of paper. It came from a retirement home in Richmond, Virginia. A Mrs Linda Miller wrote that Mrs Eve Lewis had 'departed peacefully from this world' on the night of the fourteenth of the previous month. As Mr Lewis was already deceased and Mrs Lewis had no children, nor any relatives in the US, the retirement home had decided to send the news of her passing to the only address that had been found among her documents. Perhaps the addressee could inform Mrs Lewis's relatives in South Korea? 'With sincere thanks and sympathy, Linda Miller.'

I didn't know what to say when I noticed that Yunho was crying. I stubbed out the cigarette, sat down next to him on the floor and passed him my handkerchief; it was crumpled. He took it, wiped the tears off the letter and said: 'So Eve is dead.'

'Eve.'

He repeated, this time with a trace of a smile: 'Eve Moon.'

He had never been able to pronounce her name correctly, he said, there was no W or V in Korean, just a B. He looked at me thoughtfully. Why on earth had she chosen such a difficult name? he asked.

He rummaged around in his trouser pocket and pulled out a pack of cigarettes. I said, without giving it much thought, that perhaps she had only intended to be addressed by Americans. He took a deep drag and nodded carefully, before agreeing that could be it. His silence and the crackle of the vinyl forced me to speak, and I heard myself ask: 'Who was Eve Moon?'

He looked at me, his eyes clear and still. That was a question to which there was no easy answer, he said.

'Do you really want to know who Eve was?'

He tapped the last cigarette out of the pack and lit it.

'The simple answer is this: she was Mrs Henry Lewis, Eve Lewis. But she was also Eve Moon, Yunmee Moon and Mizuki Takahashi. She had many names. I can still remember clearly the first time I saw her: in Johnny's tiny room in Seoul, over fifty years ago . . .'

★

9

From that afternoon on we met daily in that room, where all the clocks kept different times – the cuckoo clock on the wall, faster than the alarm clock on the dresser, which in turn was nimbler than the grandfather clock with its deep gong – and Yunho told the story, his voice accompanied by and never breaking free from the rhythm of that many-voiced ticking, of the events in Seoul and Osaka in the years 1959 and 1960.

Seoul, 1959

2

I remember the song drifting out through the door, the soft howl of the guitar, the drums following the rhythm in a way that seemed tentative but was in actual fact confident, nonchalant, even; yet it wasn't these sounds that filled the space, but the heavy late summer air, the heat of the afternoon, and even though the corridor I was making my way along had no windows, the sun found its way in regardless, seeping between the cracks in the doors and dividing the floor into sections, an almost black one followed by a golden-brown one, my short journey accompanied by distant music, punctuated here and there by the noises in the building, the clatter of pots and pans, the clack of a blade against a wooden board, the murmurs of the landlady who had eyed me sullenly.

Finding his door ajar, I pushed it open. Johnny and Eve were dancing in an embrace, cheek to cheek, their eyes closed, while 'Sleep Walk' played on the gramophone, sung by the brothers Santo and Johnny; the latter my friend's namesake. Back then, I was convinced that nothing could separate them, Johnny and Eve, *Eve and Johnny*, they moved on that small spot between the bed and the desk, caught in a perfect moment.

I watched them for far too long. I sat down on the floor outside Johnny's room. I didn't know where else to go; I didn't know anyone in Seoul besides him. As I waited, the scent of freshly boiled rice rose up from the kitchen on the floor below, the aroma of crushed garlic, diced chilli peppers and roasted fish. A clink of crockery, then the landlady scurried into the living room with a tray. I heard her husband's voice: what had taken her so long? She didn't answer. Had the student paid yet, he asked. She hadn't had a chance to speak to him yet, she said, he had a visitor. 'A visitor,' I heard, 'who?' 'A young woman,' she said, 'or maybe not.' 'What's that supposed to mean?' he asked. 'Don't speak in riddles!'

It was Eve Moon, she answered. 'Eve Moon,' he questioned, his voice becoming louder, 'Eve Moon?' 'Yes,' she whispered. Unbelievable, he thundered, this wasn't a brothel, what was he thinking, taking that whore up to his room! 'Quiet down,' his wife interrupted him, 'the whole building can hear you,' and she closed the door.

Only at this moment did I notice that Eve had stepped out into the hallway alongside me. I couldn't tell how long she had been listening, for her expression revealed nothing. Her face was rigid, a mask. Yunmee Moon, or, as she called herself, Eve Moon – curled hair, freckles whitewashed with face powder, lips painted red – to me, her beauty was too calculated. Later, much later, once Johnny was already on his way to North Korea, I learnt to differentiate between real Eve and unreal Eve.

She drifted over to the stairs and paused for a few seconds, as though wanting to make sure her exit would go unnoticed; me, she ignored. She slipped out of her shoes, tucked them beneath one arm and padded down the steps to the ground floor, opening the front door only slightly; she didn't need much space to slip outside.

I knocked on Johnny's door. He opened it, a cigarette in the corner of his mouth, a beret on his head, his hair glistening with pomade; he looked sleepy. When he recognized me, he laughed and hugged me again and again. 'Yunho,' he cried,

'Yunho, what a surprise, what are you doing here? Come in, come in at once!'

Johnny and I grew up in western South Korea, in Nonsan, which was just a small settlement back then, too small to appear on any map. We became friends because of the confinement of the village, and remained friends in spite of it. Johnny, who was constantly searching for ways to propel himself from Nothing to Everything, and I, so desperate to believe that time stood still in Nonsan that until my first day of school I refused to learn the days of the week; I knew only Saturday and Sunday. Rice paddies and mountains, *non* and *san*, and between the fields endless long paths along dykes wide enough for one bicycle or two pedestrians. Every day we children trekked to school in the neighbouring village, two hours there, two hours back. We walked there in the bright light of winter, which transformed the undulating valley into a sea of white, and in the yellow light of summer, when the many shadows cast onto the cracked earth by the shrubbery, grasses and thatched roofs were joined by additional, bizarre ones, abstract formations from another world. Back then I believed I couldn't live anywhere but here, and even long after I had left Nonsan it seemed to me that I deserved nothing but misery and worry, for I had left paradise.

Johnny was the youngest of five children, the only son, and I was the youngest of two sons. My mother worked as a housekeeper for his father, the school director, my father farmed his father's fields, and I spent my afternoons in their courtyards and gardens. My family's house was located by the boundary wall of their property, right next to the main entrance, for ours was the gatehouse, and one of my father's tasks was to turn away unannounced or unwanted visitors and let in the expected ones. Our house was tiny, consisting of a kitchen, two rooms and a hall area, a *maru*, which was used as a living room and mopped daily by my mother, while I sat in the classroom and learnt Japanese, maths and history. Three years later, the Japanese became Korean. Johnny's living room was cleaned by Yuri, the housemaid, as were all the other rooms belonging to the director, and she complained that she did nothing all day but sweep and scrub; this house was so big that if you peeped in from the front door, the furnishings could fit between your index finger and thumb.

'Did you know it's haunted?' Yuri asked me one afternoon as I came home from my lessons. 'That's why Mr Kim got the property so cheaply.'

For the first few months after the family's arrival, she said, the whole village had waited for the ghost to eat up the director's children, but nothing had happened. They had spied on the family in vain, peering in through the cracks in the fence. Eventually they had given up – but I should be careful, she said, fixing me with her dark eyes, the danger wasn't gone yet, if I walked along the wall at dusk I would see them, the people wanting to catch a glimpse of the cursed house and the evil spirit, they came from far and wide.

She hurried into the kitchen, giggling. I stayed and thought of the gnarled maple tree that stood on the outer limits of Nonsan, where your gaze was met by an expanse so vast that not even the all-belittling sky could dominate it. I asked myself whether this ancient deciduous tree, its lower branches tied with white strips that fluttered in even the slightest breeze, leaves in captivity, had been decorated for this ghost or for another, and whether the delicacies in tin bowls, offered to its roots at regular intervals by unseen hands, were intended to appease it: this spirit, which had its sights set on my best friend.

★

I couldn't get it out of my mind. I wanted to see it, I had to see it, and so we searched for Yuri's evil spirit, Johnny and I. We didn't find it, or any other spirits, but we did find phantoms; apparitions of grey and brown whose clothes hung off them in shreds, or was it skin and not cloth? As hard as we tried, we couldn't make them out, their hands and faces were so filthy that they were barely distinguishable from the colour of the earth, they roamed the streets like lost shadows searching for their bodies. They didn't speak, but gurgled, wheezed and gaped, their gazes clung to ours, and we found ourselves staring into a face that had melted away, that was missing a nose, the mouth deformed and the eyes too, and we ran away screaming. 'Don't go to the barley fields, never go to the barley fields,' Yuri had warned us, for that was where they lived, in between the blades of grass: the leper colonies, exiled by the healthy, hiding away in a thick pelt of barley and emerging only when children drew close. When you were least expecting it, the green curtain would part and they would jump out, as quick as lightning. They would grab your arms and pull you into the field; there, they would tickle you.

'And once you're helplessly winded from laughing, they take out a knife and slit your belly open.'

'With a knife?'

'They crave children's intestines. That's what they feed on.'

Yuri grinned as I hid behind Johnny's back. 'Don't be scared, Yunho,' she said, 'you just have to throw sand on them, then they'll run away, because it itches and stings their open wounds. But if you throw earth on them they'll follow you, because it's good for their inflamed skin.' She squatted down on the floor, filled two canvas bags with sand and pressed them into our hands.

So armed, Johnny and I dared to approach the edge of the

barley field. The grain was still young, pea-green, the sky a deep blue and streaked with veins of white, and the clouds were drifting by quickly, as though the day was being wound forwards. The sea of grain shimmered in a play of light and shadow. We stared into its density. All of a sudden, the barley stalks just a few metres away from us began to twitch ominously . . .

We ran away screaming, reaching into our bags and scattering sand all around us. Mr Im, the egg vendor, who carried a big wooden crate on his back that contained live chicks and ducklings as well as his entire assortment of eggs, got some of it in his eyes. He cried out, lost his balance, and slowly, very slowly, tipped over backwards onto the ground, crate first, paddling his arms and legs in the air like a hapless beetle. Before we could make ourselves scarce, however, he was back on his feet. He grabbed us by our collars, and for a whole month we had to walk through Nonsan for him, calling out: 'Buy your eggs, chicken and duck eggs, from Im Junbing, the Egg King!'

Beyond the barley fields lay the rice paddies, and during the rice-sowing, when the seedlings were transplanted into the flooded beds, the director's family helped: the girls would fetch their nylon stockings from their dressers, stretch their arms into the skin-toned hose and glide their hands back out with splayed fingers to find the holes through which leeches could strike. Only once they had made certain that the stockings had no holes did they pull them on. Despite the utmost care leech attacks still occurred, the girls screamed, and we boys, who had to get by without nylon armour, just laughed at them.

When I was eight years old, a year before the end of the Second World War, I fell in love with Miya Sŏng, the girl who lived in the neighbouring house. Back then Johnny was still called Mino and had no idea of my feelings for Miya, who was four years older than I was. He had no idea of how I fought to win her affection, and even she didn't suspect a thing; did she even know I existed?

Perhaps; one summer afternoon, which we spent sitting beneath the shadow of a pine tree in one of the courtyards, watching the dog and her six puppies as they raced one another in a circle – cheering on the little plump one who was so intent on catching up with his mother (we yelled to him to keep going, 'Come on, little one, keep going!') – she paid more attention to me than she did to the dogs. She was smiling; that's why I believed she loved me (that's why I believed I loved her).

In the same year, Johnny too lost his heart.

We had heard of films, but never seen one. We had heard that they were living photos; shaking pictures, we thought, shaking our heads around in front of the director's black-and-white photos until we became dizzy. In our hiding place, on the sturdy branch of a ginkgo tree, Johnny asked me if in cinemas the audience sat in front of huge photographs jiggling their skulls from side to side. He said he couldn't imagine it. I said I couldn't either, because it really wasn't much fun. Perhaps it would be different if the pictures were huge, said Johnny, and he suggested we try it out; so we gripped tightly onto the tree trunk and began to wobble our heads back and forth, slowly at first, then faster and faster.

Today I think it must have been a coincidence . . . The world held still, just for us, no wind, not even a breeze, and as well as holding its breath it paused all the other noises too. I can still picture us now, perched on the branch and rocking our heads from left to right, from right to left, laughing, because we've figured out the secret, feeling smug, because we're the only ones who have figured it out, while all the others are paying a fortune because of their stupidity. When the wind disturbs the stillness, the postcard-like stillness, we pause, and suddenly everything is alive again, we hear birdsong, the babbling of the river, the chirping of the crickets, the humming of the bees and the flies; and, far off in the distance, my mother's voice.

In August of that year, after July's monsoon rains had softened the earth and the grass roofs – transforming the air into steam and swallowing the bright, early summer light, so that when the sky finally cleared it blinded us – a vehicle, a small cabinet of sorts, rolled through the village. From the wound-down windows they called out to us that it was a travelling cinema, that they had brought films and everyone was welcome to come and see them, everyone. 'Did he say film?' Johnny asked me, jumping to his feet. I nodded. 'Come on!' he cried and set off in pursuit of the car, 'we have to find out where they're taking the cinema!'

We didn't have to search for long; the wooden poles that had been sticking out of the vehicle were now jutting out of a stretch of land which had previously been undiscovered; terra incognita. Until this day, no one else had known of its existence; we had kept it a secret, it was *our* uncharted valley. This was where they rammed the poles into the earth and built a black machine, the film projector. Johnny and I lingered nearby. We acted as though we had no interest in them, neither in the projector, which we thought was an oven, nor in the construction of the cinema, which was in full swing. 'Come here and help us!' they called, waving to us. We trotted slowly over to the men, feeling uneasy. They asked us to pass them the curtain from the bag, they wanted to fasten it to the poles.

Slowly, the rods transformed before our eyes into a wooden framework, and this in turn became a white fabric house with a curtain as an entrance. It stood there, wide-legged, as though it belonged here, as though it had always belonged. 'Tonight,' smiled one of the men, handing us two pieces of paper, 'come to the cinema and bring your parents, brothers, sisters and friends.'

They came, everyone came. The whole village wanted to know what the 'magic house' was, although they had to buy tickets, while Johnny and I just sneaked inside.

There were blankets spread out on the ground. We slipped off our shoes and sat down on the soft material, feeling the damp of the previous weeks seep through from the earth. It wasn't yet completely dark outside, some patches of the sky still gleamed deep blue, but the tranquil glow would soon be swallowed by the blackness of night. No one dared speak, we sat there silently, feeling the gentle breeze which made the fabric walls rustle; then came a gust of wind, the material billowed up, a candle was extinguished.

A cry of alarm.

Whispering? Wailing?

Soft murmuring.

The hiss of a match being struck.

The lanterns are all lit again, casting a dim light. The evening wind subsides, giving way to nocturnal stillness, and slowly the stars step out from beneath the cover of darkness, one after the other, until the entire sky is glittering.

The moon!

Everyone tilts back their head. We are lying down now, lying on our backs alongside each other, some resting on top of others, as we stare up at the firmament. We look for the moon and find it, and as soon as we know where it is in the heavens and how big it is, we see its light, its silvery, smouldering light. And I forget that I came to see a film, instead I remember one of my father's sayings: 'Even if the sky falls in, there'll be a hole to escape through.' That evening, I believe I can see them right before my eyes, the holes in the sky you can escape through; they are bright yellow. But perhaps it's the other way round, because Father also said: 'The sky is as big as a little coin.' I never used to understand this saying, but I think I do now; it seems to mean that the stars, in their compactness, are the actual sky, and not the space in between. As I lie next to Johnny on the blanket, trying to remember the sound of my father's voice, I become sad when I realize I've forgotten it, even though he died only a few months ago.

Suddenly, word goes around that it's about to start. With a loud click, the machine is set in motion. Someone asks us to blow out the candles. All at once there appears on the screen a living picture: whenever it breathes it shudders, and its sharpness is lost in the trembling. When it disappears, everything goes black before our eyes, and screams of horror come from those who think they've gone blind; when the shadow of a head hops across the film – it's like we've been wounded, like a flesh wound – we cry out for them to sit down, right now!

I was transfixed by the phenomena of light, never would I have thought that life could take on this form, be a woven fabric of light and dark, black and white, a world both fleeting and eternal, whose time is numbered; perhaps it was the awareness of this transience which forced me to surrender my thoughts, my knowledge, my memories and feelings – and, for the duration of those two hours, liberated me from poverty and hunger.

Eventually, when I could no longer follow the flashes of

light on the screen, I leant back and watched the stars shimmering.

'Yunho, don't fall asleep,' hissed Johnny, pinching my arm. I had closed my eyes, but I wasn't asleep; I was thinking about Father, how whenever he had a day off, he used to tuck his brown leather bag under his arm and trek into the centre of Nonsan; how he sat down on an old newspaper on the pavement in front of the courthouse and waited, among the street traders and shoe-shiners, for people who wanted to file a claim but were unable to write up their petition themselves – the illiterate, 'Black Eyes'. He had been their translator, the connection between mind and paper, and he had put his all into it, making two, three drafts of the same document, at home by candlelight while we slept. The rent on one of the many writing booths – wooden huts that jockeyed for position in the square before the courthouse, tiny spaces furnished with a table and two chairs, a third person would have to stand in the background – was an expense he hadn't wanted, because he couldn't pursue this on a regular basis anyway, he had said, it was only a hobby, not work. He had turned away customers who wanted to hand in their petition the very same day; he gave priority to the quiet and gentle ones, the peddlers and poets who had never learnt to read or write. 'A full bottle of water makes no sound,' he had said, listening to them and transcribing their poems. After he finished, he gave them the words he had captured for free, and they cradled the sheets of paper in their hands as though they were precious jewels. Some verses he also copied out for himself; he carried them around with him like others carry money.

'But they smell much better, don't they, Yunho?'

I was just trying to remember the smell, the smell of the paper, and the rough surface of dried India ink across which I used to love to brush my finger, when suddenly a loud rattle from the projector announced that the presentation had come to an end. Everyone stood up and searched for their shoes in the weak glow of the petroleum lamps and candles. Many had fallen asleep, they had to be woken or carried home, but Johnny was wide awake, his eyes were shining. He pulled me over to the man who had operated the projector and asked him whether he had painted the pictures himself. The man laughed, gave Johnny's cheek an affectionate pinch and said, no, he just showed them, he and his friends. He was in his early twenties and studying literature, a small, lean man whose black hair was combed into a glistening side parting with a generous quantity of oil. His body was clad in Western garments, and he wore a hat which today I know to be a beret, but back then I marvelled at the rounded little heap that hung down over the right side of his forehead.

He and his friends stayed in Nonsan for a week. Director Kim gave them lodgings, letting them sleep in the guesthouse, and by way of thanks they showed us a different film every night. At the end of the week, Johnny declared that when he grew up he was going to make films in Seoul; as he spoke he wore the beret like a woollen bowl, upside down on his head.

Johnny couldn't sit still. Again and again, he jumped up to bring me a drink – ('Are you thirsty? Do you want water or tea?') – and again and again he answered his own question ('Oh, but that's not celebratory enough, and we have reason to celebrate! You're probably hungry, I'll fetch you something to eat – a bowl of rice and a few little side dishes, grilled vegetables, sautéed roots, kimchi, maybe if you're lucky there'll still be some leftover *mandu*!'). All the while, he played with a cigarette from the half-empty box, letting it wander over and under each of his fingers, and bombarding me with questions: how long has it been since we last saw each other? Five, six years? What are you doing in Seoul? Are you planning to stay for a while? Are you going to study? How have you been these last years? I tried in vain to answer; there were many I didn't catch because we were talking simultaneously, each of us louder than the other, our conversation interrupted by questions to answers that I hadn't even given, with the result that I eventually cried out in exhaustion:

'That's enough, I can't hear you!'

We laughed and fell back onto his bed. He'd come far, I croaked; to an iron bed with a squeaking mattress. Not to mention, added Johnny, grinning from car to ear, that it was frightfully dusty yet wonderfully soft.

'It's like sleeping on my very own cloud every night.'

'And what about these feathers jabbing into my back?'

'Jabbing? Now you're exaggerating!'

'No, seriously, I think I'm bleeding.'

'That's impossible. My cloud's ribs are soft—'

'Its *ribs*?'

He hadn't changed, he was still Mino; cheeky, brazen, and far too confident considering that he was utterly devoid of talent. He could neither draw nor sing, all he could do was daydream and lie the tail off a tiger. He had remained loyal to the beret; he was wearing it on his head as he smoked. In other ways too he looked astoundingly similar to the film student from back then, perhaps because he had combed his hair with too much oil and was wearing wide-legged black trousers.

'They're too big, I know,' he said, as our gazes crossed, 'but I like them, they look as though they used to belong to Humphrey Bogart, don't you think? The only thing missing is the braces.'

He turned in a circle for me. Where had he got them from? I asked, adding with a laugh that he had probably stolen them. He smiled secretively, stubbed his cigarette out on the windowsill and tossed it onto the floor. A girlfriend had given them to him, to make amends after he was thrown out of the military academy.

'You were kicked out of military academy?'

'No. From the breeding ground of the political élite.'

His fate, he told me, had been sealed by a campus fight, from which he had, of course, emerged as victor, but which had lost him his place at the academy. They had accused him of undignified behaviour, inappropriate for one of their students, and of tarnishing the reputation of an institution so rich in tradition. 'Rich in tradition,' he had interjected, spitting with contempt. In that moment he had no longer cared about anything; hung-over and injured from the fight, with one black eye and a bloody nose, he had stood there before the 'committee of idiots', as he called them, and ranted, 'Rich in tradition?' The Americans had brought it with them, just like the cars the highly esteemed teachers cruised around in, the uniforms they paraded in, the banknotes they tossed about in bars! At this point he was grabbed by two cadets and dragged out of the room. In the autumn, he said, he had become a student at the Korea University, where life was considerably more pleasant.

He smiled mischievously.

By the way, he added, his name was no longer Mino, and hadn't been for two years now, but Johnny. 'What made you choose that name?' I asked in surprise. He reached for the lighter and lit another cigarette.

'Did your girlfriend give it to you? The tall, pretty girl in the yellow dress? I saw her in the hallway earlier.'

'Eve?'

I nodded.

He grinned. He wasn't sure whether she was his girlfriend, he said, what they had wasn't clear-cut.

'It's not?'

'You don't have a relationship with Eve, Yunho, you just meet up with her.'

His first encounter with Eve, Johnny told me, had been at his sister Haesun's wedding. She had come with an American, an acquaintance of his father's. Word got around that he had bought her services as an escort.

The skies crumbled that day, into snowflakes that were neither cold nor heavy, but dry and light, almost incorporeal. The snow's arrival was unseasonable. It was late October, and they had wanted an autumnal wedding. The celebratory dinner was relocated from the expansive garden into the narrow entrance hall of a neo-Gothic church on the outskirts of Seoul. Here, they waited for the snowfall to come to an end. It was oddly quiet. The wedding party had gathered by the window, their gazes following the children, who instead of fleeing inside had stayed dancing in the snow, trying to catch the flakes on their tongues. Johnny had lingered outside too, and was watching them; all of a sudden, just as he was about to lose all sense of time, Eve appeared. Without saying a word, she placed an orange in his hand, a delicacy only to be found on the black market. The rind was sticky, warm, the fruit bigger than his palm, and he had to spread his fingers in order to cup it.

'Thank you,' he said, 'thank you very much.' She nodded and turned to walk away. He stopped her. Was she leaving the party already, he asked? There was still so much to eat. She nodded again and gestured towards the street, saying her companion had already gone. With a smile and the hint of a bow she said goodbye, but Johnny couldn't let her go so easily. He followed her through the suburbs, from the outskirts of Seoul to the densely built-up centre, and the longer the pursuit lasted, the narrower the streets became, the wide boulevards of the outer neighbourhoods transforming into alleyways, and in the city's labyrinth-like core he lost sight of her. He only found her again because she was waiting for him. She didn't look up; she was staring into a compact mirror. When she spotted him, she sauntered over to the door of her house, turned and looked him straight in the eye.

And Johnny?

He fled, panicked, into an alley.

Johnny learnt that she worked in a dance school, one of the many that had come into existence during the Korean War in which not only the Western style of dance was taught, but also that of dress, hairstyles and speech. The resulting mumbo jumbo of Korean and English – much like that other American import, sunglasses – was donned, then discarded again as soon as one left the place. Then one would slip back into the Korean attire: the white trousers, the long skirt, the unmade-up face. Eve was an exception, she didn't contemplate surrendering her disguise; she kept her American name and the American clothes, and threw away Korean just as she had Japanese before it, not even bringing it out again on special occasions. She identified effortlessly, too effortlessly I'd say, with those who were marching through our homeland as though they had conquered it and all its inhabitants, whom they punished as they saw fit by smearing their faces with thick, red paint, writing 'Goddamn Koreans' on their backs – all that over a tin of beans or a bag of rice. When a group of youths trailed Eve, shouting 'Yankee Whore!', I considered it just.

At the entrance to the dance school were two neon signs flashing the words 'Dancing' and 'Girls'. Beneath, on a plastic chair, sat the establishment owner and ticket-seller, a slight man in his thirties with a lynx-like face, who always wore sunglasses regardless of whether it was sunny or not, and slicked his hair down to his skull with pomade. One strand, however, refused to be tamed, springing right back up into the air after being brushed, and fanning out; because of this people called him Cockatu. There was no fixed entry price, Cockatu demanded whatever and as much as he wanted, good-looking men were charged less, women nothing at all, and ugly people were refused entry altogether. If he raised his hand his partner would appear, a mountainous black man who had a name but was never addressed by it, who never needed to move a finger, instead simply standing up and stepping into the light; this was enough for everyone to make themselves scarce, even those who felt unjustly treated.

The dance hall was in the basement, and bigger than any room Johnny had ever seen up until then. Shortly before five in the afternoon, before he opened up and switched on the neon sign, Cockatu would put on a record and set it to repeat. Then the music played for an empty room, filling the twilit dancefloor from two funnel speakers. The sound was tinny, the strings barely distinguishable from the trombones, and yet – perhaps because the melodies were soft and slow, intended to rouse longing, perhaps because the room swiftly filled with women who, like Eve, wore long evening dresses and bared their shoulders, 'obligingly romantic', as Cockatu called them – this place, with its painted-on seascape, sun, water, and footprints in the sand, was a kind of refuge, if you overlooked the chaperones who patrolled among the dancing couples; and the back room. People disappeared into it in twos for a half or full hour, into that small space lit by a blackened light bulb, the walls pasted with scraps of paper, a Japanese window in the middle of one, and furnished only with a dark leather couch and a cassette player placed on the uneven linoleum floor, which creaked with every step.

'You have to bring your own condoms, but you can choose the girl and the music,' Cockatu always said, 'and you pay in advance!'

The second time Johnny encountered Eve, she was in the arms of an American soldier for whom the standing blues clearly weren't enough; he was urging her towards the back room. Her lips were as red as her dress, her hair bleached light brown and tightly curled, and her natural, brownish skin tone shimmered through the white face powder.

At that moment, Johnny lost all the timidity he had previously felt around her. 'What a cliché you are,' he said, 'the Korean cliché of an American woman. Are you proud of yourself?'

The GI, who only understood that some guy was stealing his time, was about to let his fists fly when he was distracted by another dancer who had been shooed over by Cockatu.

Eve put her hands on Johnny's shoulders, pulled him close and whispered in his ear: 'It's harder than it looks. Why don't you try it sometime?' Then she pushed him away. He was grabbed by two hands and transported out onto the street with a kick.

He was so surprised that he stayed there on the ground for a moment – stunned not that he'd been kicked out, but by her quick-wittedness. Eventually he stood up, brushed the dust from the street off his clothes and ran a comb through his hair.

Sheltering in a dark corner, he lit a cigarette. Even though he hadn't planned to, he waited for her. He bought a newspaper from one street kid, a packet of chewing gum from another, had his shoes cleaned and his fortune told by a bothersome old man (the street prophet read a short life in his palm). He had a long wait; it was almost midnight by the time she finally appeared. When he called out to her, she looked around, hailed a taxi, then declared before climbing in that she wouldn't go out with him, not with the cliché of a Korean man.

Over the next few weeks she ignored him on every corner in Jongno, as she did the postcards he sent her, the letters and drawings. He was barred from the dance school; Cockatu's giant blocked the door. Every night Johnny waited, perched on the asphalt, in front of the flashing neon signs 'Dancing' and 'Girls', while drunken soldiers passed by, refusing to leave him in peace; they all wanted a glance inside the sketchbook he had with him, some wanted their portraits done, and more than a few started a fight. He froze his backside off on this corner for a whole month, but he filled the empty pages of his book. Eventually he had to make the sketches smaller and smaller, until even the last white flecks of paper were covered with his drawings.

One night, he heard a vaguely familiar voice, a woman's voice. Did he want to be a painter, an artist? she asked. He looked up and into Eve's face. No, he answered, not really, he actually wanted to make films, but he didn't have any money, so he contented himself with drawing his films instead. He held his little book out to her. She took it, opened it and flicked through slowly, page by page, smiling at times, sighing at others, and eventually she clapped it shut and said that he couldn't draw, but she liked his films. She took a cigarette out of her coat pocket. Did he have a light? He nodded, and tried to strike a match, but it jumped out of his fingers, as did the second, and he only succeeded on the third. His fingers were numb, numb and stiff, and he wasn't sure whether Eve really was standing in front of him or whether he was imagining it, for he hadn't eaten a thing the whole day.

While he was still staring at her longingly, just as the crane eyes the frog in the swamp, she linked arms with him and said: 'Let's get out of here, Johnny.'

He asked her why she called him Johnny, but she wouldn't tell him, even though she was the reason he was thrown out of the academy. She told him she could only love him if he were close by her, so from that moment on he never left her side. She said he couldn't hide himself from her, that he had to reveal his true self, and so he confessed his secrets and introduced her to all his friends. She, however, only let him see her when she was made up; when he stayed the night she slept with a piece of white gauze over her face, as motionless as a statue. When he told her that knowing her true face wouldn't ruin the image he had of her, that even something as perfect as jade has its flaws, she seemed to understand, but still she didn't show him her original self. Instead, she told him a fairy tale.

Back when the tigers smoked long pipes, little Yunmee had suffered a broken heart. She was helplessly in love with an American whom she had met in a bar at the military barracks north of Seoul, in Uijeongbu.

Yunmee came from a reputable family. Her parents were dead, and her older sister by almost ten years, a headmistress, was her strict guardian. Yunmee loved to read, and did so avidly, but what she loved even more were films, the technicolour pictures from Hollywood, like *Singin' in the Rain* or *The Wizard of Oz*. It was less the stories that fascinated her, more the film stars' blue eyes and golden hair – she could never get her fill of watching them, and soon it was no longer enough to admire these exotic creatures on the screen, she wanted to stand close to them and touch them. With this intention, she crept to the bus station, neither knowing what awaited her in Uijeongbu nor whether, if confronted with a 'Blue Eyes', she would actually get up the courage to speak to him.

Around the military base were a number of shops, bars, restaurants and cafés, all with English names, and brothels too, so the GIs no longer had to be taken to Japan for 'female entertainment', as was the case during the Korean War. Women from good homes couldn't let themselves be seen in this neighbourhood, not if they wanted to marry men from good homes, but despite this (or even because of it) the military base exerted a strong pull on them, and Yunmee was by no means the only girl who wandered the streets in search of Blue Eyes. She had heard from a girlfriend that there was a bar frequented exclusively by GIs. She had made a note of the name, yet left the piece of paper at home.

She stepped into the very first bar she saw. It was dark and smoke-filled, the small windows shrouded by curtains. A mute gramophone stood in one corner, the barman and his two helpers were smoking behind the bar, and propped up against it were several men she hadn't been looking for. They were pale-skinned, yes, but neither blonde nor blue-eyed; their hair was the shade of pine bark, their eyes the colour of the asphalt that was currently being spread across Seoul.

Yunmee hadn't picked a good time; it was three o'clock in the afternoon and the bar wouldn't fill up for another three hours. As she was about to leave, scared and disappointed, she felt a hand on her shoulder. Not daring to turn round, she stood as still as a candlestick in a pawnshop, and the American had to walk round her to look at her face. His eyes were blue, as blue as the Sea of Japan in sunlight, and the hair beneath his dirty cap was yellow, dark yellow like the rice paddies of south-eastern Korea. The American's name was Jeff and he was a soldier. He took pity on Yunmee, and when she was unable to answer any of his questions in a language he could understand, he escorted her to the bus station. She didn't notice that she was speaking French to him. It was only once the bus arrived that she realized her mistake and thanked her rescuer in English; he promptly asked the confused young lady for her address through the small bus window. She gave it to him, less because she wanted to see him again and more because she wanted to prove she wasn't the bimbo he must think she was, after all her gibberish.

He really did come to visit her, and they managed to meet on two more occasions before he fell foul of her older sister, who had been alerted by the housekeeper to Yunmee's note about 'Uijeongbu, Bar Acapulco', and subsequently had her followed by the chauffeur. Through an interpreter, Private Jeff was forbidden any further contact with Yunmee, and he complied with the ban until one day in May, six months later, when he smuggled a note to her via a friend saying that he would be returning to the United States the following day and wanted to see her one last time; he would wait by the rice merchant in her street after sundown. The encounter took place, Jeff refusing to be intimidated by the rice merchant's distrustful looks, and at the end of the night the American went back to his base, where he boarded a plane at dawn, and Yunmee to her sister's home, where a month later she discovered that she was pregnant.

She decided to have a termination. She wanted to maintain the illusion of respectability, despite the rumours her neighbours had been spreading. The old woman, who she'd hoped would help her maintain the crumbling façade, instead prompted its collapse: she demanded such a high sum for the procedure that Yunmee was left no choice but to confess everything to her sister, whereupon she was thrown out of the house. That very same day, Yunmee became Eve – Eve like Eve Harrington in *All About Eve*. It was Henry Lewis, the American honorary guest at Haesun's wedding, who gave her the name. When he saw her for the first time, in a beige trench coat, a loose-fitting rain hat on her head with her curls peeping out from beneath, he said she looked like Anne Baxter at the beginning of the film, when she asks Bette Davis for an autograph. Yunmee liked the name, and the character of Eve Harrington too, her scheming, calculating behaviour, and so she began to dress like her, to curl her fringe and put up her hair in the exact same way.

She borrowed the money for the new wardrobe, the perm and the doctor's bill from Cockatu, who was an acquaintance of Henry's, and in return she danced seven days a week, from seven in the evening until midnight, with anyone who wanted to dance with her. She had planned to do this only until she had paid off her debt, but soon realized that she earned more in one night as a dancer than a factory worker could earn in a whole month, and so she remained true to Cockatu's Dance School.

Had she broken many hearts since then? asked Johnny. Eve laughed out loud. One admirer had ended up in the insane asylum because of her. The insane asylum? Johnny was impressed. Eve nodded. He had been the son of a high-ranking government official. The family had lived in the prestigious Angukdong neighbourhood, with a chauffeur, a cook, numerous servants and a private tutor, and made regular trips to Tokyo. The son spoke very good English, because as a child he was looked after by a nanny in New York. This early Western influence, however, proved to be disastrous: he never warmed to Korean women, especially not the ones his mother paraded before him as potential wives. Heiresses trotted through the villa's labyrinthine halls as though in a fashion show, turning to all sides for his inspection, and yet he didn't like a single one. Eve met him on one of his nightly forays, and as they danced to Glenn Miller's 'Serenade in Blue' he proposed marriage – thereby unleashing numerous dramas. For one, his mother demanded that his father cut all ties with his own concubine once and for all, claiming he was setting a bad example to his son. Around the same time, President Rhee had declared concubinage illegal and called upon all civil servants to give up their second wives. Soon inspectors would be sent out to investigate whether the ban was being obeyed, and any offenders would be fired. A ban on anything Western was also imposed in the son's household; all albums, books and posters were given away or burned. Eventually, the parents issued their son with an ultimatum: either he gave up his unbefitting fiancée or they would send him to an insane asylum, where electric shock therapy would surely burn the ridiculous ideas out of his brain. The son had laughed and said he didn't believe a word of it, they were only bluffing!

They weren't. He was led away in a straitjacket.

'And the lunatic was grinning as they took him,' said Eve, 'he even stretched his arms out willingly and slipped into the sleeves they tied around his back.'

When the paramedics pushed him onto the back seat of the ambulance it was eleven in the morning, the January light almost white, and the tips of the ginkgo trees were swaying in the wind. 'A Fool Such as I' was playing on the radio.

As the ambulance drove off, it scattered the pigeons from the pavement and careened past a pothole, a small crater filled with empty cans and bottles. A schoolgirl in black uniform, whose role it was to conduct her schoolmates safely across the street, already had her whistle between her lips and only just enough time to jump back. Then the street tram thundered past, and the ambulance disappeared from sight.

The next day, one of the family's servants came by and demanded the engagement ring back from Eve. Through her, Eve found out that a lobotomy was to be performed on him.

Johnny played with the empty cigarette pack, flipping the lid open and shut. After a while, he frowned and said: 'I think Eve lied to me. I mean, I *know* she lied to me.'

He had made enquiries and discovered that she was not only significantly older than she claimed to be (she was born in '31, not '36), but also from Pyongyang (not Seoul), and she didn't have a sister who was a headmistress in the city.

'Two years before the outbreak of the Korean War, she fled to the South. The border wasn't a guarded stronghold back then, but just a sign written in four languages.'

Her father was in jail, the reasons for his imprisonment unknown to Johnny. Perhaps he had been too wealthy, perhaps too religious, for the family was Catholic. Perhaps he had supported the Christian Democrats and not the Workers' Party. In any case, he, like many of Kim Il-sung's opponents, was imprisoned after the 1948 elections that turned the north of Korea into the Democratic People's Republic. A few weeks later, Eve set off with nothing but the clothes on her back — without her sisters, without her mother. Presumably she had

37

some jewellery with her, rings or gold chains she was planning to sell in the South. Johnny's informant found out that she had been fleeing her neighbour, a Red party functionary who was pressuring her to marry him; he wanted to get his hands on the land that had been distributed to her family after the end of Japanese rule.

Arriving in Seoul, Eve made ends meet by selling American money. The dollar trade was illegal, and so was carried out only after nightfall. Constantly on the run from policemen, and the loan sharks from whom she had borrowed the majority of her starting capital, she was driven into the darkest corners of the city, where she was beaten and robbed. When Cockatu found her, she was a complete mess; she hadn't eaten for days and her body was covered with bruises and open wounds. He took pity on her and gave her a place to stay. She was able to wash and was given food and clean clothes. Whether he had glimpsed her beauty beneath all the dirt or whether he initially offered her a job as a housemaid, my friend couldn't say. Presumably she was his go-to girl before he enlisted her as a dancer at the school.

Johnny pulled a cigarette out of a new pack and lit it. The match hissed, then flared, illuminating him, me, the floor we were sitting on; by now it was evening. I couldn't make out the expression on his face, for a moment I thought I saw disgust. The flame died out. Johnny sighed; he didn't believe that Henry Lewis had given her the new name, his guess was that Cockatu had chosen it and written it down for her.

'She can't read, after all. Presumably he scribbled "Moon" on a piece of paper and explained to her what it meant: that, my love, is your new name, Eve Moon.'

He didn't imagine that she had ever seen her family again.

'They would have been imprisoned and executed, no doubt. You can't expect anything else from Commies.'

He took a deep drag. I heard him breathe out and saw the smoke float in grey-blue plumes through the darkness. He said he found it suspicious that she hadn't told him the truth.

'Suspicious?' I echoed, unable to stop myself from grinning. 'You sound like a policeman . . . no, like a spy. Have you changed your plans? Do you want to be a secret agent now instead of a film director?'

'An agent?'

He grinned. That wasn't such a bad idea, he said. Perhaps Eve was an agent, but a North Korean one rather than South Korean. Her official biography had turned out to be false, but the supposedly true one could just as easily be false; there was no way of checking either of them.

He looked at me thoughtfully.

'How much do we really know about the people we love?'

I stubbed out my cigarette.

'Enough,' I answered, 'not to voice allegations like that. You know you're putting her in danger.'

'Yes, of course.' He laughed. Sometimes his imagination got the better of him, he said. He had seen too many films like *The Hand of Destiny*, an incredible black-and-white film by Hyŏngmo Han, did I know it? Margaret, a communist spy with a chic Western apartment – who in the eyes of the South Korean public works as a madam in a cabaret – shelters a student who is fleeing from gangsters, and falls in love with him. But, I interjected, the student Yŏngchŏl turned out to be an agent for the South Korean resistance, so he wasn't a real student anyhow, and from that moment on Margaret was in trouble. True, admitted Johnny, although Yŏngchŏl hadn't really lied; he was both, a student and a spy.

39

'Then Margaret didn't lie either. She just withheld the information that she's a spy,' I replied.

'Correct.'

Johnny nodded and pushed the cigarette pack and lighter towards me. Speaking slowly, he said: 'That brings me back to my question: how much do we really know about the people we love?'

I pulled a cigarette out of the box, but didn't light it.

'Barely anything, I reckon. Nothing at all.'

He tapped the ash from his cigarette, letting it fall to the floor. 'Take you, for example' he said, 'I don't know anything about you. And yet there was a time when I knew everything. Before you left me there in that backwater, Nonsan. When was that again? Ah yes, I remember, it was September 1953. I remember very clearly, because a few days after your disappearance a North Korean deserter pocketed 100,000 dollars from the Americans for a stolen fighter plane. He allegedly hadn't known anything about the reward, had never seen the flyers dropped all over North Korea by the US pilots. There was an awful lot written about him in the newspapers at the time, particularly about the American car he bought himself. It was a Cadillac, the only one in Korea.'

Johnny took a deep drag. Once again I felt his gaze on me.

'Back then, I thought that perhaps you'd done the opposite. That you'd gone over to the communists.'

3

No, I was drawn south, not north. I packed up the few things I owned and left Nonsan, went wherever the wind blew me and the waves propelled me; on days when it rained, I would study the colour of the rain from beneath the shelter of a tree, trying to memorize it; on other days I followed the traces of the light until it disappeared in a valley. I travelled on foot, hiking cross-country, sleeping in caves, cornfields and under bridges. My new friends were homeless like me, children, teenagers, refugees from the north, refugees from the south, people without ages or names who had become arbitrary, transparent, during the search for their families. We shared the little food we managed to beg, shared the warmth of our caves, we shared everything we owned, and yet we lost one another.

I was the only one with a goal: whatever it took, I wanted to get to Daegu. I knew from my mother's letters that I had relatives there.

Father was from south-eastern Korea. I remember his family not as people, but as addresses which I wrote on envelopes once a fortnight at my mother's request, after she had dictated the letters to me in her slow, rhythmic way. None of her syllables stood alone; they all melted on her tongue to a pulpy mass, from which the few gaps between the words stuck out prominently. Were the pauses coincidental or intentional?

Sometimes she used them to veer off mid-sentence: as though she had decided on a different ending.

She could have written the letters herself. Before her marriage, she had been taught to read and write by a student, who, like many of his classmates, had abandoned his studies and set off to mobilize the rural population against Japanese colonial rule. Officially, these dissenters instructed the villagers on the use of the 'modern appliances', as mother called them, which were intended to simplify crop cultivation, but in actual fact it was a Korean lesson. One day, the Japanese secret police, the thought police, whose task it was to track down anti-Japanese activities and whose spies were distributed across the country, arrested the student before my mother's eyes and charged him with high treason. He and his friends were tortured and executed. 'Why tortured?' I asked. She answered: 'He was an end, but the thought police were searching for the beginning.'

Later, I found out that she learnt to read and write by exchanging letters with him. She described it factually, depicting it as a purely mechanical process: 'the slow and steady filling of paper with circles and strokes'. Then, one lazy afternoon beneath the shadow of a pine tree, Yuri whispered to me: 'Yunho, you know they were love letters, right? Apparently they flew in a wide arc over the house wall and landed on the ground with an almighty plop.'

Yuri rolled onto her back and closed her eyes. For the last few days, the scent of summer had been intensifying. 'If he hadn't been arrested,' she mumbled, 'you and your brother wouldn't exist.'

My mother's silence seemed to support this theory. She never spoke of the student again, and didn't even give him a name, but he seemed close to her, closer than her relatives, of whom she never spoke and whom I never met.

42

Johnny had a large family – eight uncles and aunts on his mother's side and just as many on his father's – who overran the house twice a year. The little uncle, the youngest, who drove a delivery van for a Japanese firm in Seoul, would bring khakis, garlic, razor blades, matches or American cigarettes, carefully hidden beneath the seats, among the upholstery, and even under the cap on his head. He told us they were stopped regularly by road cowboys who lay in wait, armed with rifles. As soon as a lorry approached, they would jump out into the road and force the driver to stop by waving their shotguns about. They were crazy, he said, completely crazy.

'They drive the fear of God into you.'

He smiled at us as he opened the car door and heaved out a gramophone, which Johnny, me and Yuri were to carry into the house. 'Set it up in the living room,' he called to us, and laughed softly, 'hopefully your father won't have a fit, Mino!'

He grinned and lit himself a cigarette. Later, over dinner, he explained that the record player had been payment for a trip to Pyongyang with illegal cargo; father, mother, child-child-child, and luckily no road cowboys, for this time he wouldn't have been able to fob them off with a few cigarettes or sake. At least they weren't having such an easy time of it any more. They had been in the majority before, he told us, but now, with all the military vehicles constantly on the road, the bastards were on the defensive. He took a big gulp of *makgŏlli*. The Japanese were getting more nervous by the day, he mumbled, and Johnny's sisters, who had to spend hours sewing soldiers' uniforms, probably knew that better than anyone, as did Yunsu, my older brother, who was subjected to the military drill at school. The little uncle then withdrew into the garden with the director.

Another six months passed before the little uncle brought a record with him. Until then, the gramophone occupied the heart of the house in silence. 'The Japanese monument', my father called it, while for Yuri it was 'that stupid thing' she was constantly knocking her head against whenever she cleaned the floor; I imagined her carving swear words into its rust-brown skin when no one was looking. Six months later we could finally listen to music, and the monument ceased to be a monument, it transformed from an object into a voice from another world – into the voice of Billie Holiday.

The little uncle had brought just the one record, and for many years Billie's voice was the only one the gramophone had.

The little uncle was one of my childhood heroes, while his older brother, the big uncle, was *the* hero. Shortly before the end of the Second World War, he received a summons to work in the shipyard in Kobe. He contemplated fleeing. I remember Johnny's thoughtful eyes and the words that weren't his, which transformed his face for a moment into that of his father: 'If he doesn't obey, we'll all be punished. He has no choice. He has to enlist. At least he doesn't have to go to the front.'

Did Johnny even know what the front was? I remember knowing the word as an eight-year-old, even the three-year-olds knew it. Front – they pronounced it incorrectly, muddling up the letters, they still meant the same thing, but did they really know what it meant, did *we* know?

'Your uncle will come back, won't he?' I asked Johnny. He shrugged his shoulders as he weaved his way through the bushes. The fields had recently been fertilized, liquid manure collected from the outhouses had been spread across the soil, and now it stank so much that we had to avoid taking the paths that ran alongside. We swallowed the buoy-shaped white tablets they gave us in school, not because we really believed they would kill the worm eggs we were consuming along with the vegetables, but because we were convinced they would kill our sense of smell, at least for a short while. That evening we lit a fire in the undiscovered valley, far from all smells and people, and as always Johnny said: 'Don't fall asleep, Yunho, otherwise your eyebrows will turn snow-white.' And as always he was the first to fall asleep, and I sprinkled flour over his face.

The big uncle did come back, thinner and white-haired, the latter without any assistance on my part, and he told of his escape from Kobe, which had almost been thwarted when he and his comrade were stopped by the military police. They showed their forged exit papers – poor-quality fakes, they had thought, but the policeman accepted them, and even gave them a compass when they asked for directions. An old Japanese farmer offered them a place to stay; he was one of the many who gave them water, food and a place to sleep, then begged them on his knees the next morning to leave without delay. Despite the compass they lost their way, and only after a long search did they find a ship headed to Korea. After days – or weeks, they couldn't say which – they landed in Busan and then set off once more on foot, before finally arriving in Nonsan months later, long after the end of the war.

If he had been caught fleeing, the big uncle would have been executed on the spot, but he had told himself he had to take the risk; he didn't want to die in Japan in a hailstorm of bombs like some of his comrades, who instead of hiding in the bunkers had run out into the open air as the planes began to circle above them. They had believed the American planes would only shoot at the Japanese and not at Koreans. They had stared directly into the machine-gun fire and called out: 'Welcome, welcome!'

The bullets had torn his friends to shreds, the pieces of their flesh flew through the air and clung to the walls of the bunker.

Father, too, was drafted before the end of the war. The director's good relationship with the Japanese authorities was no longer of any use, for Hirohito was running out of men and Mr Kim out of excuses. Father had to draw up his will and pack. The last document he ever drafted was his own; he fell just a few months later. On the day the letter reached us, my mother ransacked our house for a photo of my father with a defiance I had never before seen in her.

She didn't cry, but searched instead. She searched for Father, searched and searched, then she cried because she couldn't find him, and the whole time I was thinking, why is she searching, why is she crying? There never was a photo of Father.

There is a saying in Korea: 'Time is medicine.' Is it really? The history that links Japan to Korea is a difficult one, the relationship between the countries is strained, if not broken. The situation isn't helped by the Japanese ultranationalists who patrol the islands in minivans emblazoned with Hirohito's emblem, the blood-red Japanese sun, bellowing anti-Korean slogans into their megaphones. Nor is it helped by the Korean grandparents and parents who hammer into their children Korea's role as the victim, without giving any thought to their own culpability. I wonder whether the relationship between the Koreans and the Japanese can be compared with that between the Jews and the Germans, in the sense that in the case of Korea and Japan, too, the victims and perpetrators are clearly defined – as is the guilt which binds the perpetrators to the victims, even over a century later: 1876 was the year in which 'the injustice' began, before then Japan's repeated attempts to expand its influence in Korea had always been in vain. The fact that it was possible to force this trade agreement upon Korea, referred to in the history books as an 'unequal treaty following the Western model', can be attributed to the Joseon dynasty's isolationist policy: hardly anything was known in the West about Korea, but equally, hardly anything was known in Korea about the West. The little knowledge there was initially circulated (mostly in book form) only among the most privileged of the privileged.

When the Japanese warship *Unyō* advanced into Korean waters in 1875, a heated debate broke out as to whether the members of the ship's crew, who were now dressed in British uniforms instead of Japanese ones, were Japanese or not – Japan could not be attacked, but Western barbarians could be. The regent, the underage Korean king Gojong's father, had steles put up all over Korea declaring that anyone who made peace with the 'foreign savages' would be considered a traitor. No one could read them, however, for most Koreans were Black Eyes; education was reserved for the minority in order to safeguard the rulers' power. In that respect, the civilized were no different from the barbarians.

Today there are different interpretations of this incident: some say that the Koreans, confronted with the *Unyō*, made a conscious decision to attack the Japanese in British disguise (considering them barbarians, though they felt they deserved it even as allies to barbarians), while others believe the attack was a mistake, that the Japanese really were mistaken for British. Either way, it resulted in the deployment of several thousand Japanese soldiers, which led to the signing of the trade agreement and the so-called opening of Korea, the end of isolationism.

★

Two decades later, a race began, the 'selling off'. Europe and America argued over concessions in Korea, as they had previously in China. Eventually, the US and Germany received permission to prospect for gold, Russia was allowed to mine coal and fell trees along the Yalu River on the border with China, France was to build a railway line between Seoul and Pyongyang, and the US one between Incheon and Seoul. Meanwhile, King Gojong was busy collecting technical innovations from Europe like others might collect porcelain figures; his palace was said to resemble an owl's nest. With most of the devices he bought, however, he knew neither what they were for nor how they worked. He gave the order, for example, for a telephone to be installed in the palace, the first in Korea, after finding out that one could use it to speak to people who were in a faraway place. But once he established that it was only possible to chat with living people, and not, under any circumstances, with the dead, his disappointment was considerable; he had hoped to telephone his ancestors. Many of the devices he owned were damaged and outdated, a fact that his foreign guests pointed out to him. Why was Gojong buying inferior goods? Had he been lied to? Had he been tricked? Most of the deals came about via intermediaries, where trust was obligatory. In truth, though, I think the explanation was much more straightforward: a shortage of funds. The king simply couldn't afford the latest technological marvels.

The stone house, for example, which was to replace his old palace, was only completed once Korea had already become the Japanese protectorate of Joseon. His lady chamberlain, Marie Antoinette Sontag from Alsace, used her influence at court in order to supplement her monthly allowance. She founded the Hotel Sontag in Seoul, Korea's first modern hotel, which developed into an incredibly lucrative source of income; after the fall of the Joseon dynasty, she retired to a house on the Riviera.

Madame Sontag also introduced French cuisine to Gojong's court. Even though the coffers were empty and the country heavily in debt, she served truffle pastries, oysters, caviar and sparkling wine at official events. Korea was not a trading nation then, with barely any trade structures in place. After all, Korea had hidden itself away until the *Unyō* encounter – China was its window to the world and only trade partner, with whom it exchanged valuables such as furs, ginseng, horses, silk and porcelain. As a country that was almost completely isolated, it had been self-sufficient; the system had consisted of obtaining luxury goods from Big Brother and agricultural goods from the rural population, in whose increasing poverty the ruling powers took little interest. The isolationism promoted by Gojong's father, and his grandfather and great-grandfather before him, had been the best way of suppressing the population: if Korea hadn't been cut off from the rest of the world for so long, the Joseon dynasty's exploitation of the country would have been ended much sooner. They say that modern-day North Korea is ruled by an absolute monarchy based on this model, it too strengthening its power through isolation. Kim Jong-un is not a communist, let alone a politician, but merely an heir. Even his father Kim Jong-il had no visions of his own, although he did have ideas; he knew, at least, how to perfect Kim Il-sung's legacy of the totalitarian state.

Gojong, the last but one of his kind, was a weak monarch, weak and clueless. There are numerous stories that paint him in a less than flattering light: the time, for example, when tennis was introduced to his court – guests from Europe had been invited especially for the occasion, tradesmen, diplomats, who all felt honoured to be playing for the queen and were dashing to and fro across the court with great dedication, until Gojong interrupted the match and asked with a puzzled expression: 'Why are these men exerting themselves so much? That's what the servants are here for. Have the servants play!'

But perhaps one shouldn't criticize him for his ignorance; after all, he did try to bring technical innovations to Korea, introduced to him by his favourite missionary and private physician, Horace Newton Allen from Ohio. One of these was the construction of a tram running from the royal palace to the palace garden; it was only a few kilometres long, that was all he could afford. After it was completed, his subjects spent their time not in the carriages, but on the tracks – for where could they go? The men, exhausted by the heavy work they had to carry out each day in exchange for a little nourishment, a bowl of rice and some fried vegetables, lay down between the tracks and used them as beds. The next morning, the driver was unable to make any progress because he kept having to get out and shake the men awake. Eventually he developed a method of quickly and thoroughly waking even the most persistent sleeper, upon which public officials requested an audience with Gojong and explained that it was damaging to the men's health to be woken in this way, and that his Majesty should order the driver to wait until they woke up of their own accord, a request which Gojong granted.

One day, an angry mob destroyed the tram, lynching the driver for having run over one of their family. Gojong had the 'insurgents' arrested and brought to trial. In their defence, they cited the stone tortoise, which according to Korean legend slept in front of the gates of Seoul. It shouldn't be woken, they said, for once it was awake great disaster would befall the city – and its sleep was seriously endangered by the loud hissing of the tram.

The next tramlines were built by the 124th emperor, covering Seoul with their iron net.

Many blamed Gojong's thin, pale, superstitious wife for his shortcomings. They accused Queen Min of being too dominant, of driving the king into the arms of his concubines and thereby sabotaging government business. They said she was cruel and power-hungry, that she had her rivals beaten until they lost the king's unborn children. Described by some as incredibly beautiful and by others as horrifyingly ugly, she was a poet, calligrapher and politician all in one, and, for a while, the most powerful woman in Korea. She was infamous for helping her own clan obtain riches and prominent roles in the court, although of course not for unselfish reasons: she needed people she could trust in important positions, because her father-in-law was plotting against her and tried to get rid of her on more than one occasion. After numerous attempts, he finally succeeded in disposing of her once and for all: with the help of the Japanese ambassador Miura Gorō, he had her murdered – Japan too was unhappy about Queen Min's friendly relationship with Russia, as it stood in the way of their annexation plans.

Late one afternoon, on the twentieth day of the eighth moon, a group of Japanese soldiers backed up by the Korean Kunrentai forced their way into the royal palace. The guards at the gates had let them pass, because they too were under Gorō's command. The palace guard answered to a Russian and to the American general Dye. Dye was allegedly a talented apple farmer, the orchard he had cultivated in a small corner of the palace garden was the object of great admiration. As head bodyguard, however, he wasn't so good: he was locked into his room by the assassins, and only managed to escape when help came (once everything was over). One half of the special unit stormed the king's quarters, kicking down the wooden doors, and tried to force Gojong to sign a document authorizing his divorce from the queen. Despite his fear, he refused.

Meanwhile, the other half forced their way into the queen's pavilion. Amid the confusion, the men were unable to identify her among the many ladies-in-waiting; furthermore, they knew she sometimes disguised herself as a servant. They promptly seized all the women and questioned them one by one regarding the queen's whereabouts, but despite the accompanying threats of violence no one was prepared to answer. So the soldiers grabbed the ladies by the hair and pulled them from room to room, until they eventually discovered a maid hiding behind a large commode; she too denied having seen the queen. When they were about to lead her away, she escaped their grasp and fled, crying out the crown prince's name – but within seconds Gorō's henchmen captured and stabbed her. They wrapped her still-bleeding corpse in a blanket, heaved it up into a tree in the courtyard, doused it with petroleum and set it on fire. They repeated this three times, until there was nothing left of Queen Min but a few bones.

It is said that this murder prompted the world's press to take notice of Korea for the first time; in the German empire, in particular, many young women from good families were moved by the king's fate and wrote letters offering themselves as concubines and wives. Gojong didn't answer any of these offers, for he had other concerns: he was under house arrest, imposed by his father – his wife's murderer – and his Japanese accomplice, and for weeks on end, convinced that they were trying to poison him, nourished himself solely on boiled eggs and condensed milk.

He wasn't poisoned, but fifteen years later he was forced to abdicate by that very same ally of his father's. Gojong's son, Korea's last monarch, signed an agreement which, in 1910, made Korea into the Japanese colony of Joseon. By way of thanks he was allowed to marry a Japanese princess, and he died, just as his father had before him, under house arrest.

The people could only dream of condensed milk, and avoiding certain foods in favour of others was unimaginable for the majority of the population: they ate anything they could find, even sand. Hunger drove them into the cities, Seoul, Daegu and Busan, and when they found that the poverty there was at least as bad, many took their few belongings and tried their luck in Japan or north-eastern China – Manchuria, as the region was still named when I was a child. After the annexation of Korea, this trend intensified: rumours that Tokyo's streets were paved with gold, that all one needed to do was bend down and pick it up, transformed the island kingdom into an alluring destination. Others, especially those who had issues with the colonial rulers, were drawn to China.

I grew up with stories about Manchuria; in my imagination it was an endlessly large and wide expanse, uncultivated, un-cultivable, with little forests where gangs of robbers hid themselves away. 'And communists,' my father added, 'and anarchists.' I knew what a communist was, but had never heard of anarchists. 'Your great uncles,' he answered, 'all three of them.'

That was all I could get out of him, and so I multiplied my father's face by three, added wrinkles to these triplets, gave them long, flowing hair and harem trousers and put them on horseback in a flat, wide landscape. 'No,' laughed my father, stroking my head. Not long, flowing hair, but braided and wound into a bun. And not harem trousers, but close-fitting European ones: 'Tights, you know, that cover the full length of the legs and the behind.' Nor did they ride on horseback through Manchuria: 'I doubt they could ride, who would they have learnt it from? From a goat they kept as though it was a cow?'

He laughed so hard that tears rolled down his cheeks. When he was finally able to speak again he conceded that, after numerous adventures in Shanghai, they had probably ended up in some Manchurian robbers' den.

In the early nineteenth century, Manchuria was the gathering place for the lawless, who sought and found shelter on the periphery in ever greater numbers: adventurers on the hunt for riches, bandits operating to a code of honour that would have made Robin Hood proud, the petty criminals who traded opium – out here, they had no reason to fear a regent's power. From the 1860s on, however, these profiteers were joined by Korean families wanting to protect their children from another famine. They settled predominantly in Jiandao, in present-day Yanbian, planted rice paddies and bred pigs and cattle. Seventy years later, there were allegedly one million Koreans in 'bandit land', some of them for political reasons – like General Yi Dong-whi, the first Korean communist and son of a rich Confucian academic from the Hamgyong province in North Korea. He was a typical northlander, bold and belligerent, not docile and passive like us southlanders. As a major during the Russian–Japanese war, he had looked on helplessly as his battalion was disbanded and those who protested were shot or bayoneted. He fled to Manchuria with the survivors and formed the Army of the Righteous. They engaged the Japanese army in numerous battles before retreating, significantly depleted, into the easternmost reaches of Russia shortly before the start of the First World War.

In 1919, General Yi and other communists and resistance fighters founded the Korean government-in-exile. Yi's suggestion of waging war on Japan from Manchuria – he was of the opinion that his soldiers would only need to cross the Yalu River in order to drive out, no, 'exterminate' was the word he used, all the Japanese from Korea – was rejected by most of the exiled politicians: they wanted to attain Korea's independence by diplomatic means, with the help of the US. Furious, Yi left Shanghai and travelled across Betpak-Dala, the Hunger Steppe, to Moscow. His plan was to ask Lenin for help; during the October Revolution, thousands of his men had fought alongside the Bolsheviks.

Perhaps it was gratitude, or perhaps Lenin genuinely did sympathize with Yi's plan, but in any case he gave him half a million roubles. More than half of it, however, was stolen on the way from the Soviet Union to Mongolia. The other half ended up in the hands of Yi's opponents, when his ally who had brought the money to Shanghai was shot during a rickshaw journey. This led to the definitive break between the communists and the government-in-exile, which from then on was to consist solely of the American faction, the group surrounding the man who would become the first president of South Korea, Syngman Rhee.

Shanghai in the 1920s and 1930s was a city divided between the colonial powers of Great Britain, France, Germany and Japan, where each 'concession' had its own legislative and executive.

It was (like Manchuria) a mecca for adventurers and gold prospectors, but also for the exiles and refugees who sought shelter in the French and British zones: Chinese, Koreans, and later Austrian and German Jews; the latter settled here because they didn't need a visa to be allowed to stay. Not to forget the economic migrants, the cheap labour pouring into Shanghai to find work, regardless of what kind. Their poverty stood in sharp contrast to the magnificent buildings in the Bund; it doesn't surprise me that China's Communist Party was founded in Shanghai, although at that time Mao was still a supporting character, the lead was played by Sun Yat-sen. He and his party, the Kuomintang, still backed by the Chinese communists then, fought against the trade treaties of the colonial powers. Sun wanted to transform the Kuomintang into a Leninist party, he wanted a united front in order to unify China by force. His follower and eventual successor Chiang Kai-shek saw things similarly, yet at the same time completely differently: he allied himself against his allies and had them murdered – but only after they had helped him to conquer Shanghai.

On the first day of the massacre, word spread into the narrow, labyrinth-like alleys of Shanghai, beyond the European-style boulevards, that the Kuomintang would arrest and kill all communists. Those who hadn't yet been caught hastily took off the red scarves, the communists' symbol, which they had tied around their heads. But it was a hot, muggy day, and the dye in the material bled into their skin and left a red stripe on their foreheads. This made it easy for the Kuomintang to search out their enemies – and they murdered almost all of them. The Korean resistance fighters, along with the communists who had allied themselves with their Chinese comrades, were arrested, murdered or handed over to the Japanese.

★

In 1931 (the year Eve was born), the empire of Japan occupied Manchuria and declared the puppet state of Manchukuo. Prior to this, the Korean and Chinese communists had joined forces with bandits and secret societies and hidden themselves away in the Manchurian wilderness. In order to win the sympathy of the population, on whose help they depended, they regularly sent their members into the villages and towns, where they distributed flyers and posters, held talks, put on political plays and sang patriotic songs – songs about their love for the homeland and about the imminent revolution, which would drive out the Japanese, end famine and help justice to prevail. Whenever they ran out of money, they kidnapped rich citizens for ransom. Whenever they felt that the group needed fresh blood, they recruited new members under threats of violence. Despite all this, the partisans were popular with the people, as the Japanese occupiers were amazed to discover during a survey: the relationship between the insurgents and the inhabitants was so good, wrote the thought police, that it was difficult to differentiate between the two . . .

The communists set up several base camps in north-eastern China, which were discovered and destroyed just a few years later by the Japanese. There were around six thousand men, women and children in the largest camp, two thousand in the smallest, leading a life of freedom, equality and brotherhood – allegedly no gender, race or religion was given preferential treatment. Life in the camp played out in groups: farmers', women's and youth groups. The children and young people were taught in camp schools, while the grownups continued their own education with the help of the revolutionary magazines and newspapers provided by the camp reporters. The purpose of the base camp, however, was to train guerrilla fighters and educate the next generation.

While Kim Il-sung was never a camp leader, as the North Koreans claimed, he was a notorious guerrilla fighter, and special units were even formed to track him down. The hunt for Kim was reported in detail in Japanese newspapers, and the difficulties encountered by the unit provided particular amusement in Tokyo. Kim's most prominent opponent was General Kim Suk-won, a Korean who called himself Kaneyama Shakugen until the collapse of the Japanese empire and was awarded numerous medals for bravery by Emperor Hirohito. He was never able to catch Kim, and during the Korean War he once again faced him as his opponent.

In a manner of speaking, Shakugen was responsible for my father's untimely death. Not only did he tour through Korea, giving speeches in schools and publishing articles in which he encouraged young men to volunteer for the front (for Greater Japan), but his interventions in Tokyo were also a deciding factor in Koreans being drafted into the imperial Japanese army from January 1944 onwards . . .

But I've interrupted my story; the eyewitness is no longer; I have reconstructed, even though my reconstruction is fragmentary, flawed, because I'm producing it without knowing all the connections.

Shakugen knew that the communists were reliant on the population's help. Winter was the best time of year to hunt down the 'terrorists', because it forced them to remain in their winter quarters, which the better-equipped Japanese soldiers could track down and burn to the ground; in the icy temperatures, rebuilding was almost impossible. The frost also took away the protection of the foliage on trees and bushes, and betrayed the rebels by freezing their footprints into the snow. The Japanese units followed them and cut off the paths to the settlements, forcing the partisans to make do with the little food they had on them; then all Shakugen had to do was wait. Sooner or later, the survivors would give themselves up.

The ringleaders were killed on the spot, and part of the group was handed over to Unit 731, officially known as the Epidemic Prevention and Water Purification Department, which in reality was developing biological weapons that were being tested on civilians, communists and prisoners of war. The rest were subjected to 'thought reform', an intensive form of brainwashing, and when this proved successful they were made members, or even leaders, of the white cells: of the pro-Japanese, anti-communist groups, the opposing force of the communist red cells.

Around this time, the Japanese military also created 'collective villages'. After thousands of farmers had been driven from their fields, and their houses and villages burnt down, they were deported to settlements which were in actual fact prisons; surrounded by high walls spiked with barbed wire, the buildings were kept under constant military surveillance and had just one heavily guarded entrance. The inhabitants had to be able to prove their identity at all times – their fingerprints had been taken at registration.

The villages were praised as a 'modernizing measure', in which life was supposed to be simpler, more comfortable. Nonetheless, many of the inhabitants starved to death, or died from the cold and epidemics. The letters they wrote to the authorities, pleading to be allowed to return to their homes, went unanswered.

In 1940, a large military offensive, involving six battalions of the Kwantung and twenty thousand soldiers of the Manchurian army, annihilated the guerrilla movement: most of the rebels were killed or imprisoned, or changed sides, and the few survivors had no choice but to flee; they retreated to the Soviet Union. Several hundred Chinese and Korean comrades, including Kim Il-sung, repeatedly invaded North Korea in small units, waging war on the Japanese army. More than three hundred such attacks are recorded in Chinese historiography between 1941 and 1945, but on the whole, according to the historians, the partisans' time was over.

After Johnny had searched the kitchen in vain for Mr Pak's hard spirits (our conversation had taken a serious turn, one he thought would be easier to digest with alcohol), he steered me through narrow, winding alleyways to a ruin, a halved residential building. In the undestroyed half, the inhabitants protected themselves from the wind and rain with towels, blankets and cardboard boxes. A little light flickered through the shattered windows, yet not enough to light my way; Johnny moved confidently through the darkness, while I stumbled along behind him. The steps leading into the cellar were slippery, the floor wet, it had rained just a few hours before. I groped my way forwards slowly, too slowly, Johnny mocked me and said I didn't need to take such tentative steps; he promised that the stone bridge would hold. When he opened the door to the bar I was able to see again, and it surprised me how cosy the space was: shoes were positioned neatly in front of the low platform, on which the patrons were eating and drinking on straw mats; some were asleep.

We squeezed ourselves into a vacant corner. As soon as we had sat down, the waitress brought us a bottle of *makgŏlli* and two little bowls. There was nothing else to drink here, said Johnny, looking at me intently. I nodded and took a sip; I was trying to figure out what he wanted to hear. Eventually,

I said that I had gone south, not north, I had tried to find my father's family, my aunts and uncles, as well as the noodle shop they had owned before the war, but all my efforts had come to nothing.

'My chances were poor from the start. Daegu was full to bursting. Every bombed-out house was packed with countless refugee families, whose everyday life consisted of begging – for food, for work, for money. I was lucky. My pleas were heard. I became a newspaper boy.'

Alongside that, I told him, I had traipsed around the offices and teahouses of Daegu with a shoulder bag filled with pencils, notepads and rubbers to sell, in the hope of earning a little money, enough for a meal.

It was a memory game, because back then street maps were only for the military; the cities changed their appearance overnight, numbers and street names were valid only for a day, sometimes only for an hour. I orientated myself by the highest buildings, taking note of their colour and alignment. I searched for intransient features, characteristics that couldn't be dismantled, painted over or torn away, and each day my territory expanded, until I stumbled upon Daegu's limits, on the most transient part of the entire city: the slums. The shacks, which were cobbled together from pieces of wood and cardboard boxes and no taller than a young tree (you couldn't enter them without crouching), looked so alike that it seemed as though the same people lived inside each one. The only thing that differentiated them from each other was their clothes; the fullest among them wore trousers and skirts, the hungriest wore sacks, and many children not even that.

The newspapers I wasn't able to sell, I read myself, but I dreamt of books, of being able to read more than a line here and a line there; torn-out magazine pages, discarded flyers. I lost my way because I followed the words and forgot to pay attention to the path. It was the written word that fascinated me, the difference between the spoken and the printed word, as though speech was an aberration of language and not the real thing: the real thing, the most important thing, was concealed in writing.

I preferred to go out at night, during the blackouts, when the city suddenly fell silent, and in the darkness I saw the scenes of my childhood: Johnny's house, the hill we used to make our bonfires on, the pond in the garden which always had a single water lily swaying back and forth, and the undiscovered valley. I thought of the July rains, which hadn't stunk of petrol and exhaust fumes, old fat and stale garlic like in Daegu, but instead of the meadows and trees of a hilly landscape, whose soft waves were a sea, a sea of green.

It was six in the morning when I decided to leave Daegu; six years had passed since my arrival. The Red Cross vehicles had already pulled into the train station, medics clad in white overalls, gas masks still under their arms, were awaiting their first patients. They would spray all those who joined the long line with a de-lousing formula, the American miracle disinfesting product Dichlorodiphenyltrichloroethane. They would envelop them in a cloud, and at the end of the day all those who hadn't been deloused – and who never would be – would collect the fallen insects and burn them in steel barrels, making the smell of burning spread throughout the city, mingling with the aromas of food and of life, but by then I would already be far away – or near, I thought, nearer to my home, and I couldn't wait for the train doors to open, to slip in and wait, crouched beneath a bench, for the conductor's shrill whistle.

I didn't make it as far as Nonsan. I had to get off the train in Seoul: end of the line.

Johnny waved the waitress over and paid the bill. It was ten minutes to midnight, the sirens would soon announce the beginning of curfew. We pushed our way past a group embroiled in a fight, their fists flying, and out of the corner of my eye I thought I saw a knife.

April nights were still cool back then; Johnny and I turned up our collars. Out on the street, he took a cigarette out of its pack, then left it hanging unlit in the corner of his mouth. He offered me one; I shook my head. After we had stood around indecisively in the darkness for a while, he asked where I would sleep tonight. I answered that I didn't know yet. He laughed. The cigarette dipped dangerously far out of his mouth. Evidently I wasn't a fan of carefully planned travel, he said.

I couldn't help but grin. 'No,' I replied, 'I prefer to just pick up my things and head off. I go wherever the wind blows me, wherever the waves propel me.'

His face twisted into a grimace.

'Is that what you did back then too? You just took off?'

I nodded.

'And our plan? Didn't you care about it? We were planning to go to Seoul together, don't you remember?' He lit the cigarette. 'And now that you need help, you've suddenly remembered I exist. You spit into the fountain, then want to drink from it again. Fine friend you are.'

I didn't know what to say; I had thought our plans ceased to exist the moment his father threw me out of the house with no money or provisions. Mr Kim had threatened me, told me to leave his property, because I wasn't a patriot, wasn't a true Korean, and how could I be, with a brother in prison, a Red – and I had gone, without defending Yunsu or justifying myself. Without saying goodbye.

'I'm sorry,' I said softly.

I'm sorry. I couldn't bring myself to say anything more, even though I knew Johnny was waiting for an explanation. That he deserved an explanation. But I couldn't tell him I had left Nonsan because I didn't want to put my brother in danger. You see, I was the only connection to Yunsu, the only one who could actually *attest* to his having joined forces with the North Korean guerrillas.

4

I just called you a person without history, Hanna; I hope you'll forgive me this description. It's inaccurate, because of course you have a past, I would even say *pasts*. You are here to find that part of your history which, until now, has been inadequately and only superficially addressed – in a sense, my story is yours, and Yunsu's story is ours.

I can barely remember my brother. My memories of him are in hiding, they flee from me, along with my affection for him. Dostoevsky wrote that it's impossible to love those closest to you, that the best you can hope for is to love those who are far away, and I agree. I never managed to even like Yunsu. I respected him, I feared him, but I don't think I ever loved him. I love neither my mother nor my father – or to be precise, I'm not sure whether I love them. I did a long time ago, of course, but over the years this love has dissipated, along with all the others; it has yellowed with age.

Yunsu was eight years older than me; I say 'was', because I don't believe he's still alive. For me he always existed in the past tense, even when we were children.

He was tall, almost a head taller than me, lanky and thin, with short hair that jutted out in bristly spikes, intent on breaking the teeth of the comb he always carried with him and seldom used; he said he was saving it. Yunsu had soft, full lips, and his face was as round and big as his eyes, which shrunk behind the glasses that Father finally pressed into his hand one day, to put an end to his constant stumbling over each and every root and stone, something which always amused us greatly. He was clumsy, awkward, his movements jerky, his expression full of rage, recalcitrant through and through. He never spoke to us, the younger children, nor did he have any time for the other teenagers in the village, the ones his own age. Instead he roamed alone through the meadows, fields and mountains, and sometimes he got lost, as though he had become aware of his smallness amid the vastness of the valleys and taken advantage of it: he would disappear and remain untraceable for days or even weeks on end, until Mother sent out a search party, who, instead of going to the effort of tracking him down, headed for the inn and transformed their payment into *makgŏlli*. A few days later, the men knocked on our door and asked my mother for more money. She told them she had given them everything she could spare, at which they shrugged their shoulders and said that, under these circumstances, there was nothing more they could do.

Yunsu hadn't always been difficult; taciturn and pensive, yes, but there used to be a degree of optimism concealed within his melancholy, a willingness to be content. After Father fell in the war, Yunsu distanced himself from us even more than he had before. He was looking for someone whom he could hold responsible, and he found the culprit in Mr Kim. Yunsu claimed that the director was corrupt, a boot-licker and a traitor. 'What does that make us, the people who work for him?' he asked, before answering his own question: 'Collaborating collaborators.'

'You got that from Mr Sŏng,' said Mother, and promptly forbade him any further contact with our neighbours. When Yunsu ignored her and continued to spend his afternoons and evenings with them – people who, unlike us, were engaged in anti-Japanese resistance, distributing flyers, organizing meetings and supplying guerrilla fighters in the surrounding forests with food – Mother turned to Mr Kim for help. He had to do something, she pleaded, her eldest was heading for ruin, he was destroying himself. No, her exact words were: 'Miya is destroying him'.

I now wonder whether Yunsu's misfortune perhaps began with this sentence.

Miya was the baby of the Sŏng family. Yunsu wasn't the only one to fall for her; many of the village boys did. I was in love with her too, with her long plait which reached down to her hips, with her black eyes so dark I couldn't tell where the pupil stopped and the iris began. When I found out that she had chosen my brother, I was jealous, and refused to exchange so much as a word with him for days on end. Instead, I followed him at a safe distance and tried to catch every one of his words to Miya. I can no longer remember what they said; the usual, I presume; I only remember that I was watching as he leant forwards, gently –

as she leant forwards, no less gently –

as he pursed his lips and closed his eyes;

as she did the same, lingering until their mouths met.

I cried the whole afternoon and evening, avoiding even Johnny, though I could clearly hear his calls and they eventually bored their way as deeply into my heart as the image of Yunsu kissing Miya.

They became a couple – so close that even water couldn't trickle between them – despite Mother's vehement protests, but with Mr Sŏng's blessing, for he loved Yunsu like he was his own, even comparing him with his firstborn, who, according to people in the village, had joined the communists in the North shortly after the outbreak of the Second World War, and now lived a guerrilla life. This was why the family was under Japanese surveillance, there were always two members of the secret police stationed near their house: the ugly worm that moved only sideways, and the rat with a stone in its mouth. Admittedly there was very little for them to see, because on the surface the Sŏngs lived an unremarkable life; in spring and summer the two younger brothers and Miya helped their father in the fields, and in winter the activity on the farm gave way to impenetrable silence.

On the day that Japan capitulated, all the Japanese teachers at my school lost their jobs, and those who didn't immediately pack up their belongings and depart on the very first trains – which were headed to the docks and piled indiscriminately with people and luggage – were rendered destitute; forced to make ends meet as day labourers or by begging. Their wives, who previously had employed Korean women as attendants, became servants themselves – and the erstwhile servants? They became beggars, because their husbands had been killed in the war.

While Yunsu, the Sŏng family and their allies flew Korean flags and burned Japanese ones, hacked up the Shinto shrine and set it on fire – their victory dances and songs accompanied by flutes, bells, pipes and anything they could find to bang together – Johnny's parents buried their disappointment and fear over Japan's defeat in icy silence.

Were they afraid, once the first police stations had been set on fire, that they too would be suspected of collaboration, and attacked? Usually the policemen and soldiers were the first to be affected, then the officials, and finally the upper classes, the landowners who had not only omitted to share their wealth, but actually increased it at the expense of the poor and the poorest; many had benefited from the new railway lines, which people said the Japanese had built upon piles of corpses. Before the Second World War, it was possible to board a train in Busan, Korea's southernmost city, and travel across Pyongyang, north-eastern China and the Yalu River via Moscow and Leningrad to Prague, Berlin and Paris.

How Mr Kim managed to make it through this time of fear and hysteria without being denounced by even one person remains a mystery to me to this day. Who protected him and his family? Who did he bribe? I'm assuming, though, that he was a collaborator, and perhaps he wasn't; I'm doing something that is still common in these parts even now: believing in the supposed clarity of guilt, even though the very absence of ambiguity should make me suspicious. Japan's refusal to acknowledge its war crimes made it impossible (in South and North Korea, in China, and in all the countries which had been annexed by Emperor Hirohito) to process the trauma of the Second World War; to move beyond ideology, guilt and sin.

When, on his eighteenth birthday, Yunsu announced that he was going to marry Miya, Mother dragged her son to the big house. It was a warm morning, all the cherry blossoms had fallen at once during the night, and the earth was saturated with soft white flowers, like feathers. Yunsu tried to free himself from her grip, bracing his feet against the ground, but Mother had developed superhuman strength; she said later that she had never been so angry, and there was nothing he could do to stop her.

Mr Kim had only just got out of bed, having spent the night

with friends – it was a habit of his to drink heavily until the sun came up – and so his response to being disturbed early was a sullen one. What had Yunsu been thinking, he snarled, he wouldn't tolerate, *couldn't* tolerate him risking the lives of his mother and brother and everyone else who was in any way connected to him. Didn't he realize that the Sŏng family was blacklisted? Mr Sŏng and his sons were radical communists who had been fighting for a blood-red Korea for years. What did they know about freedom, about justice? Hadn't Yunsu heard that the Reds had driven all the Christians out of the North? That they had planted agents in the South in order to turn innocent people into revolutionaries? That was how they had transformed Jeju into a communist island! Of the tens of thousands of soldiers stationed there since the war, most had gone over to the communists. They had had the island under their control for months; fending off the American soldiers, and later the South Korean ones too, with the weapons the Japanese had left behind. President Rhee had sent one division after the other, and one after the other had fallen victim to Red propaganda and joined forces with the People's Army. There was no way, Yunsu interjected, that Syngman Rhee was the rightful president of Korea, he had never been elected in the North, there had been protests everywhere, but no one had done anything about it, Rhee was nothing but a cat's paw for the collaborators who now feared having to do penance for the crimes they had committed during the colonial era. Yunsu was furious, I could hear his voice even from the garden. He screamed that the question wasn't how much *one* human life was worth, but how much thousands, hundreds of thousands, millions of thousands of human lives were worth.

Mr Kim was no longer listening, and had already summoned

his servants. They locked my brother in a room and called the police. That very same evening, Yunsu was imprisoned.

Mother was stunned, shocked. She had expected Mr Kim to appeal to her son's conscience; she had hoped he would have more success than her, had thought that Yunsu would take him seriously. He had always looked up to the director as a child, copying his facial expressions and gestures, and Mr Kim, venerated in this way, had always held him up as an example to Johnny and me.

'When will Yunsu be released?' I asked Mother. She shook her head; she didn't know. 'But he hasn't committed a crime!' I protested. She nodded, and agreed that he hadn't, but she had heard that detentions and secret executions were on the increase, that Rhee was on the hunt for communists. She was very worried. She didn't want to pester Director Kim any more, and wasn't expecting any further help from him. Instead, she overcame her timidity and crept to the neighbouring house one night, to speak to the Sŏngs.

Her effort was in vain. When she got there, she found their house empty. They hadn't even left the dust behind, she said.

That was in May.

We managed to visit Yunsu only once in prison, which was a day's march from Nonsan, before the civil war broke out on 25 June – a day I can still clearly remember: the weather was warm and sunny, and Johnny and Haesun were swimming in the river, splashing around as Mother and the women from the village washed clothes. They used blocks of soap so big they could barely hold them, and wrung out the wet clothes against the rocks, their hands and faces red from the heat and exertion, and Haesun said that she never wanted to get married, because she never wanted to have to do the washing, and Johnny said that no one wanted to marry her anyway, so she didn't need to worry about it. She lurched towards him and tried to dunk him under the water, but he was bigger and stronger, so she cried out: 'Yunho, help me!' I kept my distance from their squabbling. I sat on the riverbank in the shade and thought about Yunsu, picturing him crouched on the prison floor, hungry, defiant and in chains. I was just contemplating how I (a fourteen-year-old) could save him (together with other fourteen-year-olds), when suddenly the siren started up. Normally it wailed twice a day; at noon and midnight, one soft tone, one loud and then another low, but this time it came several hours too early and didn't stop: low, loud, low, pause, low, loud, low, pause, low, loud, low. It didn't match the yellow afternoon light; its shrill sound tore through the heat and the landscape's muted song.

I looked up to see Mother and the women speaking nervously with one another, and heard them say: 'What can it mean, something terrible must have happened, what should we do?' Haesun and Johnny had even stopped arguing, and were swimming to the shore. By now the women had decided to follow Mother home, and called us over; Johnny's family owned the only radio in the village, and they hoped to get more information from it. We went as quickly as we could. The washing, which was still sopping wet, stopped us from running; we carried it together, each of us holding a corner.

How strange we must have looked that afternoon. A procession of women in their long white clothes, and three children connected to one another by a coarse cloth, and we didn't think of letting go, we would never have let go, so long as the siren song united us.

Half the village had gathered together in front of the radio. Yuri shook her head as we walked in and told us there hadn't been a report yet, but that the normal programme had been interrupted, and it really had: only a soft rustling could be heard. We prepared ourselves for a long wait, Mrs Kim instructed Mother to attend to the guests. Suddenly she was interrupted by a voice on the radio, a man's voice, fearful and agitated, saying that North Korean troops had marched into South Korea and were en route to Seoul, that we should stay calm and leave the towns.

'Get yourselves to safety, head into the mountains. Get yourselves to safety, but stay calm . . .'

The room empties, then the entire house, until eventually only we children remain. The grown-ups have disappeared – they sighed, complained, then surrendered their visibility from one second to the next, the decision swallowing up their bodies, even their shadows; we, the ones who remain, watch them go, our bodies and shadows all too tangible; we don't know where to put them. I can still feel it today, the uncertainty that paralysed me back then, how I was afraid of moving even a muscle, for every movement seemed to have conse- quences, terrible ones. Haesun and Johnny didn't move either; we stood there in the middle of that large room, which shrunk more and more until eventually we disappeared into it.

Over the days that followed, more and more people left. In the end Mr Kim organized a horse and carriage to take us to a hideaway in some woodlands on the other side of the North– South arterial road. He told us that the communists had reached Seoul, and from there it wasn't far to Daejeon and Nonsan, so we had to leave today and he wouldn't accompany us; it would put us in danger if the Reds found him with us.

We took clothes and some provisions, a few sacks of rice, beans and dried squid. I remember the squid in particular because I could smell it throughout the entire journey, even though it was wrapped up. We left everything else behind, the radio, the gramophone, the sewing machine, the records and the director's library. With a letter signed by Mr Kim on his lap and the reigns gripped tightly in his hands, Johnny sat on the carriage and I alongside him; we didn't speak the whole time, any words had perished after we had to incessantly shoo away refugees, the old and weak, invalids and children, who followed our carriage and tried to climb up on it – we were obeying Mrs Kim's orders.

Mother refused to come with us, she wanted to wait for Yunsu. Now that war had broken out, she believed they would release him. She comforted me, saying she would follow on with him as soon as possible.

We held out for five weeks in our emergency quarters, in our refuge hut, which we knew was the right one solely because it was the only one for miles around. It was huddled in the shadow of a mountain and couldn't be seen from a distance; the ideal hiding place, the director had called it, and I had to agree with him: it was ideal, visible only if one already knew of its existence. The hut itself, however, was near-derelict, the roof had never been patched up, the wind blew through the gaps, and in July, during the summer monsoon, we had to leave all the doors open so the water could flow away. We didn't replace the paper in the windows but instead let it hang down in strips from the wooden frames. Despite this, or perhaps because of it, I felt safe in this place: I could sense any change immediately through the thin walls – which could keep out neither the morning nor the evening and had long since given up trying to do either – and in the voices of nature which ventured right up to my ears. The war seemed far, far away; it seemed to not even exist, were it not for the exchange

74

of gunshots that ruptured the stillness from time to time, the postcard-like stillness.

At the beginning of August, Mrs Kim announced that we had to pack, that we were going home, that we couldn't wait any longer. I begged and pleaded with her; I had promised Mother I would wait for her. Mrs Kim's expression hardened. She said we had no choice, our provisions had run out . . .

I try to push the gate open as quietly as possible, the others follow. I hear Johnny's breathing behind me, constrained. The front garden is white, but not from cherry blossom or snow; the ground is covered with pieces of paper, shreds of paper, of differing sizes and differing shades of white, most of them soft from the damp; many are burnt, some have dried and re-dried, their black script now indecipherable.

Everything is still.

Suddenly, a gust of wind—

A sound like whispering leaves.

The scraps fly up into the air. Johnny grabs at them, collects them, decodes their message. His voice is weak, too weak to hold its own against the wind, and is carried away. I hear only a few of his words, the rest rustle away beneath my feet.

Johnny read his way through the garden, followed the words down to the pond, and there was the source, the origin of the shredded sentences: the director's library, disembowelled.

He turned towards the house. On all the cabinets and boxes which hadn't yet been taken, there were little yellow notes: the cabinets 'expropriated', the boxes 'expropriated', the shelves 'expropriated'; everything else, the numerous little tables, the crockery, the cutlery, the sewing machine, the gramophone and the radio, had disappeared. The pictures on the walls, the calligraphy prints, the stone and wooden figurines, the ornate chests, the jewellery, even the children's clothes which Mrs Kim had sewn, as well as their underwear and shoes, everything was gone. In Mr Kim's study, a communist manifesto had been hung on the wall. I tried to read it, but Johnny pulled me outside. 'What do you want with that trash?' he demanded. 'We should take it down and burn it.'

It remained there for the next two months, until the People's Army withdrew from the South, General MacArthur's men marching closer and closer. At moments when no one would miss me, I stole into the room, a space I had never been allowed to enter before, sat down on the floor in front of the wall and made my way through the text, letter by letter, word by word. One night, when I had almost read it all, with just one paragraph to go, I was startled by the sound of a woman crying loudly. I hurried over to Johnny and woke him. Together we crept to the front door and opened it. There was no one to be seen. 'Come on,' I said. He shook his head. 'Come on,' I repeated, pulling him out into the cool night air. We tiptoed over to the garden gate, which was open, and peered through the gap.

The white light of the full moon illuminated an oddly static scene – static despite its drama: my Maths teacher's wife was lying on the ground, clinging to a North Korean soldier's right boot, her sister-in-law was hanging on to the left boot, and her son was cowering in chains at the soldier's feet. The soldier stood wide-legged, with his arms stretched out, holding a club in one hand – no, a baseball bat, Johnny's baseball bat, which the little uncle had brought back from Japan. All right, said the North Korean, in order to stop the women's crying and pleading, he would spare Mansik's life if he reported to the community house the next morning with a sack of rice. The women howled, they had no rice, where could they get so much rice, have pity, please have pity, but he interrupted them:

in that case Mansik was as good as dead. He kicked them away from him, they fell aside, and he disappeared into the darkness.

The next morning, I heard that the community house had been set on fire. All the men who had obeyed the communists' order had been burned alive, including Mansik and Mansik's father.

I still hadn't heard anything from Mother or Yunsu. Nor was there any news from Director Kim. We didn't know whether we should wait and hope, or if it was better to just give up. The uncertainty, the state of limbo in which we found ourselves, was reflected in the empty house, in the seemingly ownerless property, where there were no longer chickens, turkeys and dogs running around freely, for they had all been killed, and only rarely would a solitary cat creep through the tall grass.

We didn't dare touch the notes on the furniture, for fear that the People's Army would return and arrest us. We jumped every time there was a noise in the garden or at the front door, and Mrs Kim would whisper to us to hide and be as quiet as mice, to pretend we weren't there. And it worked, to begin with there were no problems, almost every night we wrapped ourselves up in dark blankets and shawls and held our breath as we crept beneath the sloped roofs and along the house wall to old Mrs Oh's hut, so we could sleep there. We would be safe with her, said Mrs Kim, she was among those the Reds were protecting, and in turn she would protect us. During the day we stayed inside the house, in the back rooms, whispering to one another, suppressing any laughter or coughs, and Johnny's mother didn't cook, we ate everything raw and cold, even the small portions of rice that Mrs Oh gave us. It was only when Johnny was spotted buying eggs from Mr Im that the North

Koreans, who had taken up quarters in the centre of the village, became aware of our presence. This time, the soldiers sent by the People's Army weren't fooled by the artificial silence; they wasted no time on courtesies and broke down the door. Mrs Kim pushed us towards the window, we clambered out into the open air and ran as quickly as we could towards the barley fields; we didn't look back.

She had said that we could only return once we had counted to one hundred three times. We started to count, *hana, dul, set, net,* and lost count at fifty the first time, seventy the second time, ninety the third time, and each time we lost count we started again from the beginning.

When we came back, Mrs Kim was in the kitchen. She had been crying. Her face was bruised; red, brown, blue. Her upper lip split. Haesun dashed over to her mother, stroked her cheek, and put her arms around her. 'We can stay here for the time being,' said Mrs Kim, freeing herself from the embrace, 'the People's Army have allowed it, but from now on we have to go to the meetings.' 'Meetings,' asked Johnny, 'what kind of meetings?'

I can no longer remember how Mrs Kim explained the process of the 'purification', the self-incrimination; I can barely even remember the evenings themselves, all these years I've successfully banished them from my memory, only at night do they catch up with me, in my dreams, when I am unable to defend myself. Looking back now it feels as though I dreamt the re-education, the hours we children spent on the floor behind the grown-ups, unable to see, only able to hear what was happening at the front.

The meetings began with the half-soldier – we called him 'the half-soldier' because he was no taller than Johnny –

running through Nonsan and banging a spoon against a tin bowl, which meant we were expected in the village hall. At each hearing, a different villager was called up to confess his sins; the chairman primarily targeted the men. Mr Im told of how he had charged too high a price for his wares, that he sometimes delivered fewer eggs but pocketed the full sum, and that he still didn't know the Party manifesto by heart, because he had never learnt to read and write.

His remorse was lacking, the chairman concluded, but the Party believed that Mr Im would mend his ways, so he would be called up again the following week, and in the meantime a comrade would read the manifesto out to him as often as necessary. The rice vendor and a few teachers from my school apologized for their antisocial behaviour and promised to improve. Not everyone was granted absolution, sometimes their penitence was declared to be unconvincing and the sinner violently beaten.

I witnessed one man's failed re-education, which concluded with a shot fired straight to his head.

That evening, Mrs Kim was called up. We froze as we heard her name; we had thought women would be spared. Johnny, immobilized by fear, asked me to go and see if it was his mother, perhaps this was a different Mrs Kim. I managed to push my way forward, using the grown-ups as cover.

And that was where I found him again, my headstrong, foolish brother – on the wrong side. He was sitting behind the group leaders, behind the leaders' deputies, in the fourth or fifth row. As soon as I spotted Yunsu, I barely took in anything else. I think I remember Mrs Kim being asked where her husband was and whether she knew that he was an enemy of the Party and the country; that he had collaborated with the

Japanese; that he was in cahoots with the Americans, and with Dictator Rhee; that he had betrayed his countrymen whenever it suited him. I watched Yunsu during the interrogation: he didn't bat an eyelid when Mrs Kim was knocked to the ground.

I crept back over to Johnny. He looked at me in despair; he had recognized her voice. He put his hands over his ears as his mother began to weep.

Mrs Kim survived, but had to be carried home by two soldiers. Johnny followed them, while I slipped away. I wanted to speak to Yunsu; I had to know whether he had seen Mother.

I didn't have much time – the midnight curfew was just an hour away.

It was easy to find the quarters of the People's Army, I just had to follow the noise. For not a whisper emerged from the surrounding houses, many of which were still abandoned. The air smelt of smoke, burnt straw, burnt wood. The yellow squash blossoms were wilted, brown; the last fruits hung from the chilli bushes. Besides the empty streets, our village looked no different from usual, and yet it felt different.

The soldiers had taken up residence in the school. One of them was guarding the entrance and spotted me before I had the chance to hide. When I asked him for my brother, my voice trembled, and he patted me on the shoulder to calm me down. He said: 'Wait a moment, I'll fetch him,' and disappeared inside. I heard a murmur, the clack of hard soles on wood . . .

The chirping of the cicadas.

A rustling in the bushes.

The soft call of a tawny owl.

I remember the sounds clearly because I didn't dare look up from the ground, all I could do was listen. The door opened, creaking quietly. Everything seemed muffled. That's what war does, I thought back then, it smothers all the sounds; I was still just a child.

Yunsu lit up as soon as he was out in the open air. A roll-up; a few shreds of tobacco inside a scrap of paper. It had print across it; the paper was probably from a book. I didn't know he smoked. He had always spoken so contemptuously about Mr Kim's 'decadent habits', alcohol and nicotine.

He said he was glad I had found him. He sat down, I remained standing. I asked whether he had searched for me. Without giving an answer, he took a long drag of the cigarette. I asked whether he knew where Mother was. He shook his head and exhaled the smoke. How was I doing? he asked. Good, I said, Mrs Kim had taken care of me. He nodded. Good, he said. He stood up and knocked the dirt from his trousers, with a sound that was dull yet somehow metallic, hard. He cleared his throat. Would I come by again tomorrow? He wanted to see me again, he said. I nodded. I didn't dare oppose him.

The next day, he was waiting for me. He seemed uneasy, despondent. He told me he didn't have much time, they were moving on the following day. He sighed and turned away. He said he felt he owed me an explanation. An explanation? I asked. About why he was fighting on the North Koreans' side, he said. I told him I already understood. He laughed. What could a little twelve-year-old boy possibly understand about it? Fourteen, I said. 'Fourteen,' he said, 'well, that changes everything,' and he told me to sit down next to him.

He said the prison in Daejeon had been overflowing. That in the preceding months, Syngman Rhee had already begun to arrest members of the union and the Korean Workers' Party, socialists and communists, locking away one group after the other: everyone who criticized Rhee and his government, everyone who demanded new elections because they didn't want to accept a divided Korea, everyone who thought the Americans should withdraw, that Korea couldn't return to being a colony. He said that his cellmates hadn't been criminals, certainly not 'political criminals', but innocent people, oppositionists.

In prison they had barely been fed – a bowl of gruel, once a day, containing just a few grains of rice. Those who had been tortured were unable to move or speak. Doctors had been denied access, he said. They had tried to help one another. He had ripped the sleeves from his shirt and used the material to dress wounds, but often the puss had already eaten too far into the flesh. Many died. Because their cell was so full, only the sick were able to sleep lying down, the rest had taken turns, and most just dozed standing up. He had heard that Mr Sŏng and his sons had been imprisoned too, but he hadn't seen them.

Yunsu told me he had thought he would never leave that cell; he believed he had been brought there to die.

A few weeks later, on 8 July, the prisoners from the floor below had been driven out into the yard. He heard the rattle of the chains and their shuffling footsteps on the concrete, then the ignition and hum of engines. When the chugging gradually became fainter, he had envied the poor wretches, believing they were being set free because war had broken out. Many hoped they would be drafted.

When the prisoners still hadn't come back by evening, only the drivers and guards, he thought his hope was justified; he told himself and his friends that tomorrow they too would be free.

Free at long last.

That night he had been unable to sleep, neither standing up

nor lying down. He had waited for the sunrise, for the reddish-yellow light that managed to find its way even through their small cell window. Suddenly he heard footsteps. A guard told them to get up and leave the cell; they were being transferred to the south-west, to Sannae. During the journey, some of his friends had laughed, cracked jokes; they had no idea what awaited them.

A trench, perhaps one or two hundred metres long.

Carelessly filled in, the soil just strewn on top.

Something that didn't look like earth jutted out of the pit.

Soldiers – hundreds of them? It could even have been thousands. They stood in a row alongside, guns in their hands.

The prisoners were forced out of the vehicle and instructed to line up in single file. Like when food was being handed out. The first fifty were told to squat down by the edge of the trench with their heads lowered. They pressed their faces into the backs of those in front of them, clinging to one another. The soldiers lined up behind the prisoners; each was assigned a head, but the order was too quiet and some didn't hear, they pulled the trigger too late or missed the target; some of the soldiers were crying, just as afraid as their victims.

The corpses toppled to the side, but some didn't fall all the way into the open grave. The soldiers had to help them along with a kick. Inside the trench, other soldiers were waiting. To shoot those who were still moving. Those who begged to be released from their suffering.

All of this had been watched, he said, by the American soldiers who were photographing the executions.

He could no longer remember how long he had to wait. It was probably close to dawn when the young soldier who was watching them undid their chains and told them to make themselves scarce.

He hadn't known where to go. He fell in with a group that joined the partisans who captured Nonsan. Mother had been among the villagers who had died during the battle, he said.

She had been mistaken for Mrs Kim and shot.

Later, many years later, I heard a rumour that Yunsu had killed Mother in order to prove his loyalty to the communists. I began to search for the truth. It's important that you understand: I grew up with the illusion that one truth existed, and only *one*. I believed there had to be a record of it somewhere, and so I searched, feverishly, as Mother had for Father's photo. I began to collect articles, protocols, reports; I read my way through mountains of essays. From one, I discovered that the inmates of South Korean prisons between 1945 and 1950 were mainly political prisoners – communists and socialists – and that in the days before and immediately following the outbreak of the Korean War the jails had been emptied and the inmates systematically murdered. The first emergency decree, made on 28 June 1950, ensured that these mass executions were legal. Most members of the National Rehabilitation League were also shot, out of fear that they would join the People's Army. The death toll was estimated to be around a hundred thousand: workers and farmers who had joined the league to receive fertilizer and rice from the government. The police had forced some to sign up, others they had merely hassled into doing so; they had moaned that they had quotas to fill, that every branch had to provide a certain number of 're-education volunteers', otherwise their necks would be on the line. And there was nothing to it anyway, they said, members just had to go and listen to a government representative once a month, who

84

would explain to them why communism was bad for Korea, and afterwards they would get a hot meal. They were assembled in schools, village halls and warehouses, and killed by the military, even though all they had wanted was some fertilizer and rice.

I read that when the British journalist Alan Winnington became the first foreign correspondent to report on the mass murders for the *Daily Worker*, his story entitled 'I Saw the Truth in Korea' brought him great difficulties: in America and Great Britain, word spread that he was a liar and a traitor, and in 1954 the British authorities refused to renew his expired passport, whereupon he became de facto stateless (thirty years later, he died in East Berlin, in possession of a British passport).

'Try to imagine Rangwul Valley,' wrote Winnington in 1951. I will never forget the paragraph that begins with those words: 'Try to imagine Rangwul Valley, about 5 miles south-east of Taejon on the Yongdong road. In the middle you can walk safely, though your shoes may roll on American cartridge cases, but at the sides you must be careful, for the rest of the valley is a thin crust of earth covering the corpses of more than 7,000 men and women. One of the party with me stepped through nearly to his hip in rotting human tissue. Every few feet there is a fissure in the top soil, through which you can see into a gradually sinking mass of flesh and bone. The smell is something tangible that seeps into your throat. For days after I could taste the smell. All along the great death pits, waxy dead hands and feet, knees, elbows, twisted faces and heads burst open by bullets, stick through the soil. When I read of Nazi murder camps at Belsen and Buchenwald, I tried to imagine what they were like. Now I know I failed.'

As the concentration camps had been liberated only six years earlier, it is understandable that Winnington made this association. Another factor may be that Douglas MacArthur, the general who was supposed to free Korea from the Red Menace on behalf of the United Nations, had as his right-hand man a 'pet fascist', as he affectionately called him. General Charles Willoughby (who allegedly was born in Germany and only emigrated to the US at the age of eighteen) was Chief of Intelligence for the Pacific until his discharge in 1951, and famous for two things: his 'Prussian' posture (he was said to walk as straight as a rod, as though he was staring over a high fence into the distance) and his pompous secret communiqués, which were often inaccurate, or, to put it another way, completely fabricated. He was known as an anti-Semite and a racist who, following the admission of Chinese volunteers into the Korean War, wrote of his deep regret at seeing 'uncivilized Chinese coolies wiping out American conscripts', because 'the white man is a precious and scarce commodity'. Even many years after the end of the war, he insisted on censoring the few files that were opened up to the public. Aside from Douglas MacArthur, who Willoughby lauded as a modern Napoleon, he also worshipped General Franco and had close contact with General Ishii, leader of the Epidemic Prevention and Water Purification Department, better known as Unit 731; he was also acquainted, of course, with Reinhard Gehlen and other former Nazi officers who lent a hand to the American secret service during the Cold War.

She was the only person on the road for miles, Winnington reports, all the others hid in the trenches just in time, ducking as they heard the approaching plane. There was no possibility of it having been a pilot error; in Korea, especially for someone with good eyesight, it was easy to recognize a woman even from a distance: 'Typically, this one was carrying a baby strapped to her back and a big bundle on her head, and she was wearing a long billowing white skirt.' The pilot knew that the figures before him were those of a woman and her child, but he shot at them anyway. Casually, even.

'Try to imagine Rangwul Valley.' I don't try, I refuse to — but I cannot forget. The valley, my brother's story and my mother's murder, they have merged together in my mind. The murderers are no longer many, but just one — and his face is not Yunsu's. I didn't believe the rumour years ago when I first heard it, and I still don't. Sometimes, though, I wish I could tell my brother that I'm convinced of his innocence; I wish, so hard it hurts, that I could undo that moment . . .

The moment when, as he tried to say goodbye to me that evening in front of the school, I evaded his embrace.

5

On the morning I moved in with Johnny, it rained incessantly. The heat warmed the rain, making the asphalt, the house walls, and even the tiles on the roofs seem to sweat, and a haze overhung the city. It was impossible to ride a bicycle through the streets; you had to get off and push, because the earth itself had turned to liquid.

Seoul was not a labyrinth of the indicative back then, there were only subjunctives and what-ifs; back then it was possible to have and try out numerous different lives, and often one of them would implode: the victims of the marriage fraudsters, who one day would have to defend themselves against lawful spouses, the innocent bigamists who had trusted a forged death certificate, the mix-ups that made children into orphans on a daily basis, the refugees from the North, arriving without any papers, who were branded as communists and persecuted. Back then it was inadvisable to depend upon just one life story, and it had never been easier to acquire several or exchange the one you had for another. Seldom had identity been so fragile; it could be shattered by a piece of paper.

Johnny cleared some space for me in his cupboard, where I stored the thin mat and blanket I used for sleeping; initially I didn't have even a change of clothes. I left the house early in the mornings, watching out for the landlords in the hallway. The last thing I wanted was to run into them, for Mr Pak wasn't too pleased that there were now two people living in the room, and only one paying.

At night, Johnny and I sat by the window, smoking and drinking beer, the one bottle which we allowed ourselves each week, and which we drank very, very slowly, to make it last. By daybreak, the final dregs were warm, but we drank those too, because it was still beer even if it was bad beer, and all the while music played on Johnny's valve radio. The word 'Zenith' was embossed on it, above the speaker grille, and the songs it played back were heavenly, heavenly in their acoustic excess. From the neighbourhood outside came the faint sound of voices, the muffled cries of street traders, the faraway drone of car engines, the barely audible buzz of insects. Johnny and I had got ourselves a filed-down, halved grenade as an ashtray, bought from a stall holder who specialized in taking war relics, remnants from the civil war, and transforming them into household items. He also had water buckets made from helmets with welded-up bullet holes, military signs that had been painted over, as well as tea trays made from compressed tin cans (Coca-Cola and Pepsi-Cola were his bestsellers).

From his friend, I purchased a jacket and a pair of trousers that not too long ago had been a soldier's uniform; after the end of the civil war they had been compelled to turn another colour in one of the numerous dye-works along the Chŏnggye River, for only then would they be acceptable as everyday clothes. You could see them even from a distance, the long washing lines with the sombre-looking, dripping-wet clothes and the large, steaming vat. Once a week, used uniforms were delivered and dyed black (there were innumerable corrupt officers and generals in the military who wanted to make a little something on the side; this profession's business acumen was legendary). Black was the students' colour of choice, the dyer explained, and they were his main customers, with the plethora of new universities springing up everywhere he would make a mint; his daughter had to take her entrance exam outside, sitting on a scrap of old newspaper, with the questions next to her on one of the few patches of grass that hadn't yet been trampled.

He nodded to us and went back to sorting items of clothing, trousers with trousers, jackets with jackets, checking the pockets before the wash. Most were empty, but in one he found a pencil stub, in another some old chewing gum and in another still a small photograph, the portrait of a young woman. He studied it as he stirred the dye with a pole. After the clothes had been immersed in the water for a while, he hung them up to dry on a line he had strung up between the trees and the electricity mast; he burned the photo, along with the chewing gum. The pencil vanished into his trouser pocket.

On some evenings, Eve joined us, and we would go to the small bar around the corner that made do with three drinks on the menu, and a home-made radio whose makeshift technology cut every song in half. Next door was the mini-market, where Johnny stocked up his cigarette supply and Eve bought the American gum she was always chewing, yellow Wrigley's. As soon as we were inside the bar, the owner shut the door behind us and turned the key in the lock; bars weren't allowed to open after curfew. Then, in the candlelight, we mostly discussed the details of my private life. Every one of these conversations ended with Eve telling Johnny to find a wife for me, and with me protesting in vain until, ultimately, I had no choice but to navigate the debate away from me and into the abyss of politics.

'Japan,' I said one night, 'has been sending thousands of Koreans to North Korea for months now. Have you heard about it?' Eve shook her head, grimaced and suppressed a yawn, while Johnny nodded eagerly and fished an old newspaper article out of his jacket pocket. He pointed at the headline and said that the campaign was even being advertised in the papers in Japan, 'the Great Homecoming' they were calling it, how ridiculous, the Great Homecoming! How many of these home-hungry people were really from North Korea, he said, it could only be a fraction after all, most had been wrenched from their villages in the south during the Second World War and loaded onto Japanese ships as slave labourers, forced to work from the day of their arrival – in mines, in munitions factories – but now the Japanese government wanted rid of them, to avoid having to pay compensation. Johnny spoke quickly, stumbling over his words, he was upset and thought I should be too – but I wasn't sure what to believe.

I had heard that North Korea was doing better economically than the South, that the recovery was progressing rapidly, that there were jobs, that Pyongyang was now modern and clean. I had been told all this by my neighbour in Daegu, who had disappeared soon after along with his entire family. I wondered whether he had been lying or telling the truth. Why shouldn't things be better in the North than here? It had been richer than the South even before the division; it had the natural resources, the industrial plants. Perhaps the politicians living there were more intelligent, more competent? I thought all of this, but didn't dare say it out loud; Rhee's spies were everywhere.

'Those communist pigs can't just kidnap our people,' Johnny blurted out, 'the president has to do something about it.' 'What, Rhee?' I interrupted him, 'the man who refused to take them in when Japan declared them to be foreigners and took away their rights? He could have brought them to the South, remember! Kim Il-sung just got there first.'

Eve looked around hastily; I had raised my voice. She took the chewing gum out of her mouth, disposed of it in a tissue and looked at me, then at Johnny. 'What would you know,' muttered the latter, turning his attention back to drinking his *soju*.

For three months I searched in vain for work. I did the rounds of the same shops at the South Gate Market, in Namdaemun, the part of Seoul which is closest to the main station and therefore offers ample opportunities for stealing and working, for little jobs with which one can earn some small change, enough for a meal. The market had reopened just a few years before, having burnt down during the Korean War; prior to that, until 1945, it was out of bounds to Korean vendors. It snaked its way through numerous side streets and alleyways, and everyone who set foot in this quarter had come either to buy or sell something. There was no real entrance, nor exit; the market began suddenly and stopped again just as suddenly, and it was never closed, especially not at night, when smuggled goods were brought out and offered in hushed tones, when the murmured lists of products and prices would drift from dark corners, and haggling was conducted at a whisper. As soon as a policeman or government spy approached, recognizable by the very fact that no one recognized them, the wares would disappear back into the darkness, and the candles, flickering on the stalls just moments before, were extinguished.

Dried squid and seaweed dangled from the roofs, barley and rice grains shimmered in hip-height sacks like tiny golden and white pearls, watermelons and honeydew melons lay in woven baskets. Suddenly, the light bulb that had illuminated an entire section of the street exploded, and for a second every-thing went still and I was liberated from my eyes; I sniffed my way through the market, groping past the spices, the chilli peppers, whose herbal, spicy scent never left this part of the city, past the ginger roots and cinnamon bark, past the black peppercorns and freshly roasted sesame seeds. I could hear thin rice-flour flatbreads being fried, the vegetables and the dough hissing in the hot pan, and finally my eyesight awoke again, revealing the little blue flame of the gas cooker in front of the tin containers where the marine creatures lived: the sea bream, scabbard fish, mackerel, sea urchins and spider crab which hadn't yet been sold.

I felt safe after dark, when my gaze didn't get lost in the flood of images; in daylight I was constantly losing my bearings because my feet followed my eyes. The streets were lined with little shops beneath long black awnings with white lettering; in the middle of the road sat the merchants, farmers' wives and children, they crouched on the floor and offered their wares, their baskets filled with potatoes, sweet potatoes, onions, garlic, gherkins, Chinese cabbage, tomatoes, courgettes, peaches, raspberries or apples, depending on the season – in autumn I kept a lookout for my favourite fruit, persimmon. Many of the younger women wore headscarves and caps to conceal their shaven heads; they had sold their hair to wig-makers. These could be seen at the market too, usually in conversation with their customers or the sellers, women who didn't look up if anyone came close to them, but then again hardly anyone did, not even the boys foraging for glass bottles in the mountains of rubbish that formed between the shops and on the paths, in order to wash them and sell them on. Whenever a truck drove through the market to bring a fresh delivery, old women and children went in pursuit, collecting whatever had fallen to the floor. Some even tried to swipe the fruit and vegetables directly from the loading bay, and were chased away. The same men would later devour the meals that these women had prepared, then, the next time, drive them away just as mercilessly as before.

I saw veterans who had lost both legs in the war, and now navigated their way through the narrow alleyways on a board with wheels strapped to it, balancing a plastic bowl for alms between their teeth; little old women who chewed and sucked on long pipe stems, clapping their hands and singing loudly whenever they spotted an American in their labyrinth who seemed to need Korean money; old men huddled over a small square table playing *janggi*; vendors who had fallen asleep over their wares and were being robbed blind by everyone who had noticed: the socks, undergarments and undershirts would turn up in another corner of the city, in another neighbourhood, beneath a bridge in the north, or in the slums in the west. Nothing disappeared forever in Seoul; objects had a longer life expectancy here than people.

I didn't find what I was looking for. At the beginning of October, when the trees were slowly beginning to change colour, a street trader told me to make enquiries on the other side of the city, at the East Gate. He said that factories and workshops were cropping up near the Chŏnggye River, a bicycle factory had opened just recently, and I should keep a lookout for posters; it was five in the morning, and the vendor had just washed his face with cold water from a bucket. Almost as soon as I nodded and turned around, he and the other merchants all emptied their buckets as if on command, and I suddenly found myself stood in a raging river.

From a distance, the slums looked like a pattern imposed over the city; the black of the corrugated metal roofs seemed to repeat at the same intervals as the light and dark grey of the awnings, made from clothing remnants and scraps of material, which hung over the entrances to the huts. The wooden slats in between, which were fixed to one another across great distances, looked like earth-toned brush strokes. A living creature, I thought to myself as I cut across it on a narrow, sludge-filled path, an organism that feeds on leftover wood and cardboard boxes, constantly changing its appearance, but which the rain dissolves and sweeps away, taking along with it the people who don't live but hide there: refugees from all over the country, whole families and half-families who have lost their home and possessions in the war, women, men and children who roam around searching for relatives and friends, criminals who think they can disappear here, in this place where no one pays any attention to names; everyone is nameless. There were no fixed streets; they were created when needed, through the destruction of a hut and the expulsion of a family. At night, a deep darkness fell over the slums; no one could afford to let the oil lamps burn longer than was absolutely necessary, their dark-yellow light forming small dots in the gloom whose edges just touched the adjacent neighbourhood – and as if by prior arrangement everyone began to speak in whispers, as though they had to be careful not to disturb the blackness.

It was an area that spread far too quickly, driving fear into the inhabitants of the adjacent neighbourhoods, for the poverty that lived in these wooden shacks seemed contagious. The city authorities tried again and again to tear down the settlement and forcibly relocate its inhabitants. But they didn't succeed, because the old dwellings would immediately be replaced by new ones; the supply of people was inexhaustible. And so they tried to at least do *something* to oppose the unrelenting growth of the slums, and sent officials to count and register the huts, but as soon as they had moved on, new ones would shoot up.

The factory was easy to find. It towered up amid the shacks, the only multi-storey building in the area. Inside it were the workshops, tiny chambers divided by wire mesh, where all day long and into the night assorted wares were produced on small square tables; in one cage it was trousers, in another jackets, in yet another skirts. The bicycle workshop was on the ground floor.

There were four stories to the factory, which had been an administrative building during the colonial era, albeit with only two floors, to which the owners had added two more after the war. They had lowered the existing floors to fit in the new ones, with the result that the individual levels were no longer high enough to stand upright in – but then again, that wasn't necessary. We had no time to go strolling around the enclosures, much less to stop for any longer than half an hour at midday, when we would climb up the ladder onto the roof: here we were surrounded by swathes of smoke, the roar of the traffic, the beeping of buses and cars, as well as the din and stench of the machines concreting over the Chŏnggye River, which flowed all the way through Seoul. But we heard and smelt none of it, we just threw pebbles down onto the street below and gazed after them, thinking about food: lunch, dinner, sweet snacks, salty snacks, sometimes we talked about them, but we didn't have much to say, for none of us had ever eaten anything but rice and kimchi.

I was hired without many questions asked. I didn't have to give any references or present any credentials; the only thing the foreman, Cho, asked was whether I could sew. A large order of school uniforms hadn't been delivered because a seamstress had spat up blood over a pile of them, then collapsed across the table. They had to throw them all away, said Cho, all the jackets, all the trousers, and he would have liked to throw her on the rubbish heap too. He shot a grim look into the corner, where the seamstress was sitting, trying hard to ignore our conversation.

Mihee was eighteen years old, but she looked about twelve. She collected spectacles; whenever she saw a pair, she stole them. She said she liked seeing the world around her in a different way, without it actually changing. Everything was just a question of proportion, she said with a smile; everyone knew that her eyesight was getting worse with every passing day, and that she was afraid of going blind. She had already started to use her hands more, stroking the tips of her fingers over the seam as though wanting to make sure her eyes hadn't been mistaken. When she stepped into a room, she sniffed around like a little rabbit, the tip of her nose hopping up and down, and she orientated herself by sunlight and shadow, light and dark, thereby avoiding sharp corners and edges. Mihee's hands on the surface of the table, her face in shadow, the silver of her glasses glinting as though trying to transmit Morse code – this is an image that has stayed with me.

It was the tablets, she told me that winter, after I had worked through the autumn in the bicycle shack; Cho had given them to her, like he always did when a big order had to be completed quickly, but all of them needed to be completed quickly, without exception, there was clearly nothing more pressing than having new clothes, she said, spitting the cigarette butt she had been chewing out in a wide arc, and she had taken them, just like always, and just like always her heart had started to race, and she hadn't been able to imagine ever sleeping again – as though sleep were an illness she could be healed from by these little white bombs, which steal yawns and numb the brain so you no longer feel anything and become a machine. While working on an order, she had swallowed not just one pill, no, but entire packets of that anti-sleep drug. This time she had noticed soon after taking them that she could no longer see properly, and she had taken another, which made her dizzy. Cho had allowed her to lie down on the floor for half an hour, on the mound of fabric remnants, and she had dunked the softest rags in cold water and placed them over her eyes, but she couldn't sleep, for she had killed it, after all, her sleep. 'I've needed these ever since,' she said, pointing at the glasses in her blouse pocket, which had only one lens, 'I'm just waiting for the second eye, then everything will be back to normal.'

That afternoon, she began to cough up black slime. The dry, white skin on her hands and arms bled, and by the end of the day she could no longer hold a needle, because the tips of her fingers were so swollen she was afraid they would burst. 'Do you still have fingerprints?' I asked Mihee, raising her index finger up to the light. 'I can't see a thing, could you put my glasses on for me?' she asked, and I held up her monocle. She leant over to inspect her finger. 'Yes,' she said eventually, 'I still have them.' And, more quietly: 'I have to stop while I still do.'

Over New Year, I had mine and Johnny's room to myself. He didn't come home, and I, assuming he was spending the time with Eve, didn't give any thought to his whereabouts.

I had a week off, unpaid holiday; there were barely any orders before New Year. I slept late, waking up in the afternoons to the sound of the radio from the ground floor, news reports, adverts, 'Jingle Bells', 'White Christmas' and

Mrs. Pak's unmelodious humming. As a Buddhist, the birth of Christ was lost on her, but she still decorated the living room with a plastic relief of Santa Claus and his reindeer, albeit naming him 'Christi-Claus'. Christi-Claus and his dog. 'It's a strange-looking dog,' she commented to Mr Pak, 'because aren't those horns? And horns are a sign of the devil, aren't they? At least that's what my friend said. So why does Christi-Claus have a devil-dog? I don't know, these Christians expect people to understand them . . .'

I enjoyed listening to them, the Paks, to me they were like a radio play. I knew their voices better than their faces or bodies, which I seldom saw, because whenever I passed by their door, early in the morning or late at night, it was firmly shut. But every third Sunday in the month I was able to eavesdrop on them, I would leave the door to our room open just a crack and lay down with my head against the gap; I liked the cool draught, or warm air, depending upon the time of year, which drifted into the room along with the music and the Paks' voices. That was my favourite pastime: lying on the floor, warming my back against the underfloor heating and listening to the radio; 'I'll be home for Christmas', trilled Frank Sinatra, and it was as though he was singing my thoughts – I was home. The fact that I had only badly paid work was a grievance I was willing to put up with. I resolved to begin my studies as soon as possible, perhaps even to take the entry exam next year, and if my test results were good enough I would get a scholarship too, like Johnny; back then I believed that his education was being funded by the state.

I didn't want to resign myself to spending the rest of my life cutting saddles out of leather and bending bicycle spokes; the saddle-baker, I called myself, after I had watched the pastor's wife baking biscuits, the saddle-baker and chain-knotter.

On my way into the workshop the next morning, I watched a policeman giving a speech about zebra crossings to a large group of pedestrians, some of whom looked affluent and were wearing hats, gloves and leather boots. Taking great pains to speak with authority, he said they must always use the pedestrian crossing, and anyone who neglected to do so, anyone who hurried across the street haphazardly, would henceforth have to pay a fine, because they would be endangering their lives and everyone else's; the group was to watch him as he demonstrated.

A mania for education had broken out in Seoul: everything was being taught and everything learnt. Korean, English, calligraphy, ballet, piano, bookkeeping, pottery, the correct way to use a knife and fork, stenography, typing, watercolour painting, embroidery, crochet, knitting. There were private schools for everything, state schools for everything else, and traffic policemen who gave lectures on zebra crossings, traffic lights and one-way streets.

The group trotted obediently behind him across the white stripes and back, going back and forth, again and again, until the exemplary art of road crossing was interrupted by a street trader with tin pans on his back. Ignoring the brand-new street markings, he clattered his away over the crossing, zigzagging between the cars, the buses and the tram. The smug students howled with indignation, the outraged policeman blew his whistle – once, then a second time. When the traffic sinner didn't react, even on the third whistle, but instead sauntered cheerfully on his way, the policeman signalled to his pupils and set off in pursuit. I could still hear an angry 'Stop!' and 'Stop! You're under arrest!' before the traffic school eventually disappeared from my line of sight.

Outside the new department store, I had to fight my way through a crowd gathered in front of the entrance; they had only enough money to admire the window displays and the people who were striding inside. Among them were war veterans who had never given back their uniforms, because they didn't have any other clothes; they drifted from one place to the next, begging for alms. Usually they started to drink even before they set out, and only stopped again once the alcohol had taken away their ability to stand upright. Back then I was convinced it was always the same three men begging their way through Seoul, the tall, seemingly uninjured one, the short, one-legged one with the crutch, and the one in the wheelchair; all veterans had beards, a uniform, and most a soldier's cap. Often they had abuse hurled at them, and were cursed and chased out of the bars and restaurants. No one wanted to be reminded of the civil war, everyone wanted to act as though it had never happened.

I didn't know the three men, I never approached them nor did they ever approach me; I didn't know what they had been through or what they had seen, and yet I felt as though I was one of them. The city was crawling with us 'antisocial elements' – refugees, beggars, invalids, the unemployed, day labourers, ragpickers and shoe-shiners – Seoul would have been empty without us. The section of the population that was ashamed of our kind could be found in the department store, surrounded by sales girls in immaculately ironed uniforms with little hats perched on their artificial curls.

Children crouched by the side of the street, war orphans and those who had run away from home because they wanted to grow up without being punched and kicked; little boys, eight or nine years old at most, their hoods and caps pulled down low over their foreheads, a tin can before their feet, empty, for no one was in a giving mood. Did they have it better than those newborns and small children who were abandoned on the streets on a daily basis; in dark corners, in front of police stations and churches? Not all of them were brought to the orphanage in time, many froze to death. Back then, if you saw a bundle of material, you avoided it, you didn't approach it under any circumstance; no one wanted to be responsible for another mouth to feed.

Delivery boys pushed their heavily laden bicycles and carts through the throngs of people. The neon signs on the house walls were swallowed by the first light of day, its milky-white haze, its sun-mist. Human voices were lost in the din of the city, all apart from one: a Caruso impersonator was standing on the crossing, belting out 'O Sole Mio'. His vocals hung briefly in the air before the wind blew them away.

I arrived at work late; Mr Cho muttered something about how I was never on time, how he was going to dock an hour off my pay. Before he disappeared into his office, he growled that I was to see to the new boy.

The new guy was small and compact, like the pit of a jujube. His name was Sangok, and he was five years older than me, a sunny character with thinning hair, who let nothing and nobody ruffle him. I showed him the ropes, pointing out which handlebars were his; we had divided up the work so that each person assembled just one part of the bicycle. He learnt quickly, because he knew his stuff with bicycles, he told me he'd had one himself for a really long time. 'Where?' I asked. 'In Seoul,' he answered. He had never lived anywhere else. 'The whole time?' I asked. 'Even during the civil war?' Sangok shook his head, no, he had fled south during the war, like everyone else, and had just made it over the bridge before it and the thousands of people on it were blown up into the air; on Rhee's orders, he added.

I took an instant liking to him. He was different to my other colleagues; easy-going and stubborn all at once, and warm-hearted too, albeit in a distanced way, as though he were surrounded by sick people. Mihee was the only one with whom he surrendered his reserve. He brought her little treats to nibble on, cooked sweet potato, biscuits, even Hershey's chocolate, which she loved, probably more for the packaging than the taste. When she was fired, he put his job on the line so that she could keep hers. He could find work somewhere else, he said, but she didn't have it so easy, she was half-blind after all.

Cho was in a bad mood that day. He came into the factory later than usual and barely said a word. His face was red, even more so than normal, his eyes bloodshot, and he stank of alcohol. As always, he did an inspection at midday and groused at those whose mere appearance he detested. Shortly after he made his way up to the first floor, I heard him scream, louder than I was accustomed to from him. He threw fabric around and kicked Mihee's table, making the sewing machine teeter. She had sewn all the blouses together wrong, he roared, the left sleeves to the right shoulders and the right sleeves to the left, who was he supposed to sell these to, where were the freaks of nature who could wear them? She had made a mess of things yet again, he shouted, it was always her fault that he couldn't deliver to the shops on time. While Cho raged, Mihee sat there at her workstation, thin and pale; she didn't understand that he was raging because of her. Suddenly, feeling his gaze on her, she lifted her head and fixed her weakening eyes on his.

She blinked. Cho gave a yell of anger, grabbed her by the hair and pulled her over to the stairs. There was nothing more for her here, he screamed, she had ruined him, he wouldn't be able to pay anyone, neither his retailers nor his workers! He would have pushed her down the steps, had Sangok not intervened. 'Mr Cho,' he said, trying to shield Mihee behind him, 'it's not her fault, she can barely see a thing. She's ruined her eyes, for this work, for this factory, you can't be too hard on her.'

'Too hard?'

Cho's already red face turned a shade redder. He bellowed: 'Too hard?!' He turned around, hurled the sewing machine onto the floor and kicked the table so violently that it swayed dangerously back and forth.

Sangok remained calm. Mr Cho couldn't just fire the girl, he said, she was only sixteen years old, he should at least pay her medical bills.

'Medical bills?'

Cho's face twisted into a grimace. He began to laugh hysterically. If Mr Shin wasn't careful, he spat, there would be two vacancies to fill. He should clear out of his way and get back to work. Cho tried to push Sangok aside, but he wouldn't back down. She needed the work, he persisted, she needed the money, couldn't she work in the bicycle workshop? As his assistant? He was prepared to give her part of his wages.

Perhaps Cho saw that Sangok wouldn't give in, or perhaps his high blood pressure was bothering him. Either way, he gave in, mean old Cho actually gave in. As he went back down to the ground floor, sweating and sighing, he said with a shake of his head that Mr Shin should do whatever he wanted, for all he cared he could pay the girl, what he did with his salary was his business, and he slammed his office door shut behind him with a loud bang.

★

Mihee became Sangok's shadow, not leaving his side from that moment on, and Sangok kept his word: he gave her half of his pay, even though she did nothing but sit or doze next to him on the floor. His monthly salary dwindled, but despite his generosity Mihee could no longer pay the rent for her room. She sold her collection of glasses and eventually her monocle too, and before long she possessed nothing but the clothes on her back. She even sold her shoes and her hair.

One day, I caught sight of her stubbly head in front of my house; she was calling my name. Mrs Pak opened the window and barked at Mihee to stop with all the shouting, no one with that name lived here, and what was she thinking making such a racket? 'But I have to speak to him,' Mihee begged, 'to Yunho Kang.' Why, asked Mrs Pak, what had that hoodlum done to her? 'Nothing,' she answered, 'he hasn't done anything, but I can't pay my rent, I don't know where to go, and perhaps he can help, he's a friend.' Mrs Pak was silent. As she closed the window, she muttered once more that no one by that name lived here. There were many people in the same situation, so she should stop complaining.

Mihee sighed and left. I watched her shaven head until it disappeared from sight. Ducking down beneath the window, I held my breath and waited until no more noises could be heard. Then I stood up and peered outside. She could no longer be seen. Mihee was gone.

Sangok was furious when I told him. Why hadn't I helped her? Why hadn't I interrupted Mrs Pak and brought Mihee into the warm, why hadn't I given her something to eat and some socks to wear, why had I let her down? He glared at me, his anger making him seem bigger somehow as he pulled on his jacket and held mine out to me. I had to help him find Mihee, he said, even if Cho fired us for it.

Cho kicked us out. He tossed the money for the days we had worked into the snow at our feet. It wasn't much, and probably wouldn't last until we found new jobs. Sangok wouldn't even look at me, he trotted briskly ahead, hurrying from one address to the next. I was surprised that he knew all the places Mihee normally went, when she herself had been forced to search for me in the hope of finding him. Over a cup of tea, once he had calmed down a little, I asked him about it. He didn't have an address, he explained curtly, sometimes he lived here, sometimes he lived there.

We eventually found her at the South Gate, sleeping in a corner of the market. Her body was ice cold, we had to shake her vigorously to get her to wake up. 'We're just in time,' said Sangok. He fed her some rice gruel which he had bought from a woman at the market, who also gave him a bowl of soup and some kimchi; that would wake the little one, she said, the chilli was hot as flames. Then he wrapped Mihee up in his jacket, put her over his back and signalled to me to follow him. He made his way towards a small bar near Eve's dance school, an underground establishment which had neither a neon sign nor any kind of sign – a nameless establishment without a Madame, but in her place there was a Monsieur who served beer from the can. When he saw Sangok and Mihee, he came out from behind the counter and led us into a back room.

'So this is where you live,' I said, then attempted a joke: 'It's not bad. At least, not so bad that you need to keep it a secret.' Sangok stared at me impassively. He should have told her where he lived, he said eventually.

'It was a mistake. She's very sick now. She has a fever.'

He said he hoped he wouldn't have to watch her grow weaker by the minute. He took her hand and laid it in his.

There was nothing more he could do for her, he said, he couldn't afford the proper medicine that the black marketeers smuggled out of the US military camps in their boots, only the bad stuff, which didn't heal or save anybody. He sighed, let go of Mihee's hand and began to rummage around in his trouser pocket. I held my pack of cigarettes out towards him. He lit one, took a deep drag. The South was going to the dogs, didn't I agree? I looked around cautiously. Things were slowly improving, I said.

'Improving!'

Sangok snorted with laughter. Nothing would change while Rhee was still in power, he was senile and a despot. He took a small scrap of paper out of his shirt pocket, tapped the ash onto it, looked at me searchingly. He was sorry I had lost my job because of him, he told me; that hadn't been his intention. In actual fact, he had been told to keep an eye on me.

'Keep an eye on me?'

I backed away from him instinctively, looking around. A little too nervously, a little too quickly. Sangok grinned, his mouth twisted into a mocking smile. There was no need to be afraid, he said, he didn't work for Rhee and his mob, he wasn't one of 'His Majesty's' spies. Taking a deep breath, he stubbed out the cigarette. The last, glowing remnants burned into the paper.

'Yunho,' he said, 'your brother sent me.'

Eve stood in front of the dance school, smoking. It was shortly before midnight and she had just finished her working day. When she saw me, she let the cigarette fall to the ground and stubbed it out with the tip of her shoe. 'What're you doing here at this time of night,' she called out in surprise, 'is everything okay?' Giving me a look of concern, she hailed a taxi. 'We have to get off the street, it's getting late.' She pushed me onto the back seat, clambered into the front and gave the driver her address; we drove to Nagwŏndong.

Nagwŏndong is one of the labyrinths in Seoul that has survived the two wars; there are no longer many of them left. You may have passed through it or brushed its fringes on your way to Insa-dong, it's behind the main tourist strip, behind the numerous little shops that sell plastic dolls, hand-painted fans and freshly steamed bread rolls with a sweet red-bean filling. At one time, these stores used to offer calligraphic art, paint brushes, canvases and sketchbooks, now it's memorabilia for travellers, fake crystals, T-shirts with strange quotes and baseball caps; I once even saw a portrait of Park Chung-hee in one, South Korea's most popular dictator.

Back then, artists used to go in and out of this quarter searching for handmade paper and Indian ink, most of them so poor they had to go without a meal in order to paint. Their world opens itself up in Nagwŏndong; narrow alleys which can only be traversed on foot, or at most on a bicycle or motorbike. To the left and right, low walls, overgrown with wild gourd and trumpet vines, almost entirely hide the houses from view; in summer the walls creep closer to one another, in winter, further apart. The special thing about this labyrinthine world is that there's no way of knowing where the narrow passages will lead you; they don't run parallel to each other, but in arcs, half-circles, and many of them come to a dead end. You could walk along them with outstretched arms, feeling your way, and that's what we had to do back then, on that night, because there were no street lamps, only the light from inside the low houses twinkling out through the window shutters.

We climbed out of the taxi. Eve reached for my hand and

pointed towards a dimly lit corner. 'That's where we have to go,' she whispered, pulling me along with her. As we made our way through the darkness, I moved closer to her; she let me. 'Don't be afraid, Yunho,' she whispered, 'I'll lead the way,' and she took my arm.

We walked through the black night for an eternity, or so it seemed, sirens wailed in the distance, pebbles crunched beneath my shoes, and I could feel Eve's soft breath against my ear.

Suddenly, she stopped and rummaged around in her handbag. She pulled out the front door key and turned it in the lock. 'In here,' she whispered, before raising her finger to my mouth. 'The words of the day are overheard by birds, the words of the night by rats.'

6

Until that January night, I had never pictured how Eve lived; I knew where she spent the nights, but not where she was by day, whether in a house or an apartment, whether she shared a room with a workmate, like most young single women in Seoul, or even a bed. For me, she existed only in the moments when she was sitting opposite me, in Johnny's room or in our bar; our lives ran parallel, and Johnny was the connection, without him these moments would never have occurred.

That night, I found myself suddenly in her world, and how different it was: her house, despite being one of the tiny ground-level dwellings typical to Nagwŏndong, with a small garden where tall clay pots were stored and white hibiscus grew, had the interior of an American bungalow: the tables were raised well off the floor, and the cupboards too could only be reached if you were standing up. Eve slept on a bed in an alcove, not on a firm mat on the floor; a cuckoo popped out of her wall clock on every third hour; and in her fridge she kept a bottle of milk, as well as a two-month-old stinking piece of cheese which she wasn't sure was still edible.

As I pulled off my shoes, she went over to the record player and flicked through her collection, pulling out sleeves here and there.

'You like Billie Holiday, don't you?'

She didn't wait for my answer. There was a crackle, then I

heard Billie singing, 'More Than You Know', and to my surprise Eve sang along.

Back then, like today, I didn't understand English, only isolated words like 'I', 'love', 'know' and 'you'. Eve translated many of the songs for me, the first that same night, in the early morning hours; it's thanks to her that today I know what was on Billie's mind.

Eve gestured towards a chair, then disappeared into the kitchen; I didn't sit down right away, but instead looked around. Her curtains were made from a red, delicate, almost transparent material. It was cool to the touch and smelt of flowers I couldn't name. On the shelves, which housed very few books but numerous little baskets and boxes embellished with mother-of-pearl, there was a set of porcelain figurines. I can still remember the angel holding a trumpet and the hollow ballerina on blue tiptoes. Two pictures hung on the wall, the smaller one showed the Eiffel Tower, the larger one the Statue of Liberty. Both had white frames, white like the eyes of the china doll on the couch.

When Eve came back with the tray, I hadn't moved even a millimetre. I was still standing in front of the furniture as though rooted to the spot; the chairs and armchairs seemed to exist only in order to be admired.

'They're real, you know, you can sit on them.'

Eve laughed and fell back onto the couch. I sat down on the armchair opposite her. She poured plum wine into two glasses and handed one to me. I took a sip; it tasted good, fruity. She reached for her handbag, pulled out a silver case, flipped it open and offered me a cigarette; Lucky Strikes. I had heard of them, but never seen any, they were said to be the best cigarettes one could get in Seoul (on the black market, of course) and they cost a fortune.

'So, I'm guessing you didn't just happen to be passing by the dance school . . .'

She lit the cigarette and rolled it back and forth between her index finger and thumb before taking a first, quick drag. The smoke, which she breathed out slowly and contentedly, veiled her eyes for a few seconds, and in that time only her lips spoke to me.

'What can I do for you?'

Instead of answering, I gulped down my wine. It suddenly felt wrong to have sought her out. I felt ashamed of my tatty shirt, dirty trousers and worn-out shoes. Why hadn't I looked for Johnny instead? Why had I gone running to Eve like a little child? She looked at me with curiosity, but I avoided her gaze, fearful of giving myself away. At that moment the record crackled ominously, the song coming to an end, and I became afraid of the silence and stammered: 'My brother . . . he's alive.'

She looked at me in surprise. Surprise, but not astonishment.

'He sent a message to me,' I added, 'through a friend.'

Eve frowned; it was written all over her face that she was unable, unwilling, to believe my – or rather Sangok's – words. I found it touching, even alluring, how gently she tried to lead me towards her view, her worldview. 'So,' she said, 'your brother sent you a message' – and there she'd been thinking he had died in the war.

She had no reason to have believed anything else; I had lied to her, and to Johnny. I said, trying to feign outrage, that the authorities had evidently made a mistake in informing me about Yunsu's death. There was another explanation, Eve interrupted me, perhaps this friend wasn't telling the truth. She poured more wine for us both, pushed my glass towards me.

She had heard countless stories about con artists who pretend to have encountered their victims' relatives in North Korea. Usually it was about money, the father needed this, the mother needed that, and seldom – no, she corrected herself, *never* – had these stories turned out to be true.

'Yunho,' she took my hand and squeezed it gently, 'it's very likely that your brother is dead, and that this guy who calls himself your friend is a fake.'

She lowered her glass.

'Did he ask you for money?'

I shook my head. She looked at me thoughtfully, and her gaze made me uneasy. He really didn't want money, I said; on the contrary, he had offered me some.

Suddenly she grinned.

'Did he tell you that your brother wants to *collaborate* with you?'

I nodded.

'And? Do you believe him?'

I shrugged. She frowned; sipped at her wine.

'What did you say his name was?'

'Shin. Sangok Shin.'

'Did Yunsu ever mention his name to you?'

I didn't answer; it seemed wiser to say as little as possible. Eve was no longer listening in any case. 'Because that would mean,' she murmured, 'that Yunsu has joined the communists.' She emptied her glass, swung it back and forth between her fingers, and avoided looking at me. She asked the next question in a soft voice, very cautiously: 'Do you think he has?'

I stayed silent. No, I refused to answer.

She opened her cigarette case and proffered it towards me. I couldn't bring myself to take a Lucky Strike.

'So many unanswered questions.'

She winked at me.

'Luckily alcohol makes all doubts vanish.'

We emptied the bottle within an hour, then plundered Eve's surprisingly large supply of spirits. We sat there until dawn in her 'living room' (she insisted on the American term, saying that no Korean word could do justice to these kinds of furnishings, which she'd purchased for a high price from members of the American armed forces), smoked and drowned all our doubts in sake, whisky, *soju*.

We talked all through the night. I was fearful that when the next day came I would be ashamed of my nocturnal confessions, of having ignored all warnings and betrayed to her all the things and people I had never wanted to betray, but at daybreak I felt no shame; on the contrary – I wished I had told her more.

Eve was one of those people who keep their life story hidden in the belief it will protect them. As she was unable to offer the kind of biography that would have been readily accepted by society, her background consisted of gaps, blank spaces; to her, secrets weren't something underhand, but a fundamental part of her attempt to fit in. As long as we weren't arguing, this worked fine, but as soon as our opinions differed, gaps would appear in Eve's meticulously constructed inconspicuousness, and she would reveal parts of her story that she had previously withheld.

We had got onto the subject of the US intervention in Korean affairs; I was against any kind of intrusion, she was for it; I was adamant that the Americans were behaving like colonial masters, she retorted that it had nothing to do with colonial politics, it was aid work, that I knew very well how many families were starving and homeless. I knew, I declared, because I was poor myself. She shook her head and said there was no comparison.

'You put cooked rice in your mouth, but the words that come out are raw.'

I had a home, she said, a proper roof over my head, I didn't have to sleep in a wooden shack with a sheet-metal roof, beneath a bridge or in a cardboard box in one of Seoul's many dark corners, like the genuinely poor people. I agreed with her, albeit reluctantly. 'But think about all that flour,' I countered, it didn't reach those in need, the government presumably took the donated produce, repackaged it and sold it on; the profit wandered into their pockets, like it had when the funds intended for the army had vanished into thin air. The recruits, the youngest of them just seventeen years old, had to trudge their way across North Korea in winter without warm jackets or shoes or provisions; many starved or froze to death.

Eve nodded emphatically. Syngman Rhee was corrupt, he allowed his party to get richer at the country's cost; the Liberals were incapable of leading South Korea into the modern age, what we needed was a strong man, a strong, upstanding, honest man, incorruptible and disciplined. Preferably a former soldier who was no stranger to a life of deprivation, who knew *exactly* the kind of sacrifices the population had to make during the Korean War.

I only heard what I wanted to. Exactly, I cried, Rhee had always shot down any dialogue with the North, but only through fear of losing the support of his American friends.

'Without him, Korea would have been unified a long time ago!'

She looked at me, her brow furrowed, a scornful smile playing on her lips. I should have expected that a room so swiftly warmed could cool again just as quickly. She let her cigarette fall into the glass, its glowing tip hissed in the remaining drops of whisky.

I should have seen the question coming: was I a communist, a Red? She spat the last word as she repeated it: 'a Red'. If I was, then I should get my things and disappear at once. 'Clear off to the North,' she snarled, 'there are plenty of crossing points, gaps in the border. The bastards keep them open. They creep into the South and kidnap people. Yes, you heard me, kidnap!' she shouted angrily, as I looked down at the floor. 'Haven't you heard about the turn-coat South Korean girls going back to their home villages as schoolteachers, spreading communist ideology in the schools, recruiting fresh meat? They brainwash and reprogramme their pupils to make them join forces with the North.' In her agitated state, she was snapping her cigarette case open and shut.

Wasn't all this part of the communist Master Plan? Eve asked me, her voice rising. A plan which, according to her sources, had come into existence at the end of the Second World War, and was to lead, in seven steps, to communist rule.

Step 1: All organs of the Korean Communist Party recruit as many members as possible, especially policemen and soldiers.

Step 2: They distance themselves publicly from the mother party.

Step 3: The party rulers, stunned, repentant, back down and promise to align themselves with other, predominantly right-wing, parties.

Step 4: This makes the communist organizations and groups seem neutral, while in reality they are still under communist influence.

Step 5: The communists appear weakened.

Step 6: The Americans, reassured, withdraw from Korea.

Step 7: Shortly after the withdrawal, a series of violent clashes breaks out throughout the country. The police and the military intervene in order to restore national security. By this point, however, the comrades have already assumed leadership.

Result: The Communist Party is in power.

Eve stared at me triumphantly.

'That's your friend Sangok's mission.'

She pulled a cigarette out of the case.

'He's supposed to recruit you. He wants to make you into a communist spy.'

I wanted to dismiss what she'd said as typical South Korean paranoia, but the 'communist Master Plan' was new to me. Where had she got this nonsense from? What she had described didn't sound outrageous enough to come from the media, which was fed with information solely by the government. They normally made more hyperbolic claims: RED NUNS TARGET KINDERGARTEN CHILDREN. And as soon as one newspaper published a ridiculous story like that, all the others followed suit, even down to the smallest paper in the remotest of villages; words without feet travel fast. I refused to read such things, let alone believe them, and was irritated by Eve's lecture. I decided not to tell her anything further about Sangok, not yet; I owed it to Yunsu to find out more.

So what about her, I retorted indignantly, she defended the Americans so vehemently that one could suspect she was working for them. Perhaps she even believed she was one? After all, she did call herself Eve. 'What's so bad about being Korean anyway?' I asked, 'I suppose it isn't good enough for you?'

'And what if it isn't?'

She took a match out of the box.

'After all, anything's better than being Korean.'

★

She let the match fall into the ashtray and watched it slowly burn. Was I in Seoul when the war broke out? she asked eventually. She was; she had sat in front of the radio and believed the announcements, the lies:

'Stay calm and remain in Seoul!'

'The government is *not* being evacuated!'

'The national army is beating back the enemy. Our soldiers will be in Pyongyang by lunch and in Sinuiju by dinner time!'

Even President Rhee had spoken on the radio. He told the people that the United Nations had received the mandate to respond to the North Korean invasion with military force, that it would send weapons, tanks and aeroplanes as well as soldiers, and that despite the difficult circumstances all citizens must be brave and fight; the enemy would be conquered and the country unified.

His voice sounded strange, said Eve, as though his speech had been recorded and played back in front of the microphone. She had said to herself at the time that she wouldn't trust a recording. And rightfully so, as it later turned out. Rhee's entire cabinet had fled Seoul on the seven o'clock train. The finance minister had been in such a hurry to get away that he even forgot to pack the banknotes that were hot off the press.

Eve told me she had gathered together a small bundle of clothes and made her way to the train station; it was just before nine.

There's chaos on the streets, it's impossible to tell the road from the pavement, there are fleeing people everywhere, most of them on foot. They carry the few belongings they can manage on their backs or their heads, or even wear them; multiple layers of clothing, two pairs of socks,

underpants, two vests, one blouse over the other, one pair
of trousers over the other. One family drives out of the city
on an ox-cart, having packed all their worldly possessions
onto the back, even their chests of drawers. Cyclists. Their
bell-ringing barely audible, there's too much screaming,
cursing, they're all 'traitors! liars! murderers!' There are no
cars, they wouldn't make it through the throng. A taxi
driver lies beaten on the ground, his vehicle nowhere in
sight. No policemen to be seen, but there are soldiers.
They have taken off their caps and ripped the insignia from
their jackets; they flee as civilians –

the last train has left; she's missed the last one. She looks
around feverishly, there's no point in trying the bus station,
the last bus probably left Seoul hours ago. Some of the
houses are engulfed in flames. The shop windows have
been shattered, the doors kicked in. They've been looted,
the shelving torn off the walls, the cash registers plundered.
She suddenly feels convinced that she's surrounded by
thieves. She has to get to safety. But where? Where is safe?
It's too far to go back the way she came, she doesn't dare
attempt it; the dance school is closer. She heads through
the side streets, constantly on her guard against rioters,
against stampedes of panic-stricken runaways. Finally she
sees her destination ahead of her. She can tell even from a
distance that something's not right: no Cockatu in front of
the entrance, no Joe either. The doors are wide open. She
debates whether or not to go in. There are noises coming
from inside, but she risks a glance . . . The dance school is
being looted. The gramophone has already been packed
up. A man is dismantling the ceiling lamp, another
disappears into the back room with a cardboard box, the

third has his fingers in the cash register. Before she can duck, he spots her. 'Get out of here, Yankee whore. The Reds are coming, and sluts are their favourite targets' –

Panic, panic, now she panics too, go back quickly, anywhere that's not here, Jongno, the part of the city renowned for its nightclubs, all with American names, Bar Mambo, Mambo Café, Restaurant Mambo King, Hot Mambo. Normally the signs light up in green, red and yellow, but today they're grey, and it occurs to her that she can't dance the mambo. She's relieved, but then remembers she was taught it once, that there are even witnesses who saw her dancing a mambo, that November evening when a drunk GI went over to the gramophone, dropped down onto one knee and bellowed at the top of his voice 'Mambo Italiano!', at which Cockatu sprinted out of the room – to find a mambo record, she had thought – but he hadn't come back, and they had to dance the mambo to a slow waltz –

does she have enough food at home? Some rice. How much? Not much. Probably enough for a few days, or a week if she's careful. Perhaps she can borrow something from her landlords . . . She didn't see them this morning. Perhaps they fled last night too? Fled without telling her? Unlikely. She'll look for them as soon as she gets home. She should have fetched water from the stream. She should have fetched it this morning, instead of wandering aimlessly around the city. Everyone has gone, the ministers for sure, they got their wives and children out of the country months ago . . . Maybe the People's Army is already in Seoul . . .? If it wasn't for this fear and panic in the air, it could almost be a religious holiday. Travellers are always in a hurry. Travellers always have too much luggage. It could be the day before the holiday, the day before the harvest festival, Chusŏk, when the whole of Seoul empties. She has one more day until the Red Army arrives, for sure. Yet another looted shop. No, it's on fire. Is no one putting it out? Yes. The owner and his three children –

her neighbours are out on the street, they've convened together right in front of her house. 'The bridge over the Han River was blown up, we were starting to think you'd been got!' Coming from Mr Jŏng, this sounds like a reproach. They're all shouting over one another, she can't understand a word. Many people, hundreds, thousands, were killed. They weren't warned. No one was. That's not how it's done in this country, you just get the hell out. Before it's too late. 'The Red Army is in Seoul.' Are you sure? 'Yes, I'm sure. The speech on the radio, didn't you hear?' No, I was— 'Kim Il-sung has announced the liberation of Seoul. You really missed something there.' Liberation? 'Yes. Liberation from US imperialism, liberation from hunger and suffering. WE'RE BRINGING YOU A BETTER LIFE, that's their motto.' Mr Jŏng can't hold himself back. Clearly the fear isn't great enough to make him go home. Hide or flee? That's the question on his mind. 'It's too late to flee.' 'What do we have to be scared about,' yells someone from the back of the throng, 'we're not rich and we didn't help the Japanese!' Now a teacher jumps up. 'Rhee is a dictator, we're finally shot of him!' His outburst is unexpectedly unequivocal. No one would dare contradict him, would they? No one –

★

inside the house, everything is peaceful. No one's here. She goes to her room; she has sublet it from a friend, Bongsun. She barricades her door with a chest of drawers, forgetting that she wanted to fetch water. She hears screams, gunshots; still sporadic for now. She arms herself with a tennis racket, then thinks better of it and hides it in the wardrobe. Too reactionary. She notices how thirsty she is. Remembers that she was going to fetch water. Again she puts it off, hoping for rain. She tells herself she'll put a bowl outside the window, to collect rainwater . . . She's familiar with the North Korean accent. She decides to invent another identity, a new family history; under no circumstances will she tell them her real name, they would kill her on the spot. She could say that her family died fighting in the resistance against the Japanese. No, too risky. The anti-Japanese resistance is well connected, everyone knows everyone. She'll claim to be an orphan who never knew her parents –

after the gunfire and explosions have ebbed away, she ventures out onto the street. The wind feels strangely alien on her skin. She pays attention to herself and her surroundings; to herself in these familiar yet alien surroundings. She notices that her movements seem like they're in slow motion. This frustrates her, makes her impatient and anxious. She contemplates turning back. Bullet holes in the brickwork. Smashed-in windows. Plundered shops and houses. Enormous portraits of Stalin and Kim Il-sung on the walls. North Korean flags. The ground is scattered with flyers, both odd ones here and there and piled in stacks. She picks one up. It sings the praises of Kim and Stalin, denounces Rhee as a 'traitor' and an 'enemy

of the people', and the US as 'imperialist intruders'. She puts
the flyer in her bag. A crowd of pupils comes towards her,
carrying banners and chanting: 'We're fighting for our
homeland!' Only now does she notice the placard on the
school. 'Exterminate the enemy! Join the volunteer army!'
Men in uniform march past. She turns away quickly. One of
them yells at her. 'Yankee slut!' He grabs her, tries to tear
off her skirt. She pushes him away, loses a shoe, kicks off the
other. Hysterical laughter behind her –

there's a knock at the door. Hesitant. Soft. 'Open up, it's
me, Bongsun! I have something for you.' She opens the
door just a crack. It's a straw hat. 'So you can cover your
face.' Bongsun gives Eve a scrutinizing look. 'Don't you
have any old skirts or blouses? Something worn out,
shabby? You can't let yourself be seen like that out there,
they'll beat you. Seoul was taken in a single day, haven't
you heard? The resistance was small, very small.' I thought
you and your family had left. 'We're all downstairs, come
and join us.' Later. She turns away. 'Wait! Don't ever use
the word "citizen", always say "comrade". And only refer
to the Americans as "American imperialist intruders",
otherwise you'll be for it.' She nods. She's tired. 'And one
more thing: lock the door behind me' –

she no longer washes, neither at home with a washcloth
nor in the public baths. The baths reopened after the
election, Eve voted too, she dropped her voting slip into
the white 'pro' urn; the black 'con' was avoided by
everyone. She should be happy she was allowed to vote,
for this at least means not being in the first category of
political criminals, that of Japanese collaborators and

pro-American traitors. She has swiftly renamed herself.
Yunmee has risen, while Eve lies buried beneath a layer of
dirt and long hair. North of the occupied South, the fields
and acres are being redistributed, the millet and buckwheat
crops carefully counted and the number of cows belonging
to hordes of agricultural agents increased. Yet in Seoul,
everyone is preoccupied with just one question: WHERE
STILL HAS STRAW HATS? Eve is not the only one to
demonstrate her approval of the Red regime with
unwashed hair. Long beards, dirty fingernails, tattered
shirts, trousers and straw hats, on sale for 200 won; these
are the latest craze that summer –

house searches take place on a daily basis. According to the
placards and Kim Il-sung's official newspaper, military units
of more than twenty thousand soldiers are to track down
'reactionaries' – for the public's safety, of course. Soon
afterwards, the recruitment of agents begins. Eventually an
order is given over the radio: political criminals have to
turn themselves in; the population will be divided up into
groups of five, and each member will be obligated to spy
on the others and report any suspicious behaviour. Eve,
Bongsun and Bongsun's husband, mother-in-law and
father-in-law form one unit. They promise one another
that they won't report or spy on anyone. Those who get
turned in, says Bongsun's father-in-law, will be imprisoned,
tortured and publicly executed. All state prosecutors and
members of the police force and municipal authorities who
were unable to flee are already dead –

a week later, Kim Il-sung lets it be known that he is
disappointed in his comrades. They're not trying hard

enough; there are too few raids, they have to work harder and, most importantly, not forget his campaign for self-denunciation. He makes a promise: 'No one will be punished without a fair trial. Even the worst criminals have nothing to fear. The severity of the punishment will be decided according to the degree of honesty displayed in the self-denunciation.' Self-denunciation. From now on they must fulfil a quota: each five-person unit must expose at least one reactionary; if not, the entire group will face punishment. Bongsun weeps. She is pregnant and fears for her unborn child, for her family –

Eve offers to turn herself in. Secretly she hopes that Bongsun will reject the offer, but her friend is relieved. She embraces her. 'How can I ever thank you, you're saving us all.' Eve goes to the police station, where she confesses her 'reactionary crimes' and admits having had 'regular contact with right-wing elements'. She sincerely regrets this, she says. She repeats this sentence many times, for the repetition of a repeated repetition seems to demonstrate an appropriate level of sincerity. Bongsun has promised to write a letter pleading for Eve to be pardoned. But on the day of the trial, her friend is nowhere to be found, nor is there any sign of the petition in her file. Eve retracts her self-denunciation. She says that the right-wing element she had contact with was actually her friend, the same one who pressured her to turn herself in. Eve is addressing a group, not individuals. The roles of public prosecutor, judge and enforcement officers aren't fixed, everyone is a judge, everyone a lawyer. All that counts is her red armband, no one dares to contradict that. The public prosecutor is outraged, the judge condemns Bongsun and her family in their absence; they are to be imprisoned and sent to a work camp. Eve escapes with a light re-education measure; the administration of justice is arbitrary, except when it comes to revenge –

she writes a 'self-critical autobiography', which she reads out loud, paragraph by paragraph, to an audience who spit and jeer at her. In the muggy heat of the monsoon season, she learns by heart songs about General Kim Il-sung and his illustrious partisans, and listens to presentations about the Red revolution. She watches from a safe distance as Bongsun and her family are arrested and taken away. Bongsun's property is seized by the state; the smaller items, Eve takes for herself. She is given a place to stay by a stranger whose brothers and friends were dragged from their beds and sent to the front. A few days later, he has disappeared too. She worries, hoping she hasn't got herself mixed up with a spy. Flyers rain down from the skies; Rhee warns the people of Seoul to hide their rice rations. Now she knows that the UN troops aren't far away. The next morning, female comrades collect gold and silver, hand towels, socks, toothbrushes, spoons and blankets for 'our Fatherland' –

at the beginning of September, General Douglas MacArthur recaptures Seoul. On Jongno Boulevard, the People's Army leave hundreds of corpses in their wake; they lie alongside one another on the dusty street, their hands fastened behind their backs with straw rope, silently welcoming the national army as it goose-steps in. The soldiers of the South are not saviours or liberators, they are conquerors and inspectors: all those who didn't flee in time are suspected of communist collaboration. 'We will investigate you,' Rhee's henchmen shout in chorus. 'We will investigate whether you remained good citizens or secretly allied yourselves with the enemy!' All of a sudden, there are policemen in Seoul again: policemen, military policemen and special policemen, members of the military counter-espionage force. They couldn't be found for months on end, but now they are everywhere; they patrol through the residential areas and carry out arrests; they fight over possessions confiscated but left behind by the communists. Once there is nothing more to take, they rob the innocent and have them thrown in prison and executed. The prosecution service promptly announces that legal action will be taken against 'private citizens' making false allegations for their own financial gain, yet there haven't been any civilians in a long while . . . If you are dragged to the nearest police station, beaten and tortured; if they say, 'You, you know the song of the people', then there is only one possible answer: 'Yes, I helped the Reds, I'm a collaborator. Signed and sealed' –

Eve is accused of collaboration, arrested and brought before the Special Committee for the Investigation of Collaboration. A member of the Committee for Public Security claims that she was turned during the last three months, that of course she is a staunch communist, and she probably always was, being from the North. Eve is called upon to denounce herself. She refuses. She explains that she fled from the North because her Christian family – and she emphasizes this, Christian family – was persecuted. Her family was among the first to convert to Catholicism, she says, and they didn't renounce their faith even when

the king threatened them with the death penalty and they
had to hold mass in a secret room beneath the house, in a
prayer cave which could only be accessed through a
trapdoor –

the committee is unmoved by her words. It is more than
likely, they claim, that she is a North Korean agent who
sneaked into the South even before the outbreak of war
(because she knew, after all, that there would be a war!) in
order to recruit comrades. Eve defends herself, the Red
Army arrested her, they tried to re-educate her, why
would a North Korean agent need to be re-educated?
The committee doesn't know how to respond to this
argument, so they give Eve a telling-off. 'You had yourself
arrested too late, for a true patriot!' She is ordered to submit
a journal, listing precisely what she did between June and
October 1950, and where she was living. She is kept in
custody, and has to compose her 'Document of Innocence'
on a cellmate's back, hemmed in between countless other
culprits – more than a hundred thousand people are arrested
and tried at this time, most of them in Seoul. The cellmate
is released before Eve can finish her document, a true state
citizen having vouched for her political integrity –

Eve is also one of the lucky ones; among the UN soldiers
coming in and out of the police station, she spots Mitch, a
regular at Cockatu's Dance School. She waves to him, calls
his name again and again, but he doesn't hear her amid the
din, everyone is shouting over everyone. Of the numerous
prison sentences assigned over the last weeks, most have
been transmuted into milder punishments, life
imprisonment into thirty years, thirty into fifteen, fifteen

into five, five into immediate release; otherwise there wouldn't be anyone left in Seoul for Rhee to tax. She pushes her way through the mass of people, shoving aside prisoners and imprisoners alike, and manages to grab Mitch by the sleeve just before he disappears. He turns round, is astonished when he recognizes her, and is more than willing to vouch for her. He tells the committee official that Eve is a good sort, that she would never even think of spying for the Commies. 'Eve?' responds the official in broken English, 'who is Eve?' 'Why, she is,' says Mitch, furrowing his brow. The man swiftly tries to smooth it. 'Ah, Sergeant Buchanan, I see, Yunmee Moon, is this about Miss Moon?' 'It doesn't matter what her name is,' barks Buchanan, 'she's to be released at once' –

on the day of her release, he picks her up. She has spent fourteen days in jail, any less was impossible, even with an American intermediary. There is an execution every day, sometimes two or even more; she didn't see them, but she heard each condemned person being led away. The guards' guffaws. Their jokes, as they push the prisoner to the floor. The clink of the chains. The machine-gun fire, always at the same time of day. She is nervous, afraid to enter her house. She takes Mitch's hand. 'Would you like to come in with me?' Nothing is how it was before, her clothes are missing, her make-up has been taken, the crockery, cutlery, her records, radio, nothing is in its place, and how could it be; its place no longer exists, the furniture has disappeared. Mitch promises to find out who is responsible and hold them accountable. She sits down on the floor. All the cushions are gone, she can feel the cold through the wood. Mitch turns to leave, promising to be back soon, with some blankets, clothes and something for her to eat. She lies on her back. Dusk draws in, the light inside the house fades, she watches the day's dying embers. She's hungry. There's nothing to eat in the house, they left her nothing.

A few days later, she told me, a policeman tried to blackmail her. He called her a Red and said he could rape and shoot her any time he wanted and no one would punish him, they would sing his praises, especially President Rhee, he would be given a 'Medal for Fighting the Communist Guerrilla', a medal for the death of a worm.

'As a collaborator, you're no longer a human being, but a toy. A toy for trophy hunters.'

Eve's mouth twisted into a contemptuous sneer.

'And once you've become prey, it never stops.'

She pulled a cigarette out of the pack. I lit it for her. I mumbled that this was why I hadn't told anyone about my brother joining the partisans.

'No one. You're the first.'

I trusted her blindly. How could I not have, after everything she had told me? She rested her head against my shoulder. I had made the right decision, she said, otherwise I would most likely have been murdered and my family's property seized, I would have been forced to leave my home, interrogated constantly, my apartment would have been searched and placed under surveillance, and I wouldn't have found a respectable paid job ever again. I would have been an outsider for the rest of my life; they would have punished me in my brother's place.

In the early hours of that morning in January 1960, I had thought she was exaggerating, but I later found out she was telling the truth: everyone whose relatives had fled to North Korea during the civil war or joined the communists had experienced the same thing; in the South Korean justice system, blood relatives were considered complicit under a law that was only abolished in the early 1980s.

As our eyes met, Eve blushed and hid her face behind her hands; she mumbled that she could no longer remember why we had argued.

Her make-up had worn off during the course of the night; her lips were no longer red, her eyes no longer rimmed with black. She was unmasked, and I noticed that there was a brownish fuzz on her chin, making her skin seem pale in comparison, almost translucent. All of a sudden she looked young, terribly young, and it struck me that when she danced with the soldiers she was in disguise: that the close-fitting clothes and made-up face were a substitute for seeking cover behind the palms of her hands.

I looked at her for a long while; too long. I cleared my throat and said I didn't get the impression that the South was all that different from the North. She answered quietly that she had revealed a lot, more than she meant to.

'If memories are locked away for too long, they have to be voiced, otherwise they become ghosts.'

I reached for her cigarette and took a drag.

'Why are you against the North?'

'I'm neither for the South nor against the North.'

She stood up and went over to the record player.

'I side with the strong, the ones who always have been strong and who will stay so.'

She turned the record over.

'Yunho, you have to remember that we are taken over by the rulers, we can't choose them ourselves. And our survival depends upon how convincing our loyalty is.'

How convincing our loyalty is. My pledge of loyalty hadn't convinced Johnny's father; he had forced me to leave Nonsan. I found myself thinking of that day when, after many months, I had finally reached the outskirts of Daegu, the foothills of the city. I had neither a house nor a home. The light was glaringly bright; it dimmed the pale tones of nature and gathered them together in the dark branches of the trees. To the left and right of me lay sleeping rice paddies, the outline of a landscape robbed of its third dimension, the shadows delicately crosshatched, made brittle by the light, which moved constantly, shimmering from one point to the next, obscuring the solitude of the plains. I had never seen the countryside so deserted; the emptiness had an inviolate purity which surprised me.

She placed the needle on the rim of the record and whispered: 'I'll probably hurt him . . .'

'Who? What do you mean?'

She sighed and brushed a strand of hair out of her face.

'I don't have a future with Johnny.'

Now it was my turn to be surprised. 'I thought you loved him,' I stammered.

She laughed; delighted by my naivety? She said she felt – and I could see her searching for a word that would make her seem warm-hearted – a *fondness* for him.

'And that isn't enough?'

She shook her head.

'You have to tell him the truth. You're very important to him.'

She nodded, and said she would, but not yet. When the right moment came, she would let him down as gently as she could.

She looked at me pleadingly, clearly wanting me to

strengthen her resolve, and so I did; I nodded, smiled, nodded and smiled, even though I knew that I was betraying my friend.

Billie's song interrupted our conspiracy. She sang of solitude, and Eve translated for me.

Suddenly feeling that I could stay no longer, I stood up, but Eve took my hand and pulled me back onto the couch. She stroked my face, my cheeks, my eyes.

When she kissed me, I realized that I had envied Johnny all along, and as she put her arms around me, I believed that everything would be how it should have been, and nothing made me doubt it.

When we said our goodbyes, she made me promise once again to tell my 'roommate' nothing about us; she would speak with him when the right moment came.

Johnny didn't pick up on our secret rendezvous. Just the once, he said: 'You've changed, Yunho, it seems like you've met someone, are you in love?' He laughed, tousled my hair and asked: 'Who is she, my friend? You can tell me.'

It was late morning; the sunlight was flickering through the bare branches in front of our house, casting crisp shadows onto the neighbouring building, which had been erected only recently. I loved the short days back then, I loved them because the darkness shielded us, Eve and me.

7

That February was bitterly cold, yet its light so glaring it made me believe that blindness could also manifest itself as a dazzling brightness, a white that forces its way in through the eyelids and continues in the mind. During those days I spent a lot of time thinking about eyesight and the loss of it. Perhaps the darkness left in its wake resembled the blackness I experienced in the windowless chamber of conspirators. The tiny room was accessible only through a concealed door; a bookcase, laden with hollow books and empty files, that could be pushed to the side. It was the perfect hiding place, and simultaneously the perfect trap, for it had only one exit. It couldn't accommodate more than three people at a time, and yet the four of us often sat there: Sangok, Mihee, myself and Jang, the owner of the stationery shop which housed our hideaway. A large, tall mirror leant against one of the walls, reflecting the opposite side of the room; on my first day of 'lessons', Sangok commented with a smile that we had five walls protecting us instead of four.

I had, without intending to do so, enrolled myself in communist training. Mihee and I were still beginners, gobies following the flying fish, not yet trusted by the Party, which was why Sangok alone was our teacher. Later, after we had successfully completed our apprenticeship, he planned to introduce us to the other comrades, the entire cell. It was composed of students, professors, writers and workers, he stressed, honourable comrades, not criminals like the mob from 1946, who had pumped out counterfeit money with the printing press that was also used to print the Communist Party newspaper. Twelve million yen, that was how much they'd planned to bring into circulation, but the American military police had put an end to all that. This incident had damaged the communists' reputation, said Sangok. Up until then the Party, still legal back then, had been the favourite among young workers, students and even schoolchildren.

After the war, freedom and democracy were all people talked about in Korea. Everyone was politically engaged, either as a simple party member or as a functionary, a visionary. At the newly founded universities, the Marxist reading groups and poetry circles, the Communist Youth public-speaking competitions, and lectures about Marx, Lenin and Mao Zedong drew the biggest crowds. Hajime Kawakami's *Tale of Poverty* would have been a bestseller, had people been able to afford to buy books; instead, the few copies in Seoul travelled from one hand to the next, their recipients doing their best to read quickly so that no one would be left out. In between all this reading, comrades flocked to the theatres to see Saryang Kim's *Butterfly*, a play about Korean guerrilla fighters in Yan'an, the paradise of fairness created by Mao. So much hope, so many dreams; it was a monstrous crime to destroy them. Today, we know that life in Yan'an was anything but paradisiacal; that society there was anything but equal, the party cadres were fatter, better clothed, and dozed contentedly in their spacious homes; we know that forced labour, compulsory military service, mass surveillance and inhuman executions were rife. The domination of the masses always begins with the annihilation of the individual.

'It seemed tantalizingly close' Sangok said. 'A Korea without poverty or social class. We were sure it didn't have to be a dream, that it could become a reality, if we convinced as many people as possible. One comrade calculated that in a group of sixty people general opinion would shift in our favour if just five of us were among them, engaged in efforts of persuasion.'

Sangok took a drag of his cigarette and eyed me critically. I was nervous about the clouds of smoke that he kept blowing into the air, and which must have been creeping their way outside through cracks and crevices, for I felt sure they would betray us. He stubbed the cigarette out in an ashtray and grinned.

'We're safe here. You're among friends.'

Jang (who looked like a bird with no rump, but was as quick-witted as the cat rolling an egg in front of it) muttered: 'To catch the cub you have to venture into the tiger's den.' He told us how he had distributed flyers and party newspapers year in, year out, on icy winter nights as well as on hot, sticky summer evenings; how he had convinced the workers at the post office and the electricity plant to go on strike, thereby bringing the Americans out in a cold sweat; how he had scurried through Seoul's hidden alleys to deliver secret messages, always staying close to the houses, with right-wing thugs on his heels who tried to catch him, yet never succeeded. Jang coughed, the effort flogging his lungs, and Sangok took over, as though on cue.

'Most of the operations were successful. By 1948, we had infiltrated the police and the military. We got hold of important documents, secret codes and strategy papers, and converted soldiers, ordinary as well as high-ranking; hundreds joined us. In 1949, two battalions of the Eighth Regiment defected, in their entirety, to us.'

He lit himself another cigarette.

'But we suffered setbacks too. Between '46 and '48, a few of our agents were imprisoned in the South. One had his cover blown when he couldn't prove he'd had a cholera vaccination. During the interrogation, he admitted that four Soviet officers and a Korean were running a secret agent training school in the North.'

After that, the Communist Party offices and the houses of prominent members were searched once again, and the police found classified documents on the US military bases in the South. They also discovered that North Korean agents were using Party premises as safe houses.

'We had to change our tactics. General Hodge stepped up the surveillance. It was simply no longer possible for us to operate out in the open.'

One raid followed the next. The lists carried by the soldiers in charge of counter-espionage seemed to have more names than there were people; hardly anyone didn't appear on a list, and even the dead were shown no mercy and forced into resurrection on them. In July 1947, the police in Seoul arrested prominent members of the Party, along with anyone suspected of being in league with them. To justify his actions, the chief of police claimed that a communist plot had been uncovered to take Seoul by force and overthrow the American military government. In February '48, the Party began to fight back. A general strike was called, and the workers' unions announced that they would only end it if the first South Korean election, scheduled for 15 August, was cancelled, if the US troops retreated from Korea, and if the Korean people were allowed to elect a government that hadn't been selected for them by the US and the United Nations. To lend weight to their demands, the demonstrators swiftly destroyed numerous vehicles and electricity and telephone masts, and carried out countless attacks on bridges.

A sad smile drifted over Sangok's face. Then their luck had turned, he said, along with Truman turning away from Stalin, the alienation of the West from the East. Friends betrayed friends, brothers betrayed brothers, fathers betrayed their sons. Any connection to the Party, no matter how insignificant, led to imprisonment.

'We were forced underground. We hatched out plans in rooms like this one here.'

He cleared his throat. Right now they were weak, he said. They had been weakened, but it wouldn't take much; the people were starving, they were desperate.

'I mean, how much longer will they be willing to tolerate these injustices?'

Sangok was right: the people's patience had been exhausted. Nonetheless, when the protests did eventually erupt, their intensity surprised me; I felt as though the sun were rising in the west.

Daegu was the first city to protest against Rhee's despotic rule, then Seoul, Daejeon, and finally the southernmost city of Busan. For the first time since the Korean War, it seemed conceivable that Rhee's dictatorship might end; the country desperately needed a government, not an old man who only came crawling out of his luxury lair to gab with foreign journalists or to secure his regime; the upcoming elections were for a lifelong presidency, Rhee having made a well-timed change to our constitution. It was still dangerous, however, to criticize the president out loud, not only had he laid the foundations of a police state with his army of spies, he had also passed a law enabling him to easily and swiftly eliminate his opponents. The National Security Law transformed innocent people into terrorists and saw to it that they could be locked away forever or executed without trial. It also proved useful under his successor, Park Chung-hee; and it exists to this day.

In 1948, Rhee presented himself as the ideal first president of Korea. Having taken over the administration of the country from General Hodge and the American military government, it was assumed that he would introduce reforms and relief programmes whose implementation would then be taken on by his successor. After all, his advanced age – he was seventy-three years old when he took office – made him a transitional head of state. During his rule, fledgling Korean politicians would have the opportunity to learn what it meant to live in a democracy; Rhee, who had studied in the US and lived there for many decades, was to teach them. Some people whispered that, in certain respects, he was more American than Korean; a strange hybrid, said others, neither Korean nor American. His reputation for championing Korea's independence as a diplomat, and his years as president of the Korean government-in-exile in Shanghai, assured him a magnificent welcome when he and his Austrian wife, Franziska Donner, landed in Seoul in a specially chartered American military jet following the liberation. 'My enemies are not only those who inflict suffering on my homeland, but also those who have stopped believing in its rescue,' he wrote as a 29-year-old in King Gojong's dungeon, imprisoned as a traitor for demanding reform.

At the beginning of his presidency, Rhee wasn't just popular, he was loved. People called him 'Father' and told one another stories of his benevolence and kindness. Of the many, the only one that has stayed in my memory is the Hawaiian fairy tale: in the early nineteenth century, many Koreans emigrated to the islands in the Pacific Ocean, recruited by American missionaries as workers for the sugarcane plantations. Most of the men were no more than eighteen or nineteen, many were unmarried. After they had settled, they started to long for a family, for a wife and children. They asked their parents to find brides for them and send them to Honolulu. In many cases, no photos were exchanged, and the women boarded the ships without having seen their future husbands. Before the arrival of his ship bride, one worker sought out Syngman Rhee, who at the time led the Korean school in Honolulu. 'My esteemed Professor,' he said, 'you are far and wide the only Korean who owns two suits. Apart from my work clothes, I have nothing smart I can wear. Would you lend me your second suit for the wedding ceremony?' Upon which the friendly director nodded and lent his most beautiful suit and trousers to this man, and to many others after him. Over the years, the suit was said to have been adjusted so many times that the material became threadbare from needle marks.

Rhee later revealed his true face. In reports compiled at the beginning of the Korean War, in 1950, the CIA described him as senile, obstinate beyond all measure, narrow-minded and forceful. He feared and hated communism with an iron rigidity, they said, and any hope for a legitimate opposition in Korea was futile, so convinced was he of his own messianic importance. The American ambassador John Joseph Muccio added paranoia to this description: Rhee didn't trust anyone, he declared in his memoirs, not even his own wife. This particular mistrust was justified, admittedly; it was an open secret that she sent regular messages to the US embassy, via a trusted priest, about what her husband was plotting next. The information she passed on must have been invaluable, because Rhee's professed goal was to centralize the administration of the South, or, in other words: to unite all jurisdiction in his person. Even high-ranking officials were under his control; they bowed and scraped to him and didn't dare make any decision without his approval, not even a day-to-day one like the issuing of a passport – according to the CIA, the president treated the prime minister like his personal secretary.

It is quite a challenge to take up the reins of government in a country that is not only teetering on the brink economically, but also caught in a tug-of-war between the US and the USSR. This situation must have felt familiar to Rhee; during his youth, Korea was torn between Japan and Russia. His solution to this dilemma was a simple one: he supported only those who financed his autocracy, the large property owners and businessmen who had become rich and (to a certain degree) powerful thanks to their collaboration with the Japanese. He dedicated himself to the battle against communism for the Americans, and he didn't care how many of his innocent 'children' he had to sacrifice to this war. He took over the police force, the main instrument of suppression and terror during Japanese rule, exactly as it was handed to him by General Hodge: complete with all its officers. Only a few collaborators, small fish, were charged and imprisoned; most of the other officers were able to resume their former roles in new locations. To enable the policemen to carry out their duties, he promised them and their accomplices protection from a populace thirsting for revenge.

Although the Korean War did not officially begin until five years after Japan's surrender, to all intents and purposes it started immediately afterwards: both Japanese officials in Korea and their collaborators were the targets of retaliatory operations. Driven from one village to the next, from the north to the south, the collaborators were rescued by the American military government. This minority was essentially given immunity by Rhee, who needed their economic and political capital to strengthen his own power. The public good he spoke of so eagerly was important to him only when it came to those who supported him: their and his opponents disappeared over time, one after the other; murdered on the street in the cold light of day, or publicly executed after a show trial, slandered as communist subversives.

By the beginning of the 1950s, the majority of the population were so poor that they became servants to the few who possessed more than them: the value of a human life was less than that of a bowl of rice. They also had to send their sons to a war with the North from which they would never return; only the privileged could afford their children's freedom. Syngman Rhee was indifferent to these 'citizens'. He saw to it that adolescent boys, the youngest just three years older than myself, were forcibly recruited shortly after the outbreak of the war and sent to the front, where most of them died. The rest caught a disease, tuberculosis, from which they never recovered – neither the men themselves, nor the women and children they passed it on to.

These were the voters who would decide upon Rhee's future in the 1960 election. In the market and at food stalls, Sangok, Mihee and I eavesdropped on their conversations and were surprised to find that Rhee (who would be president again in any case, because his only opponent had conveniently died of complications following a heart operation in a faraway American hospital) was still popular, significantly more so than his right-hand man Lee Ki-poong, the vice-presidential candidate – who even the government-loyal media predicted would lose, just as he had four years previously. But this time Rhee's party, the Liberals, were absolutely determined to secure the vice presidency too. They decided to strive for votes in the opposition's stronghold: the south-east of the country. Campaigners toured through the cities there, trying to overwhelm the population with sheer numbers (quantity was something the masses couldn't ignore, the election committee told itself). They decided to hold a large rally to which they would lure opposition voters, first with election promises, and if this didn't prove fruitful, with bribes and threats.

On 28 February, the Liberals mobilized their members, as well as any citizen who had the misfortune to cross the election commando's path: they were seized and brought to the meeting place in lorries and ox-carts. To ensure the rally wouldn't be disturbed, schools were ordered to stay open, even though it was a Sunday. This directive met with resistance among the schoolchildren, who saw it as their hard-won right to have a say in the country's future, and by association their own. To the young, political participation was not a promise, but a challenge, and democracy an idea that, as South Korea became exposed to American politics, had swiftly transformed from a utopia to a social model in which justice, prosperity and modernity were of secondary importance; first and foremost, it was about the hope for freedom. Throughout the twelve years in which Rhee had clung to power, he had dangled this promise before them, and they had gobbled up his every word. Now they were sick to the stomach. If freedom existed, they thought, then it always had; they just hadn't realized that they had to seize it for themselves.

This was my opinion too. When I was working in the bicycle factory, I had repeatedly tried to convince my colleagues that they had to fight, that their freedom entailed this very fight, and each time they would explain to me that their *inability* to choose freedom was actually the reason for their enslavement. And each time, after I had tried in vain to convince them of this free future, which could begin any second if only they let it, I slunk back to a room I could only afford because I didn't have to pay the rent, and cursed the stagnancy of the present, for being so far from my expectations; there was no space for justice back then, and this was what I longed for even more than freedom. I thought I was the only one – until I met Sangok.

For us, the youth protests were a miracle. We gathered by Jang's radio and waited anxiously for news from Daegu. From time to time, when the station slipped away from us, Jang had to fiddle with the dials to recapture it. Mihee kept us supplied with tea and rice, she was a better revolutionary than I, more determined, more passionate; how had Sangok put it? 'There's no such thing as a revolutionary without blood boiling in his veins. How else will he forget himself completely in the moment of self-sacrifice?' But despite this, she was assigned a subsidiary, subordinate role, while I served the few customers who wanted to buy notepads, exercise books or pencils, constantly on the lookout for the police.

The reporter announced that the seventeen-year-old pupils had deliberately chosen the Sunday of the government's rally to create civil unrest (instead of following their teacher to the cinema as instructed). Assembled in the schoolyard, their leader read out a manifesto, voice trembling. I can no longer remember the exact words, but I remember my ears grew hot as I listened. How good it felt to hear the agitation in the reporter's voice, his breathlessness, the sometimes faint, sometimes loud crackle over the airwaves; how wonderful that he stumbled over his words, because this uprising was so unexpected, so unheard-of!

Today, all I remember of that fateful speech is the pupils' demands of justice for all, free elections, an end to autocracy and the beginning of democracy, the 'reign of the people'. That's what we understood democracy to be, taking the term all too literally, but we can be forgiven for that, because this idea was still young in Korea, even though the longing for it was very old. I envied the pupils their chance to make themselves heard as a group, and I envied the leaders Yi and Kim their comrades, who shared their views and were prepared, I remember this part clearly, to sacrifice 'our teachers' careers – for no doubt they'll lose their positions because of their disobedient pupils – to Korea's future'.

What became of Yi, I don't know. Kim, despite objections from his father, who expected financial security from his only son (the eldest having fallen in the Korean War), began his studies in Western art and left the country after the spring snow-melt; with a forename like his – Supyŏng, meaning 'horizon' – how could he have done anything else?

Arm in arm, holding placards and banners, they marched through the city. At first, the policemen on patrol didn't realize that the neat rows were in fact a *rebellion*, especially as the young people's cries, 'We want fair elections!', were drowned out by the afternoon sea of noise; only after passers-by began to turn, pausing in their daily routines to watch the adolescents march in formation towards the main square, did the guardians of order take notice, but even then they didn't intervene. How could they know that the young rebels were attacking the government? All they heard was a strange cry, a Tagore verse, 'Light of Korea, illuminate the East!', which prompted them to guide the demonstrators safely over the crossing.

In the meantime the group, modestly sized at first, had

swollen by more than several hundred; all the schools had sent delegations, and the now noticeable protesters were on the home stretch: before them lay the house belonging to the governor of the south-eastern provinces. He was expecting them and had summoned police to protect him from the 'barbarians', but due to the traffic chaos unleashed by the Liberals' election rally the police hadn't arrived, and so the governor decided to personally read the recalcitrant youths the riot act. The governor had allegedly pounced into the throng like an enraged lion, lunging out around him until his 'naked fists' were bloodied, and roared: 'You cursed communist pigs, you Red dogs!' The reporter – who was so worked up that he spat into the microphone – told us that he had been unable to hold himself back, and had shouted: 'That's Korea's future, you ape!' The throng had apparently laughed raucously. When they finally arrived at the governor's residence, the reinforcements pulled him away from the 'crime scene' and began to arrest the students, one after the other.

They were released a few days later, thanks in part to the press. Even the most government-friendly newspapers praised the 'brave youth' for taking a stand against the 'scheming government'. Rhee was compared to the former Japanese rulers, and the suppression of the pupils' protest to the suppression of the March First Movement in 1919, when the entire population, even women and children, had risen up for Korean independence and the end of Japanese occupation. That peaceful protest, inspired by Gandhi, was nonetheless brutally quashed.

The next day, Sangok brought flyers with him. We couldn't let this opportunity slip through our fingers, he said, we had to make use of it. He gave each of us a flyer, which declared that that we couldn't let the students in Daegu down; we couldn't just stand by and watch, but had to fight NOW for fair elections. Jang nodded in agreement, Mihee clapped her hands in excitement, Sangok smiled. Our hour had come, he said. He pressed the stacks of flyers into our hands, and told us there were more, we could get replenishments as soon as we had distributed these. Then we divided the inner city up between us: Sangok took the eastern part, Mihee the west, Jang the south and I the centre, Jongno. 'Go and position yourself by the new city library,' Jang advised me, 'the students gather there after class in the evenings.'

He gave me a light cuff on the head.

'But make sure the pigs don't catch you. They patrol there all the time.'

I completed my mission quickly, but didn't fetch more flyers; I hadn't seen Eve for weeks, and unlike Mihee I was a lousy revolutionary, an unreliable comrade and a bad friend. To me, it was more important to be with the woman I loved than to be a cog in the revolutionary machine.

We had planned to meet in front of the Academy, a cinema that exclusively showed foreign films. The screening was well attended that evening. I slipped into the foyer alongside the other patrons and studied the poster for Luigi Zampa's *La Romana*: Gina Lollobrigida in Daniel Gélin's embrace as Adriana — a fallen woman who is besotted with the student Mino, an opponent of Mussolini's dictatorship, a young man who is unable to forgive himself for having betrayed his comrades.

How familiar this story was to me, and what a strange coincidence that the student should be called Mino! Mino Diodati, admittedly, but Mino nevertheless. When I saw the scene in which the anti-fascists drop their flyers from the gallery of a dark cinema, letting them flutter down like snowflakes, I thought to myself, why didn't I think of that? In the beam of the projector, their message falls on the heads of the spectators, one sheet of paper after the other tail-spinning through the grainy air, turning first onto one side, then the other. The audience, shrouded in words, has no idea what's happening. Only when the police charge into the auditorium does the distant present become immediate; the shadow of time steps out of the light, and Adriana loses both Mino and herself in the darkness of Rome.

It was warm in the foyer, the air heavy with the scent of soap, perfume and powder; I was surrounded by people in suits, coats and hats, who lacked only in poverty. When I spotted Eve making her way through the crowd, I found it hard to believe that I had ever been cold.

My rendezvous with Eve were as clandestine as my conspiracy with Sangok, Mihee and Jang, but it was this secret that proved fateful: wherever the needle goes, the thread must follow.

I don't know whether she felt the same way; perhaps I was only imagining that we were happy. But I was happy, and as I zigzagged my way through the narrowest alleys and darkest corners of nocturnal Seoul, which in my mind were part of Eve – for I couldn't have envisaged her in any other place in the world, Eve, the Korean woman with the American name – it seemed a miracle to me that I was able to find her, that I could fool the blackness of the night.

I told her I loved her: that I loved her like a homeless person who has finally found a true home. She laughed and said that I didn't know what love was; she didn't take me seriously, because she didn't *want to* take me seriously. If I had questioned her about her feelings for me and forced her to tell the truth, she would probably have said that she liked me, that she liked being with me, liked waking up next to me, that she even felt something for me that she would call affection, but love? No. And in due course she would end our relationship, at a time when it would hurt me less, but not today, not now.

Perhaps I'm mistaken; I hope so. Sometimes I so long to be mistaken that when I recall our conversations, I smuggle in assurances that were never given, but that today, many years later, have become part of how I remember Eve; questions and answers that I have perhaps invented, and perhaps not.

You must be familiar with them too, those motionless memories? They are neither dead nor alive, but frozen images which used to be memories. They are memories of memories, created by us in a final attempt to halt the progress of forgetting; they are the fragments that have defied corrosion. They don't *ask* us to look at them, no, they force us, and we obey until we no longer know why it is *these* pictures that torment us. I notice that I surrender other memories in their favour, even though they are merely phantoms pervaded with feelings. That is all I possess of my past; a feeling that is stronger than everything I am today. I could never leave it behind me, as much as I might try, I am stuck in its skin, its language. It makes me believe that Eve loved me as much as I loved her; she was just afraid of feeling anything other than anger. Tenderness made her weak, and weakness was something she couldn't forgive in anyone, especially not herself.

We went to the Mambo; here too, everyone was talking about the change in the air. Would Rhee's candidate win the vice-presidential election this time? Lee Ki-poong was the president's chosen successor, or in truth his *heir*, because he had let Syngman Rhee adopt one of his two sons. In spite of this insurance policy, it seemed unlikely he would be able to succeed by legal means. Lee was so unpopular that (despite the poor alternatives) he wouldn't be elected, and how pitiful was his scrabble to gain the advantage at the very last minute! He had brought the elections forward by two months, which didn't speak in his favour; instead, it stank of desperation. Even the men at the bar who spent the whole live-long day sitting around in teahouses like the Mambo were aware of this. They weren't given table service, merely tolerated at best, and most were ostracized because all they could afford was one bottle of *makgŏlli*. They would hold on tightly to their empty cups until finally they stood up; they were their sole claim to their bar stools, albeit only for a short while. These men would never make the teahouse owner rich, they took seats from other customers, and when the boss arrived they would be chased out, cup or no cup, but on the occasions when the boss wanted to join in on their conversations or when he had gone to visit his family out in the countryside, the long, black bar and the soft, worn-out stools were their home. All the drinks they couldn't afford were listed on the walls, a radio in the corner played hits and arias interspersed with piano music, Chopin and Mozart; they sang along to 'Smoke Gets in Your Eyes' and Nam In-su's ballads, cried over the many goodbyes, the green rivers, blue mountains, the wide valleys and unrequited love.

They eyed us closely as I searched for a quiet table. I ignored them as much as possible, but it wasn't easy, because Eve maintained a conversation with their eyes. I never knew whether to admire or despise her for her courage; more than a small part of me believed I had to shield her from the lustful stares.

'You always want to save me.'

She didn't need a guardian, she told me, and she certainly

didn't need to be rescued. She was right; she could handle herself better in this place than I. She picked up the flyer, my last one, unfolded it carefully and skimmed the words.

'So that's what you were doing all those afternoons when I thought you were looking for work.'

She put it in her handbag and promised to give it to her friends.

The barmaid beckoned. Eve nodded to her, and told me she would be back in a moment. Settling in for a long wait, I felt a hand on my shoulder. I turned and found myself staring into the face of a stranger. Jinman Kim was his name, he said, leaning over me slightly, he was a friend of Johnny's.

'May I join you?'

Before I could answer, he had already pulled a chair up to the table.

'How is Johnny? Is he well? Or is he sick or something?'

Jinman was tall and stocky, his hair was smoothed with pomade and combed back, he wore narrow black trousers and a grey-and-black checked shirt. A pack of cigarettes poked out of his breast pocket. He took it out and offered me one. They were Lucky Strikes.

I shook my head.

'No idea. I haven't seen him in ages.'

'Neither have I. But I could really do with his support right now.'

'Support with what?'

Jinman frowned. The opposition was getting stronger and stronger, he said; the president had been smart to bring the elections forward. He took a comb out of his breast pocket and ran it through his hair, beckoning the waitress over. He winked at her and she beamed back. When had the *makgŏlli* last been filled? It mustn't be too old, he told her, he knew his

151

stuff with liquor just as much as the students did. He laughed and held the pack of cigarettes under my nose again. This time I took one.

'Why are you telling me all this?'

'You're Johnny's friend, aren't you? His friends are my friends. In some circles that's an unwritten rule.'

'Which circles?'

'Ours.'

Perhaps I should have stood up and left, but I was curious, I believed I knew which circles he meant: the gang called itself the North-West Youth. Most of its members had led affluent lives in North Korea before they had been driven out of their homes, their families murdered. Arriving in the South, they had joined forces with Rhee and became his henchmen, seeking to exact vengeance on those who had taken everything from them. They practised political agitation through violent means, using intimidation, threats and blackmail; carried out arrests, even executions, in conjunction with the police; and grew rich by driving their enemies from their homes and land. Their professed goal was to find those who could harm 'their' president; opposition fighters and communists, traitors to their country. I had heard that they recruited informants and paid them well; even royally, some said.

I wondered whether Johnny was one of their spies, and if he was, whether, now that he was avoiding them, they wanted to use me against him. I took a big gulp of *makgŏlli*. The fragments of a piano solo drifted over to us from the radio, and I imagined the rest, the trumpet, the saxophone, the double bass, the drums and Billie's voice.

I lowered my bowl and looked around: the drunk men at the bar in their dirty suits would stagger home just before the beginning of curfew, some would fall asleep in a war-damaged building in the belief they were home; the waitress in the red blouse and the red shoes, who sent her parents more than half of her wages in the belief that her younger sisters wouldn't have to take the path she had, but instead would study, find respectable jobs and support the whole clan; Jinman, whose daily bread came from betraying his fellow man, in the belief of serving a cause greater than him – he would soon realize that this great cause had in actual fact been small, smaller than the many 'friends' who disappeared forever because of his tip-offs; in that moment, the men, the waitress and Jinman all became a memory, and lost their immediacy, their urgency. They became an image, which carries a piece of the past within it, and it seemed foolish to me, ridiculous even, that they were thrashing around helplessly, entangled in the present – when, as soon as they had escaped this captivity, it would all seem so *paltry*: null and void.

Johnny had to resume his work, said Jinman, continuing his monologue, there was only a month until the elections, and I was his best friend. If Johnny was incapacitated, for whatever reason – and here Jinman looked over at the bar, at Eve, and stubbed out his cigarette – surely I wouldn't want everything he had been fighting for to be endangered just because of some illness?

'What has he been fighting for?' I asked quietly.

'A united Korea, what else?'

Only Syngman Rhee could bring the country together, said Jinman, that much was clear, no one else could take on North Korea. Did I really believe that Chang Myon, a man with no backbone whatsoever, could hold his own against Kim Il-sung? Kim would swallow him in one go and then let out an almighty belch.

Jinman guffawed. He stood up, brushing the cigarette ash off his sleeve.

'Tell Johnny to contact me. Today.'

He gestured towards the bar.

'And say hi to Eve for me. It's unusual for her to be so shy.'

He vanished instantaneously in the dimly lit room; it was as though I had dreamt the encounter. A small group of people had gathered in front of the bar to watch a drunk man who was dancing to the music from the radio, his arms raised up high. They were singing along rowdily and clapping in time. At the tables, huddles of three or four people sat around talking, their heads close together.

Eve was still standing in the same corner, but now she was alone. When our eyes met, she came back to our table. 'What did he want from you?' she asked, reaching for the cigarettes in my jacket pocket. 'He told me to give you his best,' I answered, and avoided her gaze. She turned away, rummaged through her handbag for matches, was unable to find any and gave up the search; she left the cigarette hanging unlit in the corner of her mouth. He was an acquaintance, she mumbled, nothing more, she had seen him around once or twice, but had never spoken to him. 'That's not the impression I got,' I answered. This time I looked into her eyes. She shrugged and turned her back on me; renewed her hunt for a lighter. I held mine out to her.

'Thanks.'

She took a long drag. I said she didn't owe me an explanation. She laughed and reached for my hand.

'Yunho, he's Johnny's friend.'

'A friend? Nothing more?'

I pushed her away; I didn't want to look at her or hear her

voice. I wished I had never met Jinman. I wanted to undo our encounter, and the only way to do this was to disappear: to cut myself out of the memory.

She ran after me, for the first and only time. She hadn't known who Jinman was and who he was working for, she said. 'Yunho,' she pleaded, 'speak to me, please.'

But I couldn't. I left the Mambo and paced through Jongno in the darkness. The heart of the city was empty. Seoul was hollow, not a living soul was here besides me: I was in a ghost town that was forsaken by light, inhabited only by winds that have no hands but shake at the trees, and by a moon that has no feet but wanders the sky.

When I got home, Johnny was sitting by the window with an empty tin can. He gave me a beaming smile and told me he had spotted it on the street below and dashed down, as quick as lightning, to rescue it. He was in the process of scratching off the label, he said, holding up the can to demonstrate, but it was stuck on so darn well that he'd been scratching for an hour already. Once he was finished he would punch holes in it, just like he had as a boy.

'Do you remember?'

The fire game had been our favourite. At full moon, we used to climb up onto a hilltop, light candles inside the cans, attach them to lengths of wire and spin them around over our heads. I used to love the sound the cans made as we swung them through the night air, a humming, buzzing sound, like a swarm of bees in flight. All that could be seen of the cans were these little pinpoints of light; they went through a metamorphosis and became burning moons, while my friends became silhouettes. The buzzing wire mingled with the chirp of crickets as we stood in a current of light.

How zealously Johnny had worked on his tin cans, how zealously I had searched for cans for him! It had been my job to look for them, while his was to pierce the pattern of holes, and when his fingers became bloodied with cuts, I had teased him about his 'dragonfly skin'.

He hadn't found any wire yet, he now said, but if he kept an eye out, he would soon find some. He grinned at me. I didn't know how to tell him about the conversation I'd had in the Mambo, and so I asked, as casually as possible, if he was planning to go and see Jinman soon. Of course, Johnny answered absent-mindedly, he was probably wondering where he was and why he hadn't been in touch for such a long time; my friend didn't notice that I had mentioned someone he had kept secret from me.

The next morning, he was gone before I woke up.

He came home two days later, with dark shadows beneath his eyes, a swollen right cheek and a cut on his upper lip. Before I could ask him what had happened, he hissed at me that I was never to poke my nose into his affairs again.

'Never again. Do you hear me?'

After that, sitting on the edge of the bed, the mattress creaking as he spoke, he told me that I had to help him, tomorrow, the day after tomorrow, the whole damn week, that I owed him that.

'Help you with what?'

'You'll soon find out. And you can bet you'll be getting your hands dirty.'

8

I had a suspicion of what might be waiting for me. The previous day, the newspaper *Dong-A Ilbo* had published a police memo describing in detail how the coming election was to be manipulated. It didn't say how the document in question had made its way from the police headquarters to the newspaper's editorial office; a paperboy and a shoe-shiner were questioned but not arrested, and it was later alleged that the opposition had been behind the leak. I can still picture the article now: beneath the bold headline was a photo of the chief of police smiling into the camera, a small man in a black suit with carefully combed-back hair and silvery metal-rimmed spectacles. What had been going through his mind when he sent the 'Instructions for a Successful Election' to all the police stations in South Korea? Did he really think he wouldn't be found out?

I can still remember his instructions too. They were as follows: firstly, before the polling began, around half of all ballot boxes were to be filled with votes for the candidates of the ruling party. Secondly, election volunteers were not to allow voters to enter the booths alone, but only in groups of three or four, so that they would be able to show each other who they had voted for. Thirdly, voters were to be asked who they had selected before handing over their slips. Finally, if the above measures were to prove insufficient, the genuine ballot boxes were to be switched with the prepared ones.

The interior minister, who was suspected of being the agent

of this plan, protested that the entire story was a spiteful fabrication, a shameful defamation. What did people take him for? Some kind of primitive dog? He pounded his fist on the table. He had lived and studied in the US for years, he had been *raised* there, he knew better than anyone what democracy meant, this was a malicious imputation intended to damage his political reputation and sling mud at the government!

This particular manoeuvre was actually only one part of an extensive catalogue of measures designed to guarantee electoral victory. The interior minister had bribed every one of the eight thousand policemen assigned to guard the ballot boxes with a figure three times their monthly salary; they were to overlook any 'procedural error' in the governing party's favour. He had forced the police chiefs to hand in their letters of resignation, which he would then accept if they let his plan be exposed. He had also assigned secret agents to the polling stations to keep watch over the guards. In addition, he had paid the youth leagues to spread an atmosphere of fear and terror on election day, hoping to ensure voters wouldn't get any foolish ideas.

The president remained silent, eventually making it known through his secretary that he wasn't concerned by the affair. He reluctantly summoned the interior minister, who denied everything. For Rhee, the case was closed. But not for the members of his cabinet – they worked hard to defame this truth as a lie, as the population didn't doubt for even a second that the memorandum was genuine; it wasn't the first time the government had tried to win an election by dishonest means.

Yet while Sangok, Mihee and Jang were planning how to incite the people to protest against the imminent election-fixing, I had to follow Johnny into his comrades' office, where we marked the freshly printed ballot slips with two crosses: one for Syngman Rhee, and one for his vice president, Lee Ki-poong. Johnny had been right; I did get my hands dirty, on that afternoon and on all the following days and nights until 14 March, the day before the election. The printer's ink clung to my fingers, hands and forearms, and from there it spread to my chin and my cheeks. I felt branded, because it couldn't be washed off, no matter how hard I scrubbed; even the bar of soap I swiped from Mrs Pak's kitchen turned black. Eventually I saw no other option but to conceal my face beneath a cap, which I pulled down low over my forehead.

I would have preferred never to be seen with Johnny again; I couldn't bear his foolish talk, and pushed him away when he laughingly grasped my arm and said I looked like a GI in my get-up. Tripping around me like a ballerina, he told me he had a mottled green jacket he wanted to lend me which would match the bowl on my head, but not his soldier's boots, he added, he needed those for himself, they were the only shoes he owned. When he held the jacket out to me, I was so angry I knocked it out of his hands. I couldn't believe I had got into this absurd situation of voting for the side I opposed, over and over again. It was quite clear, however, whom I had to thank for it; when Johnny had turned up again after those two days, I had felt relief, having imagined the worst.

The North-West Youth was a paramilitary organization financed by the South Korean government, and indirectly by the Americans too. It was led by thugs who had become high-ranking officers during the Korean War; afterwards, many members found roles within the police force. Sangok had explained to me that the youth leagues, not the North Korean People's Army, were responsible for the massacres carried out during the civil war – even a worm can roll over. In addition to their brutality, the North-West Youth were notorious for refusing to spare even their youngest members: fourteen- and fifteen-year-olds were forced to bury, burn or dump into the sea the bodies of those who had been beheaded or shot by their comrades.

These 'guardians of law and order' played cat and mouse with their victims, promising them mercy, then executing them like criminals. They lured them to the execution sites with food, with the prospect of leniency, forgiveness, with the hope of a future, and they exploited their naivety and stupidity. They viewed their victims' 'newly vacated' properties as payment for the 'lessons' they provided. Is it any wonder that a hunger for education sprang up immediately after the war ended? Ignorance, the population had learnt, came at a high price.

These stories had burned themselves into my memory; I was afraid that I too would have to dig graves, and not a stranger's, but my own and Johnny's. How relieved I was when he revealed that all I had to do to save our lives was write and fold; making two crosses seemed a trivial matter – admittedly, I hadn't thought I would be voting for a large swathe of the population.

The ballot-rigging office was located in the cellar of a building whose upper floors no longer existed. It was a wide room with a low ceiling; I had to duck down slightly whenever I crossed it on the way to the stairs.

There were twelve of us: myself, Johnny, and his ten friends, whose acquaintance I didn't want to make and who didn't consider it necessary to make mine either. We eyed one another with a suspicion that was in part justified; certainly some of them had been forced into the counterfeiting, presumably they owed the gang money (this had been Johnny's undoing too). Why hadn't he gone to his father for help, I asked? I had to shout over the noise of the ballot slips being printed alongside us. Instead of answering, he lit himself a cigarette and pushed the pack towards me; I pushed it back. 'They could at least have put a radio in here,' he muttered, 'with tedious work like this it's so easy to nod off. A bit of music really wouldn't be asking much, especially as they're not paying us.'

Not *even* paying us, he had wanted to say, as though this were a job like any other – as though it wasn't necessary to carry it out in secret. We had received no instructions about what to do if we got caught, but we knew we would be in trouble if we left the printing press behind; it was worth more than all of us put together.

Johnny commented that we had many more piles of ballot slips to fill in and no time to waste. Suddenly, his eyes sparkled. He picked up a slip, drew thick crosses on the pre-printed sections and grinned.

'How many votes is the opposition supposed to get?'

He laughed and made a second, third and fourth cross.

'Those dogs will regret having forced us to do this.'

His mirthful grin gave way to a grim sneer. 'It happened after you left,' he whispered, 'but it's the government's fault that Father had to sell all of our land at a ridiculously low price.'

'Mr Kim sold everything? Sold, not leased?'

Johnny nodded. It was all gone, he told me, the rice, barley and melon fields, his mother's tomato patch, the apple and peach trees, the wild gourd and the violet trumpet vines, and the buyer got it all for practically nothing – his father had been forced to sell, otherwise he would have been dispossessed. 'The Liberals carried out the land reform to secure their victory in this election and all the ones after it,' said Johnny, 'just like Kim Il-sung in the North.'

He tapped the ash of his cigarette onto the floor and sighed.

'People say that the taste of meat emerges as you chew, and the taste of words as you speak. I can't say I agree.'

'Where are your parents living now?'

'In Nonsan still. They were allowed to keep the house.'

Through all the months that Johnny had given me a place to stay, I had never asked after his family, and he had never mentioned them; I had assumed nothing had changed in Nonsan, in my mind nothing *could* change in Nonsan. Despite my dislike of Johnny's father, it was upsetting to discover that time had wrought havoc there too.

'So then why are you letting yourself get roped in by the Liberals?'

I grabbed a cigarette.

'Because Rhee is the only one who can get the better of Kim Il-sung. He's the lesser evil.'

He gave me a wink.

'Small steps forward aren't enough for you. You want a revolution, a coup. I'm not as greedy. My navel isn't bigger than my belly.'

I couldn't help but laugh.

'Besides, I told myself that this way I'll get back from them some of the money that's owing to father.'

This line of reasoning didn't make sense to me, but as my best friend, Johnny had a right to my support; so I voted for the opposition too, and would have spent the entire day casting dissenting votes, had one of the minders not looked over our shoulders and interrupted us.

'Hey, you idiots, you've misunderstood! You'll have to start over.'

I glanced quickly at Johnny, who was practically spitting with rage. I could see that my friend wanted to lay into the guy, but he and I both knew that would only get us into difficulties, for we were outnumbered in the room. We ripped up the 'incorrect' slips and declared obediently and in unison that, yes, we had misunderstood, it had been a mistake.

'Burn them,' he said curtly, before stomping back over to the printing press. I saw the glow of his cigarette in the dark corner, and only then did I notice how silent it had become in the cellar.

The people knew what was going on behind their backs; they had been warned by that newspaper report and others, and they fought back. In Daejeon, a large group of high-school pupils took to the streets, following the example set for them by others in Daegu a week before; in Busan the unions distributed flyers; in all towns large and small people demonstrated without pause and called for the 'protection of democracy' (as though democracy was a species of animal threatened with extinction). The protesters ended up in violent clashes with the police and the youth leagues, who began to attack, and even kill, journalists and 'overcritical' citizens; and all this beneath the gaze of the guardians of the law, who preferred to wait it out rather than intervene. In Seoul, a seventeen-year-old boy climbed onto a windowsill on the fourth floor of the interior ministry and painted WE WANT FREE ELECTIONS on the façade in his own blood.

Meanwhile, Sangok and Jang were trying to unite the numerous small protests into one big operation. They were in conversation with a few students from Korea University, Mihee reported, but the latter were still hesitant, fearing the consequences of a large demonstration. She had come to ask me why I'd been absent from the last few meetings. I couldn't tell her the truth, I was too ashamed; instead I said that I had to help someone who was in trouble, but would rejoin them as soon as the matter was dealt with.

She squeezed my hand. I was a good friend, she said.

'You can count on us if you need any help.'

While the rest of the country simmered, the situation reached boiling point in the south-east, in Masan, when a former oppositionist, a shady character named Ho, switched sides and suddenly declared himself a member of the governing party. The price of his conversion was fifteen million won, thirty times the monthly salary of a National Council representative. An expensive purchase, but one that paid off, because now the governing party had a three-quarters majority. The opposition promptly announced that this election was a matter of 'life and death'. They would use all their strength and resources to keep the 'right-wing villains and criminals' from electoral victory – who, of course, were in turn doing everything they could to achieve their goal.

In principle, all citizens were entitled to vote after their twenty-first birthday, on the provision that they registered in advance. As the offices in which one could do this belonged to the interior ministry, the regime tried to manipulate the number of eligible voters to its advantage. It decreed that, prior to the election, each citizen had to seek out the voting station in his or her constituency and submit a letter to the government. Only then would they receive their ballot slip. But some families received only one slip, even though several family members were entitled to vote. We heard on the radio that this had happened to a Mr Min; he was entitled to five voting slips, but only received one. When his son requested the remaining four on his behalf, he was subjected to verbal abuse, and had to report back to his father that the license for his business would be revoked if he were to 'put on airs again'. Later, an investigation into the events of 15 March revealed that every fifth family was affected by this manipulation, always those in financial need, those without means.

There were attempts at manipulation and intimidation in Seoul too. I could have cast my vote undisturbed, for Johnny's friends pressed a voting slip into my hand right next to the ballot box, but I waived my vote, as did Johnny. We already knew the result. The previous day, we had put the prepared boxes into position, and Jinman had carried out a random check of the ballot slips, before sealing the boxes and explaining with a grin how the 'enemy' would be prevented from entering the polling stations the next day.

'The enemy?'

'You know, the opposition. They have the right to post an election supervisor in every station. We'll be taking measures to prevent that.'

'How?'

Instead of giving an answer, Jinman sauntered outside, sucking on his Lucky Strike.

I wondered whether I should confess everything to Sangok – perhaps he and his comrades could do something? Then I decided against it, less because I didn't want to betray Johnny, more because I didn't want to look bad in front of my teacher; he had already mocked me countless times for my 'counter-revolutionary' relationship with Eve.

In his opinion, the Confucian separation of the sexes should be rejected, because it engendered 'pathological curiosity', was unnatural, and had only come into existence to keep women helpless and dependent. This, he explained to me, had made it easier to reduce them to their sexuality (to their function as reproductive machines) and to deny them any form of equality. Men were duty bound to redress this injustice, but for him, anything beyond that was out of the question.

'Women are a biological and economic problem. In peacetime they are important, in wartime, detrimental.'

His eyes twinkled; I couldn't tell whether he meant it seriously.

'When a man loves a woman,' he continued, 'he doesn't just lose his freedom as an individual, but also the control over his own body.' Jang, who had been listening silently with half-closed eyes, let out a loud laugh.

'So dies the butcher. With a willow leaf in his jaw.'

Then he muttered: 'Don't listen to that madman, boy.' He had once been as head over heels as I was, he told me, and it was best to let love run its course.

He clapped me on the back.

'It will self-destruct. And then you'll be free.'

That afternoon, it was announced on the radio that the opposition party's electoral supervisors had been turned away from the polling stations with excuses like 'you're too late', or 'it's too early' or 'there are already too many people in the station and there's no more room'. There had been more of these hindrances in Masan, a reporter recounted, than anywhere else in South Korea. The supervisors had been let into only three of ten stations, where they had to watch helplessly as three people at a time were sent into the booths, one of whom then checked all the ballot slips before giving permission for them to be cast. Three votes for Rhee and Lee Ki-poong; anything else was unacceptable. Some election volunteers showed the voters where to make the crosses, others demanded to see the already folded ballot slips before they were submitted.

An elderly woman had hers torn from her hand, opened and ripped into a thousand pieces. After seeing this, two opposition members jumped into a car and drove through the streets of Masan. Through a loudspeaker, they called for the population to boycott the election, declaring that it could no longer be saved. Police officers arrived on the scene at once; they seized the jeep and the megaphone, but let the protesters go. The young men returned to their headquarters, where they painted placards which they dangled out of the window, yelling through another, not-yet-confiscated loudspeaker: 'We want new elections! Let us vote in peace! Long live democracy!'

A knot of people formed beneath the window, applauding them. When the first passers-by raised their voices to join in the protest, the oppositionist 'agitators' moved their demonstration to the street. Suddenly, a military jeep drove past, a North-West Youth jeep – their members were everywhere, multiplying by the day, they were like clones, that's how quickly they lost their individuality. Johnny's comrades jumped out of the car, armed with baseball bats, wooden poles and iron rods, and began to beat the demonstrators; the police hurried over to lend the thugs a hand.

'The citizens fought back,' reported the broadcaster, still out of breath. 'When the first stone hit the police car, the uniformed officers tried to push through the crowd to arrest whoever had thrown it. But the people wouldn't let them through. Instead, further stones began to fly through the air, and the officers had to beat a hasty retreat.'

This wasn't the only protest in Masan – the entire city rebelled and marched, spontaneously, to the town hall. There, they found their opponents lying in wait, along with the only fire engine Masan had.

★

It was nine in the evening when the blinding glare of floodlights illuminated the square outside the town hall, and the police began to shoot tear gas into the crowd. As the protesters dropped back, coughing, shielding their eyes and mouths with their hands and sleeves as best they could, the fire engine accidentally reversed into an electricity pylon. It toppled over, and the power went out.

Blackout.

Chaos.

The demonstrators arm themselves with stones, pebbles, bricks. They throw them at the police officers, who close in, still deploying the tear gas.

Coughing.

Wheezing.

Someone discovers an unexploded tear gas canister and hurls it back at the police. It detonates. Now the police are coughing, not all of them are wearing gas masks. The demonstrators cheer and search for other still-intact canisters. The police again grab their weapons, unscrew the attachments. This time they shoot bullets into the crowd.

The demonstrators rapidly disperse.

One group storms the house belonging to District Official Ho; kicks in the front door, hacks the furniture to pieces, throws it from the windows, sets it on fire. The house is empty, Ho and his family got out in time. A second group, school-children no older than eighteen, march to the police station on the northern outskirts of the city, smash in the windows and hurl burning pieces of wood into the building. The police officers fight back, shooting at the youths; two are hit, one fatally, the other loses consciousness. When he wakes a few hours later, he finds himself inside the station, surrounded by corpses. The third group, which consists of newspaper delivery boys, shoe cleaners, beggars and peddlers – those united by their hatred of the police, who terrorize them on a daily basis – exact vengeance by setting two police stations on fire and stealing guns. Most of them are arrested, beaten and tortured, having first been denounced as communists; only then is torture allowed. Screams ring out from the interrogation rooms. Prisoners dangle from the ceiling. Others are tied to chairs, the tips of their fingers attached to electrical wires which protrude from telephone sets. The torturers use this makeshift device to give the prisoners electric shocks whenever they dare to answer 'No, I am not a communist.' In the neighbouring room, baseball bats and rifle butts are used to smash in skulls. 'Evidence' is planted in the trouser-, shirt- and jacket pockets of both the dead and the unconscious, small scraps of paper with the words: 'Long live Kim Il-sung! Long live the Democratic People's Republic of Korea!'

The next morning, before all the ballot slips have been counted, it emerges that the victory has been too conclusive, so conclusive that it seems unbelievable even to the interior minister, and he instructs all his subordinates to correct the numbers, in other words, to take the not-yet-counted falsified ballot slips and tear them up or burn them, to get rid of them, no matter how! Meanwhile, on the order of the Masan police chief, two uniformed officers go down to the port and sink the corpse of a pupil fresh out of the academy, Juyŏl Kim, who was hit on the head by a tear gas canister during the protest and died; the canister shattered the right-hand side of his skull and bored into his brain. They tie bricks to his hands and feet; under no circumstances must he be found. Meanwhile, the re-elected regime makes it known that the revolts in Masan were instigated by communists, as evidence collected by the police will confirm. Responding to the accusation that police officials shot at innocent citizens, the brand-new vice president Lee Ki-poong retorts: what else were they supposed to have done with their guns? After all, they were there to be fired.

The opposition insists that the Masan riots be investigated. This time, Rhee can't have his opponents locked up in the Parliament cellars, as he did the last time he wanted to implement a change to the constitution; the US ambassador, Muccio, intervenes. Gritting his teeth, the brand-new lifelong president approves an inquiry and appoints a committee of independent experts who are sent to the south-east of the country, where the demonstrations and protests refuse to let up. The inhabitants of Masan are demanding justice for the victims of police violence, as well as a detailed list of the perpetrators and the dead. Long queues form inside and out-side the city hall, mothers, fathers, even young children and adolescents on the search for their relatives. Among them is an elderly woman from Namwŏn, a place known for its swallows, and for its white azaleas in springtime.

Juyŏl Kim's mother stands before the committee. Her name is Janju Gwŏn. She has travelled to Masan on foot, spending two days on the road, and has slept beneath trees and bridges. She has tried to clean herself up for the hearing as best she can; her face and hands are presentable, but her feet, clad in white rubber overshoes, are dirty, and wilted azalea blossoms cling to her grey hair. She plucks them out while waiting to be sum-moned to present her case. When her name is called, she needs help getting to her feet. Leaning against her eldest son, she limps over to the committee's table and sits down on the chair allocated to her. Before being given permission to speak, she says she is looking for her seventeen-year-old son, a pupil at the state high school in Masan, that she hasn't seen him since

15 March and is very worried. He is her youngest son, she says, his two sisters were killed during the civil war, struck by bombs while trying to flee, and her husband died in the war too. Since then it has been only the three of them, and her sons look after their old mother lovingly, working for the Masan daily paper on their free afternoons and in the evenings after school. Juyŏl, she says, assigns the routes to the newspaper delivery boys and draws up their schedules, and after finishing school he plans to go to university.

Once she stops talking, she can no longer hold back her tears; her older son tries to speak for her, but she refuses his help. She was so sure she would find Juyŏl in Masan, she says, but then her relatives, friends and other acquaintances described to her what had happened that night and how small the chances are that he is still alive. 'Sometimes, I think I can feel it if somebody I care deeply about is alive, even if the circumstances speak against it. It's as though I can feel their presence, sense it, just as I know whether they are well or not. Is it foolish to believe that? Or is it only foolish to hold on to it? Not to let go before the hope turns into a dark chamber, a trap?'

For the members of the committee, Janju Gwŏn's story is just one of many; during the election night, more than two hundred of Masan's inhabitants were imprisoned and tortured, many of whom were never seen again. Juyŏl's friends, in their search for him, have made enquiries in the hospital, in the police stations, even in the mortuaries; the hearing in the town hall is Janju Gwŏn's last hope. The sympathy of the committee members, however, has been exhausted: to them, the old woman standing before them is not a human being, not an individual, but a case; a file. As she speaks, she loses even the final vestiges of humanity and dignity. She becomes a victim, who – to some extent – has been trampled justifiably, for she is one of the weakest members of this society. Weakness is unforgivable.

They take a look in their files; they take at least this much time to simulate compassion. They leaf through the lists of the dead, which the magistrate officials have drawn up out of fear for their future. They read through them, then eventually shake their heads. The name Juyŏl Kim is nowhere to be found, they say, so Mrs Gwŏn shouldn't give up hope, her son may still be alive. Has she looked in the hospitals? Janju Gwŏn nods. She should enquire there again, suggests one of the members, perhaps the names got mixed up. Janju Gwŏn lowers her gaze; she can't read, so she checked all the rooms in the hospital personally. If the committee don't know any-thing, then . . . She has a suspicion, and now, with the general helplessness expanding in the room, she feels she can express it without her sanity being questioned: could her son perhaps be in one of the secret police stations that civilians don't have access to? Could he be lying in a torture chamber still, in a corner, injured, his cries ignored by the guardians of the law, who don't want to admit the abuses of that night even to themselves?

Even though the committee wants to reject this suspicion, they hand Juyŏl Kim's case over to the state prosecution service with the instruction to inspect it very closely; too many similar rumours have proved to be true, and their mandate states that they have to represent the people. In the days that follow, they will confront the fact that the police in Masan have resumed their illegal activities: that evidence and confessions are still being falsified in order to justify the events of that night. Police officers tell an adolescent boy arrested on suspicion of gun theft that they will kill him if he continues to protest his innocence, and that no one will hold them to account; they thrash a taxi driver with wooden canes when he denies having set the police station on fire, they tell him he's 'filthier than a street mongrel, viler than a Red', and threaten to wrap him up in a straw mat and throw him into the sea 'like all the rest'; when a journalist conducts research into Juyŏl Kim's case, they beat him. And the suspicion is voiced, ever more loudly, ever more insistently, that the police have dumped the schoolboy's corpse into the well in front of the city hall. Eventually, the state prosecutor orders the well to be drained. All he finds are dying fish.

The search for Juyŏl Kim unleashes hysteria in South Korea. Hardly a day goes by without a policeman being arrested, without street riots or demonstrations calling for new elections – everyone is on edge, tense, not only those who have skeletons in their closet, but also those who are looking for the skeletons.

Johnny's connection to the North-West Youth was making him extremely nervous. Whenever he heard voices coming from the floor below he would jump and ask me to go and check it out, but I felt equally anxious. We would both be arrested if even one person from the gang of forgers was caught and interrogated regarding their accomplices.

We didn't speak about our days in the printing workshop; I didn't ask Johnny how far his involvement in the league went, he clearly had no desire to volunteer any explanations, and I felt that the less I knew, the better. It was still impossible to predict when the situation would calm down, acts of police violence were still being uncovered on an almost daily basis, yet Rhee continued to govern unfazed, appointing one minister after the next, pushing his cabinet members around from one post to another.

To Johnny, that was a good sign. Everything would settle

down, he assured me. I didn't really know what to wish for; on the one hand, I wanted new elections, but on the other, if the opposition came to power they would order a thorough investigation of the ballot-rigging. This, after all, would allow them to get rid of numerous opponents in one fell swoop, and then Johnny and I would find ourselves in trouble.

Even though we were terribly hungry, and our cigarette supply was dwindling, we didn't dare leave the room.

We whiled away the daylight hours smoking; I flicked through Johnny's lecture notes. I read the Korean translation of a Japanese translation of the first chapter of *The Rebel* by Albert Camus: 'What is a rebel? Someone who says no, but his refusal is not a renunciation; he is also someone who says yes, from that first stirring onwards.' I tried to engage Johnny in debate, claiming – purely in order to provoke him – that the borderline that Camus locates in the rebel's 'no' was a no that demands nothing of him, yet denounces everything, that in fact it wasn't a borderline, but a snapping-shut, a beheading: the attempt to dethrone those who hold power by divesting himself of them. Rebellion, I explained, doesn't *invoke* a *value*, either silently or by protest, rebellion is the inversion of all values, the crossing, no, the *destruction* of all borders. Only through a destruction of the whole could the ground be prepared for the new. The new would never originate from the old, for the old spreads out its roots, seeking niches and gaps it can creep into, which it can convince of its existence, of its superiority. 'Better to die on one's feet than to live on one's knees,' I said, quoting Camus. The rebel is someone who has liberated his awareness from old-fashioned beliefs, he is the individual who has managed to connect with his consciousness. He is ruled not by the desire for change, but by the discovery of the self that was in possession of this desire. I pointed to the sentence: 'Awareness develops from the act of rebellion.'

There are some sentences that have the power to change a life, but my friend was unmoved. He merely muttered: 'I'm like a blind man looking at a picture.'

Johnny couldn't stand it in our room any longer. Surely it would be possible to stretch his legs under the cover of darkness, he reasoned. He came back after just a few minutes. He had found a *Dong-A Ilbo* on the street, and bought two packs of cigarettes from black marketeers. 'Read this,' he said, tossing the newspaper over to me. He sat down by the window and lit a cigarette. 'Juyŏl Kim's corpse found in harbour,' I read and lowered the paper. 'Can I have one too?' I asked. He pushed the pack towards me.

'So they found him.'

To be precise, a fisherman had pulled him out of the sea just off the coast. Back on land, he sent a street urchin off with the mission of informing the local media and the committee at the city hall, but not the police. Meanwhile, the sailor guarded the corpse. News of the discovery of Juyŏl Kim's body spread at lightning speed, and the inhabitants of Masan came down to the harbour in droves, among them a press photographer, who took pictures of the corpse. The dead boy was then taken on an ox-cart to the morgue to be autopsied.

The article ended here; the pathology report wasn't yet available, and as yet no statement had been issued by the city hall. It was reported on the radio that everyone, not only Mrs Gwŏn, was impatiently awaiting the result of the examination; that in front of the hospital people were discussing how Kim's mortal remains could be preserved as a 'memorial to police despotism and violence'. The reporter was breathing heavily; he had run to the studio in order to broadcast the announcement.

Another equally impassioned debate raged around police violence. A passer-by claimed to have seen a large, elongated knife wound on Kim's stomach, an injury that could only have come about through torture. When two onlookers defended the 'police measures', the crowd turned on them and drove them away, just as they did the police chief, who had hurried to the scene with a group of uniformed officers; he was pelted with stones and severely injured.

To this day I still don't know why, but back then I felt that the events in Masan were decisive; I believed that, even before the sun set that night, something would happen to turn everything upside down, to challenge everything. Johnny thought, a little more prosaically, that the people would rise up once more and demand retribution and revenge for Juyŏl Kim's murder. Everyone had been searching for him, he said – for a corpse, remember, not for a living person – and now they had got what they wanted. 'Tonight,' he prophesied, 'the world will come to an end.'

It didn't, not on that night nor on any of the nights that followed, even though a further uprising did shake Masan: once again, police stations were pelted with stones and set on fire, and the houses of hated politicians plundered and burnt down. They, of course, had long since left the city, as had most of the policemen. The few who had stayed grasped their rifles once more when confronted by the mob, but they had learnt their lesson; this time, they didn't dare shoot into the throng, and instead fired shots over the rioters' heads. This only made the angry crowd even angrier. Forty thousand people took to the streets that night, of whom most were young and unemployed, but by no means out of control: they had given careful consideration to which buildings they wanted to set on fire and which they didn't. They also left a few members of their group behind each time, with buckets of water, to make sure the fire didn't spread.

Two days later, the government newspaper, the *Seoul Shinmun* – which the Paks along with all the other citizens in Seoul were forced to subscribe to, and which I normally steered clear of but had pinched before Mr Pak had the opportunity to read it out loud to his wife – published President Rhee's statement on the incidents in Masan:

'The population cannot live in peace while there are troublemakers trying to level out society by violent means. It is my right as president to punish unlawful acts, and I advise citizens not to side with the insurgents. The government is not yet able to rule out the potential involvement of communist elements in the riots.'

Just a few days later, the *Seoul Shinmun* published an announcement that, according to foreign sources, the revolts in Masan had been planned and put into action by 'communists from outside' (in other words: North Korea) who had infiltrated the country.

'You see,' said Johnny, reaching for his jacket and slipping on his shoes. 'Everything's fine. They think it was the communists. And who knows,' he grinned before pulling the bedroom door shut behind him, 'maybe it really was?'

I too decided to go out, to no longer let my fear smother me; it had been days since I'd heard from Eve, and my longing for her, as well as my concern, drove me out of the house. I was just pulling on my jacket when I heard my name being called outside the window.

I peered through the glass. It was Mihee; she was standing on the street, rubbing her hands over her bare upper arms. She was wearing neither a jumper nor shoes, and I wasn't sure if she even had socks on. I waved her up, and a few seconds later heard her padding feet.

She came in, but remained in the middle of the room, even though I offered her Johnny's bed to sit on. She looked pale, tired, her hair was lank and dull, and a confused expression lay on her face; she reminded me of a fly that had fallen into a bowl of hot rice porridge.

I asked her what had happened. She didn't answer, instead staring past me into the distance. It was strange how quickly the room was changed by her presence. I remember reading somewhere that an adult forgets the child they once were, the child that thought itself eternal. Looking back, I believe that Mihee was broken by the world because she was unable to give up on that child.

All of a sudden, she began to sob loudly. Wanting to comfort her, I put my arms around her. She cried and spoke all at once, much too quickly, much too much, and as she cried she swallowed her words. Unable to understand her, I interrupted, but the more I interrupted her, the stronger her stammering became.

'Yunho,' she finally cried out, 'they've arrested Sangok!'

9

They came to Jang's stationery shop, she told me. 'In a black limousine. It almost ran over a child . . .'

'A child?'

'A girl, about seven or eight years old. I've seen her wandering through the city with a brown leather suitcase for weeks now. She's either a street trader or homeless.'

'Was she hurt?'

'I don't think so.'

'And then? What happened?'

'Two men got out.'

'Police?'

'I don't think so.'

'Soldiers?'

'They weren't wearing uniform.'

'Did they have badges?'

'I didn't see. But they were armed. They went into the shop, and didn't even try to be quiet. Then I heard screaming.'

'Screaming?'

'I crept closer . . .'

'That was reckless, they could have caught you.'

'Then the shop door swung open and suddenly Jang was pushed out onto the pavement.'

'Did they say anything to him?'

'I don't think so.'

'Was he injured?'

'He was bleeding. His top lip and his nose were smeared with blood.'

'And what happened then?'

'Then I heard a shot.'

'A shot? Just one?'

'Or maybe more . . . I can't remember now. Then Jang fled.'

'He got away?'

'Yes, the coward vanished into a side street. He didn't even turn when I called his name.'

'Did the men notice?'

'They weren't interested. They let him run. Then they came out of the shop pushing Sangok in front of them. His hands were tied. He was limping. He had blood over his face. One eye was swollen shut.'

'But he could still walk?'

'I should have helped him, but I was so scared.'

'No, it's good you stayed hidden.'

'Someone must have betrayed us. Maybe Jang?'

'Why would he?'

'Maybe they offered him money. Lots of it. He once said he wanted to leave Korea, to turn his back on "this miserable country" once and for all.'

'I don't think that's very likely. If he'd wanted to rat out Sangok, why did he wait so long?'

'Well, if it wasn't Jang, then who . . .?'

'Nobody. Nobody betr—'

'You. You're the traitor.'

'Me?'

'*You* betrayed Sangok.'

'Why would I do that?'

'For lots of money.'

'For *money*?'

'Everyone can be bought.'

'So where is all this money? I'm poor. I have nothing. Everything you see here belongs to Johnny.'

'After you lost your job at the bicycle workshop, you didn't look for work. Why not?'

'You know why. We were together every day.'

'Because you didn't need work, you already had it.'

'You know that's not true.'

'You're working for a secret organization.'

'No, I'm not. That's nonsense.'

'Or for a youth league. For the North-West Youth.'

'Why would I work for criminals? Do you think I have a death wish?'

'Someone betrayed Sangok, Yunho.'

'Maybe it was a coincidence . . .'

'Someone betrayed him. *Him.* Not us. They let Jang go, and they didn't even bother looking for me. But they took Sangok.'

'Maybe they've had him in their sights for a while . . .'

'They beat him. Who knows what will happen to him now.'

'I had no reason to betray him, Mihee. As it happens, I had every reason not to.'

'Oh, sure. Don't play me for a fool.'

'I'm not! Listen: he's the only connection I have to my brother.'

'Your brother?'

'Yes. To Yunsu. He joined the partisans during the war.'

'He's living in the North?'

'Allegedly. According to Sangok.'

'So why did you turn down his offer? He said again and again he could smuggle you over the border, and every single time you had a different excuse for why you wanted to wait.'

'I can't just abandon everything and run!'

'Why don't you admit it, you don't want to leave Seoul because of Eve! You probably told her everything about us, and she passed it straight on to her American friends!'

'Eve would never do that! She's on our side.'

'I bet *she's* working for a secret organization!'

'You know where she works.'

'Did she know about him?'

'I don't know . . .'

'*Answer me*: did she know about him?'

'No. Yes . . . I mean, I told her about Sangok. But she wouldn't . . . she would never . . . Maybe she told Johnny?'

'Johnny? Your friend Johnny? He knew about us too?'

'No . . . Yes? Perhaps. But Johnny would never . . .'

'Who else would never, Yunho? Who *else* knew?'

Before I could answer, she had stormed out; that was the last time I saw her. I tried to find her after my return from Japan, but all my efforts were in vain, I might as well have attempted to measure the sky with a stick of bamboo. I searched everywhere, in the cities along the coast, in the remote mountain villages, but it was as though the earth had swallowed her up, along with Jang – Sangok was the only one I found.

It was a coincidence, one of those coincidences that Koreans in both the South and the North call destiny: *your* destiny, *my* destiny, *our* destiny, an ineradicable, unalterable future which is determined at the moment of our birth. This subspecies, this *degenerate* species of the real future was invented in order to make life more tolerable . . . Or was it to make dying more tolerable? Let's say dying. Sometimes it's easier to disappear, like the world in the first hours of a heavy snowfall.

The report compiled by the truth commission which

President Kim Dae-jung convened at the beginning of this century only fell into my hands because I had been stood up by Father Matthew – the brother of the Maryknoll order who hid me from Park Chung-hee's spies on numerous occasions during the 1970s. Perhaps you know him, he's living in Seoul again now. As the brother of a communist, I led the life of a fugitive for almost three decades, always on my guard against agents of the Korean Secret Service, the KCIA, constantly searching for people whom I could trust; whom I *wanted* to trust. Sometimes I spent weeks on end holed up in a dark room, speaking only in whispers. Then I would picture what my day-to-day life would have been like in the US, or in Germany, a country that had stayed in my mind from Yunsu's *Textbook of the German Language*; when he was at school, they had to learn the language of the Japanese allies instead of the enemy language, English.

The report lay hidden among the antiquarian tomes, but only the first volume – the other three were missing. The book had clearly never been read, because the pages' outer edges were still slightly stuck to one another. Because I could afford it, I bought it, put it on a bookshelf at home and forgot that it existed. A few months later, I stumbled across it again. This time I kept a lookout for familiar names, scanning the pages in the hope of discovering something about my disappeared friends. I never thought I would actually find something, but there in the very first section, in the chapter 'Suspicious Deaths', appeared Sangok Shin.

It said he had fled to North Korea in 1949 and studied political ideology in Kangdong, a small city north-east of Pyongyang. After that he completed a one-year apprenticeship as a radio technician and, upon the outbreak of the Korean War, was deployed to South Korea as part of the People's

Army radio unit. In 1960, following his arrest in Seoul, he was sent to a prison in Gwangju, where he was asked repeatedly whether he would renounce his political convictions. During the interrogation he declared that, as a member of the North Korean Workers' Party, he could not support the Republic of Korea, but instead would do everything in his power to strengthen the Democratic People's Republic. Even after his parents visited him in prison to plead with him, he still refused to recant; he said this would be totally irreconcilable with his conscience. After that, his parents were forbidden further contact.

I checked the dates. After the end of the civil war, Comrade Shin had stayed in the South; his mission was to convince South Koreans of the communist idea and to recruit new agents. Between 1953 and 1961, he hadn't set foot on North Korean soil.

He had never had the opportunity to befriend Yunsu.

On 29 May 1961, two weeks after Park Chung-hee's military putsch, Sangok was sentenced to lifelong imprisonment, the usual punishment for political criminals. Thirteen years later, in August 1974, a prisoner named Cho, who was serving a sentence of twenty years for three murders, was placed in Sangok's cell by the prison director. The next morning, Sangok was found dead; according to the autopsy, he died of a heart attack. But of course, he was really tortured to death by Cho, after he repeatedly refused to swear loyalty to the Republic of Korea.

I should tell you that, until 1973, President Park had been almost tolerant of dissent, by his standards at least. In his 'Five Phase Plan of Ideological Conversion', the emphasis lay on 'voluntary changeover'. I had heard stories about it from political activists, young students who, like me, had been forced to flee from state repression. Father Matthew had introduced me to the Monday Evening Group; US and Canadian missionaries who helped political dissidents and smuggled news of Park's human rights abuses out of the country. They also mentioned the plan, but no one could give me specific details; those who had been 'converted' steered well clear of Father Matthew's group.

Here, in the commission's report, the plan was described in detail. Conversion apparently took place in Phase Two, which could last up to four months and consisted of lessons in anti-communist thinking. The 'candidate' had to learn texts about 'free democracies' off by heart (and this in a dictatorship, how utterly absurd). If he refused, conversion had failed. In Phase Three, he was watched for a month by other, non-political, prisoners; his behaviour was recorded in detail, and then his studiousness was taken into account alongside these surveillance reports. If the candidate managed to clear this hurdle too, in Phase Four the 'sincerity' of his wish to convert was evaluated by the prison guards and a KCIA agent. This evaluation was based upon the existing behavioural reports and a personal statement composed by the candidate, in which he had to declare the reasons for his renunciation of communism and his plans for the future. In the final phase, the successful conversion was announced on the prison radio, and extracts from the successful candidate's personal statement were read out.

In 1971, after the People's Republic of China replaced Taiwan as a permanent member of the UN Security Council, Park Chung-hee believed that a new invasion by North Korea was imminent (again with Chinese support). Or perhaps this was just a neat excuse. Either way, he modified the 'Five Phase Plan'. From 1974, 'conversion teams' were deployed, who forced political prisoners into signing a document which promised their renunciation of communism. Their tool of persuasion was violence; in other words, daily torture by fellow inmates and thugs who had been planted in the prisons expressly for that purpose. Three hundred of a total of five hundred left-wing individuals – many of whom had been incarcerated since April 1960 – changed their political convictions within days, while the rest died suddenly of 'natural' causes. Like Sangok, who – and I couldn't get this out of my head – had ended up in the clutches of the anti-communists after someone had betrayed him.

Who?

'We have to stay alert,' he had always said. 'We live in a world where you can get your nose bitten off if you close your eyes for even a second.'

Many days passed before I saw Johnny again. When he finally came staggering through the door to our room, he was so exhausted and hungry that he fell onto his bed, still chewing on the last scraps of some dried squid, wrapped himself up in his blanket and promptly fell asleep. The next morning, he was uncommunicative; he merely muttered that he had to go to the university, ran a comb through his hair, slipped on his shoes and slammed the door shut in my face.

Without hesitating, I followed him. I suspected him of having betrayed Sangok to his comrades. But I lost sight of him by the gates of Korea University, where it seemed as though every single enrolled student had gathered on the small campus: they were preparing a demonstration.

Some were carrying signs, others posters, many had a strip of white cloth tied around their foreheads; everyone was talking over one another, some were laughing and making jokes, many were agitated and anxious. They knew they were putting their future on the line with this protest, and not only their own, but their families' too: the future of the older siblings who had sacrificed their own education for them, and of the parents who had sold the family property in order to make it possible. Unlike them, I had nothing to lose. I pushed my way into the crowd and grabbed a white cloth. The students next to me laughed, applauded and clapped me on the shoulder. They didn't know me, but they saw me as one of them; I had never been able to smuggle myself into their lectures – but into their demonstration, this I managed. I heard someone whispering, close by my ear, that the dean had tried to talk them out of the protest, that he had threatened them with expulsion from the university. I turned and grabbed the student, who looked like he was in his first semester, and said that we would be doing the right thing, that this was all that mattered. His classmates nodded in agreement, jabbing him in the ribs. At that moment, the announcement came through a megaphone that we would begin our march at one that afternoon, and the crowd applauded, cheered and roared. Someone pressed a bundle of broom handles into my arms, and paintbrushes, paint and paper into Choi's, the first-semester student, and told us to make posters. At a loss, Choi held the blank sheet up in the air and asked what slogans he should paint. 'Freedom, truth and honesty!', someone suggested, 'We want freedom, truth and honesty!' Choi began to write, but I took the brush and the paint out of his hand. 'It has to say "Down with the traitors!",' I told him, 'and "We want new elections!"' I listened with one ear as the leader of the demonstration, a student named Yi, read out the students' demands. 'We're fighting for freedom, dignity and democracy,' he cried. 'We students are the only ones who can build a true democracy.

We demand that all those responsible for the terrorist acts in Masan be punished immediately and without exception. Immediately and without exception!'

His last few words were drowned out by thunderous applause. Once Yi had cried out that we couldn't let anyone stop our peaceful protest, especially not the police, the first students streamed out through the gates onto the street. From the campus loudspeakers came the dean's voice, but it went unheard. Everyone, myself included, was too busy shouting the slogans: 'Freedom, truth and honesty!' and 'Down with the traitors!'

We marched in the bright spring light. The cherry trees were blossoming, their white petals swayed in the warm breeze, and I remember thinking that Sangok had fulfilled his mission, he had succeeded in mobilizing the students, and I was happy that he hadn't been imprisoned in vain: we had made progress. We had done the right thing.

How strange it is, the right thing, its clarity so fleeting and illusory.

The police were waiting for us. Even before we reached the East Gate, we were battling against numerous troops, and they tried to arrest as many of us as possible. Passers-by looked on passively while schoolchildren called out words of encouragement, some of them even joined us.

In order to dodge the police, who had taken to the roads on foot, on horseback and in cars, we split up; one group intended to push through the side streets to the Parliament, and the other, which I joined, planned to break through the police barricade. As soon as we were positioned opposite them, we roared 'Down with the traitors!' and rushed full pelt towards the pigs. A fierce struggle broke out, the vanguard defending themselves as best they could. Many were injured, but we couldn't let ourselves be distracted, we had to storm forwards, that was our plan, the big and strong would give us cover, and we held on to this, we knew we wouldn't all make it to the Parliament. Our goal was: as many as possible.

I reached the square without any officers laying even a finger on me. Every one of us who made it was cheered and welcomed with thunderous applause. As I sat on the ground with the others, I noticed that workers had gathered on the building site near the square; they had been joined by shoe-shiners, newspaper and other delivery boys, and on the far side of the police cordon stood journalists, government workers, pupils, mothers with their children, all of them watching us, and their interest spurred us on. Someone began to sing. I hummed along, knowing neither the melody nor the lyrics. My neighbour prodded me, grinning, and said he could never remember the damn university hymn either. Had I started there last autumn too? he asked. I nodded. 'You look a little lost,' he said. 'You stick out. Like me.'

He too had started university only the previous year, he told me. He rummaged around in his bag, pulling out a pack of cigarettes, and offered me one. He hadn't been able to study before, he said, because of the war. Now I understood; Johnny had told me about them, the 'old' students, those who'd had to fight in the Korean War. Johnny had said: 'They learn differently. They know what it's all about. But we, what do we know?'

Suddenly the roadblock opened and a car approached, a shiny black Hudson Hornet like something from a Howard Hawks film. It was the dean, who had come to convince us to return to campus or to our homes. He was proud of us, he said, as he began his speech over the loudspeaker, proud that we had managed to carry out the demonstration peacefully – at this point we clapped and whistled – and he was proud that we wanted to make a stand, but now, he said, raising his hands, now it was time to bring the protest to an end, and if we did then all our fellow classmates would be released from custody, the chief of police had promised him that. 'That's a lie!' I shouted, suddenly feeling confident, overconfident. 'No one believes you! If you're serious, then prove it: bring our friends here from the prisons!'

I hadn't expected the echo. Everyone began to yell. 'Set them free!' roared some; others bellowed, 'Down with the traitor!' – meaning the dean, who beat a hasty retreat. The chief of police took his place, but we booed him away before he had the chance to say even a word. Next, the fire engines came. They were intended to intimidate us, but we remained sitting; we knew that if we stayed together they couldn't touch us, neither the police nor the firemen, nor all the deans or politicians of the world. That was our method: obstinacy. And we were good at hissing at everyone who annoyed us, at drowning out their speeches by shouting, singing and heckling.

'How much longer do you reckon they can hold the gangsters back?' someone whispered in my ear. He had heard that they had assembled in order to beat us. 'Who?' I asked. 'The North-West Youth,' he said. We had been promised police protection as far as the gates of the university, if we left now. We looked at one another, unsure of what to do. This was new information.

As we debated, an old woman wearing a red headscarf and worn-out shoes squeezed her way through the seated students and pressed seaweed rolls into our hands. She mumbled: 'Eat children, eat, you must be starving.' She also brought us beakers of water, cigarettes and sweets which she had wrapped in paper. 'Eat, children.' That was the only thing she said, and I didn't ask who she was and why she was helping us, whether perhaps her son was among us, or her daughter, I was just happy the police had let her through.

All of a sudden, the cry rang out that it was time to go back to the campus. With these words, our leader climbed into a jeep and slowly drove away. Duped, we stood and followed him, only a small group remained. The worms are crawling away, I thought, yet I couldn't stay sitting there.

It was seven in the evening when we began our counter-march, the busiest time on the streets of Seoul. The trams, buses and cars were forced to stop for us. Many pedestrians stopped too, waving to us, applauding and cheering as we made our way past. Windows were flung open, and from every one there were people smiling out at us. My feeling of having given up, given in, subsided completely: I was wrong, this demonstration hadn't been an empty gesture, we had accomplished something; we may not have won any concessions from the government, but we had taken a stand. I was still thinking in the plural, I was still a 'we', a student of Korea University, and not a penniless orphan, not an unemployed pauper who could be trampled on for the common good.

After the junction in Jongno, the police escort left us, as did the light; the street lamps weren't lit in this neighbourhood, and so the darkness caught up with us. Just as we were approaching the viaduct which led to the East Gate, figures dashed out of the darkness, masked men, their faces and hands wrapped in cloths, their fists gripping iron bars, chains and truncheons. They came towards us, attacking the front third of the march, two against one, three against one. Our comrades came to a standstill and defended themselves, causing a pile-up; we hadn't yet realized what awaited us and so we crashed into them. Two students fell from the bridge. A jeep with a reporter who had accompanied us tried to drive past, but teetered dangerously, and the photographer, who had leant too far from the vehicle, fell onto the road and disappeared beneath the fighters' feet. I dodged the brawl, the screams, the stifled wheezing and the blows, and crossed the viaduct as quickly as possible. The street traders who had been selling their wares at the other end dismantled their stands and fled. With them disappeared the scant light that had dimly illuminated this corner. I searched for a lookout point; I didn't want to desert my comrades, but I didn't know how to help them either: it was impossible to differentiate the students from the gang members. Spotting an abandoned chair in front of a shop, I climbed onto it and was able to see the police arrive, one single squad car – most of the officers were approaching on foot, but they didn't intervene. Following closely behind came high-school pupils and street kids, or so I later read in the newspaper; to me they were just black shadows that moved more swiftly through the crowd, nimbler and smaller, they fought the gang that had ambushed us, forcing them to flee.

I left my lookout post; I'd had enough. On the street I had been one of them, but now that the demonstration had come to an end, I was myself. The police began to arrest people indiscriminately, demonstrators and attackers: early the next morning, the chief of police was furious with the sergeant who had given the order; he wasn't supposed to arrest the gang leaders, this was a severe breach of the agreement with the North-West Youth! But that was still to come, for now everyone was still attacking everyone else, and I slipped into a dark alleyway in the belief I had escaped. But I was wrong;

there were people fighting here too, I could hear the pounding of fists, and then a body fell to the floor.

At first I saw only a dark mass, then a few contours, and eventually a face. It was Johnny.

Johnny didn't stay on the ground for long, he swiftly got back up and lurched towards his opponent with balled fists. I couldn't make out who he was fighting. Suddenly, the moonlight fell on the other man – it was Jinman.

They circled around one another. Jinman jumped towards Johnny, Johnny hit him in the face, Jinman crashed to the floor. Johnny straightened up, and at that moment Jinman's buddy, a scrawny little guy, began to lay into him, and I couldn't stand by and watch any longer, I had to intervene. I grabbed the little guy and dragged him away from Johnny by the ears and neck. While I held him down – I didn't want to injure him, so I just pulled his hands behind his back and clamped him between my legs – I watched as Johnny pulled himself upright, crawled over to Jinman, grabbed a stone and began to strike his face, neck and shoulders. Jinman fought back vigorously at first, but gradually his struggling weakened, until eventually he was no longer moving, only wheezing quietly. 'Johnny,' I yelled, 'Stop it! What are you doing?' 'Murderer,' shrieked the little guy, 'murderer!' He thrashed about, kicked himself free from my grip and rushed, with me on his heels, over to Jinman, who was now unconscious. Together we tried to pull Johnny away from him. 'You'll kill him! Stop, for God's sake stop!' I roared. 'Murderer, murderer!' blubbered the little guy, trying to press his fingers into Johnny's eyes. Johnny lashed out, punching first the little guy then me in the stomach; we sank down to the floor, immobilized.

By the time I got to my feet it was quiet, eerily quiet. Johnny was kneeling alongside Jinman, breathing heavily. The little guy had pulled himself up too, he leant over his friend and called his name. 'Jinman!' he cried and shook him by the shoulders, 'Jinman!' But he didn't move. 'Jinman,' he cried again and again, 'Jinman,' more despairing, louder and shriller, and when he still didn't show any sign of life, he screamed: 'You bastard, you've killed him!' Johnny stood up slowly, and took a step towards him. The little guy jumped to his feet and disappeared soundlessly into the darkness, like a rat.

'Johnny,' I whispered, and when I saw his hands twitch: 'It's me.'

He turned round.

'Yunho.'

He sounded exhausted. 'What have you done?' I asked. Only now did I see he was trembling. 'Come on,' I said, 'we have to get out of here, he'll come back with the whole gang.' I grabbed his arm, and he didn't resist. I led him along narrow, secluded paths through the city, avoiding the main roads because they were well lit; in spite of the dim light, I had seen that Johnny's face and hands, as well as his jacket, were covered in blood. We crept from semi-darkness to semi-darkness until we reached the Paks' house. All of a sudden, Johnny signalled to me to stop. A military jeep was parked on the street, a group of thugs stood in front of the door, their heads together in collusion. I couldn't make out a single word, but it was clear they were Jinman's men, and that they were planning to break into our room. 'We can't stay here,' I whispered to Johnny. He nodded.

'Let's go to Eve's.'

As we hurried through Seoul under the cover of night, Johnny mumbled again and again that he should never have introduced her to Jinman. That was all I could get out of him. We had to dodge and weave to avoid being picked up by the police patrols; the city was overrun with them.

Finally, after numerous detours and pauses, after hasty ducking and hiding, we reached Eve's house. I recognized it by the azaleas in front of the wall, which had only begun to bloom a short while before; their fragrance seemed particularly strong that night. We crept through the gate into the front garden. Johnny knocked softly.

The door opened with a squeaking sound, and Eve peered out through the crack. After one look at Johnny, she beckoned us in. As soon as we were in the hallway, she led him into the kitchen. I followed. Could I help? I asked. Without looking at me, she shook her head; she laid clean towels, iodine, alcohol and cotton wool on the counter. 'It's not too bad,' she said, 'I'm not even sure it's all his blood.' She cleaned Johnny's wounds, tended to him as best she could, then asked: 'And what about the other guy, did he come out of it badly?' Johnny nodded. 'Was he one of them?' she asked. He nodded again. 'Then he deserved it.' She sent us into the living room, then followed a few moments later with a bottle of *makgŏlli* and three small bowls. 'Sit down,' she said to me, then poured for us. Johnny reached for the bottle, not wasting his time with the bowl. She ignored him, fixing her eyes on me instead.

'Tough night?'

I didn't answer.

'I get it.'

She took Johnny's hand.

'You need to get some sleep.'

I didn't follow. She would take a thin mat from the wall cupboard and roll it out on the floor, she would get Johnny to lie down and spread a blanket out over him, she would stroke his forehead and cheeks, he would close his eyes and kiss her hands; how often I had witnessed their evening ritual.

'Is he in trouble?'
'You could say that . . .'
'Serious trouble?'
'Yes.'
'Do I have to drag every word out of you?'
'No.'
'If you don't tell me what happened, I can't help you. Come on, don't keep me waiting.'
'Jinman is . . .'
'Yes? He's what?'
'Johnny killed Jinman.'
'Jinman's dead?'
'I think so.'
'What do you mean you *think* so? Is he dead or not? Did you check?'
'Check?'
'Perhaps he was still alive! My God, Yunho!'
'We just fled.'
'Why?'
'Why what?'
'Why did Johnny kill Jinman?'
'I don't know. I only got there at the end. I wasn't able to stop it.'
'Did anyone else see you?'
'See us?'
'Yes, *see* you. Was Jinman alone?'
'No. He had a friend with him.'
'And what happened to the friend? Is he dead too?'
'No, he made a run for it.'

'So now they're after the two of you?'

'Probably . . . Yes.'

'Then you can't stay here.'

I slept fitfully that night; I had disjointed, nonsensical dreams, and kept waking up thinking I had heard a noise. At around seven in the morning, I finally fell into a deep sleep, but Eve shook me awake just an hour later, she had the *Dong-A Ilbo* open and was pointing to the headline: STUDENTS BEATEN BY MOB.

Perhaps they would believe it, I said. Who would believe what? she asked. The police, I responded, perhaps they would believe it had been an act of self-defence. She lowered the newspaper and stared at me incredulously. 'They won't,' she said eventually, gently. 'The police *are* the mob.'

She was pale and bleary-eyed, but seemed neither fearful nor nervous. How had she slept, I asked. Badly, she said, very little. She had woken up repeatedly, listening out for strange noises in the garden or on the street. She stood up and smoothed down her dress.

'You and Johnny have to flee, it's your only option. The North-West Youth is under the president's protection. As long as he's in power, that won't change. And the way things are looking right now, Rhee's rule will end only with his death.'

She lowered her gaze. I took her hand, pulled her towards me, and she let me take her in my arms. Suddenly she pulled away. She had to go out for a while, she said, and I was to watch over Johnny. Where was she going? I asked. She had an idea, she replied with a smile.

When she came back, around an hour later, Johnny was still in a deep sleep. She shook him awake, highly agitated. 'We have to go to Busan at once,' she said, 'there's a ship leaving for

Japan tonight, and we have to catch it.' 'Tonight?' I replied, 'that's impossible.' 'It's the only way,' she continued, 'we don't have a choice.'

Only then did I notice that she had said 'we'.

'We?'

'Yes, we. Johnny, you and I. The North-West Youth doesn't differentiate between Johnny and his friends, you know that.'

As she spoke, I watched Johnny. He looked dazed. She said we had to leave right away, that we didn't have time to lose. She ran into her bedroom and began to pack. After just a few minutes she was heading towards the front door. In my memory, all of this plays out in slow motion, but in actual fact it happened very quickly. We hurried through the garden, opened the gate just a crack. A bird sang louder than it had any right to, perhaps a mockingbird. Voices moved along the wall and we held our breath, even though they were female. Eve, beckoning us on impatiently, Johnny, touching my arm but avoiding my gaze.

The bird's cry followed us for a while, then could be heard no longer; it was drowned out, not by normal street sounds, but by the sirens.

The previous day repeated itself, except its double was stronger, louder, bigger. We stumbled into a demonstration, this time uniformed high-school pupils, marching arm in arm towards the Parliament with placards and banners, surrounded by children, boys and girls chanting 'Down with tyranny!' The street traders, workers and employees on their way into the office clapped and cheered the rebelling students, some even joined in the march. The police were on the scene again too; they didn't wait long before attempting to make arrests, but the pupils fell back from the henchmen, causing a wave to run through the column. A group of placard bearers at the very edge of the procession told us – just before they had to turn and run from the three policemen armed with guns and wooden truncheons who were bearing down on them – that there was going to be an address at the presidential palace; that they were on their way there. I moved to block the pigs' path, but Eve pushed me to the side. 'Are you crazy?' she hissed. 'We can't draw attention to ourselves.' She quickly dragged us back into the middle of the procession. 'You want to stay here, of all places?' I asked. She shrugged.

'It's the best camouflage we can find.'

We marched along, singing, yelling, brandishing our fists, threatening Syngman Rhee and the government, we demanded a tyrant-free future, no, a not-too-distant present where we could live in freedom, and for a while I forgot we were on the run. I couldn't see a thing from the middle of the street, the throng of people was too dense. From time to time, though, I caught a glimpse of the houses that had been destroyed by war, the walls that had once been buildings and the bullet holes, I saw the tiny shacks, improvised from cardboard and plastic sheeting, of the poor, and they too were waving, they too were running along with us, calling out new slogans like 'Justice for all!' and 'Prosperity for all!' At the crossing, a police mob with truncheons and guns laid into one of the students, trying to drag him away from his group, but his comrades held on to him tightly. Just a few metres away, some office workers had decided to hold a sit-in; they were picked up and carried off to the police cars. From the first and second floors of the buildings, stones rained down on 'Rhee's dogs'; as soon as they looked up to identify the culprits, the throwers ducked.

The whole of Seoul demonstrated. An indescribable and

glorious noise reigned over the streets, or so it seemed to me. Those of us in the middle of the procession didn't get attacked; we were shielded by the workers and war veterans at the sides. Our numbers grew at every crossing, students from all the universities of Seoul joined us, and pupils too, even the younger ones. Admittedly, our numbers also dipped at every crossing, some had to disappear into the side streets because they were being chased by the pigs, or drop back to help those who had got into difficulty. We fought our way on towards the Parliament, where we were greeted by an army of uniformed officers who shot tear gas into the air. The capsules exploded and left behind thick, grey-white clouds which drifted slowly. I heard coughing, wheezing. Eve and Johnny threw themselves to the ground, making themselves as small as they could and closing their eyes, I dropped down next to them, peering through my fingers every now and then, until all of a sudden I felt a hand on my shoulder; a young woman, not much older than I was, held a bowl of water out to me. 'Wash your eyes,' she said; she had covered her eyes and nose as a precaution with a damp, coarse-meshed cloth. She wasn't the only good Samaritan, I saw shadows scuttling through the fog, heard the clink of tankards and porcelain bowls on the asphalt, the splash of water, and I watched children, brave children, who were on all fours searching the street for stones to throw at the police.

'We have to get out of here,' mumbled Eve. She coughed, dunked a handkerchief in the bowl and covered her face with it, then vanished into the haze. My eyelids were burning so much I could barely open them. I ran after her half-blind, colliding again and again with the bodies that lay crumpled on the floor, whimpering quietly. One of them wasn't moving. I knelt down, groped around for a hand, felt for a pulse. At that moment, a strong wind picked up and blew the gas back into our opponents' faces, not all of whom were wearing masks, and many fell. The perfect moment for a counter-attack, I said to myself, reaching for an undetonated tear gas capsule that lay on the ground next to me and hurling it into the clouds of smoke. It exploded on the opposing side! We rejoiced, albeit cautiously. A fevered hunt for intact canisters began. A second capsule exploded, then a third. 'This is for Juyŏl Kim!' I heard. 'And for Sangok Shin!' I yelled, which earned me a jab in the side. 'Stop that!' hissed Eve.

Our happiness was short-lived. Rhee sent in his men. Armed to the teeth, they loaded the demonstrators one after the other into waiting trucks. The crowd hissed, booed, hurled stones, sticks, anything that could be thrown. Perhaps their missiles came too close to the uniformed officers; or perhaps just to one, who lost his nerve and began to shoot. Hearing the volley, I thought they were blanks. I had heard it was normal to fire warning shots, but when the first bodies fell and pools of blood began to spread, we ran for our lives.

Johnny, Eve and I had worked our way from the middle to the edge of the crowd, dangerously close to the trucks and the guns, and all of a sudden we found ourselves surrounded by the dying. A jeep approached, presumably from one of the daily papers. Eve waved it over. 'There are injured people here!' she screamed. 'Our friends are hurt! Can you take us to the hospital?' The reporter nodded. 'It's now or never!' Eve whispered to us, before grabbing one of the invalids and heaving him onto the back seat; she pulled Johnny and me in alongside her. I couldn't close the door and had to hold on to it for the entire journey, but we made it to the nearby bus station. Here too, there were shouts of protest, and gun-fire. We jumped out of the car, leaving the injured man on the back seat. 'To the hospital,' I said, 'and hurry!' We dashed over to the bus stop; when I next turned around, the jeep had disappeared.

'It's already left! The bus to Busan has gone!'

Eve looked at me in despair.

'What should we do?'

I quickly put my hand to her mouth. I had heard someone else say 'Busan', quietly, as though from a distance; I followed the call.

'Busan! Busan! You want to go to Busan?'

A taxi driver, sly as a fox, was profiting from the unrest in Seoul; he was planning to drive back and forth to Busan as many times as he could. Because the bus wasn't running, he would earn more in one day than he usually did in a whole month. Eve asked if he had three places left. He didn't hesitate.

'Get in, we're setting off now. Come on! Quickly!'

The haggling didn't last long. Eve gave him a few banknotes. He clapped his hand on the back seat; three further passengers joined us in the car. We were nervous, not knowing whether we would make it out in time; the driver said he had heard that the military had now taken over 'the defence of Seoul'.

'The military?'

Eve was surprised.

'That's right, miss, the military. Let's make sure we get out.'

We sped out of the city. Tanks were rolling towards us from the other direction, along with a never-ending column of jeeps packed with heavily armed soldiers.

We found the ship right away; Eve led us there. She seemed to know the captain. The cargo boat was waiting for us in a hidden bay, we and five other passengers were to be smuggled to Japan.

We spent the journey in total darkness; only twice a day did the loading bay open, allowing us out into the fresh air. Soon I no longer knew what day it was, I lost all orientation. In the beginning I fought against it, trying to calculate the day of the week and our distance from the mainland, but eventually I gave up. It seemed as though it was meant to be this way, this way and no other: as though the blackness in the belly of the ship was to suffocate all recollections of the past and erase our memories, so that on our arrival in the new land, we could be new people.

10

I looked up; Yunho had fallen silent, and only Billie could be heard. Over the past days I had become accustomed to not looking at him during his narrative, instead staring into my notebook and pretending to write. I would draw circles and squares, and of their own volition the circles and squares settled into words and formed a landscape of lines and crosshatches, yet over time it was the gaps between the grey, the blank spaces, that produced a picture.

Now he wanted to listen to me, Yunho announced, it was my turn to talk for a change, 'you, with your Japanese accent'. He wanted to know everything, he said. He looked at me intently, but after the many hours of silence I couldn't bring myself to talk, it felt as though I had lost all memory of speech. Yunho was the narrator, and I the listener; this was our division of labour. I had settled into it, and anything else felt wrong. Not knowing what to do, I evaded his gaze.

'You don't have to talk about yourself if you don't want to.'

He pushed himself up from his chair, went over to the record player and held up the sleeve that lay on the lid. He had owned this album for more than half a century, he said, and carried it with him all the way across Japan, over the sea and eventually back to South Korea. *Solitude.* He stroked the record sleeve. It had taken him years to learn the strange characters. The Latin script was pretty, but peculiar, each letter stood for itself alone, keeping its distance from its neighbours – each letter was a fortress. This being-for-itself, said Yunho, didn't exist in Korean. He turned the record over and placed the needle down gently on the edge, but remained standing next to the player. Only once the crackling and rustling transformed into music did he return to the living-room table.

'Love' was the first English word he had learnt. At first he had thought it meant 'life', because it came up so frequently in Billie's songs; he should have known, he said, that it was love, not life. 'But what should I picture with the term 'solitude'?' he asked.

'Seclusion. Isolation. Aloneness.'

'Aloneness?'

He nodded slowly. Yes, he could hear that in her music. Billie sang as though she were alone in the world, as though there were no one listening to her.

'She sings for herself. Without trying to win the audience's approval. On the contrary, I have to fight to win hers. I don't feel entitled to listen to her songs.'

'How do you mean?'

'It's like I'm eavesdropping. Spying on her through the wall, or through the crack around a door.'

He closed his eyes, hummed along for a few bars. Took his glasses off, breathed on the lenses and cleaned them thoroughly with a cloth that had become worn out with use. Johnny's father had owned a record collection, he said, all of them operas, apart from one Billie Holiday album. It had been stolen, together with all the other records. Perhaps it was somewhere in Pyongyang now, in the house of some low-ranking party functionary, for they had been given the less desirable looted objects. Or, he smiled, perhaps they had divided everything up fairly among one another, like the communists they were, and Billie had journeyed into the Diamond Mountains, well hidden in the rucksack of a partisan who understood the words on the cover just as little as he did.

Yunho disappeared into the kitchen, and returned with a bottle of mineral water, two glasses and a packet of biscuits on a tray. 'Please help yourself,' he said, 'I'm sure you're hungry.' He couldn't offer me dinner; he looked at the clock and commented that she was late. Yunho employed a part-time housekeeper who cooked for him twice a week, cleaned his house, washed and ironed his clothes, and the remaining days he fed himself from meals on wheels. Yunho didn't cook – he had tried it once, he told me, but had proved to be a hopeless case, confusing flour with salt and chicken with fish; here, he winked. I pictured him putting some roots in the frying pan, adding an egg, still in its shell, and waiting for the raw ingredients to become a meal, perhaps humming 'Pennies From Heaven' and keeping a lookout for fallen hairs.

I couldn't help but laugh; the laughter caught the words I had been searching for, and when he asked me whether I was disappointed by my homeland, they thrashed around only momentarily before leaping off my tongue. No, I answered, I wasn't disappointed by South Korea as a country, but I was disappointed that it didn't feel like home.

'So what does home feel like?'

He looked at me with curiosity.

'Different.'

'Different?'

He pressed for more, of course, so I tried to give a longer answer. I said: 'Perhaps it's me who should be asking you, not you me. What do I know about home?'

'That's precisely what I'm trying to find out. What do you know about home?'

'Not much, I don't think. I'm no expert.'

He waved his hand dismissively and said that home and expertise were a contradiction in terms. Then he blinked.

'Do you think *I'm* one? An expert on the meaning of home?'

I nodded.

'More so than me.'

'Why? Because I was born and grew up in the same country?'

'Because you never had to hear that you don't have one.'

He laughed loudly.

'You're wrong about that! That's something we have in common. Like you, I've had to spend my whole life with people telling me that I don't have a home.'

'Why?'

'Because apparently I'm on the wrong side,' he replied, clearing his throat. 'And you? Which side are you on?'

'On whichever side they'll have me. On every and none.'

'Then you're really and truly homeless?'

'I don't believe in home. Or rather, I don't believe in home as a *place*.'

'As what, then?'

'I think there are places that we love. I even think there are places where our souls feel at home. Soulscapes.'

He nodded slowly. He had once read that everywhere we go, we are always looking for our own souls. 'Does that mean,' he asked, 'that there's a connection between the soul and home?'

At that moment, Billie joined in our conversation with 'These Foolish Things'.

Yunho coughed, tapped a cigarette out of the pack and lit it. I took one too, for it seemed to me that complicity required a ritual.

'What will you ask Mrs Yang when you find her?'

'*If* I find her.'

He nodded.

'*If* you find her.'

'Who my parents are, of course,' I answered, blowing the smoke towards the window, 'and why they gave me up.'

'That's all?' he asked, looking at me with his clear, still eyes.

No, that wasn't all, but I had been afraid to speak the truth out loud: 'I want to ask her,' I said slowly, 'why my parents took my home away from me.'

Yŏnghee Jang came to West Germany as an assistant nurse. In the years after the Second World War, the rumours about kidnapped Korean women had turned out to be true; many young women, some practically still children, who had believed they were going to work in factories in Japan, had instead ended up as prostitutes in military barracks in South East Asia. As Young Maria was unable to find a job, nor had the prospect of one, her mother married her off, leaving it to the husband to provide for her. Hwang's shop, not much bigger than a broom closet, seemed to be doing well, he sold soya bean shoots, tofu, pencils, cigarettes, shoelaces and similar knick-knacks – in short: everything he could get his hands on. He was a decade older than Young Maria, and remained tight-lipped about his past. Only after their wedding did she discover that he had been married once before and had a child from the previous marriage, a daughter, who was being brought up by his parents-in-law. His ex-wife, whom he divorced only after his marriage to Young Maria, was in a sanatorium for the mentally ill; she had gone through terrible things during the Korean War and had forgotten how to speak, he said. He added that he'd been forced to tolerate similarly unspeakable things. He used to be a policeman, one of those 'regents of suburbia' who determined what school was built where, who would be the teacher and which gods could be worshipped; who could open a doctor's practice and who had to close up their shop. The Japanese colonial administration would never have been able to maintain their rule without these hordes of policemen. As a 'reward', they extended some of their power to the guardians of the law. Initially, only the Japanese were accepted into the Korean police force, predominantly former samurais who had fallen out of favour, but in the early 1940s they began to admit an increasing number of Koreans, mostly uneducated, violent types. They were the only ones permitted to carry and use guns. In addition, they alone had access to the village telephone, which was always located in the police station. They determined life and death, profit and ruin, and as a result were even more unpopular and detested among the population than the Japanese emperor, to whom every villager had to swear loyalty on a daily basis; it was not by chance that, upon the outbreak of war, Hwang headed south and transformed himself into a 'businessman'.

His business, which he had described before the wedding as 'blossoming', turned out to be a constant nuisance; not only was it far from making a profit, but it also regularly attracted hoodlums demanding back the vast sums of money Hwang had borrowed. This put Young Maria in a state of unceasing anxiety, and she lived in fear of being beaten for the sins of her husband, who one day would just take off and leave her.

Hwang didn't leave her, or at least not immediately; first she had to settle his debts for him by cleaning in the American military barracks in Uijeongbu, a job he had fixed her up with. While mopping the floors there, she overheard the conversation that ultimately brought her to Germany. The women from the early shift were whispering to one another about how

209

wonderful it would be to leave Korea forever. All one had to do was pass a nursing course, register with an agency, and this would lead to a job with a German hospital.

Young Maria listened attentively. Could this be her chance to start afresh? She could exchange mopping floors for going back to school, dedicating herself to twelve months of study (officially at least, but in reality the private schools, which had shot up in the South like mushrooms during the 1960s, would make out the certificate after just nine). It was said that there were thirty thousand vacant positions to be filled in Germany, and that they would take anyone who could show a qualification as a nurse or an assistant nurse. Young Maria had never been interested in medicine, but the prospect of a different life lured her in; she signed up without telling Hwang.

The small room on the second storey of the dilapidated building in the heart of Jongno was overcrowded, and most of the women had to sit on the floor. The lessons were purely theoretical at first, the practical side would start after the introductory phase. The group shrank within the first few days, and even Young Maria debated whether she had made the right decision; she wasn't used to listening to lectures all through the morning and into the late afternoon, but she completed the training and passed the German-language course. She dictated her CV from the telephone booth to the Korean Overseas Employment Agency which organized the nurse exchange. The next day, she confessed everything to Hwang, who refused to accompany her and forbade her from leaving Seoul; she almost missed the first lesson of the anti-communism course which was mandatory for anyone wishing to emigrate.

Nonetheless, she still applied for two plane tickets. The cost for them, she had been told, would be deducted from her salary in small instalments over the following three years, the duration of her employment contract. The fact she would have to pay for the flight herself didn't bother her, for she didn't know in any case what to make of the sum in Deutschmarks; compared to prices in Korean won the figure seemed laughably small. She also hadn't understood that the amount given in the information brochure was the gross salary, and that the actual pay was significantly lower. She only realized her mistake after her arrival, and spent hours in the supermarket adding and subtracting; everything was much more expensive than she could ever have imagined.

On the day of her departure, Hwang didn't go to work. Normally he opened his shop at around seven, but on that morning he was still home at eight. Didn't he need to go to the store? Young Maria asked, cautiously. They had quarrelled enough over the previous months, and she didn't want to argue any more, not today, the day that she had joyfully anticipated, but which contrary to her expectations now felt sad. Maybe he wanted to entangle her in another row so that she would miss the flight. Furious, she swept through the apartment, on the lookout for small things to stuff into the side pockets of her luggage: a pair of tweezers, some chopsticks, a narrow tube of salve (a cure-all), headache tablets, three handkerchiefs, a fourth scarf (there was no way of knowing whether the other three would be warm enough) and a bulb of garlic (it lay there, lonesome on the kitchen floor, and in her nervous state Young Maria shoved it into the suitcase, hoping fervently that it wouldn't be squashed).

Just as she was about to leave for the bus station, Hwang stumbled over to her, drunk with sleep. Was she leaving for the airport? he asked, his right eye still closed, his left eye half-open. Young Maria nodded. She would write, she said. No she wouldn't, he retorted, he knew she didn't like to write, and she knew he didn't like to read. He stretched out his arms. She hesitated a little, still fearing an act of sabotage. 'There's no need to be like that,' he mumbled, 'this isn't an attack', and as he spoke he tugged at the corner of his white undershirt. She couldn't help but laugh, and while he was still holding her close, he whispered into her ear that she didn't have to be sad, that he had good news. He had sold the shop, given notice on their apartment, and in four weeks' time he would follow on after her, he was starting the government's anti-communism seminar tomorrow. He grinned; he had also changed the date of his ticket. With these words, he set her free. She teetered over to the door, pushed it open and left the house without turning back.

Shortly after his arrival in Germany, even before he left Frankfurt central station, Hwang met a Vietnamese woman and settled in nearby Giessen with her; the divorce papers reached Young Maria after his wedding. In the mid-1970s, he was arrested at Gimpo Airport in Seoul; Park Chung-hee's secret service suspected him of being part of a North Korean espionage ring. The outrage caused in 1967 by South Korean agents kidnapping their fellow countrymen on German soil had made the KCIA more cautious, they began to lay in wait for 'dangerous elements' on arrival and grabbed them after passport control.

'That's why she didn't dare visit her family in South Korea for over twenty years.'

'She was probably under surveillance.'

Anyone who arrived from abroad was under surveillance back then, said Yunho. The communist danger lurked *everywhere*. He too had been spied on; spied on, but never arrested.

I reached for another cigarette. 'It wasn't until 1994,' I said, 'six years after the Summer Olympics, that she flew back to her homeland.' She gave away all her furniture, dividing it up among the people she had become close to. I got the little rattan table she had found at a flea market, as well as an antique rocking chair that she had reupholstered herself, with a fabric that didn't match its age: a cheap, flowery print. I said at the time that it was much too thin, but she just waved her hand dismissively and said that she was thin-skinned too.

'Ducks of a feather fly together.'

I didn't correct her. I had long since given up correcting her inaccurate sayings and word mutations, like 'sickness insurance' or 'cheekful'. 'Sickness insurance pays for doctors' visits,' she used to say, and 'my cheekful ex-husband.'

To this day, I still don't know whether he was cheeky or cheerful.

A thin beam of sunlight fell through the curtains, making Yunho's silvery hair shimmer. 'Do you believe,' he asked, 'that Mrs Jang can help you to find your family?'

I took a sip of water.

'I believe that Mrs Jang *is* my family.'

He looked at me in surprise.

'Your mother?'

'No, not my mother. A relative of my mother's. Perhaps her sister or cousin.'

'Because she knew that you were given away straight after the birth?'

'How else could she have known that?'

'So you think your mother sent Mrs Jang to Germany to check on you?'

Spoken out loud, it sounded crazy.

'No. I *know* that Young Maria was already in Germany when my mother's family, or my mother herself, asked her to look after me. Perhaps she even arranged the adoption.'

'Your adoption wasn't handled by an agency?'

I shook my head.

'Neither the state agency nor Holt International?'

He stubbed out his cigarette in the ashtray; it was a glass bowl, not a halved grenade.

'No. It was mediated privately.'

'I see.'

He looked at me curiously.

'And your mother's name and address weren't in the file?'

'They were, but they weren't up to date. And hadn't been for a long time.'

He nodded. In Korea everything was in motion, he said, nothing stood still; stagnation was too expensive.

'So Mrs Jang is your only clue?'

'Essentially, yes. You know—'

At that moment, I heard a key in the lock. I grabbed my notebook and pencil, put both in my rucksack and jumped to my feet.

'Aren't you staying for dinner?'

Yunho held me back with a gentle touch to my arm. I shook my head. He lowered his gaze. Was he disappointed? Relieved? Perhaps both; he wasn't used to eating in company.

'I'll come back tomorrow.'

'Good,' he answered, after a brief pause, 'so I'll see you tomorrow. Shall I get my housekeeper to make you something to eat? She could pack it up for you.'

'No, that's not necessary.'

All at once I was in a hurry to get out into the fresh air.

★

'So now you're taking an interest in your roots,' Monika, my mother, had commented with a sad smile when we were saying goodbye. 'All of a sudden.'

'Well, it's your fault,' I retorted, 'you made me into a Korean.'

'I just wanted you to get to know your culture, that's all.'

'*My* culture? And there I was thinking my culture and yours were the same.'

She blushed, stammered a few words, then turned away. 'You're right,' she said, 'it's all my fault.'

She didn't try to hug me. I knew what she thought of my trip to Seoul, she had tried repeatedly to talk me out of it. 'You'll only end up disappointed,' she had said, more than once. There was a time when I would have believed her; as a child, I had been convinced that paradise must always be out of reach; otherwise it wouldn't be paradise.

Everything was different now, and still I didn't regret anything. Admittedly I knew only one metro line, namely the one that connected my apartment to Hongik University, where I got on the green bus that took me to Yunho's neighbourhood, Yŏnhui, where the cafés called themselves Brussels or De Paris and had dressed themselves in European façades. There was also a German bakery here, a confiture boutique, a steakhouse, an Italian restaurant and a Japanese noodle bar – the rest of the world in its entirety.

When the rubbish truck came crawling through the tangle of alleyways, even pedestrians had to wait behind it, there was no room for both in the narrow streets, which for Seoul were almost unnaturally clean and guarded by uniformed men who carried walkie-talkies in their shoulder holsters; all the house entrances had cameras fixed above them. Yunho's next-door neighbours were the only ones indifferent to the air of privacy, they did their washing with the windows and doors flung wide open, hung the wet clothes up everywhere, even on their entrance gate, and cooked in the open air; they were Chinese.

Yŏnhui was the only part of Seoul I knew, I had seen neither the palaces nor the parks, museums or shopping avenues; I moved through the city as though it were behind glass. Only when I inadvertently touched the tips of the cashier's fingers in the 7-Eleven mini-market while paying for my evening meal, which normally consisted of a cheese-and-ham sandwich and a Danish yoghurt, did I notice that I wasn't in Yunho's story, but in reality. I would then take a deep breath and search for a ray of sunlight to warm myself in. But as soon as I stepped back inside his house, it was back, the wall of glass, with me trapped behind it.

Perhaps, though, it was the other way around. Perhaps the hours in which Yunho spoke about the past felt more immediate to me than the present, and it was the present that seemed to have passed by before it had even begun.

Osaka, 1960

11

While we, the cargo, were smuggled onto land in Shimonoseki without incident – the border guard's boundless patriotism no impediment to his purchasability – John F. Kennedy was in Massachusetts and Pennsylvania competing for the Democratic presidential nomination. Six months later (despite his inexperience and Catholic faith) he went on to win the election, defeating Richard Nixon, a friend of the South Korean regime; this changeover of power in the White House in Washington prompted a changeover of power in the Blue House in Seoul.

We took the train and made the seemingly endless journey to Osaka. Johnny and I initially protested that we wanted to stay near the coast, but Eve insisted on travelling further, saying there was a Korean city in the east. She hadn't realized that Ikaino was only a neighbourhood of Osaka; a few streets, nothing more.

The din of the big city chewed at our ears, its dust clung to our skin. Seeing cherry blossoms in the distance, we followed anything that moved, a bus, a taxi, a pedestrian, it didn't matter what so long as we didn't stand still, for we would collapse on the spot and die of thirst and hunger if we did.

Eventually, we arrived; I remember how happy I was to no longer have to move or flee; I hadn't expected to have to take flight again, my legs felt like stems, my feet like stumps, they didn't tread, but stalked, staggered, into the first open building.

The gate had been opened not for us, but for a petite woman

with dark skin and grey eyes. There wasn't a single hair out of place in her pageboy haircut, and she was dressed in traditional Korean costume, a long white skirt and white bolero jacket; her clothes were what enticed us over.

We addressed her in Japanese, she answered in Korean.

Ayumi Nobukawa was a quiet, friendly creature, too friendly to be human, a friendly ghost, I thought to myself, as I watched her glide through the house searching for Tetsuya Yamamoto, while whispering to us that she was a teacher at the Korean school and taught the younger daughter of the house, Eiko; only later did I find out that she came from the 'Red' island of Jeju.

She fled with her mother to Japan during the riots of 1948, her father having already made off with the family's entire fortune a few days before. The riots occurred when the Korean governor – a fanatical right-winger named Yu – joined forces with the American government to violently suppress a demonstration. During the cold winter months, mother and daughter tried to track down their defector, even hiring a private detective, but without success; they spent spring and summer on the island of Tsushima, where Mrs Nobukawa worked as an *ama*, a pearl diver. One day, she didn't return from a dive, and from then on Ayumi wandered from one Korean family to the next, along the entire southern coast of Japan, until she finally ended up in Osaka; here, she was able to stay.

It was summer and the monsoon season was over; from one hour to the next the rain stopped, the sun emerged and seemed to never want to set again. The wind hid itself away in the treetops, and the leaves barely moved – when they did, they did so only surreptitiously. Ayumi clambered a few branches higher in order to get a better view of the horizon. Since her mother's death, she had taken to studying it, with a scientific curiosity but also with an element of longing; with homesickness. To her it seemed like a destination, a place where she wanted to be when she grew up. She didn't know what she wanted to be, but she did know where: there on the horizon, at the line that wasn't really a line but a crossing – the boundary where the sky meets the earth.

Eve and I saw Ayumi differently; she thought her unyielding, and hard beneath the soft façade. 'Don't believe your ears,' she warned me, 'trust only your eyes.' Johnny agreed, he thought she was too scrawny, and said that even her voice and smile were thin, emaciated. Ayumi allocated us the middle room on the first floor, the others had already been rented, she said, and weren't big enough 'for a family'.

A family: Johnny, Eve and I had passed ourselves off as siblings. It had been difficult enough to scrape together the rent for one room, so we posed as unmarried brothers who had been forced to leave our homeland with our older, widowed sister because of 'Syngman Rhee's repressive measures'. We had prepared ourselves to embellish his 'reign of terror', to detail our reasons for fleeing, we were planning to talk about the manipulated elections, about ever-present hunger, mass unemployment, children wrapped in newspaper instead of clothes, about criminal gangs who controlled the markets, streets and banks. We were armed for hours of debate and were expecting reproaches and verbal attacks; we were convinced we would have to justify ourselves, and hoped for leniency and kindness, as well as strokes of luck.

So perhaps you can imagine our surprise, when, in the entrance to the building, directly next to the stairs, we found ourselves standing before a large, no, a *gigantic* blue-red-blue striped flag with a red star, the flag of North Korea. Johnny was so shocked that he forgot to close his mouth; Eve forgot to blink. She had heard that the Korean minority was on North Korea's side (many of the communist agents who were taken prisoner in South Korea came from Japan), but had thought the reports were exaggerated.

She was wrong. In Ikaino, the North had won the civil war. The flag was unequivocal, and it filled her with fear.

In contrast to my 'siblings', I felt like I had spotted new buds blossoming on a dead tree. I was happy to find myself confronted with the North Korean flag instead of the South Korean one. Leaving aside the fact that, because of Yunsu and Sangok, I felt closer to the communists than the fascists, the flag made it clear that the South Korean despot had no sympathizers in this house.

I was right: Tetsuya Yamamoto, a helpful man in any case, became even more so when he heard my somewhat rose-tinted (and slightly exaggerated) story. In his eyes, we were the innocent victims of persecution, and his love for his (our) homeland required that he offer us his support. Whatever we were guilty of, it couldn't be as bad as what the Republic of Korea had done when they and the US had turned the North into a sea of flames. From his point of view, we Koreans from the South may be barbarians compared to him and his kind, the Japanese Koreans, but first and foremost we were defectors. We deserved to be rescued, for we were aware of our backwardness and had chosen to flee into modernity, into civilization. And we were useful, too, because we possessed something that he and his people had lost: we were more Korean than them. It was our task to legitimize the flags they had hung up in their homes. They needed our accent-free pronunciation and the ease with which we carried ourselves in Korean, a language for which they had either lost all feeling or which they had never possessed in the first place (in Tetsuya's house, only he, Eiko and Ayumi spoke Korean; his wife Naoko and Kimiko, his eldest daughter, knew a mere few words). Was this the reason why we were met everywhere we went with warmth and kindness? Back then, I often asked myself whether human beings only love things that are useful to them, even when it comes to their fellow man. I myself stopped loving my parents as soon as I began to earn my own living; what I feel for them today, now that they've been dead for more than half a century, can at most be defined as nostalgia.

Given that Eve and Johnny seemed lost for words, I, the youngest, began to speak. I explained that we had been part of the underground resistance against Rhee ('What did you do?' 'We wrote and printed flyers'), that we had been spied on by his secret service and had to flee Seoul as a result, and that we had used the riots in the South as cover to escape to Japan, hidden in a cargo ship. ('How many of you were there in total?' 'Eight.' 'How many days were you at sea?' 'I don't know, we stopped counting. During the day we were locked inside the dark cabin. At night, when we were allowed out into the open air, we found ourselves in a dark room of a different kind. It was much bigger, but just another display of how vast infinity is.') It was purely by chance, I said, that we had ended up here in Ikaino, in this house: all because of a full, white skirt.

Tetsuya laughed thunderously. His laugh startled me initially, but over the days that followed, I realized that the wind always sang in his lungs.

★

A few years ago, I booked a flight to Tokyo and caught the bullet train out of Shinjuku. The journey lasted just a few hours, not days like it used to, the train moved through the landscape at a speed that makes humans and animals dizzy, only the houses, the ugly, grey blocks, can hold their own against its pace; their relationship to time is different. It took me a while to get my bearings in Osaka, the city had become another one entirely. I got out in Tsuruhashi, weaved my way through the 'Korean Market', as it's called in Japan, and after an hour spent wandering aimlessly through the streets in the hope of finding a white, full skirt to guide me, found myself suddenly in Ikaino.

How much the neighbourhood had changed, but at the same time how little! The canal, once filled with bobbing tree trunks propelled by workmen on rafts, was now empty, and there were puffy, white clouds reflected in the calm water – perhaps it was them I had followed? The houses still looked the same as they had fifty years ago, that was what astounded me, they looked *exactly* as they had fifty years ago: as though they hadn't aged even a little. When I looked closer, however, I realized I was mistaken, most of the buildings had been renovated or rebuilt, but they had inherited the appearance of their predecessors, so much so that I thought I had travelled back in time: except that Ikaino was empty and quiet, the few people I saw were old, like me, and the children had disappeared.

There used to be children everywhere you looked. The little boys squatted on the asphalt and played with their marbles, the girls played house, one always had an infant on her back instead of a doll, for dolls were expensive and rare; usually it was their own little brother or sister, sometimes the neighbour's offspring. I suddenly remembered the children who used to roam around the area in groups, doubtless up to no good. Washing fluttered against the walls of the houses or on lines stretched across the street, the mother's kimono, the father's long underpants; the brightly coloured blouses and shirts were part of the dark alleyway, in which the wind lost its way and became a mere breeze. Implements of all kinds leant against the walls: brooms, shovels, bicycles. The blue of the sky was dissected by power cables, making the asphalt into a patchwork. The children were always whispering to one another, they exchanged folded notes, sure to be messages of the utmost importance; a small child of one or maybe two years of age sat in a pram on the street, forgotten by its mother, she would remember it when it cried loudly, screaming for her, or perhaps she had left all her children behind and gone back to Korea.

No, not to Korea, for Korea no longer existed, there was only South Korea and North Korea. She would have avoided the South for sure, so the only real alternative was North Korea, a young democracy. In Ikaino, one heard only good things about the North. Kim Il-sung was held in high esteem, his publications on the revolution were considered fixtures of any given household, trumping the works of Stalin and Marx in popularity; his portrait adorned the Korean schools in Osaka and Kobe, which he had built and which were run by 'his' people, the members of the Sōren association. Until the 1970s he financially supported his comrades in Japan, then the tables turned; today, Sōren allegedly transfers money to the regime in Pyongyang on an annual basis, some people claim they're spectacularly large sums (1.9 billion dollars!) but – how had Eve put it back then? – never trust your ears, only your eyes.

The organization that preceded Sōren was founded after the end of the Second World War and disbanded just four years later by the American military government, doomed by its proximity to communism. Its leader, the mathematician Kin

Tenkai, had declared in his inaugural speech that he and the association would devote themselves to the service of the Japanese Communist Party, for the latter had consistently and uniquely supported the Korean minority, showing solidarity with the Korean workers and students.

This would have been bad enough, but Kin Tenkai's cardinal error was to side not with Syngman Rhee, but Kim Il-sung, thereby humiliating the US – whose president, Harry S. Truman, in response to the 'Red Threat', had in 1947 introduced a 'Loyalty Oath' which would go on to become unequivocally anti-communist during the McCarthy era. In Osaka, the pro-North league was significantly more popular than the pro-South Mindan organization, which had only a hundred thousand members; the pro-North league had four times as many. Added to this was the occupying power's belief that the Koreans, like all Asians, were susceptible to communism, and that even the Japanese were 'helplessly at the mercy' of this devilish ideology.

After Washington decided to back Rhee, Tokyo was unable to tolerate any triumph on Kim Il-sung's part, even an indirect one. General Charles Willoughby, MacArthur's little fascist, hired a Mindan member, the communist-hater Gen Kosho, to spy on the competition, poach important members with monetary gifts, and generally stir up trouble within the association. When Gen's lifeless body was found near the Ueno train station, a rumour circulated that there was a list of Mindan members who were to be murdered. What's more, there were whispers that the Soviet Union was financing Japan's Communist Party and Kin Tenkai's organization.

Both reports were bogus; yet Willoughby used them to inform the State Department that the young Japanese democracy was *extremely* endangered and must be protected *at any cost*. The ensuing large-scale surveillance operation of all suspect elements cost around half a million yen each month; even the former Kempeitai, the military policemen from the imperial Japanese army, were involved.

At the same time, Kin Tenkai and his leadership team (of which Tetsuya was a member, representing the prefecture of Osaka) searched for a way to finance the association. Most Koreans left Japan and returned to their homeland between 1945 and 1947, shrinking the number of members, and consequently the income from donations too. As the American military government in Japan had decreed that emigrants could only take a specific sum of yen with them, many of the returnees had given the rest of their savings to the organization (for the benefit of those staying behind), but this kind of financing had no future. So Kin Tenkai asked Korean business people for large donations, which flowed into his newly founded Central Industrial Company (CICo). CICo planned to use the money to expand its existing activities, which included the production and sale of soy sauce and sake, as well as an in-house publisher.

With CICo, Willoughby had found what he was looking for: a smoking gun to put an end to Kin Tenkai's 'criminal mob' once and for all. On the morning of 30 September, the police stormed all branches of the supposedly extremist organization, seized the accounts, minutes and reports, froze all the bank accounts, arrested nineteen members of the management team and dissolved CICo; the confiscated fortune amounted to 248 million yen.

Tetsuya escaped a prison sentence, but they ransacked his home, confiscated his paperwork and destroyed his possessions. He was marched off in handcuffs before the eyes of his terrified children to an interrogation which lasted several days; Eiko was only seven years old at the time, Kimiko eleven. Perhaps the precariousness of his situation is best portrayed with an image: that of a bird balancing on the tip of a blade of grass. In the end, his long-standing friendship with Osaka's police chief proved useful; the official sided with Tetsuya and arrested another Korean instead.

Willoughby had warded off the communist threat, for the time being at least. But he didn't achieve his other goal – he had hoped that Mindan would be flooded with membership applications. He hadn't considered that Mindan, following the logic of Syngman Rhee, would shy away from accepting Koreans who were now branded as communists. Many were refused membership; and with the outbreak of the Korean War, the divisions between the pro-North and pro-South Koreans deepened. Kin Tenkai fled to North Korea. Of the two hundred Mindan members who joined Rhee's army voluntarily, most were treated as North Korean spies and, after the end of the war, if they hadn't been executed as enemies of the state, they returned, disillusioned, to Japan. It would be another six years before the broken pro-North league resurrected itself as Sōren, and reached new heights of popularity. When we arrived in Osaka in 1960, two thirds of all Japanese Koreans were Sōren members.

In order to understand why, you only need to remember two dates. In 1952, one year after the San Francisco Peace Treaty returned full sovereignty to Japan, all Koreans (and Taiwanese) living in Japan lost their citizenship and became de facto stateless. Syngman Rhee, who had met with the Japanese prime minister to discuss the fate of his fellow countrymen, among other matters, cared little about the future of these six hundred thousand and repeatedly thwarted the talks; Kim Il-sung wasn't even invited to the table.

In 1954, as anti-South Korean sentiment spread, the North Korean foreign minister Nam Il announced with great ceremony that all Koreans in Japan were citizens of the Democratic People's Republic. Sōren was founded the following year, and just like its predecessor, which had fallen victim to American anti-communists, it thought little of bipartisanship or neutrality and instead swore loyalty to North Korea. Sōren, its founding father Han proclaimed to thunderous applause, would no longer support the Japanese communists, but the government in Pyongyang. They had made the mistake for long enough, he declared, of involving themselves in Japanese affairs. Their new objective was to raise the children of the Democratic People's Republic of Korea.

'To raise the children of the Democratic People's Republic of Korea.' For Sōren, the future lay not in Japan, but in North Korea — in the new old home, once more within reach.

Home: what a tricky, frightful and frightening *religion* that word is.

In Korea, *kohyang* means 'ancestral home' and 'birthplace', but the term also contains an emotional, larger-than-life component, namely that of blood, of individual and collective roots. Home is, therefore, past, but also, and this is the crux, future: destiny. Only once I know where I'm from can I know where I'm going. Exiles have a past too, but for them the future is out of reach, just as much as the home they have had to leave.

Zainichi, that's what the Koreans in Japan called themselves: 'those who are temporarily in Japan'. The Korean War changed, destroyed, their dream of one day returning to their homeland. It also worsened their living conditions; before the war, they were on an equal footing with the Japanese, at least legally, or rather, theoretically – but after it all their rights were taken away from them, in the end even their voting rights. In this existentially precarious situation, Sōren became their port of call: a place of comfort, of community and mutual support – a kind of home. A home which, despite being far from their homeland, was nonetheless a convincing placeholder, secured by the infrastructure that the exiled Koreans had built up, for Sōren knew how to use, nurture and strengthen institutions to its advantage. The Korean schools that came into existence in Japan shortly after the end of the war – which gave lessons in backyards, in peoples' homes, even out in the open air, on the streets and in fields – were over time relocated into proper buildings and equipped with teaching material and a curriculum that came directly from Pyongyang. The children learnt their language, their culture and their history (*their* history meaning that of General Kim Il-sung's glorious revolution). Their *own* history once again became a foot-note; the parents weren't bothered by this, or by the fact that they were paying for the indoctrination of their progeny. Ironically, those learning about Kim Il-sung's revolution were predominantly the offspring of the middle and upper classes, who in all likelihood would have been dispossessed and imprisoned in the People's Republic; the poorest Zainichi couldn't afford the school fees.

Sōren also founded a bank, which gave credit to families and small businesses that had been turned away by Japanese banks. The organization maintained an 'amicable relationship' with the Yakuza – most of the pachinko arcades belonged (and still belong) to them. This strengthened their power as well as the cooperativeness and engagement of individual members, who stood up for their compatriots, calling on an employer or the city authority whenever trouble arose, and also distributing food, clothing, toys and even cash in the refugee camps. Very few of them were convinced communists, even the CIA described them in their reports as 'moderately left-wing' and 'socialist-minded'; instead, they were individuals who had been united by the experience of exile – people like Tetsuya Yamamoto.

When I met Tetsuya, he was no older than forty-five, yet to me he seemed like an old man, a small, thin old man with grey, frizzy hair that stuck out from his head like a cloud, surrounding his face with the appearance of a halo. He always wore trousers that were slightly too wide for him, held up with braces, and a shirt that was usually covered in stains; splashes of kimchi stock, soup, stew, but also blue ink, black paint – everything that Tetsuya touched left its mark on him, from every street he veered into he took with him little stones, twigs and dirt, and from every floor he sat on, dust. Naoko, his wife, merely sighed; she had long since given up trying to keep him and his clothes clean, she would look at him accusingly only once a month, and then Tetsuya would link arms with me and say it was time to take a bath, and as we steered our way towards the bathhouse, he would flick the dried dirt from his clothes, humming 'Que Sera, Sera'.

It was he who gave me my favourite record; he pressed it into my hands one day, just like that. '*Solitude*, the best album Billie ever recorded,' he said, even though this was the only one he knew and he didn't even like it. He preferred Doris Day's bright, high voice to her dark, low one. 'The singing kindergarten teacher!' I protested indignantly. 'Yes, precisely!' he retorted. If he'd had a kindergarten teacher like her, he said, he would have stayed a child forever.

Tetsuya gave Johnny and me work in one of his pachinko

arcades; he owned four, and all four were well frequented. We had to polish the silver balls for hours on end. It was an important job, he assured me, because if the little balls weren't smooth enough the customers would get upset and complain, there would be brawling, maybe even fatalities, and all that over the raw surface of a pachinko ball; the police would have to be called, and somebody would lose their future. Johnny lost his patience; he resigned after two days, but without actually handing in his resignation, he simply didn't turn up at the arcade any more, and Tetsuya didn't ask after his whereabouts. I, on the other hand, was taken under his wing; I became his maid-of-all-work, sometimes his chauffeur, sometimes his secretary, always his memory, and even after we had spent the whole night adding up the takings, paid the Yakuza and washed out the sake bottles – the first rays of sunlight, still weak and pale, coming into view over the rooftops – we would sit in his office, and he would tell me stories from his life, of working in the steel factory in Kawasaki, when a black smog dominated the city and he hadn't needed to wash his clothes, because they were constantly being dyed grey, over and over again, by the breath from the chimneys.

He described how he had learnt to distil schnapps in order to earn money. 'Yeast, rice, sugar, water and fire, that's all you need,' he said, showing me how he had slowly stirred the mixture in what would later become Naoko's soup pan, how he had added fresh water drop by drop and tasted the alcohol. He had made a living from slaughtering too, he said; whenever he wasn't in the kitchen making schnapps, he had driven out into the countryside and made his way from farm to farm, slaughtering cows and goats. He hadn't had to pay for the heads, hooves and innards, the farmers let him have those for free, and he handed them to his mother-in-law, who cooked them for an entire day, seasoning them with hot spices. He then gave these to his customers. 'Try them with a little glass of schnapps,' he told them, and the list of orders grew and grew. Business went well and the amphibian became a dragon: word got around that Tetsuya knew a thing or two about distilling schnapps, and after five years he was able to hire an employee. He should never have done that, he said, shaking his head; it had been a big mistake. The employee, an unseasoned dimwit, forgot to destroy the order slips, the police found them during a raid and had proof of Tetsuya's illegal trade. They arrested him, and he was brought to trial. Luckily, he said with a smile, his niece, a sweet little thing, had cried throughout the entire hearing. The judge probably thought she was his daughter, Tetsuya held her in his arms because she refused to leave him, and so he had got off with a small fine. Perhaps, he grinned, he had let the beak believe she was his child, perhaps – and here his grin widened – his brother had advised him to do it and threatened the little one: 'If you don't cry your eyes out the whole day through, I'll give you what for!'

His brother had gone back to South Korea with his family after the end of the Second World War. He had wanted to go with them, but his brother told him: 'Tetsuya, manage my pachinko parlours for me and send money when I need it.' He hadn't heard anything from him since the outbreak of the Korean War, he still waited every day for news. Tetsuya fetched a wooden crate from the cupboard and opened it. I was surprised to see how much money this unassuming box contained. He would go home one day too, he said, because even fish love the seabed they used to play in, but only when the time was right; once Korea was reunified.

★

233

I hadn't been alone with Eve since that disastrous night when we ran into Jinman in the Mambo; on board the ship we were constantly surrounded by the others, and in Osaka I never arrived home until morning, once she had already left the house. She had found work in a beauty salon in our neighbourhood, where she washed, blow-dried and curled hair in a small space with flowered wallpaper and turquoise plastic chairs. The brand-new full-length mirror didn't have wheels, so it had to be arduously lifted and carried from customer to customer by Eve and her colleague. The radio was never turned off, but constantly warbled or chattered away in the background, sometimes slipping into the voice of Elvis Presley, sometimes Perry Como or Patti Page; when Hibari Misora sang, the volume was turned up, for there were rumours that she was of Korean descent, and whenever a Japanese song came on, the dial was turned in the opposite direction, but there always remained a barely audible hum, a human voice which clung to the notes regardless of which language it sang in.

Eve had adopted a Japanese name for her job interview, Mizuki Takahashi: Mizuki meant 'beautiful moon', and she had seen 'Takahashi' on a delivery truck. She had forgotten her surname from the colonial era. She didn't need a Japanese name in Ikaino, the Korean one was sufficient, because apart from a handful of Japanese people – petty criminals and low-paid workers who couldn't afford the rent in the nicer neighbourhoods – only Zainichi lived here, most of them for over fifty years already, they had migrated there at the beginning of the last century.

Immediately after Japan's annexation of Korea, workers from Japanese textile factories, as well as from the coal mines in Fukuoka and Hokkaido, had travelled through Korean villages hoping to sign up as cheap labour.

Then, during the First World War, when the Japanese economy went through an incomparable boom, thirty thousand low-wage Korean workers were hired during over eighty 'promotional tours'. They received a third less pay than their Japanese colleagues, and on top of this the police alone had access to their savings books; the full amount was paid only on completion of the contract. This was to ensure that the workers didn't get any foolish ideas about taking off.

When the recession hit in the 1920s, it affected the Japanese economy too, and the government banned this form of mass recruitment (they feared hordes of unemployed Koreans would join forces with the communists and anarchists). Still, it continued to exist until the 1940s, and in the final years of the war it was practised openly again, sometimes the work detail was announced by postcard, sometimes the military police simply came by and took the unlucky individuals along with them.

Our neighbour Yun was one of the 'voluntary idiots', as he put it. On 5 January 1942, in Seoul, he went along with a Korean who was looking for men keen to earn money in Osaka. The man said they were recruiting workers for the construction of a railway line, although Yun would have to decide at once, for the train was already waiting. Because Yun lived right behind the station, he was able to say goodbye to his family, but most of the men climbed aboard the train without having told their loved ones. On the platform in Shimonoseki, said Yun, the group was met by an old, bald-headed Japanese man, who took their papers and forbade them from disembarking the train when it stopped in the stations. They weren't even allowed to look out of the windows. It was night once they reached their destination, and so cold that Yun thought he had landed in *jigoku*, in hell. Only once he was standing before the gates of the coal mine in Hokkaido did it dawn on him that he had been tricked.

Seven men guarded him and the other forced labourers, all of whom were Koreans. They had to slave away from six in the morning until eight at night, and received three servings of barley gruel per day, mixed with rice, miso soup and pickled radish. They were allowed to bathe every few days, for no longer than fifteen minutes at a time. There was no alcohol or tobacco, and the door of the sleeping quarters was locked from the outside at the end of the working day. The dormitories were ruled by a 'Big Bossu'; whenever he considered himself to have been insulted, he dragged the unlucky individual out into the freezing cold and beat him with a wooden club. As the months passed, the club was stained blood red.

After the end of the war, the 'Big Bossu' returned to Korea. He was lynched on the day of his arrival.

Yun fared better than our vegetable trader Mr Ri: he also ended up in a coal mine, but on the island of Sakhalin, which Japan had annexed in 1905 following their victory over Russia. He worked there in the toughest of conditions for two long years, always in the belief that he would take the money he had saved back to Korea once his contract ended. But after the capitulation of Japan, his savings book became worthless, and the landing of the Soviet troops made escape from the island impossible.

In 1946, the first Japanese were sent home from the island ('And I had thought we Koreans would be the first to be called onto the ships – after all, we were the war victims!'); he waited in vain to be summoned. Only once Ri married a Japanese woman and the Soviet–Japanese peace treaty was signed ten years later, was he able to embark by steamer to Maizuru: on his arrival in Japan, he was disappointed not to see one single Korean flag among the many Japanese ones.

'I stormed into the Mindan office and asked the secretary: why were none of you there to welcome us? And why did you leave us to rot for all those years on that devil's island?'

The secretary, without a flicker of emotion on his face, replied: 'All Koreans on Sakhalin were enemy spies.'

Perhaps it was because of this cautionary tale (which Mr Ri never tired of telling), that all Zainichi were in agreement that they wouldn't return home until Korea was reunified. Until then, most made a living by collecting scrap metal: discarded iron poles, rusted railings, old car parts; hoarding inside and in front of their houses anything that could be taken apart and was worthy of being described as metal, with the result that Ikaino looked like one big open-air scrap storehouse. Many Koreans sold native food products: the ingredients required for kimchi, as well as rice cakes in varieties which, although they seemed Japanese to me, Naoko assured me were in fact Korean. The rest worked in the factory a few streets away, where rubber soles were produced. I had heard that the work was hard, but the pay not bad. Our housemate, Misaki Satō, was a money-lender; she was widowed, her husband had died of a lung infection just a few months after the end of the war, leaving her and her two children without means, and so she made private loans, cash in exchange for interest rates that were higher than Mount Fuji; Johnny said she would squeeze the blood from a flea and drink it if she could. He had tried to convince her to give us a small loan at a lower interest rate. She sent him packing, but offered Eve a job. 'Where,' Eve had asked, 'in a factory?' 'No,' Misaki had answered, 'in my salon.'

Missu Satō, as everyone called her, was a spherical woman. Everything about her was round: her face, her hair (a jet-black curly wig), even her nose (as round as a clown's), and the only exception was her gaze, which was sharp; piercing. She had fled Osaka in 1945, as the hailstorm of American bombs became ever stronger, her train stopped outside Hiroshima and was unable to go any further. At first she waited for a truck that had been promised to the passengers, but when it still hadn't arrived after six days, she decided to walk to Shimonoseki with her children. She couldn't wait any longer, she didn't want to miss the ship to Busan. They were on the road for three days, in a surreal landscape of ashes and embers, a lunar landscape, as she called it; little fires blazed here and there, steel rods protruding out of the earth glowed red, the ground was so hot that it singed the soles of their feet. The injured who were still able to move tried to help those who were half burnt; their skin blackened with soot, you could only tell from the whites of their eyes that they were human beings. In the midst of this inferno, a woman had given birth to a child and then died, said Missu Satō, and she had searched for leaves and grass to cover the newborn and protect it from the sun. Eventually she left the infant with a pastor, a Frenchman, and resumed her journey. Initially she had tried to find a path among the dead, but before long she began to just clamber over the charred bodies, barely noticing the corpses and their stench any more.

She missed her ship. It exploded shortly after it left the dock, and everyone on board lost their lives. Missu Satō stayed in Shimonoseki until the trains began to run again. Back in Osaka, she found a family of strangers living in her house; her neighbour, in the belief that she would never return, had sold it for a hundred yen. Missu Satō took the hundred, wangled another hundred out of her, begged a larger sum from Tetsuya and then began to lend money – until, that is, Sōren sabotaged her trade with its flow of North Korean capital at ridiculously low interest rates.

Our room was normally empty when I arrived home from work, apart from the cigarette stubs Johnny had dropped on the floor, letting the ash mingle with the dust and drift through the room in small clouds. One morning, though, I was able to finish earlier than usual, it must have been just before six o'clock; I remember that the sun had already risen. Eve was lying on the tatami mats in her pyjamas, with the small record player Tetsuya had lent to me alongside her, and because it was crackling and rustling and Eve was humming along softly, I barely noticed Billie.

I can still hear Eve today, if I close my eyes, for her voice has taken root in my ears, or perhaps I captured it the first time she touched me, her low, soft, fragile voice; I always loved it, and I probably always will – I'm unable to forget it. She sang that she was a fool and didn't get beyond that line. She sang again and again, louder each time, until eventually she couldn't help but laugh. I stood outside the door, peeping through the crack. She reached for a glass of water, took a sip and lifted the arm of the record player back to the beginning of the song. With a scratching sound, the instruments struck up, and Eve sang along with Billie, Billie in English, Eve in Korean.

I couldn't interrupt her, I couldn't and didn't want to. She was happy; in that moment she was happy. I could feel her happiness, almost grasp hold of it, and who was I to spoil her happiness for my own?

I sat down outside the door and closed my eyes, exhausted. I fell asleep immediately.

★

A touch awoke me. I thought I was dreaming, but when I opened my eyes, Eiko was sitting next to me. She was four or five years younger than I was, slender and tall. 'Tall?' Eve had said. 'You only think that because you're a dwarf.'

Eiko had a rounded face, high cheekbones and large, oval-shaped eyes; 'exquisite' was the word that came to mind the first time I saw her, I was astounded that a human being could be so pretty. 'Clothes are wings,' Eve said, rolling her eyes. I countered with a saying of my own: 'One still has to sleep first in order to dream.'

Eiko had huddled up against my back; I edged away a little. She had come to trust me, often linking arms with me or slipping her hand into mine. Whenever she did, I gave her a little push and whispered to her that it was inappropriate; that she wasn't a child any more, after all.

Once I was able to hold my eyes open for longer than a few seconds, I noticed that she was smiling, no, beaming, as though she had a large, steaming sweet potato in front of her.

'What's new?' I mumbled.

She grinned.

'Nothing.'

'Come on, spit it out.'

She shook her head, hiding her face in her hands.

'Okay, so don't tell me.'

I yawned demonstratively, and she immediately gave me a little shove.

'Don't fall asleep, Yunho, you can't sleep now. I have great news!'

'And there was me thinking it was nothing.'

'Oh, I was just saying that.'

She moved closer. At that moment I spotted Kimiko; she

was watching us. As always, she looked confused, like a fish that had accidentally hopped out of the sea: helpless, disorientated, clueless. But she had another side to her too.

Iron eats iron, flesh eats flesh: not a day went by when the sisters didn't argue, Eiko in her high, screeching voice, Kimiko's soft and barely audible. She was a master of silence. I often felt that quietude was subject to her command, that she could dispatch it wherever she wanted: she could reduce people to silence or envelop herself in a soundlessness as thick and impermeable as a wall. Thus protected, she crept up and eavesdropped on everyone and everything. It was impossible to have a conversation away from Kimiko's ears; Johnny and I called her 'the invisible one'.

I signalled to Eiko to turn round. Smiling, she followed my command, then froze. She mumbled an apology in Japanese and jumped up quickly. At the stairs she turned round, once Kimiko had vanished from sight, and whispered to me: 'I'm going to study, Yunho. I'm going to study soon!'

Before I could answer, she interrupted me by putting a finger to her lips.

'But it's still a secret. Please don't tell anyone.'

'You're going to study where? In Osaka?'

'No.'

'In Tokyo?'

'Wrong again.'

She smiled at me mysteriously.

'In Seoul . . .?'

'Almost.'

She grinned. She would give me a clue, she said, even though I didn't deserve one.

'On the other side.'

'The other side?'

'Exactly,' she answered, 'north of the 38th parallel.'

Discarded by South Korea, picked up and given a home by North Korea: for most Zainichi, North Korea was Korea. Mindan couldn't change that, though from 1965 onwards they would issue entry permits for the *Republic* of Korea, and South Korean passports. Sōren, in turn, couldn't organize North Korean passports, but they could offer a future in the homeland.

Now I was wide awake.

'You've signed up for the Great Homecoming?'

Eiko nodded.

'Pyongyang in August!' she replied, and ran, laughing, down to the ground floor.

12

Only now did I notice the scent of grilled meat, chopped garlic and crushed chilli peppers that was slowly spreading through the upper floor. So this was why Tetsuya had sent me home early; the Sōren committee had called an emergency meeting. Tetsuya hadn't mentioned anything about it, but then he hadn't ever tried to convince me to join either, perhaps because I had South Korean citizenship. Ever since Gen Kosho had been exposed as a Mindan agent, a certain paranoia had prevailed among the Zainichi. I had explained to him that I hadn't had a choice, if I had claimed North Korean citizenship I would have been locked up, and the key to my cell flung in a wide arc into the sea. Instead of answering, he had given me an odd smile that made him look like a hawk with broken wings.

The Japanese government had declared it an issue of 'humanitarian' importance that all Koreans return home. More than half a million human beings, many of them unhappy and liable to resort to violence due to their impoverished circumstances, were yearning for their homeland (yes, homesickness was brought into it). To deny them this would be inhumane, the government claimed.

They didn't mention that they had abolished welfare benefits for the Zainichi. The once imperial subjects, Hirohito's 'children', had become stateless, and as 'foreigners', as Koreans, they had lost their right to Japanese support. (How long must you be a foreigner before you can call yourself a native? How natively born must a person be before they can outgrow their foreignness?) Nor was there any mention of how the Zainichi came under general suspicion at an official level. Whenever the Japanese police issued warnings of criminal gangs and violent behaviour, they put up the South Korean flag; the presumption of innocence was (and is) exclusively reserved for 'natives'.

A 'humanitarian issue', they called it. This issue ridiculed any sense of humanity. Was it humane to deny human beings, who could no longer be exploited under the law, their livelihood, and at a time when Japan – not least because of the trade resulting from the Korean War – was experiencing an economic boom? How humane is it to push the helpless to total helplessness? Very, it seems. Or deeply *human*, at least, to cheat others to benefit oneself and then call this the 'fight for survival'.

Even before the outbreak of the Korean civil war, plans to forcibly relocate the Zainichi had been pored over at length by the US occupiers in Japan. They weren't put into action because their legal section opposed the handing over of citizens who showed solidarity with North Korea to a South Korean government which, in all probability, would have interned them in prisoner-of-war camps or executed them. Those who had no problem with that did have a problem with sending suspected communists into an American zone of influence. They repeatedly referred to the 'successful relocation' of Mexicans in the early 1930s – an incredible euphemism considering that over half a million men, women and children practically sprinted across the border out of fear for their lives; the failed repatriation of the Filipinos in 1935 wasn't mentioned.

Now Sōren, an organization supporting these 'unwanted

migrants', had taken up the matter. This must have been a cause for celebration for the Japanese government, especially Prime Minister Shigeru Yoshida, who was renowned for his Koreaphobia. Japan never did rid itself of all six hundred thousand Koreans, but a good 15.55 per cent left nonetheless. The 93,340th returned home in 1984.

The housemaid stepped into the hallway with a tray groaning beneath the weight of small and large bowls of fish, meat, seafood, vegetables and roots; as I hadn't yet eaten, my mouth watered. I heard a soft voice behind me say that none of them would emerge before the evening. They would spend the rest of the day gobbling and guzzling without pause.

Ayumi sat down alongside me on the stairs; I had never noticed before that a dimple formed by the right-hand corner of her mouth when she smiled. A strand of hair fell across her face, she clamped it back behind her ear. There wasn't much for them to discuss anyway, she said, the Great Homecoming was proving so popular that it didn't need to be advertised. In the beginning they had distributed flyers, begged the journalists to take notice of them, and now they were swamped with interview requests.

'And all of them want to speak to Yamada.'

Yamada, *Comrade* Yamada: he boasted that he was the mastermind of the Great Homecoming, and he was astonishingly quick off the mark when it came to decorating himself with others' feathers; in truth it was far from clear who had brought the campaign into being. In 1958, a group of Zainichi in Kawasaki had written a long letter to Kim Il-sung, asking to be admitted into the Democratic People's Republic of Korea. Just one month later, to everyone's surprise, General Kim had announced that North Korea would open its 'doors and hearts' to all Koreans in Japan. The following week, Foreign Minister Nam Il had worded the invitation more precisely: all home-comers would be welcomed with housing, work and training. Sōren publicized this offer in their newsletter, unleashing a veritable flood of articles. The Japanese daily papers in particular seized upon it and reported the news, which was helpful, because more than half of the Korean minority in Japan spoke no Korean. In order to remedy this, Sōren employed additional Korean teachers to teach the mother tongue to children and young adults who wanted to undertake the journey to the motherland. This initiative had come much too late, Yamada said; the language classes should have started years ago, someone with a vocabulary of just a few hundred words was far from a true Korean. 'So what makes someone a Korean, Mr Yamada?' I asked, unable to stop myself.

Yamada looked at me scornfully.

'Parentage is important, but it's not enough.'

'What's more important: having the right biology or knowing one's homeland?'

Both were equally important, he declared, for if one of the two elements were missing, the person was incomplete. *Incomplete.* But, I replied, weren't there incomplete Koreans too?

Yamada gave an irritated laugh and retorted that I was cheeky, rude and disrespectful! I was like a tree frog, he said, hopping from one pumpkin leaf to the next.

'Watch out you don't slip off.'

Yamada was the Sōren chief for Osaka, the city with the largest number of Korean immigrants. He had spoken in favour of a return to the homeland ever since his election to the committee, he told me, and now his efforts were finally bearing fruit.

Though he himself wouldn't dream of embarking on the *Tobolsk* or the *Krylion*, the passenger steamers which Khrushchev had put at his Korean comrades' disposal; he loved his refrigerator and his WC far too much for that.

Yamada was married to a Japanese woman who everyone simply called 'Madame Chiang Kai-shek': a large, broad woman with a large, broad voice and large, broad gestures. She owned numerous clothes shops and was the editor of a women's magazine which she herself wrote for, as she claimed. Madame was constantly surrounded by three assistants who carried her bags, rummaged around in them for her glasses when required and placed them on her nose, held umbrellas and parasols protectively over her head and brought along her newest hats whenever Madame had difficulties, as she often did, in choosing just one. But these weren't the only people under her command: there were also the servants in her house, the tenants she protected from homelessness, the workers in her husband's restaurant, her husband himself – in short: everyone who didn't manage to get out of her way in time. It was rumoured in Ikaino that she knew about her husband's affair, but tolerated his lover because the woman hadn't yet achieved what she had already accomplished: Madame had given Yamada a child, albeit a daughter, Senko.

Yamada wasn't dissimilar to his Madame, although he was of calmer temperament. Like her, he trampled over everyone with his decisions. His beginnings as a businessman had been humble, making shampoo powder in the backroom of his parents-in-law's house. It sold surprisingly well, Madame having played a not small part in his success: she had gone from door to door, unaccompanied by assistants, singing the shampoo's praises in her unique, irresistible way.

Yamada sold the company shortly before the war broke out

(a wise decision, as most factories didn't survive the US carpet-bombing) and found work with the Americans after the end of the war; 'lackey services', as he never tired of saying, which nonetheless led to the contract which established his fortune: he supplied the American troops with dried blood plasma during the Korean War. Two life-saving tin cans; one contained distilled water, which was blended with the contents of the second, dried plasma. It took only three minutes to form the donated blood, and it could be used for up to four hours. The business collapsed when suspicion arose that the blood, which was mostly given in exchange for a hot meal, could be infected with hepatitis, but by this point Yamada had already made a fortune. He used it to open not one, but four *yakiniku* grill restaurants: in Osaka, Kobe, Kyoto and Tokyo. By 1960, he ruled over a *yakiniku* empire.

It had been Yamada's idea to recruit Tetsuya as a committee member, Ayumi told me. Most of the comrades had been against it, claiming that Tetsuya was better suited to the South Korean sympathizers, to Mindan, that he had, after all, fought on Rhee's side in the civil war (which was a lie). Yamada had to work very hard to convince them, he had talked until his mouth was raw, saying it was worth accepting Tetsuya even if only because he could support a number of projects with large sums of money – the schools which were still to be built, the banks which were lacking capital. This argument eventually tipped the scale in his favour, and Tetsuya was admitted, but the suspicions never vanished. When flyers with death threats were pasted onto Sōren buildings and individual members threatened and even beaten by Mindan activists, the committee wondered whether they had let in a traitor, a spy who was working for Syngman Rhee and doing everything within his power to sabotage the Great Homecoming. Their concerns were unnecessary, Ayumi told me, she could personally guarantee that no one needed to doubt Tetsuya's loyalty.

I studied her surreptitiously. Was she spying on Tetsuya? Was that why she lived in a small rented room and not in official lodgings? Was it possible that she was an agent, posing as a teacher? If Mindan had spies, then so did Sōren. When she turned to face me, I quickly lowered my gaze. I often found myself unsure of how to act in her presence. Johnny had already pulled me up on it, as had Eve, but both of them were barking up the wrong tree: I found Ayumi neither attractive nor unattractive – I was afraid of her. It was easy to underestimate her, for she seemed pliant at first, but only at first. Johnny was right when he said he had seldom met a harder woman. In my opinion, she lived alone because she was unable to forgive, and I believed she was unable to forgive because she was unable to forget. She had phenomenal powers of recollection, nothing ever slipped her mind; she could read through her memory like a schoolgirl through her books.

She seemed to have taken a liking to me; she spoke to me whenever she saw me in the house. Sometimes she had nothing to say, and would interrupt herself mid-sentence, apologize and walk away. If I tried to stop her, she warded me off and fled with her hands in the air. She couldn't engage in conversation without stroking her hair, she smoothed it down strand by strand as she listened to me or answered a question that I hadn't even asked. 'She's an odd creature,' said Eve. 'Incredibly odd, and lonely, terribly lonely. I feel sorry for her, this small, odd woman.'

I asked myself whether this characterization did justice to a person like Ayumi; yes, she was odd, and yes, she never mentioned a sweetheart, her family were all far away or dead, and yet she never seemed lonely to me. On the contrary, she was always lost in her thoughts, in a kind of trance – a glow often emanated from her. She had no time to feel something like loneliness, she planned to transform the world in accordance with her ideas and values; she was, in her own way, religious. She possessed a conviction she was unable to break away from without abandoning herself.

What she had devoted her entire being to was neither communism, the 'unrelenting course of history' of which she spoke so often, nor was it General Kim Il-sung, whom she worshipped. No, the belief that had fully pervaded her was a different one: she believed, passionately and unwaveringly, that there was a paradise on earth. And this Elysium was North Korea.

'I was with the first homecomers – there must have been a few thousand of them – when they took the train to Niigata. I'll never forget that day. It was the 18th of December 1959.'

She enunciated the date solemnly and deliberately, as though it were a spell.

'I boarded with them in Osaka, and travelled through a foggy, snow-covered landscape.'

Past solitary fields, through black forests, the darkness sometimes perforated by the weak glow from a farmhouse. Whenever the train stopped, there would be a group of people on the platform waving and smiling at the travellers, singing songs from the new (and old) homeland and waving the flags of the People's Republic. Among them were young men selling rice balls and roasted chestnuts, the sweet scent pushing its way into the compartments of the train.

'Just picture it, Mr Kang,' she whispered, 'the dark yellow gleam of the train stations on a pitch-black night, and above it all hangs the scent of warm chestnuts, fried rice and freshly fallen snow.'

She accompanied the group only as far as Niigata, her task was to help fill out the emigration forms and 'to comfort the heavy-hearted'. They reached the last station at around eight in the morning, with half an hour's delay, and put the final kilometres behind them on foot, accompanied by a police escort; Mindan members had laid down on the tracks in order to stop the train from travelling any further.

'Presumably the first ship wouldn't have been able to set sail without police protection,' explained Ayumi, 'Mindan threatened to blow up the Red Cross station in Niigata – along with "all the traitors".'

She beamed.

'Today there are more than fifty thousand.'

Fifty thousand people had refused to let the terrorism intimidate them, she told me, and had been living in North Korea for five months now, in beautiful, clean, modern apartment buildings, built especially for them by General Kim Il-sung. They no longer had to worry about where their next meal would come from, or how to pay the rent; their children would receive an education, the younger ones could go to high school, the older ones to university. Jobs for everyone. *Education for everyone.* Eiko too had been hooked by this dream. If I had been braver, I would have considered studying at the university in Pyongyang myself.

Ayumi pulled a carefully folded article out of her jacket pocket. She told me it had been published recently in the *Asahi Shimbun*, and was part of the series 'North of the 38th Parallel'. Even if I didn't believe her, she surmised, surely I would trust a Japanese person.

I scanned the article. When enthusiasm failed to appear on my face, she told me to wait a moment. She came back with numerous issues of the magazine *Korea*, which was published by the propaganda office of the North Korean government. She only had the Japanese editions, she said, but the magazine was also published in English, French, Russian, Chinese and Korean. It was full of illustrations . . .

Beneath a photo of Pyongyang – the newly paved streets so straight and clean that they looked like a scene from a painting, as did the pedestrians, who were relaxing after their carefree workday in twos or threes, with poker-straight backs and beaming smiles (even smiling was a serious practice) – and alongside a floor plan of one of the numerous apartments that were being constructed along the Taedong River, there was a guest contribution by a recent homecomer, describing his new life: 'The government of the People's Republic of Korea gave me everything I need: an apartment, a job and some cash for immediate expenses. My wife, who is Japanese, has found a job as a nurse in the maternity ward of the university hospital in Pyongyang. I teach at the vocational high school. But there's one thing that clouds my happiness; the more wonderful life in my Fatherland becomes, the more I think of my friends in Japan who are anxious to return home too.'

She nodded to me, content in the belief that she had convinced me, but I was fascinated less by the words and more by the colourful photos, which were carefully composed even though they were supposed to be snapshots, unadulterated proof of a carefree existence.

When I commented that the images looked staged, Ayumi called me an uneducated lout.

'As limited as a frog in a well.'

She leafed through one of the issues and showed me the first few pages, which documented the travels of North Korean politicians. Could something like that be faked, she asked?

'Here we talk to Nikita Khrushchev from the Soviet Union,

here to Otto Grotewohl and Walter Ulbricht from the German Democratic Republic, here to Władysław Gomułka from Poland.'

Then she read out the names of the countries that 'we' were friendly with: Bulgaria, Hungary, Albania, Romania, Mongolia, Cuba, Czechoslovakia and Iraq. In addition, 'we' had received numerous visits from foreign delegations: from Indonesia, France, Colombia, Nepal and Vietnam. 'We' were friendly with all of these countries, she said, with half of the entire world.

'These pictures are proof of North Korea's political and economic superiority, Mr Kang. Or are you telling me that South Korea has this many factories?'

Textile factories, chemical factories, steel factories, rice factories. Factories whose purpose and definition have now slipped my mind. Factories that made the label of 'factory' seem old-fashioned. Factories that were more like monuments than workplaces, so shiny were their numerous machines. I had to agree with her; the South didn't have that level of industry. Nor were we proud of our work, like the comrades in the photographs: proud of the early accomplishment of the five-year plan, of the numerous irrigation plants, schools, hospitals, theatres, cinemas, shops and restaurants which they had rebuilt since 1953 – and always with a smile.

I'll admit that I was sceptical; I suspected that the happiness in their faces was posed. So much joy isn't natural, I thought; it isn't *realistic*, not in this concentrated form. I had to hold back from making sarcastic comments or jokes – about the apparently eternal sunshine in North Korea, the bright-blue, cloudless sky, the polite grins that were welded to the faces of the citizens, and the statistics which studded the text like sweet beans in white rice cakes:

'Since 1953, 1.6 million trees have been planted.'

'There is an 80-year-old elephant in the Pyongyang Zoo.'

'In 1959, a kolkhoz sold 14,000 rabbits.'

'The average tobacco plant in the People's Republic has 18 leaves. Each leaf is around 70 to 80 cm in size.'

'A hen laid five eggs within 26 hours. 17 of 20 hens laid three in the same time period.'

On the photo safari through North Korea that Ayumi took me on, I saw workers standing before glittering and gleaming machinery, their chests emblazoned with medals; fishermen out at sea amid a swarm of silver bream; women harvesting seaweed on the coast; housewives out shopping as the shelves behind them buckled beneath the weight of the food; dancing workers in a forest glade, complete with butterflies and pumpkin blossoms; holidaymakers hiking in the Diamond Mountains, staying in a hotel with sauna and full board ('I haven't been able to stop eating since I got here!', declares a member of the North Korean Workers' Party); and singing performers from the Kwangtung opera in front of a large audience in Pyongyang. After a while, Ayumi began to turn the pages faster and faster – the quicker she leafed through, the more the photos blurred before my eyes, transforming into a film, the rigid life becoming an animated one.

Suddenly, my gaze fell on a picture of a group of workers standing by a furnace in the Hwanghae steel factory, they had been photographed in profile and were wearing caps that cast shadows over their eyes, but I thought I recognized Yunsu. I asked Ayumi to stop; she thought I was interested in the article, and began to read it out loud, but I wasn't listening. Was it him or wasn't it? For a few seconds at a time I felt sure it was, then I was overcome with doubt once more and couldn't establish even the slightest resemblance to my brother; at times I had difficulty remembering Yunsu at all, as though someone was erasing his face as I tried to call it into my mind.

Eventually, I gave up trying. I needed a sharper picture, one that showed him in sunlight, or, even better, an interview, an article with his name and a photo. At least ten comrades were interviewed for every issue, and the magazine had been in print for three years – perhaps he had been photographed or interviewed for one of the thirty-six editions? I wondered whether he had changed much, and tried to imagine to what extent. Was he thinner? Was his hair starting to grey? Did he live in a large, modern apartment too? Did he have a good job, or was he studying? Was his life there a good one, a happy one? In the mid-1960s, in Park Chung-hee's South Korea, people sang: 'We too want a good life, a good life at long last!' I couldn't help but think of Yunsu whenever I heard the kindergarten children warbling this propaganda, this 'hymn'. Was Yunsu living a good life at long last?

I took the magazine from Ayumi's hand and searched for him in the photos, studying every face. People used to say that he looked like Mother and I like Father, but I had always thought the opposite: in my mind, he looked like Father and I like Mother . . . Worked up by the idea of finding him, I searched myself into a frenzy, I forgot Ayumi, forgot that she was sitting next to me on the steps, talking to me. Whenever a noise startled me out of my concentrated state, the caw of a crow, the clatter of pots and pans, a door being opened and closed, I took in only fragments of sentences, 'day nurseries for working mothers' and 'excursions to the sites of the Revolution'. Then I would give her a brief nod before turning my attention back to the hunt for Yunsu's face, which, in my excitement, sometimes transformed into my mother's face, and then my father's . . . Eventually, I was searching for my entire family.

'Mr Kang.'

Ayumi laid her hand on my arm, and I wanted to shoo her away like an annoying fly. She had to go now, she said, she had an appointment. I asked her to stay a little longer, ten minutes, five, I begged, pleaded with her; I wanted to finish looking through the magazine. She shook her head, that wasn't possible, she couldn't keep the person waiting, but – she added with a smile – I could hold on to all of them, she would lend them to me.

With the stack and the promise that I could borrow the remaining issues as well, I retreated to our room. I laid the open issue on the floor, and leant over the pages with a magnifying glass that I had coaxed out of Naoko; I wanted to make sure I didn't overlook a thing, even the smallest detail could be important.

I didn't take an afternoon nap that day; normally I had to leave at five, and my shift didn't end until around eight the following morning. I laid down on the tatami mats, but couldn't sleep for excitement and nerves, just half an hour later I was kneeling in front of a magazine again, moving the magnifying glass across the faces; I worked slowly and systematically.

Johnny teased me when he found me there, hunched on the floor. He said I looked like his grandfather, that I would ruin my eyesight. He ventured a glance over my shoulder, puffing cigarette smoke into my face, and declared that it was all staged, 'composed spontaneity'. After that, he ignored both me and my obsession. As the days passed, however, he became suspicious, and his pointed remarks more frequent. It said 'magazine' on the cover, he said, they weren't novels, but something to be flicked through quickly and then tossed aside.

Was I trying to learn all the issues off by heart? Eve defended me. Of course Yunho is interested in North Korea, she said, that's normal. 'Normal?' Johnny interjected, 'I find his behaviour disturbed. He sits there by the window every free second he gets, crouched over those magazines, and only puts them aside when darkness falls.' 'Maybe he wants to improve his Japanese,' countered Eve, 'it's good practice to read a text over and over. He's only learning the language.' She was trying to placate Johnny, but he couldn't be calmed, because he had a terrible suspicion: he believed that I was engaged in North Korean studies because I was planning to take the next ship to Chŏngjin. I overheard them talking one day when I arrived home before breakfast.

'I bet he's already filled out the emigration forms,' I heard Johnny's voice through the wall. 'He can't,' retorted Eve, 'we're illegal immigrants.'

I moved closer to the door.

'He's working for Tetsuya.'

Johnny sounded impatient.

'If there's anyone in Ikaino who can get the necessary papers, then it's Mr Yamamoto.'

I was just about to walk in when Eve spoke again.

'He won't leave us.'

'Why not? Because of how much he loves you?'

Johnny guffawed.

'Why don't you find yourself some rich American? It shouldn't be that hard for you. Just ask your informer friends.'

'My what?'

'Spare me the pretence. I know your secret, Jinman told—'

'Jinman? You believe that idiot?'

'I didn't at first . . .'

'And now?'

'Now – now I think his accusation has at least a kernel of truth to it.'

'Truth? Jinman was a professional liar, you know that.'

'Well, you organized our escape to Japan pretty quickly.'

'The escape route was already set . . .'

'The yen appeared out of nowhere.'

'I had some at home . . .'

Johnny cleared his throat.

'That certainly makes sense.'

He cleared his throat again.

'What doesn't make sense, however, is how you, *you* of all people, could lead us straight into this communist den.'

Silence.

Eventually, Eve murmured: 'Everything's completely different here.'

Everything really was completely different here: here I had a job, a boss who trusted me, who was even divulging the inner workings of his business to me. Here I earned more than Johnny, here *he* asked *me* for money, not I him. I had changed; the escape from Seoul and the boat journey had changed me, as had the people I had got to know in Osaka. All of a sudden, I saw South Korea, my home, with different eyes, it shrunk and shifted into another time, another dimension: my past became *unearthly*, unreal.

I wasn't the only one who had gone through a transformation. Eve, who used to stride through the streets of Seoul as though she were its queen, acted like a maidservant in Osaka. She didn't look anyone in the face, took care to keep her gaze lowered, and when she spoke Japanese she sounded like a child. The uncertainty that dominated her words in the foreign language infected her Korean too. She, who had never shied away from confrontation, now evaded everything and everyone. An exile now, the only thing she cared about and took an interest in was her homeland, even though in Ikaino it was called the Democratic People's Republic. Johnny too, formerly a loudmouth and a rebel, behaved impeccably in Japan, he followed all the school regulations, and didn't even comment on the portraits of Kim Il-sung that adorned the teachers' lounge and all the classrooms, even though in Seoul he would never have tolerated the Supreme Communist as a hero.

In some respects I understood my friends' metamorphosis; they were playing roles; here they weren't my friends, but my family, Johnny my brother and Eve my sister – it had seemed only logical when, even while we were still aboard the escape boat, Johnny had suggested they adopt their Korean names again, because they needed a disguise. So why not invent the names, I interjected. 'Isn't it silly,' I had asked, 'to use the real names if they're supposed to be covers?'

Johnny had laughed and called me a bad liar. I had given myself away even back when we were children, he said, by blushing before a lie even crossed my lips. I should trust him, he said, he was more experienced in such things. It was much smarter to not distance oneself too far from the truth. In Korea, they were known as Johnny and Eve, and hardly anyone knew their Korean names, but we would remember them easily, because they weren't made up, but our actual names. 'And what about my cover name?' I had asked. 'You don't need one,' Johnny had replied, 'you've never done anything wrong, and you never will. A hare doesn't need a hare costume.'

I pushed the door open; today I think that if I'd eavesdropped on their conversation for just a few minutes longer, perhaps I would have found out the whole truth, and everything would have turned out differently . . .

Instead, I blustered into the room and into the conversation. 'Calm down, both of you,' I muttered, 'I won't leave you.'

Johnny stared at me, whether angrily or nervously, I couldn't say. He started to answer, then seemingly thought better of it and stomped out of the room. Eve tried to lighten the tense atmosphere with a joke.

'Speak of the tiger, and he appears.'

She smiled with embarrassment. They hadn't expected me back so early, she said, I had startled her. Without giving her another glance, I pulled off my jacket and crouched down next to my pile of magazines. She stood there indecisively, seemingly unsure as to what she should do; eventually, she sat down next to me.

'You really are looking for something in these magazines, aren't you?'

I looked up. Johnny's presence changed her. She was less sure of herself when he was around, shy and vulnerable. I caught myself feeling repulsed by her weakness, it disgusted me and filled me with loathing. I wanted to grab Eve and shake her, scream into her face, demand to know why she was putting on an act, why she was hiding herself away. I couldn't understand how her wonderful strength, sovereignty and self-confidence could be completely extinguished, suffocated, by him. I didn't understand her, I didn't understand him. I had no idea of how love operates and what it unleashes.

I answered reluctantly that I wasn't looking for something, but someone. Who, she asked? She wanted to help, she added. I shook my head and said that wasn't necessary. She nodded. Fine, then she would just keep me company, the clientele at the salon would have to make do with her colleague today.

She took a cigarette out of her handbag and offered me one. They were Japanese, not Lucky Strikes. I took one and lit both, hers and mine. We smoked in silence, then I pulled the first magazine from the pile and began to leaf through it.

By the time I had worked through almost the entire stack, dusk had fallen, and Eve was asleep. I knew I would have to leave soon, but I didn't want to, my body refused; it was good to feel her presence, and I wasn't ready to surrender the illusion that everything had stayed as it once was: that we were still in Seoul, and it was night-time, the streets empty apart from the occasional shadow darting through our labyrinth.

Her soft voice strayed into my daydream. Had I found what I was looking for, she whispered, her eyelids still heavy with sleep. 'No,' I said, ' it was probably a stupid idea to look for him anyway.'

You can't imagine how I felt. I had been convinced I would see, *finally* see, my brother again. I had hoped for so much from the photographs. If Eve hadn't been with me, I would have cried, I would have cried all night long. I told her about my hope of finding Yunsu in the magazines. She took my hand, squeezed it and leant over to me until her lips brushed mine. She kissed me, a hesitant kiss, as though she hadn't known me long, and I reciprocated as though I were kissing her for the first time; we couldn't stop ourselves. We knew we were being reckless. What would happen if we were caught? How would Johnny react? But in that moment, we didn't care about anything else; I held her tightly and didn't want to let her go, I held her more tightly than I had ever held her before, and she clung to me: we tried to save one another.

Suddenly I heard a noise, a scraping or rustling. I opened my eyes, expecting to see a rat or the greengrocer's cat, but instead I saw a pair of human eyes, watching us through the crack in

261

the door. I pushed Eve away and jumped to my feet. 'What's wrong?' she asked. I had no time to answer, already pursuing the footsteps in the hallway. The spy ran down the stairs, I chased after. Arriving at the bottom, there was no one to be seen. I dashed out onto the street. There was no one there either. I headed towards the school. Someone had been spying on us, I had seen their eyes, I wasn't imagining things. I sped up; I thought I could catch up with the person if only I were quick enough, I tore down the main street out of Ikaino, following its path and racing through the city as though in pursuit of the devil himself: I was convinced that Johnny had caught us kissing, but was too cowardly to stop and face me.

'Stop,' I screamed, 'Johnny, stop! Stop, for God's sake!' I called his name again and again. I ran through Osaka, bellowing a name he no longer used.

As was to be expected, the police stopped me. For disorderly conduct. I had been moving on the pavement at an 'improper speed', they said. 'Highly suspicious.' As was my strong accent and my Korean name – Yunho Kang could only be a criminal, for he was Korean, a Chōsenjin.

Tetsuya was waiting for me outside the police station. He leant against the car door, smoking a cigarette. When he saw me approaching, he took one last drag before throwing it (half smoked) onto the street. Some poor wretch would pick it up and finish it, he said, and gestured towards the car.

'Get in.'

He'd had to leave the meeting early on my account, he told me. I had cost him the evening meal, the only good thing about meetings like these, which were a waste of time, he grumbled, nothing but a waste of time, always the same questions, the same answers, he wouldn't carry on with it for much longer. He sighed.

'They said you were running riot.'

I shook my head. I wasn't, I said. I was merely running. That was my crime: moving too quickly.

Tetsuya laughed. I wasn't the first person they had booked for moving too quickly, he said. I should be careful; there was a speed limit for pedestrians in Japan. He grinned and told me not to worry.

'You were in the wrong place at the wrong time. It's happened to all of us.'

And it happened to Koreans far more frequently than all the rest, he added with a sigh. What other choice did they have but to emigrate? All public administration roles were reserved for natives. Koreans couldn't be officials or train drivers. They even had a hard time in the private sector. The large companies either excluded them from the application process or fired them as soon as they found out their heritage.

'It doesn't bother me that I'm not allowed to work for one of the Zaibatsu monopolies,' said Tetsuya. 'My dream was to become a doctor. Even as a child, I was fascinated by illnesses. In Andong, where I grew up, my grandfather was a healer. He brewed tinctures and potions, sold herbs and made a fortune doing it. One day, out of the blue, he died, and a fight broke out over his inheritance.'

The inheritance dispute lasted many years, and by the time a settlement was made, nothing was left of the fortune. Tetsuya's father, unable to find work in Andong, had to emigrate to Japan. People said that the streets of Tokyo were paved with gold and that no one need go hungry there. That wasn't quite the case, but he did find a job. Whenever he managed to save some money, he sent it back home. The medical books, tables and pictures were all that had remained from the inheritance, and Tetsuya grew up among them.

'I wanted to follow in my grandfather's footsteps, but my mother sent my brother and me – he was fifteen, and I twelve – to join my father in Japan. I started work in a shoe factory. Then my father died, and a short while later my mother too, and I was released from the responsibility of sending money to Korea.'

We had reached a district I was unfamiliar with. The houses were bigger, the façades new, the streets clean. There were no beggars on the corners, no hunched old women. No scrap metal in the alleyways. No groups of children running through the neighbourhood, left to their own devices. The only resemblance to Ikaino was the washing fluttering on the line, but even that seemed whiter.

The Sōren headquarters had sent numbers, said Tetsuya carefully, quotas that they were supposed to meet within the next six months. The rebuilding was far from complete; the People's Republic needed teachers, doctors, engineers and labourers, especially labourers.

He asked: 'Have you heard the saying: after a house burns down, hold on to the nails? Well, they're currently in the process of pulling the nails out of the ruins.' I shouldn't believe everything I read in the papers, he said, the reports were exaggerated, sugar-coated. His cousin had emigrated to North Korea a year ago, on the very first ship. In the beginning he had written often and regularly: he reported that his family of four had been allocated a one-bedroom apartment in the north. It was on the fourth floor, the building new and even equipped with a WC. But then they had discovered they couldn't actually use the toilet, because there was no running water. The taps and basins were merely decorative, useless mock-ups.

They had to hurry down to the river at daybreak to fill buckets; it had to be at first light, because later the villagers would wash their clothes in the river and the water would no longer be drinkable. The used, dirty water had to be carried back down all four floors and discarded behind the building. The food wasn't good either, he and the children were sick in turns; they were constantly requesting a doctor's visit, but even that didn't help much, because the medicine was useless.

We came to a halt in front of the pachinko hall, but Tetsuya made no move to get out of the car. He didn't want me to get the wrong idea, he said, the homecomers wouldn't starve, but they certainly weren't getting meat every day either. The beautiful apartments in Pyongyang had all been filled, and from now on the rest would have to live in barracks or repurposed gymnasiums.

'And how could it be any different? It's not even seven years since the end of the civil war, the country hasn't yet recovered from the devastation.'

He pulled the key out of the ignition and opened the car door. We got out and paused in front of the unremarkable grey door to the pachinko hall; the small, angular neon sign wasn't yet holding its own against the remaining daylight. Tetsuya seemed lost in thought. When I reached out to open the door, he grabbed my arm.

'I tried to find out whether they were just rumours, stories circulated by Mindan activists with the intention of scaring people away, but no one wanted to comment.'

He offered me a cigarette, I shook my head.

'They're the good American ones,' he said, 'I'd never offer you the bad Japanese ones.'

He produced a lighter out of his trouser pocket; let it rest on the palm of his hand, stared at it. With the unlit cigarette in the corner of his mouth, he said that perhaps North Korea had taken on too much, fifty thousand hungry people, thirty thousand unemployed and twenty thousand children, all of them wanting to be cared for; this avalanche had descended on the People's Republic from one day to the next. It was one thing to feed, clothe and give money to fifty homecomers, but five hundred was a different matter, five thousand a completely different matter, and fifty thousand . . .

'The locals are afraid they'll have to move out of their apartments to make room for the newcomers. After all, hospitality demands that guests be offered the best and most beautiful of everything. And the newcomers, for their part, could have behaved better . . . Just because they have papers giving them special rights, it doesn't mean they should exploit the situation. It's not wise to push in front, waving your ID round.'

He lit the cigarette and threw the match onto the street.

'The government has begun to question the new comrades' beliefs. Whether they've come from Japan because they believe in the communist state, or because they want to get ahead on false pretences.'

Ideologically impeccable comrades or political criminals? This was the question that would be asked more and more frequently, he said. There had already been arrests . . .

Tetsuya took a long drag of his cigarette. He had been waiting six months now for a letter from his cousin, he told me. He put his hand on my shoulder.

'My advice to you, Yunho, is not to sign up. Stay here.'

13

It was cold on that May day, surprisingly cold and stormy. Tetsuya's hair billowed in the wind and blew into his face; he had given up on brushing it out of his eyes, and so it seemed like I was talking to the back of his head – which was fine with me, because I didn't know how to tell him that it wasn't me who was planning to emigrate, but his daughter.

All of a sudden it began to rain. Just isolated, oval drops at first, yet they soon turned into round, heavy ones. Bit by bit the rain smoothed down Tetsuya's rebellious curls, even though they put up a valiant defence, balancing the water buds on their arches.

It was clear to me that I owed him the truth; of all the practices between humans, the one most familiar to me is that of recompense, the business of debt. Before I had begun to owe Tetsuya something, I had been indebted to Eve, Johnny and Director Kim. I had owed the latter for a roof over my head, food in my belly and clothes on my back, and thanks to the others I at least had a home. My entire life was and is an accumulation of debts; ever since my birth, I have led the existence of a debtor.

I live a life that does not belong to me, but instead to those who make it possible; it is a cold, distant life, the life of an outsider. Again and again, in such a life, you find yourself beneath a glass globe with just a limited number of feelings and reactions at your disposal, because only these will guarantee that the glass doesn't shatter; for this, your benefactor's face is a seismograph. Avoiding the tremble of the needle is the commitment you have made, the contract you were born into. Time, chance, moments of sadness and of happiness, even destiny; these things are no longer available to you, they don't belong to you and they never did. Everything that you are is merely borrowed, whether you are content, hopeful, melancholy, joyful, cocky, exuberant, inconsolable, in love – especially in love. As a debtor, it is impossible to love truly and wholeheartedly, because the act of loving will inevitably lead you out of the glasshouse, thereby endangering the system and your very existence.

Gratitude is the only feeling the debtor can possess and give, in exchange for a little freedom.

I knew what my obligation was, and I fulfilled it, brushing aside the scruples I felt. I didn't owe Eiko anything, but I owed her father everything. Why had I hesitated? Probably my salary had gone to my head, my financial security. It had made me believe I could lay gratitude aside, renounce it.

Tetsuya barely reacted to my revelation. I was expecting shock, indignation and fury; I expected him to jump into his car and drive home to read his unruly daughter the riot act. Instead, he nodded; he didn't seem surprised, or even angry, just sad. His youngest had always been very independent, he said, she had her own mind and only listened when it suited her. To change her would be as impossible as driving a herd of cows through a mouse hole. She had inherited this stubbornness from him, he added with a sigh. Along with her admiration for General Kim Il-sung. And how could she fail to idolize him; in class she was told unceasingly about his heroic acts and the 'glorious revolution', the school walls were plastered with his pictures. She had learnt from a young age to be grateful to him, after all, he had fought for an independent Korea, for her homeland. She probably thought she owed him for a lot of things, no, for everything: every Korean word she knew, her entire Korean self. Tetsuya shook his head slowly. He couldn't blame her for that, it had been his mistake, he should never have let things go this far.

Tetsuya was talking more to himself than to me; he seemed to have forgotten I was there. He didn't exchange another word with me that evening. When I went to look for him in his office the following morning, Hiro, the bookkeeper, said he had gone home hours ago; there was a dagger concealed in his smile.

I could hear them even from a distance. Tetsuya was speaking calmly, as composed as ever, Eiko was upset, her voice cracking, and Naoko was silent; I was sure she was there, she just preferred not to take sides. I waited outside the front door, even though I knew that loitering on the street would make me look suspicious; I was certain there was a law against Koreans 'idling in public spaces'. But I didn't want to go to my room until the argument had subsided.

I can no longer remember how long I eavesdropped for, but I do remember that their voices transformed increasingly into independent people the longer I listened to them: Eiko's changed from the voice of a girl into that of a mature, courageous woman, a resistance fighter, fearless and unflinching. Naoko's was drained, tired and fearful, like a withered old woman in the semi-darkness, giving thanks for the blows and mouldy food thrown her way. Tetsuya's developed from the voice of an impassioned, energetic idealist to that of an embittered opportunist, cowardly and weak. By the end, I was

269

on Eiko's side, not her parents', although admittedly I didn't understand every facet of their argument; I filled in the gaps later.

Tetsuya and Eiko were arguing about an event in Japan that was unknown to me, because it had taken place long before my arrival in Osaka – long before my birth, even – and had made its way from mouth to mouth in Korea in the form of half-truths; back then, those who stayed didn't care about the fate of the émigrés, no different from today. Once you leave the inner circle and break the bond with your homeland, you are no longer welcome; you are unwanted, a foreigner.

From father and daughter Yamamoto, I discovered that this event was of great significance for the Zainichi, still influencing their view of Japan even forty years on, and, as a result, also their decision whether to leave the island or stay: the Great Kantō earthquake, which in 1923 flattened the port city of Yokohama as well as large parts of Tokyo. After the earthquake (measuring 7.9 in magnitude) had torn apart the densely built-up areas, crumbling even the modern brick buildings, large blazes ravaged the Kantō plain for two whole days, fed by exploding underground gas lines and the strong winds of the approaching typhoon; Sagami Bay was engulfed by a tsunami.

The earthquake occurred at lunchtime, an unfortunate moment. While the inhabitants of Honshū were busy preparing their meals over the tamed heat of their stoves, the flames were suddenly set free. The furnishings were the first to catch fire, followed by the external walls, then the neighbouring dwellings. The wooden Japanese houses turned into torches and set both themselves and their immediate neighbours alight, until the only buildings left standing in Tokyo were those made of steel. Because the water mains were destroyed, it took days before all the flames were extinguished. Two million people became homeless, more than half of Tokyo's population, and a hundred thousand died, the majority of them in firestorms.

Many Zainichi, however, fell victim not to the earthquake, but to the self-proclaimed vigilante groups which formed in the hours following the first shocks. These groups came together to check everything was in order in their neighbourhoods and to protect the inhabitants from the Koreans, who they alleged had poisoned the well water. This lie unleashed hysteria, and the hysteria, in turn, unleashed new rumours. Subterranean explosions became bomb attacks or 'signals' from 'enemy forces', others believed that the thick clouds of smoke in the south originated from an exploded powder house, and the clouds in the north-east from a detonated arms factory. In the days that followed, the police received reports of 'mysterious symbols' found on the side of a building, written in white chalk. Could they be secret messages, or military communications calling for an attack on Tokyo? The police investigated and came to the conclusion that the symbols really were a code, albeit a civilian one: the abbreviations served as memory aids, left behind by tofu deliverymen and newspaper boys, who didn't want to forget where they needed to collect payment and where they didn't. That very same night, small flyers were distributed, strips of paper bearing allegations that the Koreans had left the symbols, that they were planning a number of attacks on the population. Someone claimed to have witnessed one of them painting the signs on a building wall. Another 'witness' testified that he had seen a Korean steal a police uniform and, disguised as a guardian of the law, rape ten women. This one rapist then turned into an entire gang, clad in stolen police uniforms and with red cloths

271

tied around their arms (communists, therefore?), rampaging through Tokyo.

After that, most people were no longer willing to wait for protection: in the name of safety, the self-appointed vigilante groups hunted down anyone who looked Korean, who was dressed like a Korean, acted Korean or had a Korean accent, even if he came from Okinawa; the innocent were stabbed with improvised spears carved from bamboo, or impaled with inherited swords – a massacre broke out. If war is a system that forces those within it to accept dying and death, then this one took a toll of several hundred; some say thousands.

On 9 September, eight days after the earthquake, the police arrested four people in Tokyo who they believed had put the murderous rumours into circulation: a shop boy, a rickshaw driver, a nanny and a launderer.

'Your lips may be curved, but mind you speak straight words.'

It was, of all days, on the 35th anniversary of the Great Kantō Earthquake, on 1 September 1958, that an eighteen-year-old Korean boy called Ri was arrested, accused of having raped and murdered two Japanese schoolgirls. He became famous not just for the murders, but also for the fifty-three books, all translated works of world literature, which he had stolen from the school library – not to sell, but to read. Camus' *The Outsider* made a particular impression on him; he compared himself with Meursault and declared that he, like that character, was a murderer without motive. Ri's Japanese defence lawyer tried to cast his crimes in a different light: Ri had killed the girls because, as a Korean, it was the only way he was able to express his rage and frustration towards the society that oppressed him, his family and his fellow countrymen.

Ri immediately disagreed. He wasn't merely comparable to Meursault, he *was* Meursault. He insisted that he had killed the schoolgirls without reason. He also rejected the resulting speculation that it had to do with his Catholic faith, or, in other words, with his 'barbaric religion'.

Sōren, of course, was quick to distance itself from him. Ri had never been a member of the organization, they said, and neither had his parents nor his brothers. He had grown up as the only Korean in a purely Japanese neighbourhood and didn't even speak Korean. Yamada even made it known that any Sōren member who gave Ri financial or emotional support, visited him in prison (Ri began to learn Korean during his imprisonment) or corresponded with him would be expelled from the league.

Despite her loyalty to Sōren, Eiko was convinced of Ri's innocence. It couldn't be a coincidence, she cried, that he had been arrested on the anniversary of the earthquake. In response, Tetsuya referred to the diary entries that had been found, in which Ri allegedly described the murders in detail. His daughter countered not with Camus, but with Dostoevsky: the murders served a higher purpose, and were therefore justified and couldn't be judged as senseless. What higher purpose? asked her father, shocked. To inform the Japanese people about the deplorable state of affairs and terrible conditions the Zainichi were subjected to in Japan.

'If Ri hadn't turned himself in, we would still be suffering, condemned to silence.'

'We?'

Tetsuya was staggered.

Just like in Meursault's case, Ri's guilt wasn't questioned, explained Eiko. He was a Korean, therefore he was guilty. He was condemned even before they arrested him and broadcast his likeness all over Japan, not just in the newspapers, but on television too. In every shop window that had a television for sale, people saw the face of a murderer. And just like Meursault he would be executed, all that remained was for the verdict to be enforced. But he gave himself up and confessed to the murders, Eiko's mother quietly interjected. He denied the rapes to the last, retorted her daughter.

'Will we ever be anything other than the people who destroy the balance of the day?'

She was tired of being afraid of every natural catastrophe, she said; tired of being told that she *had* to be afraid of nature's rebelliousness. She had been born into this situation, this conflict; she had never had a choice, until now. Now it was down to her to no longer belong to a weak, vulnerable minority, but instead to a strong, prominent majority. At long last, she too had the opportunity to lead an independent existence! And she was able to correct the mistake made by her parents, who were content with living life as 'intruders'. How could she let a chance like this slip through her fingers?

I don't know whether she noticed me as she ran past into the open air, for I quickly looked away. I was ashamed of her behaviour, of this tirade of disobedience, even though, and I can admit this now, it impressed me too; perhaps I was ashamed of my budding admiration for her.

When I went inside the house, Tetsuya and Naoko were nowhere to be seen. I crept up to the first floor, nudged open the door to our room and left it ajar; I didn't want to risk breaking the silence which had suddenly descended upon the Yamamoto family residence.

The following day was like any other, with one exception: Tetsuya asked me to drive him to the Korean school, apparently he was expected there. As I didn't know where it was, he had to guide me through the tangle of streets; finally it appeared, on the outskirts of the city.

A school bus was parked in front of the new building, which had concrete walls and steel railings. It would resist any earthquake, said Tetsuya proudly; he had contributed a 'considerable sum' to its construction. The large windows sparkled in the sunlight, and in the schoolyard the children were playing in their new uniforms. Although the classes were separated by gender, the schoolhouse wasn't.

I looked around, but couldn't spot Eiko. Tetsuya didn't even look for her; he strode ahead of me into the building, and I hurried after, so as not to lose sight of him. In a long corridor, he veered to the right. Next to the coat rack with its many wall hooks, there was an inconspicuous door, which he knocked on. 'Come in,' called a voice from inside. He waved me over, signalling for me to join him, and stepped in.

The man, who had been sitting in front of an immense wooden desk, stood up; he reminded me of a viper slithering over a wall. He made a prolonged and deep bow before Tetsuya, and Tetsuya did the same before him, which gave me the opportunity to quickly look around. The director's office was sparsely furnished: there was a long shelf unit along the wall at shoulder-height, with the books piled up on top of each other. In the centre of the room stood two dark leather armchairs and a narrow couch, and between them was a low, dark-stained table, stacked with magazines which I recognized as the ones from North Korea. On the whitewashed wall hung a portrait of a man whom I had heard a great deal about, but whose face I saw properly for the first time that afternoon: Kim Il-sung.

In South Korea, images of the General were forbidden. If

you were caught with a photo of him, you could be locked up in prison for life for 'communist agitation'. Only malicious, anti-North Korean caricatures were permitted, and the focal point of these drawings was the boil on Kim's neck, which was alleged to be a malignant tumour; probably even they, the caricaturists, had never seen a picture of Kim. Any foreign publications to be distributed in the South were inspected by the censorship authority and all pictures of Kim adorned with a large black splodge, just as any articles about North Korea were removed from the magazines, leaving behind only the inside edge of the pages. They were sometimes cut out with a knife, but often simply torn out, meaning that a part would be missing from the subsequent *Newsweek* article. Kim Il-sung's existence contaminated all life in South Korea, even the everyday life of privileged foreigners.

I was astounded by how young he looked; compared to his adversary, Syngman Rhee, he was a child.

'That's General Kim Il-sung,' said the director, noticing my stare. He invited us to sit down on the couch.

'Is this the first time you've seen him?'

Clearly he was familiar with South Korean practices, but before I could answer, there was a knock at the door. He quickly got up and opened it.

Ayumi's face was red, as though she had been running, and her hair was dishevelled. She had a tray in her hand, bearing a pot of tea and *daifuku*, Japanese rice cakes with a sweet bean filling. She poured the tea and sat down on the vacant chair.

'I presume this is about your daughter?' asked Director Masaki.

Tetsuya nodded.

'She's signed up for the emigration,' explained Ayumi. As

she spoke, she kept her eyes lowered as though to avoid Tetsuya's angry stare.

'And that's a problem?'

Masaki took a sip of *genmaicha*. He didn't touch the *daifuku*.

'The problem is that she acted without authority,' says Tetsuya. 'She added her name to the list without discussing it with me or her mother.'

'That was a mistake. She should have consulted you, of course.'

Director Masaki shook his head slowly. He took a pack of cigarettes out of his jacket pocket and nodded to Ayumi, who jumped to her feet, took a heavy glass ashtray down from a shelf and placed it on the coffee table. Masaki proffered the open pack first to Tetsuya and then to me. We both took a cigarette. He didn't offer one to Ayumi; women weren't supposed to smoke in public, especially not in front of a superior.

'Can't my daughter's name be taken off the list?' Tetsuya exhaled the smoke towards the window. 'Sometimes the simplest solutions are the best ones.'

Masaki shook his head slowly. That wouldn't be possible, he said. The lists with the homecomers' names and signatures were in the Red Cross's possession. This was to deter any suspicion that they could be manipulated.

'Manipulated?' asked Tetsuya in surprise.

Masaki nodded.

'Once there were names on the list that should never have been there: the family hadn't applied to leave. The matter culminated in a murder and an arrest.'

He took a long drag of the cigarette.

'Since then, we don't keep the lists ourselves. A simple but effective measure.'

He smiled.

'So the list with my daughter's name isn't in the school?'

'No.'

'The Japanese Red Cross has it?'

'No. The International Committee of the Red Cross.'

'The International Committee of the Red Cross?'

Tetsuya looked stunned.

'An organization that is beyond any suspicion,' replied Masaki.

'So what does that mean for my daughter?'

'It means she can leave if she wants to. No one will stop her.'

'No one?'

'If she has all the necessary documents with her, she'll be allowed to board the ship.'

Tetsuya's eyes widened.

'There's nothing we can do to stop her leaving the country?'

Masaki glanced at Ayumi.

'You can ask your daughter to reconsider. But you can't have her name removed from the list, no.'

Suddenly, Ayumi spoke up.

'It wouldn't look good, either, considering that Eiko belongs to the Homecomers' Brigade.'

'What's the Homecomers' Brigade?'

I went red; the question had slipped out. Ayumi gave me a reassuring smile.

'Only the best schoolboys and schoolgirls are part of the Homecomers' Brigade. They inform their fellow students about the Great Homecoming and are available to answer questions.'

'Yes, exactly, "they're available to answer questions". It was never agreed that they'd board the ships themselves.'

Tetsuya was furious. I knew him well enough to know that

he was only pretending to be calm; in truth he was boiling with anger. He had been trembling inwardly even as he stepped into the director's office, but now that Masaki and Ayumi had told him to his face that nothing could be done, he was struggling to contain his rage.

He dropped his cigarette onto the rug, stubbed it out with his foot and headed towards the door without any word of goodbye, his hip colliding with the metal edge of the desk as he went; the resulting sound, an oddly high-pitched tone, filled the room like a gong announcing the conclusion of a ceremony.

To my astonishment, Masaki extended his hand to me in farewell. He was sorry, he said, that he couldn't do more for the Yamamoto family, and asked me to pass this on to Mr Yamamoto. Eiko would change her mind, she just needed to be persuaded. She or her friend. An idea seemed to strike him. He squeezed my hand a second time. It would be much easier to convince her to stay if she had to undertake the journey alone. Was she not alone? I asked. Masaki shook his head. Her friend had signed up too. He looked at Ayumi questioningly.

'Senko Yamada.'

'That's right. Little Yamada.'

He nodded to me.

'Perhaps she might be easier to convince.'

Tetsuya had left without me, the car park was empty. Only then did I notice that the building site was actually like a small desert – one could also say: a deserted sandy beach. It would fill over the months and years to come, with companies that would spring up from one day to the next and end their existence from one day to the next, and every few years their dwellings too would be torn down, making way for other new buildings and new companies, for the winners, not the losers, of modern Japan.

I stood there, undecided; I didn't know how to get to Ikaino or which bus I should take. Suddenly, I heard a familiar voice.

'I didn't expect to see you here,' said Eiko, 'Father, yes, but not you.'

She eyed me closely.

'Has he stood you up?'

Her laughter was infectious; I couldn't help but laugh too.

'He drove off without me. It's your fault.'

'My fault? Why is it my fault? What have *I* done?'

Perhaps it was because I treated her like an adult, but she behaved differently with me. She was more confident, more self-assured. I, on the other hand, was still grinning idiotically like a schoolboy. A moron.

'You know very well that your travel plans aren't exactly to your father's liking.'

'My travel plans!'

She laughed so hard that she had to lean against me. Then, all of a sudden, she turned serious.

'And you know very well that once I'm there, I can't come back.'

'What do you mean? Why not?'

I knew, of course, that it wasn't possible to simply travel from North Korea to South Korea. But why shouldn't someone be able to travel from North Korea to Japan? Was the Great Homecoming not a normal departure?

Eiko shook her head emphatically. Before boarding the ship, she told me, they would have to sign a declaration that they would never again set foot on Japanese soil. Besides, it wasn't possible anyway, because the ships only travelled in one direction.

'And in North Korea they just evaporate into thin air?'

'They continue on to the Soviet Union, you clown. Back to their homeland.'

I certainly wasn't trying to crack jokes. Now I understood why Tetsuya had been so worked up; he was on the verge of losing his daughter. Unless he accompanied her, that is, but he had no interest in the North, he wanted to go to the South, as he had told me many times, to find his brother and give him the money he had saved and which he was sure to urgently need. And besides, he wasn't a North Korean, his family was from the south-east, from the Daegu region; he had embraced me when I said I spent the post-war years there, before ending up in Seoul. We had drunk *makgŏlli*, one bottle after the next, and I had told him about the hut, the tiny hut made of cardboard, a few wooden slats and mud, which I had called my home, and he patted me on the shoulder and mumbled that I had a new home now, not a home country, perhaps, but a home nonetheless, here with him in Ikaino.

'It will hurt your father a great deal if he can't even visit you . . .'

Her expression darkened. She turned away from me and stared into the distance. I couldn't help but think of the sentence: 'I realized that I had destroyed the natural balance of the day, the exceptional silence of a beach where I had once been happy.' I wondered whether this silence resembled the one that Meursault had experienced.

Suddenly she turned to me and said: 'I don't have a choice. I'm not deciding against my family, but *for* a future. I'm choosing hope. I'm sick of not having any, do you understand?'

She wrapped her arms around her bulging schoolbag, which

refused to close. I offered to take it for her, but she shook her head. She was used to taking her books for a walk, she said. She brushed the strands of hair that had fallen into her face behind her ear – the gesture reminded me of Ayumi. 'Of course I could pretend to be Japanese,' she continued, 'disappear into the crowd. That would probably be the easiest solution.'

'How would you do that?'

Sometimes I really was as simple-minded as a frog in a well.

'I already have a Japanese name. All I would need to do is marry a Japanese man and move away from Osaka. I would never be able to tell my children where I come from, of course, or what their roots are. And I'd have to pray that the in-laws wouldn't ask any awkward questions before the wedding. I wouldn't be able to see my parents any more either. I would have to disown anything Korean, and forget the existence of this land I once called home.'

She rolled the circular stone in front of her feet back and forth.

'Perhaps it wouldn't even have to go that far, perhaps I wouldn't have to completely deny my roots – I'd have to keep my children's heritage a secret from them, sure, but not from my husband. Mother and Father speak Japanese most of the time anyway. And they can't read either in Korean or Japanese.'

A Black Eye, Tetsuya was a Black Eye! As soon as she said it, it was like the scales fell from my eyes. Of course! That was why he took me along with him everywhere, why I had to read everything out and write everything up for him; it wasn't just about having a witness, about making himself look important, he needed me because I translated the world of strange symbols into sounds that he could respond to.

'You see,' Eiko bent down, picked the stone up from the

282

ground and placed it in the palm of her hand, 'I'll have to say goodbye to my father either way. As a Japanese daughter-in-law I might not want to see him again even if I had the opportunity. I'd be embarrassed by him, him and his Korean habits. But as a North Korean daughter I would write letters to him, I would remember him with pride and speak lovingly about his idiosyncrasies.'

She took my hand, opened my fingers and placed the stone in the centre of my palm.

'I know Ri is guilty. Of course he's a murderer, and of course the girls didn't deserve to die so young and in such a terrible way.'

She lifted her head and looked at me. Behind her, the sun was setting, and I didn't know in which direction lay the only street I knew in Osaka.

'But I stand by what I said. He's also innocent, because he was dead already when he murdered them. He's a victim, just like them. He was killed bit by bit by the society he was born into: every time they rejected him as an outsider, an intruder.'

The day's remaining light was reflected in her eyes.

'I've read *The Outsider* a good three times, perhaps even four. I know the Japanese translation off by heart. At first I didn't understand Camus. The last sentence in particular confused me. I read it again and again, but still didn't understand it. Not because I'm not clever enough, but because I didn't *want* to understand. Meursault gives in to hopelessness. He surrenders himself to it. Becomes one with it. But *I* choose hope.'

She laughed; I listened to her laughter, her contagious laughter.

'Can you blame me for choosing hope?'

She turned on her heels like a child, like an unburdened

283

child. She turned on her heels with her arms up in the air, an unburdened, happy child.

'Yunho, yesterday was a great day for Eiko Yamamoto! She changed her destiny!'

She bowed, as though she were standing on a stage. The imaginary audience and I were about to applaud when cries rang out from the other side of the street.

'The bus is here!'

Eiko clapped her hands.

'Would you like to ride with us?'

The girls formed a guard of honour, letting Eiko board the bus first and choose the best seat. She guided me to the back row, to the seats in the middle, clearly wanting to keep all her fellow passengers in sight. One of them she waved over: she wanted Mio Kobayashi to sit between us.

Mio was the opposite of Eiko, small and plump with a round face and metal-rimmed glasses perched on her nose. The red clasp in her hair made her look very young, no older than fourteen; I was surprised that she and Eiko were in the same class. She was very shy, and didn't study me like her classmates did – with a certain relish, with unconcealed curiosity – the kind of curiosity one might apportion to an object, not a human being. She had a heavy stutter, which made it difficult to get her to speak, but in any case it was Eiko who spoke, who dictated the answers to Mio.

Had she made a decision at last, asked Eiko, had she spoken to her parents? Mio shook her head. Eiko gave her a reproachful stare, yet seemed unsurprised. She couldn't put it off forever, she said. Although, Eiko corrected herself, that depended on her age.

'How old are you?'

'Seventeen.'

'When are you turning eighteen?'

Mio didn't answer.

'In two days,' called the girl on the front seat, Eiko's best friend, Senko Yamada, 'it's her birthday two days from now!'

Eiko gave Senko a contented nod.

'Then we don't need your parents' approval, your signature will be enough – *if* you want to come, that is. And you do want to, don't you?'

Mio didn't look up. She stared at the school bag in her lap; I had the feeling she was praying.

Eiko's mouth contorted into a mocking smile. Mio was afraid, she explained to me, and that was understandable considering her mother was Japanese, albeit one who was willing to spend her life with a Korean. But her father, and at this point Eiko's voice and expression cooled noticeably, was worse than any Japanese person. He was a writer, she continued, who had published his final essays in a Korean journal that was swiftly banned by the Americans, by General Douglas MacArthur, the man who had the People's Army in Incheon run down by his tanks.

'It's fair to suspect that Minoru Kobayashi wrote these texts in Korean because he was out of luck with his Japanese ones.'

She turned to me.

'You see, Yunho, in the early 1930s, shortly after Japan founded Manchukuo, Mio's father was considered a major literary talent. He was one of the literary stars of Greater Japan! He had all the right prerequisites: a foreign birthplace and "exotic" stories.'

She giggled.

'I'm not the one who thinks they're exotic! That's what the Japanese critics called them. And not just the stories, but also the way he used the Japanese language. He learnt it in Korea, as the son of a *kisaeng*, a Korean geisha. Allegedly his father was a distant relative of the king.'

She gave Mio a little shove –

'This is your grandfather we're talking about!'

– and winked at her.

'He probably grew up in well-to-do circumstances, but apparently your geisha grandmother was very unstable. Tantrums, screaming fits. No wonder no one wanted to marry her. But thanks to his papa he had enough to eat, and silk shirts and trousers, and when he got older he studied at the Japanese high school. Presumably he learnt Japanese from the children in the neighbourhood, the migrants who had come to Korea in the early 1920s.'

You couldn't blame the critics for calling his stories exotic, I felt the same way when I read his work; Kobayashi wrote autobiographical texts, and his life story was certainly impressive. After finishing high school, like so many Koreans back then he went to study in Tokyo. At university, he befriended Japanese communists and anarchists, and after news had spread that the anarchists' bomb attack had been successful, that General Yoshinori Shirakawa had been killed, he followed them to Shanghai in order to take part in the revolution. These 'successes' lured in young men like Kobayashi, because they also attracted young women – the Korean anarchists were very popular with the female sex, and had no shortage of amorous propositions.

After two years of pursuits and adventures, Kobayashi was summoned back to Korea by his mother, to get married. But instead of focusing his attentions on his bride-to-be, who was certainly to his liking, he began an affair with an older, married Japanese woman. The romance was exposed, his engagement to the Korean virgin called off, and the betrayed husband hauled young Kobayashi in front of a judge. Only on the condition that the criminal leave Korea and never return was it possible to lay the matter to rest.

Kobayashi decided to settle in Tokyo. He had considered Shanghai, but his novella, which had been published in a prestigious literary journal in Japan, had garnered so many good reviews that he believed he had a more interesting, glittering future in Hirohito's capital. Soon after his arrival, he was disabused of this notion: not only were his other texts rejected with the justification that his Japanese wasn't 'ripe' enough for a 'writer of distinction', but as a Korean and former anarchist he was watched around the clock. He couldn't take a single step without being followed by a spy, and the secret policemen who followed hot on his heels made sure he didn't forget he was under surveillance. They stormed into his home on a weekly basis, threw him out onto the street regardless of whether he was half-naked or dressed, rummaged through his drawers and cupboards, emptied his bookcases and scattered his books all over the apartment; his notebooks and literary drafts were all confiscated. Then the Second World War broke out. A few years later, he met Mio's mother and married her.

'During the Second World War, he returned to Korea and travelled through the villages, recruiting the hungry and desperate. Men and women.'

Eiko's eyes narrowed.

'People say that most of them worked in Japanese ammunition factories. But some, especially the young women, were locked up in brothels and forced into prostitution.'

She grabbed Mio's chin.

'Your father was a rotten traitor who got rich at his

countrymen's expense. Who knows how many yen he got per girl. He was a vile, miserable traitor.'

Eiko pinched Mio's mouth together.

'Or do you see it differently?'

Mio shook her head. 'N-no,' she stuttered. Eiko loosened her grip.

'You owe it to your homeland to make reparations. And you owe us your loyalty. Are you ready to give us proof of it?'

Mio nodded vigorously. Eiko signalled to Senko, who pulled a piece of paper and a pencil from her bag and handed both to her friend.

'That's enough.'

I couldn't stay silent any longer. Eiko looked at me, stunned and affronted, but immediately let go of Mio. The girl slowly rubbed her damp cheeks and closed her reddened eyes. I put my arm around her protectively and tried to calm her down. Eiko shot me a contemptuous glance, then jumped up and went to sit in the front row with Senko. Both of them pretended to ignore Mio and me.

After we had stared out of the window in silence for a while, Mio asked shyly: 'You're from South Korea?'

I nodded.

'Are you in Japan on business?'

'No.'

I couldn't help but smile.

'Then you're on holiday?'

'Holiday?'

I was bewildered. Raucous laughter rose up from the front seats.

'Sure, Mr Kang is on holiday!'

Mio stuttered.

'Be–be–because . . .'

'Because?'

I was keen to hear the explanation.

'Be–be–because . . .'

She guessed I wasn't a refugee, she said, because there was no longer any reason to flee, not now that the dictator had abdicated and the 'democratic spring' had been proclaimed . . .

'Abdicated, did you hear that? Rhee has abdicated!'

Eiko and Senko held their stomachs with laughter. 'Mio,' they cried out eventually, 'Syngman Rhee can't abdicate, he's not a king!'

Mio's cheeks flushed a deep red.

'Yes, of c–c–course. Step–p–p–ed down. Rhee has step–p–p–ed down.'

I was only just able to fit in the question, 'When?', and catch the answer, 'Two or three weeks ago', before the bus stopped, 'Last stop!', and the universal decampment, the industrious locating of jackets, bags and hats, made any further enquiries impossible.

I had to speak to Eve right away. Did she know about Rhee stepping down? And if she did, how long had she known? Why hadn't she said anything to me? And what about Johnny? Did he know that Rhee was now a thing of the past? Did Eve want to return to South Korea without us? Or did she not want to go home at all? Did I even want to go home still? Was my home still my home?

While a typhoon of seemingly unanswerable questions raged in my head, I struggled to get off the bus, an impossible task considering that the numerous chattering girls began to move in slow motion – even the bus driver, a broad, good-natured fellow with a sun-tanned face who had smiled throughout the entire journey, raised his voice: 'Quickly quickly quickly! Bballi bballi bballi! This is a bus, not a café!'

Finally, I found myself in the open air. In the distance, I spotted a four-storey building which looked familiar. I looked around for Eiko. She and Senko had planted themselves in front of Mio. I looked at the list in Senko's hand; the schoolgirl was clearly being forced to sign by the Homecomers' Brigade . . .

But I couldn't help Mio, I had something more important to do.

14

It must seem absurd to you that a complete stranger, especially someone from a lost time, is telling you about the life of a dead woman. A woman who, as he can say today with the confidence that only age brings, was the love of his life. It's painful for me to say this; I'm ashamed of my past and present self. I didn't know it back then; back then I thought she would be one of many, the first, but not the only. I fell in love again, of course – more seldom than I expected, for how often do you encounter a person whom you trust implicitly, to whom you want to entrust yourself unconditionally? – but the state of being in love never transformed into love, never absorbed me: I stayed *I* too much, let too little of myself go.

I remember reading that happiness destroys us, that it takes away our identity. Perhaps you will understand my unhappiness better if I tell you that I experienced this happiness only with Eve.

I persuaded myself, convinced myself, that she hadn't yet heard of President Rhee's resignation, that I would surprise her with the news – even though this was unlikely, because she lived and breathed her homeland. On the other hand, I couldn't imagine that she would have kept this news from Johnny and me, perhaps from Johnny – I had noticed that they barely talked any more, that they avoided one another – but not from me.

I was worked up, incredibly so. My hands were cold and damp from nerves. Would she hug me with relief? Would she kiss me for joy? Would I return her kisses? My legs quickened, without me having expressly ordered them to, and I tried to slow down; I didn't want to be arrested a second time for a pavement-speeding violation, but even at a walking pace I fidgeted to such an extent that I feared attracting the attention of a policeman.

Missu Satō's tiny shop finally appeared ahead, but moments before I reached my destination, heavy doubts descended. Was it really possible that Eve hadn't heard about Rhee's resignation? If she knew about it, why hadn't she told me? Why had she never spoken to me or us about it? Was she planning to return to South Korea alone? The fact that she didn't want to stay in Japan was common knowledge, to me and everyone she talked to; not a single day passed when Osaka didn't fall short compared with Seoul. Even though, recently, she had begun to complain more fiercely and loudly about 'the Koreans', who she considered more insolent and bad-mannered than the Japanese. Did she want to secretly flee her exile? Had she had enough of Johnny and me? Enough of *me*? If that were the case, I thought to myself, completely deflated by this point, it would be better not to confront her, for then I could retreat from our relationship without losing face, and since our arrival in Ikaino it could no longer be called a relationship anyway; affection has to arrive before it can depart.

I watched Eve through the shop window, which held a display of rosy-pink plastic heads topped with wigs. Above the black manes were photographs, cut from magazines and stuck onto cardboard, of prominent, well-coiffed women. Eve was stand-ing in a cone of light, illuminated by the sunbeams that had found their way into the salon despite the jumble of heads.

Strangely, I have the feeling that this took place in autumn, for in my memory yellow, reddish-yellow and brown leaves lie at my feet; the trees are bare, and a cold, damp wind carrying the scent of the approaching winter streams into my nostrils. Then the afternoon dies, the setting sun turns into a moon and I into a part of the street, all I can hear is the gentle rustle of the leaves, which are whirled up before they flutter back down to the ground; I shiver.

Eve is busy sweeping the cut-off hair, the tips, curls and strands, into the middle of the room. She brushes the hair into a dustpan and empties the contents into the waste bin. Then, with a mop that she plunges repeatedly into a bucket of water, she begins to scrub the linoleum floor, which is starting to curl up at the edges. She mops not in straight lines, but in loops, painting circles and numbers, an eight, a three, a nine, numerous zeros; some spots remain untouched, but that doesn't bother her. Once she's finished, she takes a step back to survey her work – an image that is visible only for a short time, and exclusively for those who know of its existence.

Only now do I make my presence known. I tap on the windowpane. She looks up, waves and signals for me to wait outside until the floor has dried. I stand in front of the door, she at the other end of the salon, on the spot which is furthest from me. She shrugs her shoulders regretfully, shakes her head slowly from side to side and smiles. I return the smile, to show I understand why she isn't opening the door.

Suddenly it's early evening, and spring, the trees haven't yet shed their summer coats, even the cherry trees are still covered with a white fuzz; the alleyway is dry, not damp with fog, and the sun is shining down brightly from the sky. I'm wearing a short-sleeved shirt that Tetsuya gave to me, or was it Naoko who left it outside my bedroom door? My face is covered with sweat, I can taste it on my upper lip, feel the dampness in my armpits, my rib cage rises and falls heavily, my lungs barely keeping up with the breath, and out of the corner of my eye I see butterflies: blues, gossamer-winged. Once I realize that I'm sweating heavily, I hope that it will be a while longer before the floor can be walked on.

She bends down and checks it. Not just once, but a second and third time too. In more than one spot. She dabs at the surface with the hemline of her skirt. Eventually she looks up and signals to me that she's about to open the door. She approaches cautiously, still mistrusting the speed at which the floor has dried. She turns the key in the lock, pushes the door open vigorously and says, in an unfamiliar, honeyed tone, more cheerful than usual: 'What a surprise! I wasn't expecting you to come by.'

I nod eagerly while trying to discreetly wipe the sweat from my forehead with the back of my hand, with my fingertips, with the hems of my sleeves, and as I do this I stare at the walls, the floor, anything that isn't in her proximity; I don't know how to bring up the topic of Rhee's resignation and our possible return home. Noticing that something is weighing on my mind, she asks whether I'm in trouble, whether I need help. Whether something bad has happened. The concern in her voice is comforting, it coaxes the first words from me, and the next follow closely behind.

P-president Rhee, I stutter, Syngman Rhee has stepped down, had she heard? Oh, she laughs, as her shoulders relax and her back straightens, of course she had heard, two or three weeks ago now.

'Did you only find out today?'

I nod.

'Really?'
She looks at me in disbelief.
'It was in all the papers!'
I feel my face turning red.
'So you don't know what happened?'

I had not only missed the end of the First Republic, but the beginning of the Second too, the 'Red takeover', as Eve called the 'democratic spring'; evidently Washington had had enough of Syngman Rhee's caprices and governing style, and his declaration of martial law in Seoul was the final straw.

The Americans had wanted shot of him even during the Korean War. In 1953, when Rhee did everything in his power to sabotage the ceasefire negotiations with North Korea, they hatched the emergency plan Operation Everready. If the stubborn president continued to reject and even obstruct the ceasefire, the South Korean troops, who were still devotedly loyal to him, were to be disarmed, their freedom of movement drastically curtailed and the chief of state arrested and replaced with a cooperative general. On this occasion (and every other), Rhee had been able to hold on to power, but in the spring of 1960 the Americans felt the hour had come to free themselves of the despot once and for all. And the industrious US ambassador and future Far East expert in the State Department, Walter P. McConaughy, believed he had found Rhee's successor: a general by the name of Song.

General Song had endeared himself to the population during the April uprisings, because instead of subjecting the demonstrators to gunfire, he repeatedly strove for 'de-escalation'. He was said to be calm and level-headed, 'the general with a heart'. His soldiers and tanks weren't feared; on the contrary, people cheered at the sight of them. He was asked twice to become South Korea's next president, once by the student leaders, and the next time by the US ambassador in person. On both occasions, he refused; in an interview many years later, he said that he would never have been able to make peace with his conscience, for he had been just as guilty of corruption as the governing party: he helped Syngman Rhee to victory by ordering his regiment to vote for Rhee, in exchange for concessions for the military – a common practice at the time.

On 25 April 1960, just six days after Eve, Johnny and I had left Busan, the university professors and intellectuals followed in the footsteps of the students, pupils and workers and held a demonstration; they gave the flagging rebellion new impetus. The small group swelled to become a march of more than fifty thousand protesters, some of whom again headed straight for the house of Vice President Lee Ki-poong and once again wrecked it. The next morning, McConaughy and General Magruder pushed their way into the Blue House and tried to convince Rhee to step down. This one meeting turned into several, and so the rumour began that the US was forcing Syngman Rhee to renounce his presidency. During these days, a small group of demonstrators could be seen in Incheon decorating the iron feet of General Douglas MacArthur's statue with a magnificent floral wreath, out of gratitude for the American intervention.

Four days later, on 29 April, Syngman Rhee and his Austrian wife Franziska left Seoul; the years of Hawaiian exile had begun. Rhee was to die in Honolulu, at the age of ninety. His widow, who used the Korean name Buran, eventually returned via a circuitous route to South Korea.

Rhee's political career ended on a tragic note. Rhee's vice president, Lee Ki-poong, also saw his personal and professional future in the land of opportunity. He had asked McConaughy for safe passage from South Korea, and it had been guaranteed. But before he was able to put his escape plan into action, he was shot by his oldest son, Kangsŏk. Kangsŏk then killed his younger brother, his mother and himself. Some believed that he was unable to get over the shame his father had brought upon the family by allowing the electoral fraud to take place. Legally speaking, however, Kangsŏk was Syngman Rhee's son at the time of the murders – Rhee had adopted him because he and Buran had remained childless.

The end of the Rhee era unleashed euphoria, yet at the same time there was violent grief at the departure of the former president and his wife. 'What do these Koreans actually want?' McConaughy was reported to have muttered in response to these contradictory emotions. 'Goddamn Koreans.'

As the general with a heart had declared himself unwilling to play president, the loser of the election, Chang Myon, whom Rhee had accused of being in cahoots with the communists, was given the dubious honour of forming a government. Following a brief and chaotic transition period, Chang's party, the Democrats, took over government business. Rhee's party, the Liberals, sank into obscurity after their leader's emigration.

The new premier was a soft-spoken man; he came from a respected academic family and had received a good education, graduating from the Catholic Manhattan College in the US (with a scholarship from the Maryknoll order), and spoke fluent English. The CIA described him as an 'incredibly devout' Catholic, intelligent, capable, sensible and 'subservient'. It was said that he lacked the passionate nationalism of his country-men, but also any will of his own: during his time in office, he was unable to make any decision without first discussing it with the American ambassador and the chief of the Seoul branch of the CIA.

Despite all this, the Second Republic was a democracy, the first real one South Korea had experienced. The presidential rights anchored in the constitution were abolished, and the post was made a purely honorary one, without power. Freedom of the press was established, and commissions were convened to investigate the massacres which had taken place not only during the American occupation (such as the mass murder on the island of Jeju), but also during the Korean War; in the early 1960s, the blame hadn't yet been laid entirely on the communists. The police force was rigorously purged: all those who had held important positions during the colonial era were fired or forced to resign. Some became victims of mob rule and violent reprisals; one policeman was boiled alive in a pot of oil.

Plans were forged to stimulate the languishing economy. Chang's indecisiveness was useful for South Korea's few industrialists, the former profiteers of Greater Japan; they preferred a weak prime minister and a hesitant government they could shape to their liking. The foundation for Samsung's present-day success was laid back then, as well as that of other family-owned Jaeböl conglomerates like Hyundai.

In the National Assembly, it was once again possible to express an opinion without having to fear for one's life. This led to an undreamt-of diversity of opinion: wrangling and squabbling soon became the order of the day, while the demand to initiate negotiations with the North for a peaceful reunification intensified. Students descended upon the National Assembly to campaign for talks with North Korea or to demand a meeting with students of the Kim Il-sung University. The Mindong association, founded by students of Seoul University, which had wholly dedicated itself to the 'establishment of unity', experienced a tremendous surge in popularity that gave the right nightmares.

When, in August 1960, Kim Il-sung presented a proposal for a federalist Korea following the Swiss model, the anti-communists believed that the Reds were planning a stealthy takeover of the South, and when the famine in rural areas reached new heights the following spring, they claimed that the 'Red Revolution' was imminent.

In this critical situation, many saw the military as the only salvation.

The army had purged itself too; the younger generation had dismissed their elders or sent them into early retirement. The generals had been plotting their move for a long time, waiting for an opportune moment. They used the transitional period to present themselves to the people as 'honest, honourable patriots', and 'servants of the Republic'. Eve worshipped them; whenever our conversation turned to 'our young officers and generals', she rhapsodized about their honesty, discipline and patriotism. In her view, they were the only ones who could save South Korea.

The Americans saw things much the same way. When the all-too-acquiescent Chang Myon was overthrown by Brigadier General Park Chung-hee and his fellow officers, General Magruder merely sent a telegram to Washington giving the all-clear that the communist junta was by no means imminent. This reassurance was necessary; during the interwar years, Park had been in a regiment that defected to the communists in its entirety. Park had been caught and was subsequently deployed by military intelligence to hunt down communists; even including his own brother, people said.

A frightened Chang begged the Americans for help and even wept, but Magruder rebuffed him. Perhaps Magruder really believed that – as Park and his thirty co-conspirators claimed – the Chang government would be no match for the communist threat.

In May 1961, the purge of South Korea began. Members of the opposition were banned from practising their professions or (like Chang) imprisoned. More than thirteen thousand civilians and members of the armed forces were also placed under arrest. Three quarters of all daily newspapers were forced to close down. The National Security Law, which had previously propped up Syngman Rhee, was reintroduced, and all socialist and communist countries were declared enemy states. Park transformed the South into a military dictatorship. He ruled the country for eighteen years, towards the end as 'president for life'. The parallel with Kim Il-sung is striking: like him, Park wanted to possess his own nuclear weapons, and loudly voiced his plans to build an atomic bomb, until the South Korean nuclear programme was stopped by Kissinger.

After numerous unsuccessful attempts – the axe always strikes the straightest trees first – Park would be murdered at point-blank range in 1979, during a dinner at a KCIA safe house, by one of his closest confidants, Kim Chaegyu, the head of the Korean secret service. Moments beforehand, Kim had shot Park's bodyguard; a small, square man with no neck who was said to kill his enemies with his bare hands, and who had an astonishingly strong influence on the dictator. As he shot him, Kim cried out: 'How can anyone govern with an insect like this?!' The murder came as a surprise – yet at the same time it didn't.

The KCIA and Park had grown together: the secret service

owed their existence to the man who would later become the 'eternal president', but on the other hand had contributed significantly to the construction and preservation of Park's power. Without the KCIA – who, among other things, also obstructed any attempt to investigate and come to terms with the massacres of the 1940s and 1950s, by declaring citizens who searched for their disappeared relatives enemies of the state (communists) and mercilessly persecuting them – Park's downfall may perhaps have occurred sooner. Besides this, Park *allowed* the KCIA to use funds which appeared out of nowhere for political purposes: many a financial godsend rained down on the opposing side just in time for the election, and incited it to split – which of course proved advantageous for Park. KCIA agents infiltrated the opposition parties as agents provocateurs, demanding a change in party leadership or nominating additional candidates for election in order to provoke internal squabbling. These operations were financed partly through manipulation of the stock market in Seoul, and partly by national – and later an increasing number of international – firms like the Gulf Oil Corporation, which were forced to 'make donations'. Such dealings were often mediated by members of the CIA.

In the early 1970s, the KCIA had morphed into a criminal institution which, in part, was more powerful than the government. Despite the power struggles inside the organization, collaboration with its allies (for example with the police) went smoothly. KCIA agents not only sneaked their way into other parties, but also into newspaper editorial departments, radio and television stations and unions, as well as universities in South Korea and in the US (where they tried to influence and even steer American Korean studies). Not even churches were safe from the men in grey; standing in a corner, they enthusiastically transcribed the sermon – as well as who had attended the mass.

The origins of the KCIA, however, can be traced back to the 1950s, when the CIA supported Syngman Rhee's freshly inaugurated (and exonerated) South Korean government in educating and unifying both the state and military intelligence, which, until the Park regime took them under its wing, worked more frequently in opposition than in unison . . .

'The only way to catch the cub is to go into the tiger's den.'

'What do you mean by that?'

Eve blinked at me in confusion. She had just told me we should stick it out in Japan, because the situation in South Korea was anything but clear; if we went home now, we would risk being thrown in jail for murder. She had ignored my protest that the judge would surely understand we'd had to defend ourselves against a fascist like Jinman.

'It's nothing,' I said, 'just a favourite saying of a friend of mine.'

'You mean the communist?'

'No, I mean Jang. Sangok's friend.'

'You never mentioned he had a friend.'

She gave me a distrustful glance.

'Did he plan the actions with you and the others? The owner of the stationery shop? Is he a Red too?'

I was confused; I was sure I'd never mentioned either Mihee or Jang to Eve, let alone Jang's shop. For the first time since I'd known her, I began to doubt her stories. Was she really who she claimed to be, or was she a spy? Was that why she had so many names, because she needed them as a disguise? As aliases?

Before I had the opportunity to dig deeper, she said – and this sentence burned itself into my memory, it still sounds like a death warrant, even today: 'Patience, Yunho, patience. Your friend Jang will get the shock of his life.'

It took its time coming. A year went by before it revealed itself as a military dictatorship, one that was tolerated – or, and this is more likely – supported by Washington. Yet the appearance of democracy had to be maintained. The Kennedy administration invested considerable effort in convincing a reluctant Park, who in the meantime had transformed from soldier into civilian, to hold free elections. In 1963, after numerous threats that they would stop sending aid, this was finally achieved; Park won with an absolute majority.

Eve must have been back in Seoul for over a year by this point, happy among her old friends.

But I'm getting ahead of myself . . .

That evening, in Ikaino, she insisted on staying in Japan. She gave all number of reasons, even enthusing about the safe, clean streets in Osaka and her work as a hairdresser.

Noticing my growing scepticism, she declared with a contrite expression that she wanted to be frank with me, and no longer deceive me. She had to stay because of Johnny, no, *for* Johnny. Almost as soon as the words had left her mouth, I felt as though I understood everything: their strangely cool, yet familiar way of interacting with one another, the secret glances and signals they exchanged which shut me out.

Eve still loved him, she had only ever loved him. I pictured them before me, Johnny and Eve, dancing between the iron bed and the small window, locked in one another's arms, cheek to cheek, with Santo's yowling guitar in the background; 'Sleep Walk'.

She had never split from him, had never given him up, and there I had been thinking she was just play-acting the older sister, playing the role masterfully well, but in actual fact it was our relationship that had been like one between siblings. She felt liking and affection for me, but love? I felt hollow, *emptied*. Played for a fool. And ridiculed by the still-echoing memory of wholeness.

Eve evaded my gaze. I tried to evade hers too – which was a mistake, because our eyes met in the middle, and I saw in hers no trace of sadness or regret, only amusement and scorn. I wonder what she saw in mine; the fear I had been unable to shake since I confessed my feelings to her, back in Seoul, in our labyrinth? I hadn't used the word love, even though I have never loved anyone but her with such desperation. Such obstinacy.

A kind of peace overcame me once I understood that this love, which had never had a future, was over. Perhaps this was why I didn't let it go right away? I wanted to watch as it slowly became weaker, invisible; perhaps I was hoping it would linger a while before it disappeared for good.

I told her that I understood her decision, that of course I understood it. Then I said nothing more, and she fell silent too. I wanted to leave the salon, where the prints from my shoes could be seen on the floor. They stood out between the stripes that the dried soapsuds had left behind. But we stood there in that room with the badly washed linoleum floor as though we were rooted to the spot; it slowly turned dark, the sun set, and with it disappeared the day's last light. I am convinced I saw a fiery glow, which slowly devoured the horizon until, eventually, all that could be seen was Eve's shadow.

Once the light was extinguished, she came towards me. She came towards me, put her arms around me and pulled me close, and I knew that it was over.

★

As I turned towards the door, she held me back with a question I hadn't expected: did I want to have dinner with her? I looked up in surprise, in shock. Had I been mistaken, had I misunderstood everything? For a moment I didn't know whether to be pleased; it would be a lie to claim that I wasn't a little relieved about the end of the relationship. Perhaps she just wanted to be kind, make sure that I was okay? In my confusion, I nodded.

'Yes, sure.'

'Do you want to go to the Lees'?'

Mr and Mrs Lee ran our favourite restaurant, a cafeteria with a back room where the food was served on low tables. At the bar, one could watch Mr Lee (he insisted on the English 'mister') grilling the *okonomiyaki*, an Ikaino speciality. *Okonomiyaki* are essentially omelettes with offal and vegetables, the dough is made from flour, egg, and dashi, a fish stock. The pancakes are prepared on the *teppan* grill. Mr Lee flipped them deftly with a small spatula, while behind him Mrs Lee, with her back to the customers, peeled the carrots and onions and sliced the white cabbage into strips.

The Lees, who were known as the 'young Lees' even though no one knew the 'old Lees', had both been born in Japan. Mr Lee dreamt of opening a second restaurant, preferably in Tokyo, but he would settle for Kobe. He was a small, stocky man with a round face and large, gentle eyes. As he grilled the pancakes, he would smile away to himself, completely in tune with the world, and only rarely would he frown, grab a bowl and place into it the flawed *okonomiyaki*; nothing was ever thrown away. He was older than me, in his late thirties, as was his wife. The couple had three children, two daughters and a son, who spoke to one another in a mishmash of Japanese and Korean. Mrs Lee could express herself better in English than in

305

her parents' language, which she herself defined as her mother tongue – just as she also refused to be deterred from regarding Korea as her homeland. But she didn't even have the faintest idea what Korea looked like, I protested irritably, and besides, the Japanese colony of Chōsen had ceased to exist a long time ago; she was in love with a fairy tale, a land that existed when the tigers smoked pipes. She blinked at me in confusion and looked to her husband for help, who translated my words for her. Once he had finished, she began to laugh loudly. She wiped the tears from her cheeks and said, before turning back to the carrots and cabbage, that 'Mister Kang' told the best jokes.

Mrs Lee (hers was spelt 'Ri') came from a different family of Lees to Mr Lee – they weren't related, even though the rumour had made the rounds in Ikaino that they were cousins. She was almost a head taller than her husband, and it was said she had to make her own shoes, because there weren't any that would fit her in the whole of Honshū. The circumference of her hands was another topic of enthusiastic debate. Missu Satō had told me, even in the very first days after our arrival in Osaka, that gloves were something Mrs Lee couldn't wear; that not even the men's sizes would fit her, so she knitted herself some from unpicked Salvation Army jumpers, donations from the Americans which the Japanese passed on to the Koreans. Mrs Lee genuinely did often wear gloves made of a coarse, dark green wool, her fingertips peeping out from the cut-off fingers, and the knitted fabric didn't completely cover her wrists. Her daughters were the spitting image of her, tall and slim, while the son, the baby of the family, looked like his father.

For the Lee family, returning to North Korea was out of the question, because Mr Lee didn't want to give up his restaurant. Besides that, the Lees weren't admirers of the General or of communism; they weren't enemies of theirs either, but they certainly weren't comrades. When their acquaintances and customers, who were Sōren members, cautioned them that they couldn't afford to be unpolitical, they shook their heads and laughed off all the warnings. When they were caught serving sake and *okonomiyaki* to Mindan members, their windows were smashed in the following day. The restaurant had to close for an entire week because no one in Ikaino was prepared to take on the repairs. Mr Lee was furious. He tried to convince Sōren to own up to the attack and pay compensation. With a bright-red face, he screamed that he didn't see why he should only be allowed to serve customers who were of the 'correct' political orientation! What did political views and dinner have to do with one another?

Sōren gave Mr Lee short shrift. Tetsuya, who felt sorry for the little man, was prepared to make good on the damage, but the other committee members refused, saying this would be tantamount to an admission of guilt. When I told Tetsuya of my suspicion that Yamada was behind the attack, that his competitor's restaurant had been a thorn in his side for a long time, he grabbed me by the arm. I couldn't ever say that again, he said. Not ever.

Mr Lee's *okonomiyaki* were sizzling and steaming as we entered the restaurant. When he saw us, his mouth stretched into a broad smile, and he bowed several times in our direction as though wanting to make sure he wouldn't be regarded as impolite. Then he called his daughter, who came hurrying out of the back room as he washed his hands, dried them on his apron and came towards us. 'Please,' he said, pointing towards the backroom, 'take a seat in our guest room. It's quieter there.'

I was surprised that Mr Lee led us into the adjoining room,

for we normally sat at the bar; I enjoyed watching him work, I liked the meticulous way he tended to the pancakes, assessing their degree of goldenness, testing the crispiness of the crust with the edge of his spatula.

Eve gave me a glance I couldn't decipher. Did she want me to refuse the table and ask for our regular seats? Too late, Mrs Lee was already waiting for us with an equally broad smile, and had served our drinks. She knew our usual order: a bottle of sake. So I thanked Mr Lee, who then returned to his place by the grill.

Eve sat down on the mats. 'What's he planning?' she whispered to me as she crossed her legs. 'What do you mean?' I whispered back. 'This is clearly in preparation for something,' she replied.

'He probably wants to ask you a favour.'

'A favour?'

Before she could reply, our host came over with two large, aromatic pancakes. He put them down before us and wished us an enjoyable meal, adding the assurance, as he sat down at our table, that this was only the starter. Then he fell silent, and I thought he was studying us, but in actual fact he was staring at the tabletop. Eve and I fell upon the food, and I realized with surprise that I was very hungry; conversation faltered and soon dried up completely. The silence wasn't uncomfortable for me, on the contrary, I happily surrendered myself to the scent and taste of the *okonomiyaki*.

Eventually, Mr Lee cleared his throat. He had something on his mind, he began hesitantly. Clearly he had been debating this whole time whether he could burden us with his problem.

'As you're Mr Yamamoto's confidante.'

'I work for him . . .'

'Yes, and you're always together.'

'That's because of the jobs I do for him.'

Mr Lee looked at me despondently.

I conceded.

'I think he trusts me and I him.'

Mr Lee nodded to me with relief. His older daughter attended the same school as Eiko, and was in the same class, he said. He shook his head slowly, and said he didn't know how to formulate his request, that it would sound like an accusation, and he was well aware that there was nothing Mr Yamamoto could do about it. 'About what?' I asked. Mr Lee sighed. About his daughter's behaviour, he answered. Eiko was forcing all the girls in her class to emigrate to Pyongyang. 'Forcing them?' asked Eve. Mr Lee nodded. She was blackmailing them. She had threatened his daughter that she wouldn't be able to graduate from school if she didn't agree to return home. The teacher was in cahoots with her. The two of them had pre-dominantly targeted the affluent girls, because once someone decided to leave Japan, they had to make their entire fortune over to Sōren.

'Make it over?'

'Yes. You're only allowed to take clothes and household goods into the People's Republic. The rest goes to Sōren. Or to the North Korean state.'

He grimaced. It was also a way of filling the state's empty coffers, he said. Was he sure? asked Eve. She had never heard of this practice. He nodded enthusiastically when he sensed that she believed him, saying that in the beginning it had probably been an exchange, the house in Japan for the house in North Korea, the savings left to General Kim for the wages that one could expect as a worker or employee in North Korea. In the beginning, the financial aspect had been secondary, but now it was all about that, now it was chiefly the more affluent

Zainichi who were being called upon to return home, but, and at this point Mr Lee took my hand, he didn't own much, he had taken out two loans which he still had to pay back, and besides that he couldn't abandon his elderly parents. His daughter was a sensible girl and hadn't wanted to sign up, but she had given in to Eiko's dictate – partly out of fear of being beaten. He had heard that violence and even death threats were commonplace if someone refused the homecoming. He edged closer to my ear. Apparently the Sōren members had a quota to fulfil; they had promised Pyongyang a certain number of immigrants.

'But people are refusing to go. They've heard too many bad stories. You must have heard them yourself, the bad food, bad medicine, bad housing.'

I reached into my jacket pocket, pretending to have been gripped by my nicotine addiction, because I needed an excuse to move away from Mr Lee; he put a pack of cigarettes on the table and pushed it towards me. I took one, lit it and looked around as I smoked. The back room where we were sitting was cosy and, I now noticed, attractively furnished. The walls were freshly papered, the lamps tasteful, even the table was well crafted. The bowls we drank from and the plates we ate from were made of porcelain, and the cutlery of steel. Mr Lee was wearing his work clothes, but even these, if you overlooked the old, oil-spattered apron, looked better than anything I had in my wardrobe.

He was lying; his financial circumstances weren't as bad as he claimed. Everyone knew that he worked like a man possessed because he wanted to open a second restaurant. Everyone was aware that he wanted to leave this restaurant to his daughter, the very daughter who had signed up to emigrate to North Korea. Whether these threats had really occurred, or whether Mr Lee had lied to me, I couldn't say. I had seen for myself how Eiko had treated Mio Kobayashi; it was possible he was telling the truth.

What did he want from me? I eventually mumbled. Could I speak to Mr Yamamoto? he asked. Could I ask him to forbid his daughter from driving fear into her classmates? Mr Yamamoto was, he said, of course free to emigrate to the People's Republic if he wanted to, but his daughter didn't need to throw the whole of Ikaino into turmoil in the process. Mr Lee fell silent and thought for a moment. No, he corrected himself, I couldn't say that to him. I should just ask him to talk her out of making the threats.

I nodded and stood up; I assured him I would speak with my boss. Mr Lee beamed at me, took my hands, squeezed them and bowed deeply. 'Thank you,' he said, 'thank you very much. Thank you very, very much. You have no idea of the service you're doing my family.'

As I reached the doorway, I turned round, unable to stop myself. 'What if your daughter has decided of her own accord to live in Pyongyang?' I asked. 'What if she doesn't want to run your restaurant?' That, Mr Lee declared decisively, was certainly not the case. Tomoko, or rather Sumin, he corrected himself, had never wanted anything else.

It was warm that evening, the mild breeze carried a hint of the summer which would soon overpower the last spring chill; the spring didn't want to yield, perhaps it always lingered on in Japan, I thought, perhaps its aroma never faded on this island.

I reached for Eve's hand. As I touched her, I realized I had crossed a line which hadn't existed before, and flinched. She laughed softly and grabbed my index finger, as she often had in Seoul, enclosing it with her childlike hand. I let her, even though I didn't know why; probably out of nostalgia. In a quiet side alley she stopped, asked for a cigarette and hid herself away to smoke beneath the boughs of a maple tree.

Had I spoken to Johnny recently? she asked. I nodded. A few days ago. The usual school gossip. I tried not to let on how flustered, hurt, and also how suspicious I was. He was very interested in the running of the school at the moment, she said slowly, and especially in the schoolgirls.

She took a long drag.

'He's seeing little Lee.'

'Little Lee?'

I could tell, despite the darkness, that my slowness to catch on was annoying her. 'Mr Lee's daughter,' she said impatiently, 'Tomoko Sumin Lee.'

'She's having an affair with Johnny?'

'Shhh.'

She laid her hand on my mouth.

'Not so loud.'

'Since when?'

I made an effort to whisper. Eve shrugged, she couldn't say. How did she know? I asked cautiously. She smiled mysteriously and stubbed out her cigarette on the tree trunk; once again, she gave me no answer. 'And you're sure?'

'Absolutely sure.'

'Mr Lee has no idea?'

'I guess not.'

She pulled me into the glow of the street lights and made me walk on. Maybe he had made his plea to me because I was friends with both of them, with Tetsuya and Johnny, she said. I pulled away from her. None of this has anything to do with me, I mumbled. Whatever Eiko, Johnny and Sumin Lee were doing was their business, not mine.

Eve studied me.

'You know Mr Lee's lying.'

'What do you mean?'

'The savings he was talking about. It's much more money than he's letting on. He can clearly afford a new restaurant in Tokyo already, but he wants to manage it himself, not leave it to a stranger.'

'And the one in Osaka?'

'Sumin is supposed to take over, with the help of her younger sister.'

'And the son?'

'He'll be able to study. Mr Lee has great plans for his son and heir.'

Eve laughed at the expression on my face; she enjoyed filling me up with gossip –

'What kind of plans?'

– and I was helpless to resist.

'A university degree in the US.'

'He really must have saved a fortune.'

'Young Lee also got a scholarship. From a Presbyterian mission.'

She lit another cigarette.

'Mr Lee isn't the kind of man you can mess with. Who knows what he's capable of when it comes to his family or his life's ambition. Apparently he was once a boxer and has friends among the Yakuza. You should warn Johnny.'

Even as a child, Mino had always done whatever he wanted, and it had been my job to put him on the right path. I had always found that difficult; his carefree and easy-going nature was precisely what made him lovable. Being friends with him meant living in a world in which neither 'good' nor 'evil' existed. Johnny inhabited another time, a time without memory; for him, the only thing that existed was the Here and Now – perhaps because he only understood the present.

Many people, his father more than anyone, had reproached him for his behaviour, accusing him of not respecting – no, fearing – life enough. And so often I had defended him, and each time I did Yunsu shook his head and said to me: 'Yunho, don't dance to someone else's tune.'

15

To this day I remain fascinated by the Zainichi's pliant identity, their talent for disguise which allows them to disappear into anonymity, to become one with the majority, the *masses*. I often envied the ease with which they were able to don and discard their visibility. People like Johnny, Eve and I were the opposite of invisible; we were conspicuous, splashes of colour in an otherwise homogeneous, harmonious world; our clumsy Japanese, our gestures, which, as much as we tried to assimilate, were different, *abnormal*; we even seemed incapable of wearing the local clothing like natives. In Osaka, I always felt as though I was walking in the beam of a spotlight, I imagined myself to be under constant observation, even though I moved solely in the shadows.

Yet the protection their camouflage granted them was fragile: if the Zainichi, the putative foreigners, suddenly became visible or were exposed, their existence was endangered. It wasn't uncommon for this new visibility to bring terrible consequences: dismissal from work and even family rifts, for example with in-laws who felt betrayed and used. Nor was it without its risk, to jump between the assimilated existence and the primary, original existence (but what does 'original' even mean in this context? How original can it be if you've never even known it?). It wasn't uncommon for the unlucky ones to get stuck in an in-between space which didn't permit an answer to the question 'Who am I?'. For a member of a minority seen as either aggressors or victims, nothing was normal, or a matter of course, and it was twice as hard to withstand the pressure of having to identify with just one group: to conceal, suppress, a part of the self.

For the first generation, explained Missu Satō, the distinction between the true and the false self was easy. Their roots, their origins, were clear; when they thought of home, they were picturing a definite place. For the second generation, for children like Eiko who were born abroad, their origins were less clear, and their names were a symptom of this turmoil. The Japanese, and therefore inauthentic, name felt more real than the genuine Korean one, which they used solely in class, in an artificial world created especially for them. How much greater must this conflict be, Missu Satō said, for those who go to Japanese schools and spend their entire lives as pretend Japanese people?

Missu Satō may have been the kind of person who would bleed even a louse dry, but she had her moments of insight. This was why, she concluded, there was so much sadness among the Koreans in Honshū; for many, suicide was the only escape.

Just a few days after my arrival in Ikaino, a twelve-year-old boy hung himself, and five months later an eighteen-year-old girl took her own life, the girl I had met on the bus journey: Mio Kobayashi. People said she killed herself because she saw herself as a *hāfu*, a half-breed.

As subhuman.

Mio's death put Eiko in a very difficult situation. Most people, admittedly, thought that the parents weren't without blame; after all, the mother in question was a stepmother, who had been incapable of loving someone else's offspring, and the perpetually absent father had been indifferent to the child. Nonetheless, the suspicion was voiced that the Homecomers' Brigade had put too much pressure on Mio, and had thereby driven her to her death. Expressed hesitantly at first, this supposition soon transformed into a fact that no one wanted to contradict. I too blamed Eiko for Mio's suicide; I had seen her in the act of recruiting, and her dictatorial behaviour had disgusted me. I had avoided her ever since, and resisted all her attempts to patch up our friendship.

Eiko didn't comment on the accusations. Perhaps she was afraid of speaking to the worried parents of her classmates, for whom Mio's 'sacrifice' came at an opportune moment, giving them a reason to descend upon the Yamamoto residence. They came in hordes and besieged Naoko, some even camped out in the entrance hall, refusing to leave until Eiko called off the 'compulsory emigration'. Eventually, Tetsuya had to summon his men (the other men, of whom I wasn't one, my muscle strength was insignificant even back then), to 'escort' them out of the building.

Through all this, Eiko remained silent; I couldn't say whether she was affected by the less than flattering descriptions of her person and appearance, which were said to be a reflection of her bad character. I wondered whether she had heard the stories which were being spread about her, and whether she found the false and increasingly exaggerated accusations hurtful. I also wondered whether Mio's death was eating away at her; whether she blamed herself for it.

She remained stubbornly silent. It was astonishing, almost admirable, how she kept to her silence, turning herself into a stone, a fortress. I suddenly recognized Kimiko in Eiko; the younger sister had the same talent as the older one, she had just never revealed it before. Or had her voice abandoned her?

317

Perhaps her wordlessness really was an admission of guilt, as people were saying. Or was she afraid of clothing her doubts and fears in words? If she responded to the questions and accusations, it might stop her from following her dream, and she would remain stuck in a country she couldn't accept as home, her world being composed of too many opposites: White and Black, Good and Evil, Korea and Japan.

Naoko was the first to admit defeat. Their daughter was beyond help, she said, in her soft, melodic voice. She sounded like a little bird complaining about a cloud covering the sun. Her resignation infected Tetsuya. He stopped trying to talk Eiko around, and instead summoned all the involved parents to concoct a plan.

Their daughters had decided to emigrate as a class, and this unity, said Tetsuya, was their strength, but also their weakness: If they could convince just one of the girls to withdraw their signature, the rest would follow, and Eiko's plan would collapse like a house of cards. One agitated mother promptly announced that not all of them had signed yet, that Senko Yamada's name was missing on the list of homecomers. This, Tetsuya rejoiced, could destroy Eiko's plan; all they needed was for one more schoolgirl to join forces with Senko and the mood would turn.

That evening, the parents set off home full of hope. They thought they had found a way to stop their daughters. Among them was Mr Lee, who pulled me aside and thanked me for my intervention; I had protected Tomoko, no, the entire class, from catastrophe.

I had successfully dodged Mr Lee's mission. Talking to Johnny, however, was something I couldn't avoid; Eve was breathing down my neck.

In preparation for this no less onerous mission, I tried to

sound out the all-knowing Missu Satō for information on the Lee girl. I knew nothing about her and had never spoken to her, I was familiar only with the sight of her back and the back of her head, the yellow headscarf she wore while she was working in the restaurant, and her vibrantly patterned blouse, which added a splash of colour to the dark interior – whenever she moved around the kitchen, a patch of sun seemed to dance back and forth between the sink and the vegetable rack.

'A sparrow may be small, but it lays many eggs,' was Missu Satō's brief response when I asked what she thought of Tomoko. She added that she wasn't shy of hard work, and had a heart as delicate and soft as silk brocade. That was all I could get out of her.

I knew the younger sister a little better; we had exchanged a few words here and there, although I had never asked her name. Perhaps they were alike? Eve called her 'the chicklet'. She was two years younger than Tomoko and had long, black hair with a bluish shimmer, friendly hazelnut-brown eyes, and unusually pale, almost white skin. She was known as the pretty daughter, I'd been able to figure out that much; all the customers remarked on her beauty, which, if you believed the comments, was increasing by the second. This tendency for exaggeration is deeply Korean, and absurd, but I enjoyed watching the chicklet blush at the compliments and lower its head right down, as though wanting to hide beneath its wing.

There was no doubt that Mr Lee wanted only one thing for his younger daughter: for her to marry well. He would ensure that she married into a family he could conduct business with in Tokyo, and in this way her value (for the marriage was undoubtedly a trade) would bring her father's *okonomiyaki* empire closer and closer to reality. And one day, in the not too distant future, the great-grandchildren would say that the family's wealth existed solely thanks to the willpower, vision and wisdom of the great-grandfather; they would build an altar in his honour and pay tribute to him, as was proper for good Korean descendants, and they would be proud of their names, the Korean and the Japanese ones. The chicklet would be forgotten, as would Great Aunt Tomoko, whose fate it was to grill pancakes in a badly ventilated kitchen in Ikaino until the day when, never having been allowed to develop a will of her own, she would be banished into an old peoples' home by her nieces and nephews.

Carrying on with a penniless refugee from South Korea played no part in the future that Mr Lee had so carefully orchestrated.

I began to watch Johnny furtively, waiting for intimations, observations and slips of the tongue that I could latch on to, sentences that hinted at a longing to confide in me. Ideally I would have liked a confession, a discussion between best friends, in which he would reveal to me his feelings for Tomoko, but the longer I had to be patient, the more annoyed and frustrated I became, and my episodic flare-ups of jealousy didn't make the matter any easier.

In my eyes, he was the man who had taken Eve from me (even though I had been the one who wanted to steal his lover from him); to me he was an intruder and an enemy. I dissected and judged his behaviour, noting every tiny mistake and adding it to the others I had already found, so that, collectively, they lost their harmlessness and consequently their charm too. Then I could no longer understand why I had ever been his best friend, and why I had forgiven all his slip-ups over the years, which I now reinterpreted as acts of nastiness: his habit of making trivialities into secrets and innocent matters into schemes; his sudden spite, which I imagined to be vengefulness; his malicious put-downs, in which I detected arrogance, and contempt for his fellow man, devoid of any lenience or mercy; his ridiculous conceit, which meant he couldn't walk past a reflective surface without checking his hair and tidying it with a comb. I sniffed out an opportunist who had ensconced himself in the life of an affluent woman, with the aim of using her and casting her aside – just like he had used and cast aside Eve when she was no longer of use to him. I couldn't form a single clear thought; I was suffering from the break-up with Eve, suffering more than I wanted to admit to myself. Whenever she worriedly asked me how I was, I answered that I was fine, that I had never been better, but my lie was like the morning mist, thin and sparse.

I was quiet during those days, horribly quiet, barely leaving our room, remaining motionless on the floor until the shaft of light from the setting sun reached me, and only then would I turn towards the wall. I led a double existence: one self was slumped on the tatami mat, while the other lived in a world made of countless layers of images, traces of memory. They settled over the present moment one after the other, as light as an accent; each trace buried the previous one beneath it, but did not destroy it, they all remained intact.

It is said that to pursue convention is to pursue time itself; I was in pursuit of the past. I moved cautiously, tentatively, in order not to scare away my memories. I avoided making any sound, for sounds inhabited the present, and as such I couldn't tolerate them; only inhabitants of the past were permitted to ignore the Here and Now. Invisibility was my refuge, and I did everything I could to build a wall that enabled me to remain *been*.

★

Johnny interpreted my behaviour differently; he thought I wanted to reconcile with him but didn't know how. Since our escape from Seoul, I had been curt and brusque with him, on one occasion even screaming that his stupidity had cost us our lives. One day he blurted out that he was pleased I had forgiven him, that he had given up hope, thinking I couldn't forgive him for having wrenched us from our homeland.

He smiled at me. It was a small, despondent smile, and I was touched to see a glimpse of Mino in it. I realized that he had changed, he was calmer, more thoughtful, his words more considered, his attitude no longer brash and quick to anger (in his arrogance and disapproval), but instead reserved. Humility, that's the word which springs to mind now. These days it's a virtue from another world, but back then it was required as a sign of maturity, arising from the understanding that there's a higher principle, one that governs the cycle of nature, and nature itself, including mankind, the animals and everything else that was thrown into the universe. Some call this God. I shy away from giving it a name, but one thing is certain: it is neither a human-like being, nor does it need our adoration.

It was the right moment, I didn't want to wait any longer; I told him I had heard about his relationship with Sumin Lee. Johnny looked at me in surprise, then he grinned. So that's why I was taking an interest in our friendship, he said, for the sake of gossip, and there he'd been feeling flattered, believing my concern was about him, whereas in actual fact it was directed at his girlfriend.

'Sumin?'

He lit a cigarette, the last in the pack. He called her only by her Japanese forename, he said, Tomoko. She didn't even look Korean, he remarked absent-mindedly. He exhaled the smoke, tapped the ash onto the clean floor, paying no attention to the embers, which burned their way into the wood. He stretched, letting out a yawn, and rolled up his jacket to use as a pillow, taking care not to mess up his hair.

She was more beautiful than Umeko, the younger sister, murmured Johnny, except no one knew that, because she was always ignored. She didn't fit into her family, just as he hadn't fit into his, he said, blowing the dense smoke in my direction, but no one noticed, unlike him she hid it well, she was very clever, his Tomoko, as smart as a hare.

He sighed.

'A man with an axe is weaker than a woman with a needle.'

He had been a bitter disappointment to his parents, he said, especially his father and grandfather. Every time yet another of his ventures had failed, they had looked at one another and said:

'When will the boy finally stop trying to ladle the kimchi broth with chopsticks?'

He looked at me thoughtfully.

'Your brother was the glorious hero.'

'Yunsu?'

'Yes, Yunsu. Do you remember?'

He pulled himself over to the wall and sat up against it.

'Do you remember how much Father loved him?'

'Father?'

'My father.'

I remembered, but in my memory the image was always shrouded by another – that of his arrest.

Johnny took several short drags on the cigarette, breathing quickly in and out.

'Did you know, by the way, that Father adopted Yunsu?'

His fingers, with the smouldering cigarette clamped between

them, were shaking so violently that the ash snowed down onto his knee.

He winked at me.

'So technically speaking, your brother is my brother.'

Back when the tigers smoked long pipes, the director developed a longing to make the young Kang boy his son. His own boy was frail and sickly, and he wasn't sure he would make it to adulthood. Yunsu, on the other hand, was clever, robust and strong, and the Kangs had a second son, while Mr Kim only had his three daughters; a fifth child was out of the question due to his wife's advanced age.

With the intention of one day adopting Yunsu, the director insisted on sending the little boy to school, kitted out with a brand-new uniform, schoolbag and a pair of handmade leather shoes. He took care of the school fees and Yunsu showed his gratitude by learning more quickly than all the other children and getting better grades. His favourite subjects were Maths and History, and even when it came to Japanese, which he hated, he was the top of his class. He also sang well, with a lovely, bright voice, and was a skilled craftsman; only his body resisted any dictate, he was a lousy athlete.

That hadn't bothered Father, said Johnny, for he had seen in Yunsu the ideal son, the firstborn that his wife hadn't given him. That's why he talked Mr Kang into a trade: a good education for the children, as well as a secure future for the entire family, and in return Yunsu would officially be the Kim family's son and heir. Mr Kang didn't hesitate for long; he quickly prepared the adoption papers.

'Then the unexpected happened: Mr Kang refused to sign.'

Johnny's mouth twisted into a thin smile.

'Father didn't know how to handle the fact that his

insubordinate servant was endangering the future of the Kim clan out of pure sentimentality. He was as mad as a hornet. He couldn't haul his slave in front of the beak through fear of alienating his future son, but nor did he have any intention of giving in. For him, it was a matter of principle.'

Johnny pulled a match out of the box, struck it and watched as the flame flared up then died out.

'The years passed by, but the conflict wasn't settled. Neither Yunsu, nor you, nor I caught wind of how much the argument was straining the relationship between our families. Once the time came for Yunsu to move up to the final year of school, Father refused to pay the fees. At least not without the guarantee of being able to call Yunsu his child. That must have been in 1943 or 1944.'

Johnny paused, as though he were waiting for an interjection on my part, but I had nothing to say; I was waiting for the grim denouement his hushed tone seemed to promise.

'Just a few days after this argument, Mr Kang was ordered to report to the front as a soldier of the imperial Japanese army. He was instructed to draw up his will, as was the practice back then. But your father didn't just write his will; he also signed the adoption papers and handed them over. My father inspected every signature, tapped the tips of his fingers against the dried ink and nodded contentedly. The next day, Mr Kang left Nonsan and never returned.'

Johnny slid back down to lie on the floor, clasped his hands behind his neck and said: 'Some time ago, my mother told me that your father was called up because mine arranged it. The old man put in a special request.'

He stared up at the bedroom ceiling, seemingly lost in thought, as though he were staring into a cloudless sky.

'The Director always got what he wanted.'

I didn't know what to say or how to react.

What did I feel?

I was staggered. Horrified. Furious.

Furious at the hard-hearted, high-handed man who was so eager to call himself the father of a particular child that he would allow someone to die for it. And I felt hate and contempt for the revealer of the secret, no, hate and contempt for the *friend* who took such delight in provoking my misery, but Johnny wasn't done, his enjoyment was only just approaching its climax.

'Do you remember that hot and humid day in May, shortly before the war broke out, when Father had Yunsu arrested? It rained incessantly that afternoon. The thunder and lightning came first, then broad, fat drops that pelted down onto the dried-out earth, not soaking in right away, because the ground was so parched and the raindrops so immense. The truth, even if you don't like it, is that Father had no choice; he had to call the police. In the eyes of the law he was responsible for his adoptive son, and he had no intention of sacrificing himself for a Red.'

He pulled a fresh pack of cigarettes out of his trouser pocket. 'And your mother,' he informed me, raising his index finger, 'couldn't help your brother, because she had already sold him when he was a child – and not even to the highest bidder.'

'You don't know what you're talking about!'

Eve's voice came from another dimension; it was distant, but close too, right by my ear . . .

'You should mind your own business rather than tear open old wounds.'

'And you,' retorted Johnny, 'should take your own advice. Otherwise I'll tear open a few of your old wounds!'

He had jumped to his feet; the cigarette was still unlit between his fingers.

'Be quiet and listen to me,' hissed Eve. She was angry, and had to struggle to keep her voice down. 'Your girlfriend Tomoko is going to leave you. She's signed up for the Great Homecoming . . .'

I can no longer remember whether Johnny answered or not, I remember only his thundering footsteps and the slam of the door. I was consumed by a pain that, while I was subjected to it, seemed ridiculous and absurd; ridiculous, absurd and bizarre, because it was over and done with, *expired* – I had thought I'd put it behind me years ago.

Why did his story upset me so much? Was it because it was plausible? Because it explained a lot of things that had puzzled me back then? Because I finally understood the magnitude of the tragedy my parents and Yunsu had been involved in? They had told me nothing of all this. I too had been an outsider in my own family. Like Johnny.

Eve and I sat by the window with a view of the setting sun, its last rays shielded by the roofs of Ikaino. She pulled me towards her and put her arms around me. I felt safe and secure, and was grateful that she hadn't left me, that she had rescued me. She always rescues me, I thought to myself.

She always rescues me.

The uproar surrounding Eiko hadn't died down. On the contrary, after Senko added her name to the list of home-comers, concern escalated. The parents had originally thought they could resolve the matter by means of some persuasive conversations and a few concessions, but the girls proved to be stubborn, and the parents, especially Yamada and Madame Chiang Kai-shek, found themselves faced with a dilemma once more: on the one hand, they couldn't publicly retract their approval of the Great Homecoming, particularly since Yamada was the leader of Osaka's Sōren branch, but on the other hand Senko was their only child, and Madame, who had never had any notion of living in North Korea – even though she expressed her admiration for General Kim Il-sung at every opportunity and called for solidarity with the North Korean people – dreamt neither of a North Korean son-in-law nor of saying goodbye to her daughter forever. But the signature that Senko had given couldn't be withdrawn without the active support of the signatory herself, and she refused to do this; she claimed that she was following her friend's orders, that she was only doing what Eiko was doing.

'Do what Eiko does' became a catchphrase and, over time, an unwritten rule. Eiko, who had been infected by Ayumi's enthusiasm for the Great Homecoming, soon surpassed her teacher in importance and became the girls' figurehead. She became everything that the parents couldn't be: she liberated herself from the mothers' class-consciousness and the fathers' capitalist interests. She became free in every sense, but in one above all – she no longer saw herself as bound by gender roles. The fact that she was rebelling against the parental ban gave her a modern aura: that of the emancipated woman.

As Yamada didn't want to upset the Sōren committee with an emigration ban, he tried to manipulate Senko through Eiko. Tetsuya had to ensure that his daughter did the right thing, he declared at the next parents' meeting, meaning that his committee colleague should do what he himself, on account of his position, couldn't: forbid Eiko from leaving the country. The legal guardians breathed a sigh of relief; if Mr Yamamoto forbade his offspring from emigrating, their own would be sure to abandon their plans.

Tetsuya wasn't convinced by the suggestion. He suspected that he wouldn't get anywhere by imposing such a ban on Eiko, but he tried nonetheless.

While the wrangling voices on the ground floor refused to abate – Tetsuya's growling and booming, and Eiko's shrill, defiant – I sat on tenterhooks in our room and waited for Johnny's return. In truth, I would have preferred to avoid him; I had looked for reasons to extend my stay in the arcade, where I curled myself up in a corner and slept on the ground, hoping not to be discovered by anyone to whom I would have to explain my behaviour. Eventually I had been unable to delay coming home any longer, I needed a change of clothes and was desperate for a proper place to sleep. I had also come to the conclusion that there was no point in punishing Johnny for the sins of his father, he had suffered enough under the man himself. I resolved not to challenge him again, but instead to talk things out. We lived together in a very small space, as far as the outside world was concerned we were siblings, and if Johnny's version of the family history was true, we really were something akin to brothers, even though Yunsu had been disowned.

I felt like an ant preparing itself to shake a tree, faint-hearted and nervous, but I didn't leave my post. Most of the time I just dozed, I didn't want to sleep through his arrival. I waited the whole morning, the whole afternoon, the following morning. I played through our encounter in my mind – sometimes it was so friendly, so amicable, that I almost looked forward to catching him unawares with my generosity, my *magnanimity*, and then it would escalate once more, transforming from a harmless exchange into a war of words; once the imagined verbal duels in my dream had run out of ammunition, I gave in to the urge and laid into my 'half-brother' with my fists.

I was awoken by someone shaking me roughly. How could I sleep through all the noise, asked Eve, quickly closing the door to our room, I had missed Yamada and his 'immeasurable' rage.

He stormed into each and every room until he found Eiko, said Eve. Then he dragged her out of bed and threatened to kill her if she didn't stop the campaign at once. He asked her again and again whether she had understood him and would do what he asked, but she refused and called him a capitalist pig, a monster, a piece of dog shit, everything that came into her mind, and so he began to hit her. At every refusal, every 'No', he gave her a slap, and she screamed her head off and tried to free herself from his grip, but he didn't let go. When she began to bite him, he grabbed her by the neck and squeezed, and who knows, whispered Eve, what would have happened if Naoko hadn't called Tetsuya.

Tetsuya pulled his 'comrade' away from his child. Eiko fell to the floor, wheezing. Yamada's fingers had left a fiery red imprint around her throat, she was gasping desperately for air, Naoko wailed for a doctor, for someone to get a doctor, and Missu Satō ran off. Meanwhile, Yamada stood there panting next to the girl, and spluttered amid profanities that he hoped she would die, that it would do them all a favour. Tetsuya promptly lunged at him, and they laid into one another like two fighting cocks, the doctor had to pull them apart before he could tend to Eiko. Yamada left the Yamamoto house cursing, spitting and kicking all around him, yelling that he would kill Eiko if she wasn't dead already, and Tetsuya threatened that General Kim Il-sung wouldn't tolerate this betrayal, that Eiko had acted as a representative of Sōren, she had been given the task of recruiting schoolgirls for the Great Homecoming, and

Yamada should make himself scarce and never show his ugly face again, otherwise—

How was Eiko now, I asked; I too was whispering. She had recovered a little, answered Eve, although Yamada's handprint, which she was wearing like a medal, was still emblazoned across her neck. Eve smiled. The girl was plucky, she said, some might say *too* plucky. Unlike me, I mumbled, I was pathetic and cowardly, afraid even of my best friend.

Perhaps it was Eve's sympathetic expression that gave my brain a jolt – all of a sudden I became aware of an inconsistency that had eluded me until that moment . . .

'Why didn't Johnny know that Tomoko had signed up? As her Korean teacher, he should be the first person to find out.'

Eve rummaged around in her coat pocket, found her cigarettes and pulled out two. She lit mine, then hers. We both took a drag, inhaling and exhaling the smoke at the exact same moment. 'He hasn't been working at the school for a long while now,' she said eventually.

'Was he fired?'

'No. He resigned.'

'Resigned?'

'He said he was offered a better role.'

'By who?'

'Yamada.'

She laughed softly when she saw my surprise. She had already wondered, she told me, whether he had made a move on Tomoko under Yamada's instruction – in order to sabotage Mr Lee's plan to open a second restaurant. She sighed and smoothed down her clothes, the black skirt, the dove-grey blouse, then looked at herself in her compact mirror, reapplied her lipstick, dabbed her lips and put the tube back in her handbag. She put on a headscarf and tucked some rebellious strands of hair beneath the fabric.

She had to go, she said, she was late and Missu Satō would be cross, it was the third time this week already, she would scold her and ask whether Eve had changed the salon's opening hours without informing her, the owner. After that she would spit into a handkerchief and scrub Eve's cheeks with it. Too much rouge, she would mutter, why the war paint, this was a beauty salon, not the Wild West! She would eye Eve's clothes critically, pluck at the neckline and lecture her: 'True beauty isn't aggressive, it doesn't need to be put on display. You should be able to fit two fingers between your bust and your blouse. Two fingers, Miss Moon, two fingers. Mend your ways!'

When Johnny didn't come home the following day either, I assumed that he – like me – was avoiding a confrontation, and secretly felt relieved. Eve, on the other hand, was worried; she said it wasn't like him. I was just about to point out that in Seoul he sometimes hadn't come home for weeks on end, but realized in the same moment where he had been, and fell silent.

We had to look for him, she said. Not understanding why she was so worried, I protested that he was a grown man and knew how to look after himself. She gave me an admonishing look. I shouldn't confuse him with his family, she said, he was a good person, and he had always stood by me. Even when his parents had wanted me out of the house.

'He told you about that?'

I couldn't imagine in what context.

'The Kims planned to throw you out right after the outbreak of war. Your brother had been arrested, after all. And the entire village knew that Yunsu was close friends with a communist. They couldn't risk you going down the same path.'

'And Johnny stopped them?'

'He stood up for you. He asked them to let you stay for a few months at least.'

She cleared her throat.

'He thought the fighting would never end. Or only much, much later. He tried to win time for you.'

'Time?'

'So you could grow up and stand on your own feet.'

'He told you that?'

She nodded. He had told her a lot, she said, a lot about his best friend.

'And when did he tell you this?'

I was furious now.

'Before or after you had sex? Or was it during?'

I couldn't bear the fact that she was taking his side. And that I, 'the poor little orphan', had been the subject of their pillow talk.

Eve took my hand. I couldn't turn my back on Johnny, she said, he was my oldest friend.

I pulled away. I didn't believe her, neither her nor Johnny. I no longer knew who was telling the truth and who wasn't; both of them seemed dishonest. When I stood up and tried to leave the room to get some fresh air, she started up again, saying it was my duty as a friend to look after Johnny.

I had had enough.

'He killed someone!' The words burst out of me. 'It's the world that should be afraid of *him*, not he of the world!'

At that moment, I heard a gentle cough. Kimiko was standing in the doorway. Her eyes were slightly reddened, as were her cheeks.

'What do you want?' I yelled. She was looking for Eiko, she stammered. 'Eiko?' I asked in disbelief. That wasn't the answer I had been expecting.

'She's not in her room. And she's not in the kitchen or anywhere else in the building either.'

'In the garden?'

Kimiko shook her head.

'And at school? Have you asked there? Perhaps she's hiding in the gymnasium.'

Kimiko looked at me doubtfully and said she hadn't thought of that. Then she asked: 'Has Mr Kim disappeared too?'

I sighed loudly. I wasn't in the mood to talk about Johnny. 'He probably got held up at a friend's place,' I answered.

Eiko was the spitting image of Kimiko. The older sister lowered her gaze, only to stare up at me moments later, with the eyes of her younger sibling, and murmur: 'But he doesn't have any friends here . . .'

16

On the way to the school, I couldn't get Kimiko's remark out of my head. Did Johnny really not have any friends in Japan? He had a lover, and who knows who else he was closely acquainted with, whom else he had befriended. After all, I had only found out about his 'chums' in the North-West Youth once it was too late.

What did I really know about Johnny?

Nothing.

But perhaps Kimiko's statement had been a question, perhaps she had meant 'I *thought* he didn't have any friends here.' How much of our conversation had she overheard? All of it? Then she would know that Eve, Johnny and I weren't really siblings; she would also know that Johnny had murdered someone. What would she do with this knowledge? Certainly she wouldn't keep it to herself, Kimiko wasn't known for her discretion . . .

But I didn't have time to worry about it. Tetsuya had sent me to the school; he wanted me to speak with Eiko's classmates and Mrs Nobukawa. That he hadn't gone himself, I understood; he had thrown Ayumi out of the house after I told him about Eiko. For him, the teacher was clearly responsible for the North Korea plan. He had accused Ayumi of brainwashing Eiko, yelling that her influence on his children had to be kept to a minimum, that he had no desire to keep seeing her nauseating face in his house day after day. Ayumi had retorted that he should come to terms with his daughter's decision, that even the wise man follows the conventions of his era. But perhaps she was overestimating him, she said, perhaps he was more like the simpleton who couldn't count past the number one.

Before the fight got out of hand, Eiko had stepped in. She had begged her father not to make her 'commendable' teacher homeless. Eventually, losing her temper, she had declared angrily that it was like talking to a wall, and stormed out of the room. Tetsuya had called after her: 'Go ahead! Leave the path to heaven and take the path to hell!'

That was ten days ago. Since then, Ayumi had found a place to stay close to the school. An improvement, she said, because now she could walk to work instead of having to wait for the bus.

The residential building belonged to the school; the accommodation had been designed exclusively for the teachers. In front of the building was a narrow strip of undeveloped land where they could plant potatoes, garlic, pumpkins or onions, Ayumi reported enthusiastically, or even breed rabbits if they wanted to, rabbits and hens; she was fascinated by self-sufficiency.

In each one-room apartment, there was a kitchenette alongside the bed-sitting room. The building even had a communal bath, a water closet and a bathtub. What tremendous luxury! Now she would no longer have to make the pilgrimage to the public baths every week. Although, she sighed, she would miss the over-filled pools, the loud chatter, the hot steam which made it impossible to see who one was gossiping with. There was a bus that went directly to the baths, I pointed out. She shook her head in horror. No, she wouldn't trek all the way across Ikaino, she said, she was happy with her new, clean bathroom and its gleaming white tiles. She was grateful to General Kim Il-sung for his gift.

Infinitely grateful.

Because the class was still in session, I waited in the corridor. During my last trip, Tetsuya hadn't left me any time to take a proper look around.

Like Ayumi's new home, the school building had been constructed by order of Pyongyang. It was only two years old and its edges still looked sharp, the grey of the concrete had a silvery shimmer; it was yet to be painted. The schoolyard wasn't asphalted, but rather an overgrown garden with wild-flowers, shrubbery and an old maple tree in its centre which seemed gigantic, picturesque, and even bucolic with the numerous butterflies, tits and sparrows that were flitting around it. It was as straight as a lamppost, wonderfully symmetrical, the kind of tree that my mother would have claimed had spirits living in it; she said you could tell by the breadth and length of the branches and by their shape. It would be chopped down soon for sure, but the task of removing its widely ramified roots wouldn't be an easy one. I pictured how the workers would need to use all of their strength to pull them out of the earth, a great army of full-grown men with a thick rope that they had bound around their waists; they would fail in their mission, at least one root would survive. But perhaps, given that the space wasn't big enough for a baseball field (they had become ubiquitous since the end of American occupation), they would plant grass instead, remove the weeds and wild-flowers, some of the bushes and shrubbery, and leave the tree standing; during break time, the children could gather around its trunk and exchange news, messages and small treasures such as glass marbles . . .

'Mr Kang.' I was torn from my thoughts. 'Mrs Nobukawa will see you now.'

The staff room was on the first floor, but just as I was about to go up the stairs, the secretary held me back and pointed towards the director's office. I was surprised, but didn't let it show, and followed her in.

In the entrance of the director's office stood two half-empty moving boxes, which I had to walk round. They didn't contain much, just books and magazines. Ayumi was sitting behind the desk, and stood up as I walked in. She bowed briefly; it was just a hint of a bow, any exaggerated politeness towards me was unnecessary.

She gestured towards the black leather chair I had sat in on my previous visit, and took a seat opposite me. The portrait of Kim Il-sung grinned down at me benevolently. In my memory it had been a deep yellow, with his face hovering in front of a magnificent, dazzling rainbow, the glorious hero in front of a glorious sunrise, but in actual fact he was posing in front of an azure sky, and the relatively compact sun was tucked away in the right-hand corner of the picture. His mouth and eyes were twisted into a smile, but his gaze was directed into the distance, into the future.

'How can I help you?'

Ayumi straightened her glasses.

'Are you covering for Director Masaki today?'

She smiled in amusement.

'You could say that.'

She laughed.

'I'm his successor.'

'Successor?'

I couldn't hide my surprise.

Mr Masaki had decided to emigrate to North Korea with his family, Ayumi explained, and would become director of a school in Pyongyang, where the lack of teaching staff was still acute. She was taking over his position in Osaka. She was the first female director of a Korean school, until now only men had been appointed, but General Kim didn't make empty promises; equality wasn't a foreign concept under Communism.

I congratulated her; I was genuinely pleased, I knew how long she had been waiting for an opportunity like this. I commented that a popular teacher like her was a good, no, the *natural* choice. She waved her hand, dismissing my words, nothing was natural, she said, everything was constructed by society: gender roles, the function of religion, even the superiority of the strongest. Surely, as a student of philosophy, I must be aware of that.

'But you never went to university, did you, Mr Kang?'

She fixed her grey eyes on me. I wondered how she had found out; apart from Johnny and Eve, no one else knew that my biography was a lie.

'It doesn't matter, Mr Kang,' she continued, 'you're still young, you can catch up with your studies any time. And you're well read, so studying won't be hard for you.'

She sighed.

'The university fees, of course, are a different matter. Not everyone can afford to pay for education.'

All at once, I felt as though I was being watched . . . Even though she seemed to be interested in anything but me (she repeated that she had a lot to do, that she didn't even have time to draw breath), I felt exposed. But perhaps it was the other way round, and I was just imagining that she was staring at me, when in truth I was the one staring at her.

'Don't gawk like that, Mr Kang,' she reprimanded me suddenly, 'I'm sure you'll get used to the director being a woman.'

She sat up straight, poker-straight like the maple tree outside her window, and looked at me expectantly. I wondered whether, now that she had become director, she would let her hair grow and put it up; with her shoulder-length hair and fringe she looked barely any different from the schoolgirls, her hairstyle made her look less important, harmless. And hadn't Machiavelli written that we humans are primarily driven by two emotions: love and fear? Though a person for whom we feel affection and love dominates us just as much as one who scares us, fear alone leads to 'lasting obedience'.

'So, Mr Kang,' Ayumi seemed impatient, 'what can I do for you?'

It seemed Eiko's favourite teacher hadn't heard about her disappearance. Once Ayumi had been appointed director, the class had been assigned another form teacher, and Mrs Ikeda hadn't mentioned to her that Eiko Yamamoto had been absent from lessons for five days now . . .

Ayumi was stunned. Of course she would do everything in her power to get to the bottom of the matter and help the family, she assured me, that went without saying. Eiko's well-being was very important to her, regardless of the argument that had occurred with her parents; after all, without her she would never have got this role. What did Eiko have to do with her promotion? I asked. Without young Comrade Yamamoto's enthusiasm, initiative and commitment, Ayumi answered, she would never have fulfilled her quota, and her application would have been ranked lower.

'Quota?'

'Mr Kang, don't play dumb. You know very well that there are quotas we have to fulfil. They're not obligatory, of course, more like guidelines.'

'So your assignment was to send a certain number of schoolgirls to North Korea?'

'My assignment *is* to inform the girls and boys in my school about the educational and vocational opportunities in the Democratic People's Republic. The decision to emigrate is theirs, not mine.'

'And Eiko helped you to bait the girls?'

'There was no baiting involved.'

'Eiko was promoting the campaign?'

'With great success. The entire class signed up, all thirty.'

'I heard she was having difficulties convincing the last ones to sign . . .'

'No, not really.'

Ayumi smiled.

'Never underestimate the power of the collective, Mr Kang.'

'I'll be careful not to, Mrs Nobukawa.'

'I take it that you want to speak with the class and their teacher?'

I nodded. She lifted the telephone receiver from its cradle and summoned her secretary into the room. She hoped, she said jokingly, that Mr Yamamoto didn't suspect her of being involved in his daughter's disappearance?

When I didn't answer, she shook her head gently. In order to convince Mr Yamamoto otherwise, the secretary would write down her new address for me and explain how to get there, and she would see me there this evening. Then I could inspect her apartment – no, the entire building – and convince myself that she didn't have little Yamamoto hidden away. But everything in good time, first I should speak with the schoolgirls and Mrs Ikeda, and after that, she said, escorting me out into the corridor, Mr Yamamoto wouldn't be able to accuse her of anything.

'Then we can call it quits.'

The secretary told me to wait in front of the closed classroom door; Mrs Ikeda would call me in. When the school bell announced the end of the lesson, the doors to all the classrooms opened simultaneously, and the children who streamed out – there were many more than I had thought – threw me curious glances, some of them furtively, but most overtly. One asked me: 'Are you the new Korean teacher?', another answered him: 'He looks like one!', and from the crowd I heard the muttered words: 'Go home, Chōsenjin!' followed by raucous laughter, reminding me how painful it sometimes is to be a Korean among Koreans.

Eventually, I was addressed by a petite woman, who introduced herself as the new teacher and led me into the classroom; she had told the girls about my visit, she said, I could now ask them my questions. To my surprise, the schoolgirls weren't seated at their desks, but standing in two rigid, orderly rows in front of the board, the fifteen shorter girls in the front row, the fourteen taller ones in the second. The classroom was deathly quiet; like a house in mourning, I thought to myself.

As the teenagers were wearing uniforms, I found it hard to distinguish them from one another, and to complicate things further most of them had pageboy haircuts. What helped me to tell them apart were the different voices, the registers and accents which were sometimes less Japanese, sometimes more, depending on whether or not their families spoke Korean at home. Yet they almost all said the exact same thing – as though they were aware of their uniformity and using it to send me off down the wrong path.

Eiko had last been to school five days ago, the group were in agreement on this, and since then no one had seen her, she hadn't appeared either in class or in the school building, or in the grounds. Everyone had thought she was sick, and no one, including the teacher, had thought to ask her parents.

I asked whether Eiko had seemed any different on Monday, perhaps unusually nervous, agitated or subdued. The class unanimously, harmoniously, shook its head. No, she was the same as always: cheerful, energetic, in high spirits. Ever since she had handed in the list, she was always in a good mood, they said. I seized on this.

'What list?'

'The list with the signatures of all the homecomers.'

'Where is it now?'

This question provoked confusion. The girls exchanged clueless glances, some blushed. Mrs Ikeda declared, after conferring with a few of the girls, that it was either still in the director's office or had already been sent to the Red Cross.

I sensed that the teacher wanted to bring the questioning to an end, that she – unlike me – was content with the answers, when suddenly a voice spoke up from the second row; it belonged to Eiko's best friend: 'Has there been an accident? Has something happened to Eiko?'

Her very lack of suspicion suggested Senko Yamada to me as a suspect. Was it possible for best friends to not talk for five whole days? For one not to have the slightest clue where the other was? 'Mr Kang,' her innocent expression seemed to say, 'believe neither your eyes nor your ears, I know more than I'm letting on.'

'Hopefully not.'

343

'Will the police be informed?'

'That depends,' I countered, 'if she's found soon, then probably not.'

'What does "soon" mean?'

'In the next two or three days.'

I genuinely didn't know how Tetsuya would react if I couldn't report back to him tonight with at least one promising lead. Senko nodded, and said that made sense. To me she seemed calm, almost peaceful: as though she knew exactly where Eiko was hiding.

As far as Mrs Ikeda was concerned, the matter was dealt with. She was waiting for some concluding words of thanks and comfort, but I didn't grant her that favour. I told her I now wanted to question the schoolgirls individually.

'Individually?'

She looked at me in shock. It was essential, I explained, because some girls wouldn't have the courage to tell the truth in front of the group, surely she must realize that. Of course, she assured me hastily, but she still had to discuss it with the director, so if I could just wait in front of the classroom again. 'Please.' After steering me into the corridor, she hurried down to the ground floor. I settled in for a long wait, perhaps I would even be summoned to the director's office again, I thought, lighting myself a cigarette.

I was wrong; barely three minutes later she was standing before me once more, asking me to put out the cigarette. Mrs Nobukawa would permit me to question two schoolgirls of my choosing, she announced. Two. No more. Agreed, I said, Senko Yamada and Tomoko Lee, all the others could go. Mrs Ikeda nodded, signalled to me to wait in the corridor, and hurried into the classroom.

344

After the girls had left the room, I was waved inside. Mrs Ikeda told Senko and Tomoko to wait outside until I called them. No, I interjected, she should keep the girls company in the corridor. 'Please.' Mrs Ikeda glanced at me nervously, but left the room; Mrs Nobukawa wouldn't approve, that much was clear. But I didn't care about being considerate of Ayumi's feelings, nor the schoolgirls'; on the contrary: I had no intention of making concessions for them, much less reassuring them. I calmly looked for a piece of paper, in case I needed to note something down. When I didn't find any in my trouser pockets, I searched through the low cupboards in the room, and took my time about it. I opened every door and every drawer. I found paintbrushes, tubes of paint, notebooks, text-books, wax crayons, coloured pens and some paper. Not much, but enough for my purpose. I pushed open a window and lit the cigarette which I'd had to extinguish before; I had tucked it into my pocket, never would I have thrown it away.

I leisurely smoked it to the end. Then, and only then, did I open the door and ask the first girl to come in.

Senko Yamada didn't look the slightest bit like her father, leading me to wonder whether perhaps she had been switched at birth or bought from another family. There were rumours in Ikaino that she wasn't Yamada's child, but the result of an affair with a Japanese man; Madame Chiang Kai-shek had done everything in her power to quell the rumours (she had sweet-talked, bribed and threatened the gossip-mongers), but the story had proved to be immortal.

I thanked Senko for her willingness to speak with me, knowing full well that this was just a pleasantry, for she had been given no choice. Her words – 'Of course I want to help my friend' – were even emptier than mine.

As I watched her fidgeting around nervously on her chair, it occurred to me that she was a seated giant; a person who looks tall only when sitting. Her upper body was longer than her lower body, her head large in relation to her shoulders. Aside from her defective proportions, she was a perfect Yamada: even the simple uniform made from cheap fabric looked like an expensive outfit on her. But perhaps her mother had helped by having it re-cut from an expensive yarn? I wouldn't put anything past Madame.

Senko seemed to be afraid of holding eye contact; she clearly felt more comfortable with eye-nudges; a battalion of quick glances, none of which lasted longer than half a second. I wondered whether she was simply feigning this shyness, this timidity. Perhaps she was putting on a naive act because she was involved in Eiko's disappearance?

She repeated her statement from before. She had last seen her friend on Monday afternoon. 'After class, yes, that's right,' she nodded emphatically (a little too emphatically, in my opinion), they had exchanged a few words, then Senko had been picked up by her driver as always. She had said goodbye to Eiko and the other girls and was then driven home, where her piano teacher was waiting for her. The lesson had begun before she even had time to put her school bag in her room. 'An anomaly, yes,' she nodded again, somewhat more slowly, less emphatically; normally she had half an hour between the teacher's arrival and the start of the lesson, she couldn't say why it had been different this time, she hadn't even had time to consult the clock.

Senko looked at me thoughtfully, and it was as though I could see her running through all the possibilities in her mind: was there a connection between the premature piano lesson and Eiko's disappearance? Was the music student a possible kid-napper? Or an accomplice, perhaps? Were he and Eiko lovers?

346

The lesson had ended after two hours, she said, like always.
'What did you play?'
'Hans von Bülow called it "Suffocation".'
'Suffocation?'
'Chopin's Prelude in E minor, op. 28, no. 4.'

I knew the piece well; on rainy evenings, Tetsuya listened only to Chopin. When the nights were warm and the moon as bright as the sun, he cranked up his gramophone and listened to prim and proper Doris; if he was in a good mood, Billie and I were granted our turn.

I liked the preludes very much, but Tetsuya and I disagreed when it came to their interpretation: I preferred a more tranquil performance, while Tetsuya insisted that the individual notes had to 'cascade in pearl-like droplets', they couldn't blur into one another.

Senko grinned; her teacher was a hard taskmaster too, she told me. Yet she deliberately slowed her playing, she waited for the tone to fade. 'The thing is,' she said, 'I'm not so much interested in the fusion of notes, the composition itself, but more the individual notes, how they are struck and gradually fade. It amazes me every time, the suddenness with which the chords become visible, only to slip back into nothingness once the breath leaves them.'

She leant back.

'They attach themselves to time, that's how they stay alive. I wouldn't like to shorten that by striking a new note too hastily.'

She sighed. Her teacher wasn't satisfied with her, she said. A strand of hair fell into her face, she tucked it behind her ear and looked at me. Eiko may have called herself her best friend, she said, but they hadn't been close for a long time now. Eiko had focused her attention on the other girls, she had wanted to be good friends with *everyone*, and she, the Yamada girl, had stood in her way. The girls avoided her because of her father; they wanted nothing to do with her, out of fear he would hurt their families if they argued. She knew how her father earned his money, she added, and she wouldn't be surprised if he had had Eiko kidnapped.

I looked at her in surprise. Yes, I had heard right, she said. After she had repeatedly refused to call off her journey, her father had threatened the Yamamotos. He had hoped that she, Senko, would give up her plan if Eiko were no longer interested in North Korea.

Senko laughed. And yet she had no intention whatsoever of staying there, she told me. She had signed up because she wanted to emigrate to Poland, her destination was 'Warszawa' as she called it, and Warsaw, she explained, was easy to reach from the People's Republic; or easier, in any case.

'They can't change my mind. Neither my parents nor Mr Yamamoto.'

She picked her school bag up from the floor.

She felt bad about Eiko, she said, and was sorry if she was making my life difficult, she knew very well how ruthless her father could be; she apologized for that too. But she wouldn't go back on her decision.

Before I could assure her that I wasn't working for Mr Yamada, she had darted out of the classroom.

Tomoko was different to Senko. For one thing, she was almost three years older, and for another, she claimed she had nothing to do with Eiko and Senko's clique; it couldn't be ruled out, however, that she was just trying to deflect any suspicion from herself.

They were expecting her at home, she declared before she

348

sat down, Father was sure to be waiting for her already, she was responsible for the vegetables, for the washing, peeling and chopping, she did her homework late at night, once all the customers had left and the restaurant was closed, that's why she'd had to repeat two years. But she was happy that she was able to finish high school at all, it was something she'd had to fight for, and it had been worth it; one day, when she no longer had to help out in her parents' restaurant, perhaps she would study.

Like Mio Kobayashi (who she claimed to have been good friends with) she had a slight stutter; the fact that her vowels and consonants lingered on her tongue longer than they should have, and doubled and tripled between her teeth, had the odd effect of making her Korean more melodic. She was taciturn; presumably she spoke as little as possible to avoid exposing herself to the danger of stammering. Her stutter had got worse recently, she said carefully, it was as though the words had submerged and were directly beneath the surface of a body of water, which, whenever she approached it, transformed into a raging maelstrom and pulled her into it; it was becoming more and more difficult to free herself.

'If you really think about it, it's the inability to say the necessary thing at the right time which makes somebody a stutterer,' she said.

'Then we're all stutterers,' I answered.

She smiled shyly.

Most of the time, she said, her tongue was blocked even by the mere presence of words, both the spoken and the unspoken.

'Yours and mine.'

'Mine too?'

'It's the words that aren't yet spoken, the words waiting in line, that really take it out of me.'

349

I took an instant liking to Tomoko; she was completely different to the girls Johnny normally fell for, she seemed more mature, more grown-up – more grown-up, even, than Eve, who was seventeen years her senior.

What did she want to study, I asked. Medicine, she replied. She'd wanted to be a doctor, an ophthalmologist, ever since she was a child.

'Is that why you signed up for the Great Homecoming? So you can study medicine at the Kim Il-sung University?'

She shook her head. It had been an impulse, just for fun, she hadn't taken it seriously, no one had taken it seriously, only Eiko. She looked at me thoughtfully. The whole class had signed to please Eiko . . . but no, she went on to correct herself:

'The first ones signed because they were tempted by the idea of living in a country where they could be themselves, where they wouldn't have to hide. The next ones signed because Eiko's enthusiasm was contagious. A few of them wanted to give their parents a scare, others hoped to win more freedom by provoking them.'

The final group signed, she said, because Eiko pressured them into it, mocking and bullying them. In the end, no one could take it any longer.

'I said to the girls, just sign. No one will take you at your word.'

'But that's not true, is it? Isn't the signature binding?'

'Yes and no. It only becomes binding once you stand in front of the Red Cross committee in Niigata and swear that you're leaving the country of your own free will. So you s-s-s-ee, all the f-f-fuss was over no-th-th-thing.'

She cleared her throat.

'But now Eiko is g-g-gone.'

As Tomoko massaged the hinge of her jaw with her fingers, I looked down at the floor.

She didn't believe, she continued, that Eiko had been kidnapped. No one would dare touch a hair on the head of Mr Yamamoto's daughter. Eiko had probably run away from home out of fear her parents wouldn't let her travel to Chōngjin; she had probably ensconced herself with a small travel bag at the home of a friend of a friend on Monday, after dinner, so that she couldn't be traced. She would only emerge again on the day of the departure, to ensure that her parents wouldn't stand in the way of her plan.

'Or maybe she f-f-fled straight to Niigata.'

'Fled?'

Tomoko blushed. She must have got hold of the wrong word, she said, she often made mistakes in Korean. She meant that perhaps Eiko had set off straight from school, without going home first.

'What makes you think that?'

'Because I s-s-saw Eiko getting into a b-b-big b-b-black c-c-car. It looked like the limousine that picked Senko up, b-b-but it was more s-q-q-quare and dark g-g-grey, not b-b-black.'

'Anthracite?'

'Anthra-c-c-cite.'

'When was that?'

She raised five fingers.

'Why didn't you say that before?'

'To s-s-start with I th-th-thought that Mr Yam-m-mamoto had s-s-sent a c-c-car.'

'But?'

Tomoko blinked.

'I j-j-just remem-b-b-bered that Eiko always t-t-takes the bus.'

★

Tomoko's statement was the first and only one to support Tetsuya's fears. No one, neither the school caretaker nor the two cleaning ladies, nor the owners of the grocery shop near the school, had seen a grey car, only the black one which had picked up Senko.

I didn't know what to make of Tomoko's story. On the one hand, I believed, like she did, that Eiko had run away, and that Tetsuya and Naoko were just refusing to admit this to themselves and the neighbourhood – because children from good homes didn't do such things. On the other hand, I wasn't sure whether I could trust Tomoko; perhaps she was trying to lead me down the wrong path with a lie. Perhaps Eiko had been kidnapped by someone Tomoko knew, and because I was making enquiries, she now thought she had to protect this person.

I pondered whom she would cover for. Her father, certainly. Mr Lee definitely had a motive; he didn't want his daughter to be forced to emigrate to North Korea, but would he go to such extreme measures? He wouldn't have been able to carry out the abduction without an accomplice . . . Who would help him? He wouldn't pay much, he was too tight-fisted for that.

Johnny.

I hadn't seen Johnny since Sunday, and had thought that I was the reason he hadn't come home. What if it was because he had to keep watch over Eiko? Perhaps the concerned father had got wind of Tomoko and Johnny's love affair and had incited my easily influenced friend to perform this 'heroic act'?

I decided to try a ruse. 'I'm not working for Mr Yamamoto,' I lied, hoping that Tomoko would buy it. She looked at me in surprise. She couldn't breathe a word of this under any circumstances, I said in a hushed tone, edging closer to her. She nodded. Had she taken the bait?

I whispered in her ear: 'I'm supposed to find out whether Sōren is trying to force individual members to emigrate to North Korea. Apparently it's already happened on numerous occasions.'

Her eyes widened.

'I'm working for Mindan.'

As soon as I had uttered the sentence, I regretted it – I sensed Tomoko's resistance. If Eiko really had been taken away by force, she said quietly, then wouldn't Mindan members be the more likely suspects? Who else would be interested in sabotaging the Great Homecoming? She stood up slowly. Was I accusing her family of being Mindan agents, she asked?

She had spotted the trap; it had been a mistake to invent the story. Nonetheless, I tried to save face and said that not all Sōren members were in favour of the homecoming, Mr Yamada, for example, had resisted pulling up stakes for a long time already, even though he had been repeatedly advised to. Yamada, cried Tomoko, Senko Yamada was the worst of them all, even more fanatical than Eiko. She was the one who had pushed Mio to suicide, she, not Eiko. Whoever had made Eiko disappear should have taken Senko too.

'*S-s-she* will make sure that everyone goes – whether they want to or not!'

With these words, Tomoko grabbed her jacket and ran out of the classroom without looking back; had she given me the opportunity, I would have apologized . . .

There was one thing, however, that she would prove to be wrong about: Senko would be the first to remove her name from the list. After that, the girls called off their Great Homecoming one after the other – with one exception.

I said goodbye to Mrs Ikeda, ignored her anxious questions and hurried out into the open air. I wanted to question the children that hung around on the streets of Ikaino; if anyone had spotted the grey limousine, it would be them.

It wasn't hard to find them. As always they were grouped together on a street corner near a convenience store. From time to time they would run in and scrounge sweets of some kind off the leaseholder. If he gave in, even just the once, his peaceful working day was over and done with, from that moment on he could count on a different boy trotting into his shop each hour to beg for something to nibble on. The only salvation he could hope for was the street trader, who, once a week and for a few hours at a time, armed with a sack of home-made sweets and lollipops in all the colours of the rainbow – as well as a seemingly inexhaustible supply of fairy tales and legends – would distract the children and wheedle their hard-saved pocket money out of them.

The boys were kneeling on the pavement, bent over their game of marbles. They held the glass pearls up against the orange-yellow light coming from the street lamps, compared the different whirls of colour held captive in the hearts of the orbs, and debated at length the question of who owned the most beautiful specimen. As a boy I had owned seven marbles; Johnny had given me one so I could play with him, and I had won six additional ones off him. After that he had rejected me as an opponent and claimed that I had a trick – he couldn't say what, but he was convinced of it – and that was why I was so good at shooting. Perhaps, though, this had been an excuse and he simply hadn't wanted to lose his supply of marbles. He had guarded the little balls as though they were treasure, always keeping them on his person, like I did my seven, which had also been the only property I owned; I lost them when we fled from the People's Army into the mountains.

I sat down on the ground with the boys, who were playing not with a heap of marbles, but a whole mountain of them – I had never seen so many at once, and was alternately envious and happy to see so many colourful spheres before me; I grabbed one and shot it at one of the others.

Its owner, a stubborn, wiry lad who, as I found out, was a very good shot (even a little fish has sharp bones), burst out laughing. I had shot his marble at the one belonging to his nemesis. A debate broke out as to whether my shot counted or not. The owner of the victorious marble, my new best friend, insisted it did. His opponent protested that I had joined their game uninvited. Which was true. 'Uninvited only from your point of view,' answered my friend. Which was also true.

And so it went back and forth. The squabbling rivals would have started a fist fight, had I not intervened and offered to play for the one who would give me some information. 'Information,' they echoed, 'what information?' and they promptly loosened their grip on one another. I told them that Eiko, a schoolgirl, had last been seen on Monday in front of the Korean school, I described her face, her hair and her uniform, and asked whether the boys had been near the school that day. I hoped for a 'yes'. After all, it was right round the corner from the shop.

Both of them nodded emphatically, they knew Eiko. The bigger and older boy was hopelessly in love with her, said my little friend mockingly, he always hung around the bus stop at the end of the school day to see her and exchange a few words.

Haruki blushed. He wasn't hopelessly in love, he mumbled, he just thought she was pretty, really pretty. His friends rolled around on the floor laughing, blowing air kisses at one another. She was nice too, said Haruki, in an attempt to rescue his dignity, she was a good sort, easy to talk to, and she didn't send him away like the other girls did. On Monday – and here he frowned, struggling to remember which day today was, he had to count them off on his fingers – on Monday, he was smiling broadly now, she hadn't got on the bus, but instead said goodbye to her stuck-up friends and then walked past this shop, where he caught up with her, and they chatted for a while, mainly about the new teacher, then he walked her to a house and said goodbye to her in front of the gate.

'Which house?'

Haruki smiled cunningly. If I played the next round for him, he would show me. But, just so it was clear, any marbles I won would be his.

'Agreed.'

We sealed our agreement with a handshake, and the game began. Before long there were only three of us, all the others having slipped away. My little despairing friend put all his efforts into winning back the lost marbles, all the while being mocked by Haruki and supplied with good advice: 'A sparrow's foot this year is better than a leg of pork in the next' was one of them, and 'The lost fish is always the biggest.'

After an admittedly unfair match, Haruki led me to the concrete building that Sōren had constructed for the teachers at the Korean school; this was also where I had arranged to meet Ayumi. Eiko had gone through this door, said Haruki, pointing towards the entrance, she had told him she urgently needed to speak with her old teacher . . .

And with the new marbles in his hand, he waved goodbye to me, then disappeared into the darkness of a side street.

17

'You're an hour early.'

She was wearing an apron, a ruffled, white apron, which, she pointed out, would make Blondie proud. 'Who?' I asked. 'Blondie,' she repeated, expressing surprise that I didn't know the American comic-strip housewife who had been causing a stir in Japan's newspapers since the end of the Second World War, persuading women to buy bread instead of cook rice.

She was stammering; I had caught her off guard. But the loss of equilibrium didn't last long, the smile that was strangely familiar to me soon appeared on her face, harbouring warmth, but hardness too.

'I hope I haven't come at an inconvenient time . . .'

'Do you know the saying: "Work like an ox and eat like a mouse – that's the way to happiness"?'

She smiled in amusement.

'Well, tonight we'll be eating like mice.'

She ushered me into the only room there was besides the kitchen and the small hallway, and told me to take a seat; she still had some things to finish.

The room was sparsely furnished: an empty wicker basket stood in one corner, a fan in the other. The fan looked new, while the sewing machine, on the other hand, must have been an heirloom; it was almost completely coated in rust. My gaze wandered over to the wall, to the North Korean flag fastened to the wallpaper with pins, its arrangement giving the impression it was fluttering artistically in an imaginary wind. But it was the carefully framed picture alongside it that opened my eyes: finally I understood why Ayumi's smile looked so familiar. Ever since the first time I met her, I hadn't been able to shake the impression that it was copied; as though she had flicked through a catalogue of smiling mouths, chosen one and learnt the smile off by heart.

It really was a copy, and the original beamed out all over Ikaino, in every school, in every financial institution. Its rightful owner was Kim Il-sung.

'You interrupted me while I was cooking, but I don't want to keep you waiting, so I hope bread is okay?'

I hurried to assure her that bread was one of my favourite foods, but in truth I was disappointed. From Ayumi, of all people, I had expected a warm evening meal.

She set the low table with two gleaming white plates, silver knives and forks, and asked me, worriedly, if I preferred chopsticks.

I shook my head. She nodded, disappeared into the kitchen and came back with a platter containing numerous round bread rolls, as well as kimchi, spicy marinated tofu, and spinach tossed in sesame oil; then she sat down.

Unfortunately, she told me, in Osaka things weren't as they had been on her home island of Jeju, south of the Korean mainland. Back when she went to school, the girls' mothers and grandmothers had always brought the teaching staff little dishes; her teacher had never had to cook for herself, not even rice. On the last day of term, the classrooms were always filled with the scent of food, of black and white pepper, ground chilli and garlic, roasted vegetables or chicken, and sometimes, albeit rarely, steamed sweet potatoes and roasted chestnuts. She sighed; in Japan other presents were customary, soap and silk stockings.

Had she wanted to be a teacher even back then? I asked, while dissecting a bread roll. She shook her head. She had started working at a young age, with her mother, in an armaments factory after they moved to Japan. She had met a Korean there, a teacher who had been barred from his profession for being a communist.

'The rumour went round that he had been a· resistance fighter in Manchuria, one of General Kim's people. The police were constantly taking him away for interrogations, he often didn't come into work for days on end. Eventually, the factory owner fired him. I stuck up for him, explained that none of it was his fault, but the owner wouldn't relent. So Mother took him in. We shared with him the little we had.'

In order to return the favour, he gave her lessons in Korean literature, philosophy and history. After the emancipation in August 1945, he was appointed director of the first Korean school. Sōren secured the position for him, and he had secured this one for her.

'Now I'm the director.'

Laughing, she brushed her hair out of her face. I spotted grey strands beneath the top layer of black; so time did leave its mark on her after all, even her.

'So you won't be emigrating to North Korea any more? I thought that was the plan.'

'It was more of a dream.'

She leant forward. Her grandparents were dead, she told me, as was her mother; she still hadn't found her father, and had never met the rest of her family, she didn't even know how many cousins she had.

'Money is such a wretched thing. On the search, the hunt,

for it, fathers leave mothers, mothers leave children. It's no coincidence that there are barely any children in Ikaino growing up among their families. Many of my pupils and colleagues have never met their parents, others have been separated from their siblings.'

She tore off a piece of bread and topped it with tofu.

'I used to be ashamed of having grown up without a father. Nowadays things are different. General Kim has freed me from shame. He's put an end to the discrimination against single mothers and widows. He is against large families.'

She poured a spoonful of kimchi broth over the tofu-topped bread and garnished it with a leaf of Chinese cabbage.

'You've been rehabilitated too.'

'Rehabilitated?'

'To our General, the fact that you're a war orphan is one more reason to welcome you with open arms.'

The chilli marinade dripped onto Ayumi's lips, colouring her teeth blood red, if only for a second.

'I can assure you that the war orphans in the North are doing significantly better than those in the South. They weren't sold to foreign families, their existence wasn't denied out of a false sense of shame.'

'Sold? I thought they were adopted.'

Ayumi ignored my question. Triumphantly, she explained: 'General Kim Il-sung did away with the family register. He abolished it.'

This was news to me. With the help of the family register, which had been reformed in the South (daughters as well as sons were now included, for example), it's essentially possible to trace the evolution of a family back to its origins. Director Kim (as the firstborn son) had kept his family's register, numerous volumes which listed the names of all his male ancestors; after the civil war, he announced with relief that he had been able to save it from the People's Army.

The register records nothing but names, yet these carry either pride or shame. In this way, the sins of the fathers, grand-fathers and great-grandfathers are captured for the descendants, as are their achievements. Would it be going too far to suggest that the Korean obsession with history has its roots in this register? That's what I believe, anyway. Our fixation becomes less absurd when you consider that the official written history consists of individual biographies taken from the family registers of kings and princes. Is the register an attempt to record the individualized history, the alternative and, essentially, true history? The truth, the particular, is hidden within the general; the wise know to trust the former over the latter. As unofficial official history, the register constitutes the foundation of identity, not only of the individual, but the entire clan. The members shape their lives in accordance with the register – even if they rebel against the past, they still look to it for reference; the ancestral tree doesn't merely represent the past in concentrated form, but also points towards what is to come, to the future.

'The abolition of the family register in the North took place just two years into the North Korean revolution, after the land reform and the division of the large landowners' estates among the tenant farmers. You are free, Mr Kang. Your worth is no longer contaminated by your family. From now on, you define your story, your destiny.'

She turned on the radio, yet immediately lowered the volume, making the programme barely audible; I thought to myself, she brings the music to life and stifles it in the very same moment.

Ayumi poured more tea.

361

'While we're on the subject of destiny: General Kim Il-sung, the man you keep glancing at so curiously, grew up under circumstances that aren't too dissimilar to ours. He began his migrant life at seven, I at fourteen, you at twenty-two.'

The Kim family emigrated to north-east China, to legendary Manchuria. What Yan'an was for the Maoists, Manchuria was for the Koreans: it would become Kim Il-sung's base for the next twenty-one years, and he didn't return to his homeland until his mid-thirties. I tried to filter the stories I heard about his life before committing them to memory – history was pursued so intensely by both the North and the South, that most of the facts were obscured by propaganda and lost to the shadows.

Kim really did come from a family of resistance fighters, as the North Korean hagiography claimed. His father and uncle were imprisoned for anti-Japanese activities, his older brother died in a Japanese prison, the two younger brothers were also active in the anti-Japanese resistance. The 'Great Leader' was only able to become a great leader, his biographer later noted, because he grew up under the 'ideal conditions'.

Because Kim Il-sung attended the local Chinese schools, he spoke fluent Mandarin. In 1930, two years before Greater Japan annexed Manchuria and proclaimed it the Empire of Manchukuo, he was imprisoned as a terrorist for the first time, and in 1931 he became a member of the Chinese Communist Party. After the Comintern issued the 'One Country, One Party' directive in December 1928, the Korean communists in Manchuria had been absorbed into the Chinese Communist Party, even though the majority of the officially Chinese party members were Korean. Most Koreans in exile lived in eastern Manchuria, as the Kim family did, and saw themselves as communists. Yet they opposed the Party's authority and saw the emancipation of Korea from Japanese rule as their true objective. They joined forces with the Chinese Communist Party only because they had a common enemy – beyond this there was considerable mistrust between the groups, which in the 1930s culminated in a purge costing hundreds of Korean comrades their lives.

The catalyst was the Minshengtuan. Translating as 'The People's Food Corps', the organization was founded by those Manchurian Koreans who were favourably disposed towards the Japanese rulers, on account of having received land and privileges from them. They asked the colonial administration for support and protection from the communists and the Chinese authorities, and demanded to be allowed to administer themselves, albeit under Japanese sovereignty. Having never received an answer, the corps was disbanded a few months later, but the suspicion grew among Chinese communists that most Koreans secretly belonged to the Minshengtuan and were therefore allied with the enemy. Between 1933 and 1936, more than a thousand Korean comrades were arrested and expelled from the party; half of them were executed.

Kim Il-sung was also detained, yet cleared of all charges after just a year's imprisonment; people say he managed to call in an unpaid debt.

He resumed his partisan life, spending the years that followed as commander of a unit of around three hundred guerrilla fighters. All the independent liberation armies and the secret league of Dadaohui ('Big Sword') had joined forces, but they were no match for the imperial Japanese army, and suffered crushing defeats in numerous battles. The survivors retreated to base camps in the Soviet Far East. From there they carried out numerous attacks, yet the communists of East Asia expected something on the scale of liberating Japan to come only from the Soviet Union.

In the last week of July 1945, after Kim was appointed captain and thereby officially became a member of the Red Army, the Chinese and Korean partisans were informed that they would soon be sent back to their homelands for the recovery.

On 6 August, Little Boy was dropped on Hiroshima; on 8 August, Stalin declared war on Japan; and on 9 August, after Fat Man had razed Nagasaki to the ground, Soviet troops reached the north of Korea. On the night of 10 August, the decision was made to divide Korea along the 38th parallel, which would keep the Korean capital within the American sphere of control. Washington was concerned that US influence in East Asia could be diminished by the Soviet presence; they feared the Soviets would occupy Korea at the end of the war with the very resistance fighters who had already fought against Japan in north-east China. The Americans wanted a re-strengthened Japanese state as a loyal partner, and even an economy as battered as Korea's could serve the rebuilding of Japan, while a Soviet occupation of Korea in its entirety would impede not only this, but the re-establishment of the pre-war order. The fear of Soviet expansion and Japan's concern that the communists could exploit the power vacuum in Korea to seize control was so great that the American troops' entry date was brought forward three times; when the moment came, 25,000 US soldiers marched into South Korea.

Moscow was in agreement with Washington's suggestion that they occupy Korea together, and also accepted the division along the 38th parallel. Stalin had little interest in Korea, after all, and was more concerned about a recovered, re-militarized Japan. Korea couldn't be permitted to slip under Japanese influence again. Instead it was to resume the function it had had since the days of Tsar Nicholas II, as a buffer zone between the USSR and their enemy.

Stalin entrusted the liberation of Korea to the Soviet Koreans rather than the Manchurian partisans, who in the meantime had elected Kim as their leader; in Stalin's opinion, the former were more trustworthy due to their long-standing connection with the Soviet Union. Stalin's mistrust had already led to the execution of numerous Korean Comintern agents back in 1937, and to the forced resettlement of two hundred thousand Koreans from the Soviet Far East to Kazakhstan and Uzbekistan; many died as a result. Stalin had presumed that there could be Japanese spies among them, and also considered them to be too influenced by Japan, 'unreliable' and 'indistinguishable from the Japanese'.

When the Joseon republic, as Korea was initially named, was proclaimed in September 1945 by the interim government in Seoul, Kim Il-sung was on his way to Vladivostok to board a steamship headed for Wŏnsan. A bombed bridge was blocking the land route. He and his men didn't reach Pyongyang until 22 September.

Immediately after his arrival, he discovered that the North Korean provinces were ruled by more than a hundred *komendaturas* and committees formed of the native population, which, in contrast to those in the South, were recognized by the occupying powers and even included in the occupation plan. The number of *komendaturas* was halved during the first year of occupation, and supplanted by the Grazhdanskaya Administratsiya ('Civil Administration'), whose role it was to ensure that Stalin's economic and international interests were protected.

The degree of Soviet influence in North Korea is a topic of extensive debate. Some historians speak of absolute influence, while others, including official North Korean histories, see little to none (after the Korean War, Stalin Street in Pyongyang was renamed Victory Street, a clear sign of the increasing alienation between the USSR and the Kim regime at the time). An undeniable fact is that the Soviets sent many political advisers to North Korea who worked in close collaboration with the interim government, as well as numerous teachers, technicians and doctors, in order to educate and train the population. Japanese engineers who were caught unawares by Hirohito's capitulation and unable to flee in time were prohibited from returning to their homeland; they too had to pass on their specialist knowledge before they were allowed to go back. It is also an established fact that the USSR used its influence to place loyal Korean communists in powerful positions within the people's committees. One of them was Kim Il-sung.

At the beginning of the Soviet occupation, there were a number of political players in North Korea. As well as the Red workers' unions, there were numerous left-wing, left-wing nationalist and also right-wing nationalist parties. In Pyongyang, for example, the Democratic Party of Joseon exerted the greatest political influence, led by the Presbyterian Cho Mansik; he was known as the 'Korean Gandhi', for his peaceful resistance against the Japanese colonial government. The Communist Party, by contrast, having operated underground until only a short while before, was still relatively weak. Kim clearly wasn't keen on being a party functionary in a union that had little influence: as the CIA discovered, he had suggested to Cho that they form a new party together, but the latter had turned him down. Whether Kim made this offer with or without the consent of the occupying power is unclear. There are sources that claim the Soviets chose him as Cho's partner because they didn't want to antagonize the middle classes in the capital city, and the young Kim, on account of his Presbyterian uncle (on his mother's side) was therefore seen as the ideal babysitter for Cho. The immediate formation of a new party, however, can't have been what they had in mind.

Kim's attempt to shake off the occupiers failed – or had it actually been the communists' goal to divide the Christian-Democratic camp? In any case, just a few months later, Kim was appointed party secretary of the Communist Party. He allied himself with the former guerrilla fighters from Yan'an, who had founded their own party, and baptized this fusion the Workers' Party of North Korea. Together with Cho's Democrats and the New People's Party of Korea, they belonged to the interim government, which was quickly dominated by Kim and his allies. When the Soviets put Cho under house arrest for 'lack of cooperation', Kim made one of his closest friends Cho's successor. After the outbreak of the Korean War, he got rid of his political opponent once and for all: he had him declared an enemy of the state by a people's court and executed.

Tragically, it was Cho who had helped the then-unknown Kim Il-sung onto the political stage. He introduced the 'renowned guerrilla fighter' to the population at a mass rally organized by the Soviets; this was the start of Kim's sun-like ascent. In 1946, just one year after his arrival from the Soviet Far East, his portrait was put up at public fairs alongside Stalin's (and sometimes Marx's and Lenin's too); behind it fluttered the flags of the USSR and South Korea – North Korea received its own two years later.

★

'If you really think about it, the North Korean revolution is about family.'

Ayumi came back from the kitchen with a cloth bag, from which she pulled out a syringe and an ampoule.

'Would you like one too?'

Vitamin injections were common in Japan back then, even in Ikaino. Tetsuya couldn't live without them, and liked to say: 'Work hard, drink hard, play hard, and look after your mind and body with bennies and vitamins.' The ever-present benzedrine cannulae gave me the creeps.

'You just said there aren't any families in the People's Republic.'

'No *big* families. The clan system is harmful to the state. It entices people to prioritize their own well-being over that of society as a whole.'

She smiled, the exact likeness of the man in the frame.

'Nuclear families, on the other hand, are good, and important too. The state,' she puckered her lips, in order to enunciate the next words as clearly as possible, 'is the natural extension of the nuclear family.'

The room was bathed in candlelight, and the flickering golden glow, together with the quiet hum of the radio, had a calming, hypnotic effect.

'The state consists of a multitude of families. They are bound together by birth, by the still-pure blood that flows in their veins. Each family forms one unit, a cell, within the state's organic structure. The group that controls the state's destiny is the head, and at the same time the heart, of this organism.'

Ayumi reached for my hand and squeezed it, quickly and firmly.

'"One heart, united." That's the motto of the People's Republic, our motherland. The heart we're talking about here is General Kim Il-sung's. We, the propertyless, the oppressed, the outcast and abandoned, we orphans and half-orphans; we who have no home to call our own, no money, no education; we who have been exploited, discriminated against, mocked and ridiculed: we are no longer alone. We no longer have to starve and freeze. We have a father who clothes us, feeds us and educates us. Who shows us the right way to think. And who teaches us what it means to have history, to live history. To *be* history. General Kim has given us his family and restored our dignity. How can we not love him for that?'

She looked at me intently.

'Let me ask you this: what sort of child doesn't love its parents?'

In 1945, most of the Korean population was bitterly poor. I remember that many children used to run through the streets of Nonsan half-naked, even in the freezing winter. One boy had cut a shirt from a sack and wore it until it fell from his body. Every year, Johnny's mother gave the first women from the village to knock on her door her old, unwanted clothes and fabric. Even though she convinced her friends to donate their worn-out things too, it was – and I say this today with great shame – the norm to see on the streets the bodies of children and adults who had frozen to death. We shared the little we had, but it wasn't enough. Every spring, between the rice and the barley harvests, there was a famine that claimed a great many victims.

Houses were broken into in search not only of rice, barley and flour, but also of items of clothing: trousers, jackets, shirts and shoes. If the front door was wide open, you could be sure the wardrobes would be empty. I remember that a friend of mine, unable to afford woollen blankets, slept beneath mats that his father had woven together out of reeds. During the monsoon season, when the clay walls became porous with the humidity, insects crawled out of them, falling onto his face, chest and arms at night. Splat. Splat. Splat.

The fields belonging to Director Kim were farmed by tenants. They gave him a certain share of the harvest in return; usually half, sometimes more, never less. Many of them had once owned their own fields: they had been dispossessed after the annexation of Korea, because they hadn't registered their claim to ownership with the Japanese colonial administration quickly enough; they couldn't fill out the forms, because they had never learnt to read and write.

Kim Il-sung knew these peoples' struggles, he had grown up with them, witnessed the hardship in North Korea and north-east China. Whether the impulse to help them came from a sense of justice or the shrewd calculation that they, the overwhelming majority of the population, the proletariat, were potential voters, no one can say. Against the counsel of his Soviet advisers, who wanted to sell the property confiscated by the 'traitors' to the impoverished comrades for a low price, Kim made the propertyless into property owners without taking anything in return: they were given the fields for free. They repaid his 'magnanimity' with boundless gratitude, admiration and, in 1946, his first electoral victory.

The redistribution was carried out with relatively little bloodshed, because most of the big landowners had fled to the South within days of the Red Army marching in. Those who stayed bitterly regretted their decision: the 'liberators' weren't popular, quite the contrary. They didn't shy away from physically castigating the population, beating them on a whim, and also helped themselves to whatever they wanted, with a particular fondness for money and machinery – and women:

by November 1945, the number of rapes had increased so drastically that a quarter of the male Soviet soldiers had to be swapped for female ones. Meanwhile, the remainder of the imperial Japanese army tried to destroy the industrial plants in the North, flooding the mines, letting the steelworks go cold, taking away the trains and smashing up the tracks. They were even told to blow up what was then the biggest chemical factory in Hŭngam. Eventually, however, the saboteurs' game was brought to an end. After they were sent to the Soviet Union as prisoners of war, their countrymen who had remained in North Korea had to atone for this destruction: they were drafted into forced labour by the occupying Soviet power.

In order to escape this fate, thousands of people took flight from the North. Ten thousand Japanese refugees were counted in the port of Wŏnsan alone, most of them women and children; many of them died, apparently ten a day. Those who didn't make it onto a ship fled to South Korea, in order to escape from Busan to Kobe or Shimonoseki, accompanied by those North Koreans who feared being persecuted as collaborators or Christians.

Between August and December 1945, half a million people crossed the then invisible border into the South.

Under Kim's leadership, the interim government turned its attention to building up a labour force. Even though there were a number of industrial plants in the North (all nationalized after 1945), there were barely any workers to support the kind of revolution the 'Great Leader' had in mind.

Kim solved this problem by recruiting employees from across the social strata. He enticed them with higher wages, free medical care, two-week-long free spa stays (in one of the numerous leisure resorts where members of the Japanese colonial government used to escape for the summer), as well as larger food rations, which were, of course, particularly desirable in the post-war era: according to the productivity and intensity of the work in question, there was the opportunity to earn a greater quantity or better quality of food. Generally speaking, mine and factory workers received more food than office workers, experts more than entry-level workers, and 'Stakhanovites', extra-diligent workers who exceeded their quota, received more and superior food (like the highly coveted white rice) as well as medals or financial rewards presented by the General himself. This kind of food distribution was also a highly effective measure of control, because only salaried workers employed in state-sanctioned businesses were entitled to food rations: the threat of these being suspended hung over everyone who complained or dared criticize the regime; this practice (hunger as punishment, food as reward) exists in North Korea to this day.

The new proletariat in North Korea was formed predominantly of young men, the erstwhile farmers and farmhands, as well as young single women who had previously been unemployed. As early as 1946, Kim, supported by the occupying Soviet power, had issued a law to guarantee gender equality, or in other words, to liberate women from the 'triple oppression created by family, society and politics'. From then on, women were allowed to play an active role in politics and the economy, they could be cited as the legal owners of property, and also choose the spouse of their liking. Polygamy was forbidden, as was the sale of women as wives or concubines. Education was to play an equally important role in their life as work – fair salaries, maternity leave and childcare made employment more attractive.

But the ideal North Korean woman was first and foremost a

housewife and educator of children, whose greatest and only true fulfilment lay in raising her sons for the revolution. With this in mind, divorce was possible but not seen in a favourable light; when the number of dissolved marriages climbed rapidly between 1945 and 1955, the regime expressed its displeasure, after which the separation craze waned significantly.

Kim Il-sung's emancipation programme for women had just one goal: to increase the working population. Nonetheless, the labour shortage in North Korea persisted until the late 1960s. Because the proletariat were paid not only by the number of hours worked but also according to the quality of their output, even equal pay turned out to be nothing but propaganda.

At the start of the North Korean revolution, Kim's regime declared four groups within the population to be 'particularly oppressed': poor farmers, labourers, women and adolescents. For the emancipation of the latter, education played a major role.

To be accepted into a state educational establishment, be it basic, intermediate or higher education, it was essential to be a member of the North Korean Democratic Youth League (which was modelled on the Soviet youth organization, the Komsomol). Without this membership there was no education, without education there was no work, and without work, no food rations and no money.

The youth league (to which Kim devoted a particularly high level of attention) therefore held a strategically important function: that of preliminary selection. 'Reactionaries' were rigorously discarded and denied the chance of progressing to higher education or the Kim Il-sung University. As part of this process, the applicants' family backgrounds were carefully vetted. 'Reactionary religious enthusiasts' were considered particularly problematic and 'dangerous', because even though they weren't trying to recruit members, they were nonetheless 'idolizing the Western culture of the American imperialists'. As a countermeasure, they were prescribed two additional hours per week at Political School, where lessons were given in Marxism–Leninism, USSR politics, Korean history, economics and political organization.

The Political School was of interest for non-reactionaries too: anyone who successfully completed a course there could apply for a teaching role at one of the many newly founded schools (as well as in factories, for the further education of young labourers) without the necessity of additional peda-gogical training; most of the new teachers who taught at the high schools had themselves never progressed beyond basic education. Just as with the selection process for labourers, teaching skills and qualifications were less important than social class, which was carefully checked before acceptance. The rule of thumb was: the older the pupils, the more important the appropriate – or rather, proletarian – background of the staff. In order to even out the lack of knowledge among the local teachers, Kim asked Moscow to send professors to North Korea along with the technical experts they were already sending. In addition, an exchange programme was set up, enabling North Korean students to undertake a study programme in the USSR. Education was free – at that time in North Korea, this was genuinely revolutionary. There were even state scholarships for higher education. The regime was unflinching in its belief that education should be not the privilege of a minority, but a fundamental right. Illiteracy, the 'enslavement of the spirit', was fought with great determination, and just one year before the outbreak of the civil war Kim Il-sung declared to a jubilant crowd that the illiteracy rate had dropped by more than two million.

Education was also the key remedy for transforming a disparate society into a unified one. Correctly administered, it would anchor the state in the consciousness of the individual and create a new identity; the borders that had once separated state and individual would disintegrate, and society would develop into a 'network of arteries'. The consciousness was to be transformed through propaganda, education, control and (if necessary) brainwashing, an unruly 'I' was to become a tamed and loyal 'we': 'one heart, united'. Even the neo-Confucians, the orthodox rediscoverers of Confucianism, believed in the power of the mind above all material things: if, after self-study and years of striving for virtue and harmony, one understood how 'to be human without the need for shame', then one was qualified and entitled to be a teacher and leader – and, ultimately, a creator.

The obsession with controlling the mind was also – despite the Kim regime's efforts to detach itself from the Japanese past – an inheritance from the colonial era, when the guerrilla fighters were persecuted and imprisoned by the thought police, and either forced to convert or, if they repeatedly refused, executed. You were only a real partisan if you had experienced imprisonment and been taught communist ideology by cell-mates; real comrades were made in prison.

'You were talking about freedom . . .'

I searched for my matches and a pack of cigarettes.

'The truth is,' said Ayumi, 'that only the state is free or unfree. Only the free state determines whether its citizens are free or unfree.' She took the matchbox out of my hand.

'That means: only the freedom of the state is real.'

With a smile, she confiscated my pack of cigarettes too.

'Individual freedom is an illusion. It's a fabrication. Propaganda. It doesn't count. Only the freedom of the state counts. That's why General Kim Il-sung fought for the independence of the People's Republic. Everything he did, he did to save and protect Korea's sovereignty, its freedom. The history of humanity, he once said, is the history of humanity's struggle for autonomy, the battle between the I and the Not-I.'

She watched me closely; she knew that I wanted to grab my cigarettes back from her.

'Equality is a myth too. We children of the state are talented and clever to varying degrees. To deny these differences would be disastrous. It's our parents' mission to utilize us for the well-being of the family according to our abilities. They are responsible for fostering our talents, for recognizing our value. And if a particular child proves to be useless, a wise father will find an activity for him or her that isn't a waste of time or resources. We are not all equal, Mr Kang, and we never will be.'

I couldn't stay silent, I had to interrupt.

'But education is supposed to make us equal. You said so yourself earlier. Don't you see the contradiction?'

'Just because someone wants and thinks the same thing, it doesn't mean they're capable of the same thing.'

Ayumi's mouth twisted with scorn.

'Let's not delude ourselves: every human being has a value, and no one is above valuation. In that sense we're all the same.'

She struck a match –

'A close relationship with one's parents, their love; these things have to be earned.'

– and blew it out.

'And woe betide the child who disappoints them.'

★

376

The land and education reforms proved to be a huge success for the Kim regime. Within two years, the Workers' Party became the largest in North Korea, with almost one million members. As it controlled the coalition partners, and the opposition was weak, it defined government policy single-handedly. After the obvious reactionaries and collaborators had been ousted or eliminated, and the population divided into one of three camps (core, wavering class and enemy class), they set about transforming everyday life into a communal life. Individuals who weren't members of at least one organization were regarded as suspect, there being no need for the private sphere – I'm using Ayumi's words now – within a happy family circle; secrets only disturb the harmony of cohabitation. General Kim, the 'wise teacher', made social control the most effective weapon in his guerrilla state; not for the well-being of his children but to boost his power. In the beginning, leading officials still complained about tardiness, inattentiveness and lack of interest at member meetings, and allegedly there was skiving and gossiping too, but eventually the disciplined mind took over the task of disciplining the body.

The disciplined mind was – after education, propaganda and indoctrination – the product of a security apparatus that shared a motto with the recruited teachers: 'From the people for the people.' In contrast to the South, where 'patriotic comrades' were murdered by the police and military (an allegation that was irrefutable even back then), in North Korea the police and comrades were on the same side. A policeman, in the view of Generalissimo Kim, had to 'come from the people' and 'feel boundless love for the people'. During recruitment, therefore, great care was taken to ensure that the strata of society formerly known as the lower classes were over-represented. A special unit was created – a successor to the Japanese thought police – to monitor 'political thought', as well as a secret police force modelled on the NKVD, whose responsibilities included tracking down any gatherings consisting of more than four people. The addresses of any 'suspicious elements' identified by these means were marked on a map (organized into administrative zones), as was the distance to the nearest regional Office for Internal Affairs – this was how the Japanese police had hunted for partisans. The surveillance and reporting was undertaken by units of between three and ten informants, usually members of the youth league or the Workers' Party.

In the prisons too, which were named 'educational facilities', as they had been in the early Soviet Union, the disciplining of the mind was the key focus. The re-education of prisoners who had committed less severe political or social crimes took the form of forced labour, in mines and factories. Perpetrators unwilling to mend their ways were kept in solitary confinement, given almost nothing to eat and, if their re-education failed, were as good as dead.

In present-day North Korea, the exploitation of the people has reached new heights. Without those designated guilty, the unlucky ones who lead a miserable existence as slaves, the North Korean economy would be unable to produce the junk that funds a Western life in the isolated East for a small, privileged group; meanwhile, we Westerners loudly express our indignation about the 'pariah state', but are more dependent than ever – if we want to maintain our standard of living – on this kind of slave labour.

On 9 September 1948, Kim Il-sung proclaimed the foundation of the Democratic People's Republic of Korea, thereby cementing the division of the peninsula. Allegedly this was a reaction to the separately held elections in the South, but in actual fact the People's Republic is older than this; the red, blue and white flag had already been presented to the population that July. At the same time, Kim heralded the glorious conclusion of the North Korean revolution, while pointing out that the South was still waiting impatiently to be liberated.

As we know, he failed to liberate South Korea, but Kim (like Syngman Rhee and all South Korean rulers after him) used the ceasefire, the never-resolved war, to make the crisis part of everyday life, and to persecute all his opponents – even unthinking individuals who were merely parroting defamatory poems – with great brutality and mercilessness.

The Democratic People's Republic became a fortress: impregnable, hidden from view. Over the years, the autonomy Kim had promised in 1948 became a state ideology; like every ideology, its sole purpose was to veil the fact that the despot's power existed only as long as nobody raised the curtain concealing his true self. But in contrast to the rule of Park Chunghee, who chose as his role models not Stalin and Mao but Hitler and Chiang Kai-shek, and who reached similar conclusions to his colleague in the North, Kim's 'Great Sun' never set.

Ayumi stood up. She held my jacket out to me. I didn't take it.

'You spoke with Eiko before she disappeared. She came to see you that evening. Why did you keep quiet about that?'

She smiled, this time looking pained.

'I didn't keep quiet about anything.'

'Eiko came here to see you. I have a witness.'

She was silent.

'What did she want? It must have been important if she went to your apartment straight from school.'

'It's only a stone's throw away.'

'Why did Eiko want to talk to you?'

Ayumi leant against the wall and turned her back to me. I had no intention of letting her get rid of me. I moved round her to look into her face again; to my surprise, she was smiling in amusement.

'As I already said: we're not all equal. Some are more valuable than others. Some are more valuable than most. My task is to find the most valuable.'

'The most valuable . . .'

'. . . to our state.'

'And Eiko belongs to this group?'

'She understands what it's all about. She has internalized the principles of our glorious revolution.'

Her smile broadened.

'And our revolution *was* glorious. We may not have succeeded in freeing you from the yoke of oppression in 1950, but we won't abandon you.'

She took my hand and squeezed it. Suddenly, I realized the real reason for my invitation to dinner: She had never had any intention of helping me and Tetsuya look for his daughter. She wanted to recruit me, just like she had recruited Eiko.

I shook her hand off.

'Did you help Eiko? Are you hiding her?'

Her grin disappeared.

'You've seen my apartment. Where would I hide Eiko? And why?'

'To protect her from her parents.'

'Her parents only want the best for her. There's no reason to protect her from them.'

'They don't want their daughter to leave them. They're so desperate that they would have found a way to forbid her from leaving. Perhaps Eiko asked you for help . . .'

Ayumi gestured towards the door.

'It wouldn't be wise to go up against Mr Yamamoto. I tend to avoid doing foolish things.'

'I know you're involved in Eiko's disappearance. She probably stayed with you that night, then you helped her get out of the city the following morning. Who knows where she is now. But I'm sure of one thing: that she'll be embarking on that ship in August.'

'If I'm correctly informed, your brother works for Mr Yamada. Mr Yamada is known for being the kind of man who doesn't hold back. How far do you think he might go to stop his only child from following Eiko to North Korea?'

Before I could answer, she interrupted me.

'How far would your brother go?'

The bus took an eternity to arrive, and came only after my fourth cigarette. The traffic lights were against me tonight too; the driver had to step on the brakes at every intersection, and the red phases lasted so long that I began to count the seconds in order to calm my nerves.

Ayumi wasn't wrong. Johnny would have had the opportunity, and he had a motive too: chronic financial difficulties. He had beaten a grown man to death, so compared to that, kidnapping a teenager, especially one who knew and trusted him, would be easy.

How far *had* Johnny gone?

But perhaps I'm exaggerating. Perhaps I'm even lying? Don't believe everything I tell you. Don't believe a face from which age has erased all guilt. Instead, ask yourself: is he abusing my trust? Is he taking advantage of me in order to reinvent reality, to rewrite history? Is he using his position in order to depict as inevitable something that was not so?

Perhaps Ayumi wasn't a fanatical follower of Kim Il-sung, perhaps she was just a naive, gullible teacher. Perhaps Yunho Kang only invented the character Ayumi Nobukawa in order to make his story more plausible? 'One snake is enough to muddy the waters of an entire lake.' And as you are listening to him, as you are granting him this power, he controls the past.

In the end, history belongs to the one who makes his voice heard.

18

Tetsuya intercepted me at the front door. He was uneasy, tense, jiggling the coins in his trouser pocket. Not even giving me time to step inside, he asked if I had discovered anything. Naoko appeared behind him, her eyes red and swollen. I had been hoping to speak with Eve first, and so I lied. 'No,' I said, 'nothing.' He nodded and turned away. Naoko disappeared back inside. Tetsuya mumbled that his men were combing through Ikaino, and Sōren had been informed too, perhaps Eiko was hiding away with one of its members. He turned to face me again. So Mrs Nobukawa had nothing to say, he asked once more, nothing at all? She hadn't seen Eiko since she was appointed director, I said. A lie, but hopefully one as white as a magpie's belly. I kept Ayumi's suspicion about Johnny to myself. Tetsuya muttered that he felt like the monk who couldn't shave his own head. Perhaps I had found a small clue, I said, trying to comfort him. A small clue? he asked. I nodded. He instructed me to pursue it and report back to him later. He had to go; he had a meeting with the Sōren committee.

Eve had overheard our conversation through the open window. She was nervous, pacing up and down, kneading her fingers. There were dark shadows beneath her eyes. She had slept badly last night. I hadn't slept a wink either.

I made sure no one was lurking in the corridor. Closed the wooden door. Pulled Eve into the furthest corner, and told her in whispers about my conversation with Ayumi. Eve declared that she didn't trust her. Why would Johnny kidnap Eiko? It made no sense, she said. I replied that it made sense if he'd been ordered to do it. By Yamada or Mr Lee.

She looked at me thoughtfully. Eventually she nodded. It was certainly possible, she said, Johnny was always in financial straits, and when he needed money he wasn't choosy about who he worked for. But why would Yamada get Johnny to do it when he had so many men working for him who were more appropriate for the job? 'Because Eiko knows and trusts Johnny,' I replied. Perhaps the idea had been for him to convince her. 'Convince,' said Eve, 'convince is just another word for kill.'

Over the next few days, the search for Eiko intensified. Tetsuya even contemplated informing the police, but then decided against it. They wouldn't help, he said, not for a vanished Chōsen girl, the missing person's report would be conveniently lost. In any case, Sōren had notified the Japanese Red Cross, who were helping to organize the Great Homecoming. They had promised to keep a lookout for Eiko at the port of departure in Niigata, and to put up a description and photo of her in all the Red Cross offices. If she turned up, they would immediately inform Tetsuya and Naoko, even if she tried to board using a different name. A different name? Naoko had queried. With false papers, they had replied. Eiko wouldn't be able to get false papers, her mother had objected. Perhaps not, they said, but 'certain individuals' could.

I had joined the search party, which consisted of ten groups, each containing eight people. We divided Osaka up among us. Each unit was to search a neighbourhood, penetrating even the darkest corners of the city. We scoured the places where beggars and the homeless gathered, risked being beaten, because they weren't fond of interrogations. We moved from one ghetto to the next, from one collection of untouchables to the next.

During these days, my image of Japan both changed and remained constant. I discovered that society's discrimination of the Zainichi was not an isolated phenomenon, but rather the renewal of an old practice: the Burakumin, also referred to as *hinin*, non-humans, as well as *eta*, filth, were, despite their 'pure' Japanese ancestry, ostracized in a similar way to the Koreans. I knew some of them by sight, as Tetsuya employed them in his pachinko halls, but we had never spoken; despite their pariah existence, it seemed to me that they were happy to have found outsiders who were even further from the core of society than they were.

Their blood, Tetsuya had explained, had become 'impure' because their ancestors had spent their time washing corpses, digging graves, tanning leather and slaughtering animals; the Koreans' blood, on the other hand, had never been pure in the first place. Until the Meiji Restoration, life had been relatively good for the Burakumin, as they took on the jobs no one else wanted, but after 1871 all Japanese nationals had been declared citizens and the Burakumin 'new citizens'; in the process, they lost their monopoly on low-paid work. Their status as 'new citizens' was noted in the family register, which anyone could access. Even if, against all the odds, they did well in school and graduated from university, big companies still refused to hire them once their private detectives had researched the candidates' background. Flicking the ash of his cigar from the sleeve of his jacket, Tetsuya had said: 'And that's when they end up with me.'

I barely spoke to the men from my search troop. I kept my distance, because I was on the lookout for Johnny; I hoped to find him before the others did. By now, Tetsuya had noticed his disappearance and was asking a lot of uncomfortable questions, most of which I didn't answer. I wasn't even able to tell him exactly how long it was since Johnny had come home. This prompted Tetsuya to turn away with a sad look on his face – he thought I didn't want to betray my brother.

By the tenth day of the search, hope of finding Eiko had dwindled significantly; by the fifteenth day, it was barely existent but for a few remnants; on the twentieth day, we walked up and down the boulevards, streets and alleyways only so that we could tell Tetsuya and Naoko, in all honesty, that we still didn't know what had happened to their daughter.

The Red Cross workers telephoned at regular intervals to say that nobody fitting Eiko's description had been reported in the office. Naoko had stopped crying by now and resorted to pleading instead. She wanted to notify the police, but Tetsuya refused every time. 'Why?' she screamed. 'Because it's our own affair; we have to settle our own affairs,' answered her husband.

The couple, who had never argued prior to this, could no longer manage to be in the same room without having at least a small verbal feud, and Naoko was always the aggressor. In the absence of a known enemy, she had decided to attack Tetsuya instead. When she ran out of words, she resorted to physical blows and launched herself at him, hitting his back, chest and arms and kicking his legs. Initially, he restrained both himself and her, pushing her calmly away from him, but with time the pushes became shoves, and eventually, blows. Naoko, that petite, slender woman, was stronger than I had thought possible, she developed the strength of a tiger; she wanted to hurt Tetsuya, and she succeeded. She blamed him for Eiko having run away, and couldn't understand why he refused to involve the police. The police had resources that they didn't, she roared, even if the police did nothing and ignored their enquiry, even then she would at least feel that she had done everything she could! What utter nonsense, retorted Tetsuya. If all she had to contribute was nonsense, she should just stay quiet.

These fights were what drove Kimiko to betray me; on the twenty-first day, she made her move. Yunho hadn't been honest, she said, interrupting her parents' fighting; Yunmee wasn't his sister, and Mino, she added quietly, her voice barely audible, was a murderer.

Naoko was the first to awaken from her state of shock. She dragged Kimiko and me into the kitchen. What was this about, she barked at her daughter, all the while keeping me firmly in her line of vision, what did she mean they weren't siblings? She had seen him kiss his sister, answered Kimiko. Kiss? Naoko flared with anger, she would kiss her brother too, if he were still alive. 'No, Mother,' Kimiko shook her head, nervous and panicked, 'he didn't kiss her like a brother, but *like a man*. Like a man in love,' she added meekly.

The scene isn't without its comical side: the prim teenager unable to pronounce the word 'kiss' without blushing; the indignant mother, no less prim, who considers it an affront – at a time when she believes her younger daughter, the baby of the family, to be in danger – to have to listen to rumours about alleged love scenes between siblings. Naoko, already running out of patience, now loses her temper completely, and instead of being pleased at her exemplary daughter's attempt to help, begins to rant and rave at her. 'You're making it up!' she screams. 'Once again you can't bear not being at the centre of everything, so you've fabricated some scandal to get our attention. What were you thinking? Your sister is in mortal danger, but instead of taking part in the search, you're blurting out ridiculous accusations!' 'I only wanted to help,' whines the golden child. 'If Yunho lied once, maybe he lied a second time too!' Amid this hubbub of screeching, whimpering and whining, Tetsuya's baritone sounds baffled, confused beyond belief; who kissed whom, who did Eiko kiss, no, who did Kimiko kiss, or had Kimiko kissed Eiko? Together with Missu Satō's mezzo-soprano, proclaiming melodramatically that 'Mr Kang has to straighten this out, he has to explain whom and when he kissed whom and when, oh, oh, oh, all this uncontrolled kissing!'

Once everyone had calmed down, even Missu Satō, who this had nothing to do with, Eve and I revealed our 'family secret'. 'So you didn't flee for political reasons?' asked Tetsuya. He seemed tired and uninterested. We did, I assured him, glancing at Eve; I hoped she would confirm my lie, but she ignored me. Almost as soon as Naoko gave her a chance to speak, she admitted that the reasons had been more personal than political. 'Personal?' asked Naoko, suspiciously. Eve nodded. The real reason we had fled, she continued, was because Johnny, or rather Mino, had murdered a member of the North-West Youth. If we had stayed in Seoul, we would have been killed ourselves.

'Mino *is* a murderer! I was right, he's a murderer!' exclaimed Kimiko. Her voice was higher than normal, from horror and delight. She didn't even try to conceal her triumph; she had been right to expose the kissing incident.

Eve's confession made things complicated for me. Tetsuya turned his back on me once and for all, disappointed that I hadn't confided in him, that I had kept from him something as important as the presence of a murderer in his house. He would neither look at me nor speak to me. Naoko, on the other hand, stared at me as though she hoped her blazing eyes would burn holes in my heart. I felt like an owl at dawn, completely abandoned. When Eve came near me, I avoided her; I couldn't believe she had put Johnny and me in this difficult situation. She defended herself by saying that she'd had to unburden her conscience, that we should never have concealed the real reason for our escape, not in a household with two children. I retorted that it hadn't helped matters to broadcast to the entire world that her lover was a murderer. Besides which, the children in question were actually adults. Nor had it escaped my notice, I continued, that she had elegantly concealed her own role in all of this . . .

We tried to engage in a muted battle; we argued in whispers in the seclusion of our room. Naoko hadn't immediately expelled us from the house, but it was clear that even a trifle like talking loudly could catapult us onto the street.

This was the night, of all nights, that Johnny chose for his return.

Eve was already asleep; how, was a mystery to me. I was wide awake and listening to her steady breathing when the door to our room opened. Thinking that it was Kimiko spying again, I said in a friendly but firm tone that she should leave us in peace, that there was nothing left to expose . . .

'No, Yunho, it's me.'

I struck a match, held it up to his face, to make sure I hadn't misheard, that I wasn't imagining things, then quickly blew it out again. I believed we would be safe in the dark, and even he seemed more comfortable that way; perhaps, though, I'm ascribing this comfort to him because I only wanted to confront Johnny as a voice, not as a person I had to betray. We stayed silent for a while, even though countless questions were burning, *incinerating*, on my tongue, but I didn't know how to voice them without accusing him.

My silence intimidated Johnny. When he finally spoke, his voice sounded high, delicate and fragile like a spider's web. He said he regretted what he had burdened me with weeks before, that he should never have told me the truth. 'Not like that,' I answered. I was bitter and hard. I couldn't back down. Couldn't and didn't want to. He doesn't deserve my forgiveness, said my intransigent self.

Johnny nodded. He had wanted to tell me the truth about Yunsu and his father sooner, he said, but hadn't been sure whether it was the kind of knowledge that would change my life for the better.

'But then you decided to use the knowledge as a weapon.'

'It wasn't meant like that.'

'So how was it meant?'

I took out my anger on him, even though I knew that it wasn't him I was angry with, but his parents; like me, he was a victim. I remembered how much he had suffered when the director had compared him unfavourably with my brother. How often he had been told that Yunsu was the one he should emulate, the perfect son, the perfect brother, the favourite of all fathers. That in comparison to him, Johnny was a pitiful creature: a pitiful, spoilt brat whose only talent was for extravagance.

Perhaps my fury was rooted in the knowledge that I could no longer help Johnny. I sensed that we had reached a crossroads, that our paths were going to diverge whether we wanted them to or not. The sensation of the parting was still indistinct for now, lurking in the background; Eve was still asleep in a corner of the room, and Johnny was sitting on the floor next to me. Eventually we both moved closer to the window, and in the weak moonlight I saw how exhausted and gaunt he looked, and felt compassion for him. I told him he couldn't stay here, that Eiko had gone missing. He remained silent, whether out of concern or tiredness I can't say. When he responded, he didn't comment on her disappearance. He seemed more intent on assuring me that he had done everything in his power to find me back then, after his parents drove me out of the house through fear of being associated with a communist; that he had pleaded with his father to bring me back, but to no avail.

'I might as well have been asking a tiger for meat.'

When I think back now to that night, the scene is accompanied by music, the first few bars of 'Solitude'; the plucked guitar tones that herald Billie's voice, soft, hesitant, but unwavering. The room is bathed in a bluish grey and has lost its boundaries, its walls; the silver light of the moon fumbles through the window, and I can see Johnny's profile before me, the tip of his nose and his lips, his eyes are in shadow. I say: 'Everything will be okay. Everything will be like it used to be. Do you remember?'

He smiles, and everything is okay, everything is like it used to be, for just a second − and in the next we're sitting in glaring bright light, and Tetsuya is brandishing a gun at Johnny, while two of his men force me out of the room. I go, stunned, confused. At first I don't know what's happening, then I spot Eve in the hallway and everything becomes clear; I had thought she was next to me, in a deep slumber, but she had gone to get Tetsuya.

There's a saying: 'No one knows which cloud it will rain from next.' This cloud was known to me; I should have watched it more closely.

From then on, everything happened in quick succession. Naoko insisted on informing the police, convinced that 'this Korean' had killed her daughter. He defended himself; I spoke up for him too, but the Yamamoto couple refused to listen to or even look at us, Eve was the only one they would tolerate in their presence, and they locked Johnny and me in the house. I was only allowed to leave the room and the property with express permission. My friend had it worse; he was put in a small closet alongside our room which served as a storage space. We were no longer able to speak to one another, but I saw through the crack in the door that one of Tetsuya's thugs entered the broom closet numerous times that day. Even though he closed the door behind him, I could hear that he was beating my friend.

I didn't dare make contact with Johnny. I was afraid they would take him away if I tried to outwit the thin, permeable wall with my voice – so I sent Billie instead. I put the gramophone right up against the wall and hoped the speaker would be a match for the wood. I didn't turn the volume up fully, out of fear the guards would see through my plan and take the records or the player from me. They didn't seem bothered by the music, though; on the contrary, the fat one even hummed along. After that, I turned the volume a little louder, just slightly, and as though its reception was being confirmed, I heard a distant knocking . . .

Johnny was knocking along, keeping time with 'I Only Have Eyes For You'.

★

The next day, Yamada came to see Tetsuya. Johnny was interrogated in his presence. Missu Satō told me later that Yamada had been unable to convince Tetsuya he had nothing to do with his daughter's kidnapping. He had, however, admitted that Johnny was working for him, and had demanded his release. Tetsuya, as was to be expected, had refused. If it were up to his wife, he said, he would have handed him over to the police a long time ago, but he was letting mercy prevail over justice. He forbade Yamada from ever setting foot in his house again.

On the evening of the fourth day of Johnny's imprisonment, a Sōren meeting took place without Yamada. The committee discussed whether or not Yamada would still be welcome in Sōren. He was unanimously expelled.

On the morning of the sixth day, the news reached us that two *yakiniku* restaurants had been set on fire. The blazes had spread, destroying the neighbouring houses. Four people had been gravely injured, an elderly woman died. The restaurants belonged to Yamada.

During the days that followed, I heard that the Korean community, reeling from the arson attacks, were demanding that Sōren distance itself from the 'criminals'; the police had also been informed. The Japanese began to hunt for the arsonists, but the files and evidence swiftly disappeared. They only resurfaced after a European, a member of the International Committee of the Red Cross, intervened in the investigation.

In the early hours of the eighteenth day, a special police unit stormed the Yamamotos' home and arrested the men who were guarding Johnny's prison. Apparently evidence had been seized which pointed towards Tetsuya as the arsonist, or at least towards those he had connections with. Thinking they had come for Johnny, I had positioned myself protectively in front of the gramophone.

At the end of the third week, Tetsuya gave in to my pleas and allowed me to see my friend. The police raid had left him subdued. In addition, he suspected that his wife was behind the arson. I eavesdropped on one of their many arguments. As always, Naoko reproached her husband for not having relented, saying he could at least have *pretended* to Eiko that he would consider going to North Korea. Tetsuya retorted that she couldn't accuse him of anything, not after she had put the entire family's future at risk with a childish act of revenge that had cost an innocent woman her life. And to make matters worse his men had been accused of the crime, they weren't even being released on bail. So what? screamed Naoko. What were their lives in comparison to their daughter's?

Johnny looked better than I had expected. He was haggard and filthy, but the cut on his mouth was healing, and the bruise beneath his eye was already starting to fade. The blood on the floor had dried. He had been given food and drink, he assured me, and he thanked me for the songs, for Billie's songs. I nodded, not knowing what to say; I suspected I had come to listen, not to speak. Did I have a cigarette I could give him? he asked. Tetsuya had taken his away, probably as part of his punishment. A punishment, he added, that he didn't deserve. He laughed. I gave him my pack; a new one that I had bought from Missu Satō that morning.

He was in a real fix, said Johnny with a cigarette in his hand, the ash falling to the floor in long flakes. Did I remember the conversation we once had with Yunsu about destiny? He laughed again. He seemed in good spirits, upbeat. I answered that I could barely remember, the memory was hazy, like a dream where you're not sure if you actually dreamt it or someone told you about it. He said we talked about destiny; he had asked Yunsu what it was, and my brother, my *wise* brother, said it didn't exist, that destiny was an illusion. To which Johnny had responded that he didn't buy that, that his mother was always talking at great length about destiny; in her opinion, it was everywhere. Everywhere was nowhere, Yunsu had answered, the idea of destiny as something unpreventable and unavoidable was a delusion, endemic to the people. It was firmly within the realm of the possible and probable to change the ever-shifting, fragile future.

'Fatalism is a tough destiny.'

Johnny took a deep drag. Back then he hadn't understood what Yunsu meant, he said, but he did now. He could have changed himself, and thereby his fate, at any moment, but he had neglected to do so; now he couldn't tell his story without piling one sin onto the next. I asked whether he meant the incident with Jinman.

'The "incident" with Jinman.'

He laughed. That sounded nice, he said. Detached. Diplomatic. Yes, that was the incident he meant, that and many others. He stubbed out his cigarette with a sigh.

'Everything began with Eve.'

Johnny really had met Eve at Haesun's wedding, followed her all across Seoul and begun an affair with her; this much was true. Yet she had never been a dancer, the whole dancing thing was just a cover; when she disappeared into that small room with her partner, she was interested not in his money, but in the information he had promised her. Eve worked as an informant for the secret service of the South Korean military. In the early 1950s, she worked in close cooperation with the

Americans and was even paid by them, then she switched to a group of young officers who were planning a coup against the government. Their leader was Park Chung-hee.

On that autumn day in 1950, after Eve had been freed from the clutches of the overzealous anti-communist special unit, Mitch, her rescuer, returned with a proposal, a job offer, which she accepted. A few years later, she was taken along to Haesun's wedding by Henry Lewis, not because he needed a date, but because he was supposed to introduce her to Johnny. The Americans hoped that Johnny would prove to be a good source of intelligence and give them information about the Koreans, who were increasingly doing their own thing and then lying through their teeth about it. At that time, numerous rumours were circulating around Seoul, and it was vital to differentiate the true ones from the false in order to survive. Eve's mission was to assist – with Johnny's help, but without his knowledge.

Johnny disappointed Eve's employers: he fell in love with her and was thrown out of the military academy on account of his 'escapades'. But they didn't want to drop the two of them just yet. Johnny, they now knew, had strong feelings for Eve, and even though it had proved to be counter-productive before, they decided to exploit this. Eve was instructed to talk Johnny into enrolling at Korea University as a Philosophy and Politics student. He'll refuse, she told them; he can't afford the fees. A few lousy dollars, scoffed her handler. She barely managed to force the smile onto her lips. For those few lousy dollars, Koreans had to work an entire year, she replied. The American with the cigar and the whisky glass in his stubby fingers backed down. His red jowls hung down almost to his shoulders, and he no longer had a neck, because he did nothing all day but sit in his leather chair making phone calls or yelling at his secretary, who, every time she heard his puffing and panting from the adjacent room, would hold her hands over her ears. Okay, okay, he appeased her, they would pay the fees, but Eve would have to pretend that she was the one supporting Johnny financially. He won't accept it, she replied. Then they would give him a grant, declared the American. That won't wash, she answered, his grades were bad, they didn't just kick him out of the academy because of his liaison with a prostitute, but also because he was a useless student. 'Then make him useful!' the man barked, before disappearing out of Cockatu's little room.

That very same evening, she declared her love to Johnny. She wanted the best for him, she said, that's why she was insisting on paying his university fees, because she felt responsible for his expulsion. Her declaration and the accompanying cash injection came at a good time for Johnny; he had secretly been worrying about what would become of him now he had been kicked out of the military academy under such dishonourable circumstances. Even if he had been prepared to sacrifice a glittering military career for Eve, he still regretted his decision (and his loutish behaviour); before long, good jobs would go only to university graduates, and the better the reputation of the university, the greater the chance of a well-paid post.

He accepted her declaration of love and her money. Without protest.

Eve knew that Johnny was a member of the North-West Youth, that's why she had been assigned to him. Generally speaking, neither the Americans nor the Korean military were that bothered by the league, because it was rigorously anti-communist. The fact that it was led by war criminals and continually terrorized the population with its criminal activities was, admittedly, nothing to rejoice about, but its loyalty to the president made it a nuisance at most.

Syngman Rhee wasn't considered a good partner by either the US or the Korean military: he pursued his own agenda and had put his allies' noses out of joint on more than one occasion. They were in agreement that Rhee and his henchmen had to be watched; perhaps there was even the possibility of luring Rhee's partner onto their side? Eve was to sound this out, with Johnny's help, and report what the North-West Youth had planned for Seoul.

At her request, Johnny introduced Eve to the group. Jinman, who as a regular at Cockatu's dancing school had had his eye on Eve for a while, congratulated Johnny on having an older woman as a lover, quipped about the experience of age, and promoted him; Johnny became Jinman's right-hand man. Through her lover, Eve got to know the other members of the group, but was excluded from their discussions. She came under increasing pressure to supply useful information; perhaps she had changed sides and that was why she had nothing to say? Her Korean handler stormed angrily out of the dance bar. The next day, she threatened to break up with Johnny, claiming that he had too many secrets.

On the afternoon when I saw them dancing in Johnny's room, he had just been placating her, begging her not to leave him. He had poured his heart out to her and confessed everything, and she had taken him in her arms and danced with him: slowly, as though his urge to reveal all would ebb away with any sudden, loud movements. A gentle questioning, that was how Johnny described it, she had breathed the questions into his ear as they danced.

I turned up at the right time; Eve hoped to glean information from me too, albeit different to the intelligence she got from Johnny, because I moved in working-class circles. She thought she would be able to use me for her purposes, that's why she told Johnny she was happy to pay my part of the rent, and he took me in because he wanted to do an old friend a favour, and because he felt indebted to me.

I didn't disappoint her. I gave her Sangok, without knowing what I was doing. That was all she needed, just his name and a description, and with that military intelligence had him in their sights. The agents let Sangok operate undisturbed for a while, wanting him to make himself known through his actions. Even after he had tried to recruit me, they left him untouched. They were sure he would build up a communist cell, and had their sights set on the entire group. Back then rumours were circulating that the government planned to manipulate the elections in the spring. There was, after all, a lifelong presidency at stake; Eve had discovered this from Johnny.

Sangok was imprisoned even though he posed no danger, for neither the present nor the future rulers. His 'terror cell' was tiny, his plans insignificant in comparison to those of the students in April 1960; he would never have been able to organize a demonstration of that size, would never have received this level of support from the population, but he was a Red and, as such, only valuable as a *contained threat* – as a national security service statistic.

It didn't take long before Jinman had put two and two together and uncovered Eve's secret. He thought, however, that she was spying only for the Americans, not for Rhee's Korean enemies. Suspecting that his buddy Johnny knew nothing about it, he decided to warn him. He told him the truth about Eve and suggested that they conspire together: to blackmail the spy. They could use the money to emigrate to the United States, to New York.

Johnny was stunned. Horrified. He confronted Eve. She swore to him that she was innocent. She claimed that Jinman was jealous, that he was seeking revenge for all the times she had rejected him. She said that Johnny had to protect her from the lunatic, that she wouldn't pay him off, because if she paid once she would have to do it again and again, and she was right, Jinman was greedy. She convinced Johnny to get rid of him once and for all. Eve saw it as a patriotic act. Like everything else she had done in the name of the Republic of Korea. She wasn't working for herself, nor for the allies, the US, but for South Korea, the bisected state. She was fooling herself, of course, herself and everybody else. Eve was no more a patriot than I am a Buddhist. She had simply found a niche for herself, in which she could live life in the way that was closest to how she imagined it should be. She had a very precise perception of how the world worked, and didn't concern herself with the facts, because they were complex, ambivalent, confusing. In her tiny universe, everything was simple, two-dimensional. She was the good one, and the others, those she was spying on, fully deserved to be betrayed. Even if she stole the socks from their feet, they were still the bad guys. I wonder whether she ever gave in to her feelings, whether she even possessed anything akin to feelings, and not just an instinct: the instinct to survive.

Jinman's pal and I thwarted her plan. The escape had been planned for one person, not two, let alone three. Nor had Johnny and Eve expected Jinman to bring someone with him to the handover. They had thought him greedier than that, less concerned about his safety than the considerable sum of money, which he wouldn't have to share if he went through with it alone. But perhaps they had forgotten about his best friend. Most of the time, the little guy was simply invisible, not a spectator, no, but part of the backdrop. When 'little Jinman' attacked Johnny, Johnny believed he couldn't feel his blows, as though they couldn't harm him. And when he pulled out a gun and aimed it at Johnny, he thought it was a toy gun, and knocked it out of his hand. Only when it hit the ground did Johnny notice that the boy was shaking; this shaking made him an inhabitant of this world, who Johnny suddenly felt compassion for. And the compassion transformed Jinman's death into a killing: into murder.

My suggestion that we find Eve was unnecessary; Johnny had been planning to do precisely that, albeit without me, but now there was no way he could shake me off. The little guy would set Jinman's group on us, on us and Eve, that much was clear to Johnny, as it was to Eve. She understood and changed the plan. We had to flee the country, all three of us. Rhee was stubbornly clinging on to power, Eve's friends in the military didn't believe a changeover would come any time soon, and the timing was bad for a coup. They advised Eve to sit out the riots. Eve said she needed money for two additional passengers, for herself and two friends. Two friends? The handler wasn't best pleased. Her cover would have been blown if her friends hadn't defended her, she said. She couldn't leave us behind. We would be arrested and interrogated. The handler reacted sullenly. He grumpily opened the drawer to get the petty cash. He wasn't a people smuggler, he said, and she wasn't an escape agent.

Johnny took my hand. He didn't have much time, he said. Tetsuya had given him an ultimatum. An ultimatum? I asked.

As Eiko hadn't reappeared, he either had to turn himself in to the police as her murderer, or board the ship to North Korea. He hadn't killed Eiko, he repeated, he hadn't so much as touched a hair on her head. I tried to calm him down, assuring him that I believed him.

He lit another cigarette. He had soon realized that Jinman was telling the truth, that Eve was only using him to get information. A secret agent, he said with a laugh, and he'd thought he was having an affair with a call girl! Perhaps the academy would have held on to him, given him a medal, he said, grinning half-heartedly, if they had known about his 'invaluable services' to the Fatherland. He took a long drag and puffed out the smoke in small clouds. His mistake had been to not make do with confronting Eve. He had gone further, and blackmailed her.

'Blackmailed?'

He nodded. He had needed the money urgently, he said.

'What for?'

'For Tomoko.'

He had wanted to free Tomoko from the clutches of her family. Eve's money was intended to finance the journey to the US, two one-way flights and a small sum for getting themselves established. He had never planned to continue blackmailing Eve, it was a one-off sum that he described as 'a fee' for having helped her out of the fix with Jinman. If Jinman had betrayed her, she would have been executed; Rhee showed his enemies no mercy.

Eve had laughed at him and said that he wouldn't get far. She refused to pay him. She didn't have any money, she claimed, only the little that she earned as a beautician. Did he really want the ten yen she had? Well, here was her handbag, he could help himself! He retorted that he wasn't in the mood for jokes, that as soon as she handed over the sum he was requesting, she would be rid of him and Tomoko once and for all. If not, the whole of Ikaino would discover her story, especially Tetsuya Yamamoto. An anti-communist South Korean agent wouldn't be shown much understanding around these parts, he said. Nor would her accomplice, she responded.

The next day, he had to carry out a job for Yamada in Tokyo. When he came back, Tomoko was waiting for him with the news that Eiko had disappeared and that he was suspected of kidnapping her. He had gone underground, fleeing repeatedly from Tetsuya's search troops. Eventually he had realized that he couldn't carry on like that; he returned and came to an arrangement with Eve. He couldn't say how, but he was convinced that she was behind Eiko's disappearance. Ingenious as she was, she had immediately directed the suspicion towards him, he said, so that no one would believe him now if he told the truth.

He sighed and pulled a folded-up note out of his trouser pocket. For Tomoko, he said, pressing it into my hand, the letter was for Tomoko. Could I do him this one last favour and give it to her? I didn't need to wait for the answer, he said.

I took it to her that same evening. Tomoko read it hastily. There was great sadness in her eyes as she shook her head. Slowly, but firmly. She had no words of farewell for Johnny.

I couldn't describe Tomoko's reaction to my friend, because I wasn't allowed in to see him again, so I played 'You Turned the Tables on Me' for him. I thought the lyrics were about betrayal; in my mind's eye, Johnny was buried beneath a shattered table, because I believed Tomoko had turned down his request. I didn't know that the expression actually meant:

'You switched roles with me.' Johnny knocked against the wall a few times to thank me.

The day before his departure, Tetsuya informed me that I could accompany my friend to Niigata. After that, I would no longer be welcome in his house. My 'sister' – he uttered the word with contempt – had sneaked away like a thief a week ago. I had noticed that her clothes, shoes and the few things she had brought with her from Korea had disappeared, as though swallowed up by the ground. Johnny's and my things, on the other hand, were still there; I packed up Johnny's worldly possessions and tied them into a bundle. In mine I put only *Solitude*.

'We cling to one another like leeches,' she had once said to me, a long time ago. When I took the record out of the sleeve, banknotes fell out. Eve must have smuggled them in; when, I don't know.

The train journey lasted an entire day. We were to spend the next three days in Niigata, in the Red Cross dormitories. I kept a lookout for Eiko at first, but gave up when we were put in a men-only dormitory. Tetsuya had ordered one of his men not to let us out of his sight. His name was Otake, he was also planning to go to North Korea, and had promised my former boss he would keep watch over us. In truth this wasn't necessary; the other travellers from Osaka knew our story and eyed us distrustfully, kicking our beds whenever they passed.

Immediately after our arrival, Otake collected Johnny and took him to the 'special rooms'; the doors of which had been pulled off their hinges. The doorless hallways echoed with the voices of would-be homecomers being questioned before their journey by three men: one Japanese, one European and an interpreter. 'What is your name? How old are you? How old are your children? Is it your wish to leave Japan and spend the rest of your life in the Democratic People's Republic of Korea? Have you made this decision voluntarily? Without force or external pressure?'

As Johnny didn't have a passport, he was to emigrate as Otake's brother. On the form he had to fill in, he entered his nationality as North Korean. I eavesdropped on his interview, on the oath he swore, his answer that he wasn't being forced into emigrating but was embarking on the journey voluntarily. I didn't see him sign the Red Cross document or the exit papers, but I heard everything being stamped; the impact echoed off the walls. The next morning, I accompanied him to the medical room, where he was examined by a Japanese doctor and two nurses.

I tried to convince Johnny to tell the truth. I suggested confiding in the European, surely he couldn't be in cahoots with the Koreans, nor the Japanese, but Johnny just laughed at me and asked how, in what language was I intending to explain his situation, this horrendously complicated situation? He had made his bed, he said, and now he had to lie in it. I was astonished by how calm he was, how composed; it wasn't he who was the prisoner, but me. When the children began to sing General Kim Il-sung's song for the third time, I wanted to yell at them 'Be quiet, for God's sake be quiet!' but Johnny just hummed along.

He was to depart at dawn, he and the other two thousand passengers. In the middle of the night, he disappeared from the dormitory for a while; I can't say that I was happy when he returned. I had been hoping he had found an escape route. Instead, he pressed a piece of paper into my hand. We should agree on a code, he said. A code? I asked. He nodded. He would write to me, keep me updated on his adventure in North Korea. He smiled. So when should I ride in with the cavalry, I asked jokingly. He closed his eyes; pondered. If he mentioned his father, he answered.

'If I tell you how happy my father is.'

The last thing I remember is Johnny standing there by the railing. He lifts his hand but doesn't wave right away, he hesitates, as though this will delay the goodbye. I too merely lift my arm, hold it motionless in the air, I too want to suspend his departure. All of a sudden I spot a small, slender figure in a yellow headscarf, making her way slowly and resolutely through the crowd. Tomoko Lee stops next to Johnny, and tucks her arm through his.

Johnny gives a beaming smile. He pulls Tomoko close to him. He is happy. He kisses her. Again and again. They're happy. Now I'm laughing. I jump up and down and laugh, waving with both hands. He takes off her headscarf, waves it high above their heads. Then they are gone. I wait, hoping to see them one last time, one final time, but the *Tobolsk* doesn't grant me my wish.

19

Yunho fell silent; towards the end his voice had failed him, he'd had to clear his throat again and again, cough the sentences out of his mouth. Outside it was still light, the sun bathed the sky in a reddish yellow; he had managed to finish his story before the onset of darkness.

He said he was pleased that he didn't have to send me home at night, as he had the previous times, and pressed some money into my hand.

'For a taxi.'

I tried to give him back the banknotes, but he shook his head with a smile.

'So that it stays light.'

I said that the darkness didn't bother me, but he insisted, thrusting his hands demonstratively into his trouser pockets; all of a sudden, they seemed disproportionately big, as though his arms had neglected to grow into the broad palms and long fingers.

I reached for my rucksack. I wouldn't be coming back tomorrow, nor on the days that followed. Today was probably the last time I would see Yunho. Now I understood why he had told me the truth about Eve; precisely *because* we wouldn't see each other again. Confessing to a stranger like me was harmless, because the grammar of this society was unknown to me. I knew too little of it to punish the sinner, I wasn't even capable of gauging the true severity of the crime that Johnny,

Eve and Yunho had been mixed up in. Besides this, Yunho had made me his accomplice: by confiding in me, by my having believed his every word. 'Words,' says an old Korean proverb, 'become seeds.'

He turned towards the door.

'Wait.'

I had reached out to grab his shoulder, but only caught his arm.

'You haven't told me what happened after that. How did you come back to South Korea? What became of Johnny, and Eve? And what about Eiko?'

I shifted across to the other side of the couch, and he sat down next to me: for the first time, we were sitting next to one another, on the same level.

'I never heard from Johnny again. He had promised to write, and I to answer. We agreed on a code, remember. He was going to mention his father's happiness if I was supposed to rescue him . . .'

He smiled.

'We knew that the North Koreans censored the homecomers' letters.'

Yunho leant back with a sigh and clasped his hands in his lap.

'If he wrote that everything was wonderful and he couldn't wait for the arrival of my daughter and I—'

'The arrival of your daughter?'

'Yes, my daughter. Didn't I mention I have a daughter? An imaginary daughter?'

He laughed mischievously.

'Then I was *not* to board the next ship to Chŏngjin. The daughter was a warning.'

He looked down at the floor.

'I contemplated going with him, you know. To search for my brother in North Korea. Johnny stopped me. He said he would sound out the situation first, find out whether life in Pyongyang was worth living. He was going to tell me in encoded letters what things were like over there.'

Yunho tried to remember, to gather together the different threads of his perceptions from that time and see into his own mind. The present, unlike the past, is active, and and has a tendency to pervade what came before. This is the principle of memory; its elusiveness becomes evident once it has been cleansed of the remnants, the traces of Here and Now. He shook his head sadly; he had forgotten most of it.

'All I can remember is that pine trees stood for people. Healthy pine trees for happy people, sick pine trees for unhappiness and suffering. And he was going to mention a stray dog if he was being watched by the secret police.'

Yunho looked up.

'He didn't write. I went to the post office every day and checked. That's what we had agreed.'

He leant over to the coffee table and tapped a cigarette out of the pack.

'I have Johnny to thank that I never ended up in the People's Republic. In a way, he sacrificed himself for me. He went in my place. It would have been much more logical if I had gone to North Korea, with my communist brother.'

'You didn't go back to Seoul right away?'

He had hung around in Osaka for a while, he said, sleeping in wooden huts where hens used to nest. He tried his hand as an ice vendor, riding his bicycle through the neighbourhood in the early hours of the morning, selling blocks of ice to housewives. Some days he helped out in a factory or workshop, binding paintbrush bristles, sticking envelopes, cleaning shoes, selling newspapers, so that he could afford a night in a brothel, a night in the warmth where he could sleep straight through; most pimps made more money renting rooms than by renting whores. Eventually, he gave up waiting for news from Johnny and went home; immediately after his arrival he had to go underground.

'Why?'

'I arrived in Busan in 1961, which luckily was during the monsoon season. The heavy rain disguised things, and the humidity made people lethargic, inattentive.'

He lit himself another cigarette. Took a long drag.

'Park Chung-hee was in power.'

He smiled a hard, cynical smile.

'Eve finally had the president she had betrayed her friends for.'

Park had it in for communists, and Koreans arriving from Japan were put under particularly close surveillance. Yunho was lucky, he returned before the great wave of persecution in the 1970s, but even he was shadowed by a security official, a man in a suit, tie and trench coat, who made no effort whatsoever to conceal that he was a spy. Yunho made himself scarce; he had no desire to be interrogated or tortured. Nor did he wish to spend years vegetating in a tiny cell, awaiting a death sentence. His efforts to lead a life of invisibility eventually brought him back to the south-east of Korea, to his father's homeland. In Chilgok, a village which back then was small and nondescript, but today is a suburb of Daegu, he found work on a chicken farm. It was run by a curious collective: a group of former lepers.

The inhabitants of the colony were against taking him in, they harboured a strong resentment towards the healthy; the group had been persecuted not long before, and some of them murdered. But a nurse from Europe managed to talk them into being more tolerant and trusting – an Austrian, Emma. A tall, slender young woman with light-brown hair and silver glasses perched on her nose, who had arrived there, in the middle of nowhere, shortly before him, and liked the fact that he brought a little disorder into the community. Her Korean was soft and melodic; 'Japanese-sounding'.

Rice paddies as far as the eye can see; those who are permitted to cultivate them have drawn the winning lot, for they have work and money. They fear the creatures that live on the edge of the fields, whose bodies, it is said, have been possessed by evil spirits, disfiguring their faces. People avoid the colony, no one wants to get too close to 'the infected', the few doctors around refuse to treat 'the damned', there being no cure for a curse; even the agents and secret police steer clear of Chilgok, the place doesn't even appear on their map. The young nurse with the Japanese accent sets off every week with bandages, salves, creams and tinctures in her shoulder bag, wading through streams, fighting her way across the overgrown path to her patients, to save lives.

'The bulging shoulder bag became a mobile nursing station, the two pigs and five hens became numerous pig and egg farms. Only after a year did I realize that I had bribed the inhabitants of the surrounding villages with American flour in the name of the Catholic Church, so that they would stop sabotaging the construction of the first brick houses in the leper village. And so that they would accept the children of the sick into their schools.'

Today, he said, these villages have become towns. Soon they will be absorbed, swallowed up, by Daegu. These things happen quickly in South Korea, muttered Yunho, in the land

411

of economic miracle. When you considered the South Koreans' close ties to the Americans, the exploitation of workers continuing into the late 1980s and the country's participation in the Vietnam War, it was no wonder the world spoke of a 'miracle'.

He brushed the ash from his shirt.

'But we probably need miracles so we don't have to explain things.'

The record, *Solitude*, had come to an end.

How often during these last days had I heard the crackling which announced that the album was finishing, the brief rustle before the needle was lifted by the arm with a *tock*? What followed was a distant rushing sound, which didn't belong to the music, yet unleashed a sequence of movements, a choreography of words and actions; Yunho's voice would become quieter and quicker, he sounded more austere, more detached, as though it was a stranger's life he was analysing.

Whenever he had finished a part of his narrative, he got up; this upwards movement was accompanied by a short groan. He went into the kitchen, fetched a bottle of water, emptied out the ashtray, put another bowl of biscuits on the tray, then set it down on the living room table. He shuffled over to the record player, pushed the arm to the side, turned the record over and lowered the needle onto the outermost groove.

A gentle rustling and crackling started up once more, and we moved into the preparatory phase: Yunho sat down next to me on the carpet, crossed his legs, lit himself a cigarette and laid the open pack on the table. I leant back, made myself comfortable against the backrest and waited, my eyes closed, for the next part of the narrative, which always began with the same apology: that he had tired me out with his stories. I replied that it was just my eyes that were tired, they had been ever since my arrival in Seoul, but my mind was wide awake, and he answered with a smile: 'If your ears get sleepy, tell me.'

'East of the sun,' sang Billie Holiday; I had barely paid attention to her words, but now I heard them loud and clear. Involuntarily, I whispered.

'What happened to Eve?'

'Eve?'

Yunho stubbed out his cigarette. There wasn't much to tell, he said. After betraying him and Johnny, she slipped away. From that day on, she no longer existed, and it had felt as though she never had – like she had never been part of his life.

He had tried to forget her, had rejected every memory of her. But one day, just as suddenly as she had disappeared, she had resurfaced, little by little. First he had by chance found himself back in the alley where Cockatu's Dance School used to be. The windows, once caked with dust and dirt, were clean, glittering and gleaming, and the entrance was guarded by a doorman. Cockatu's establishment had been brought back to life, with a new name and a new pimp. In all those years, no one had taken any notice of the place, and one day it had suddenly reopened its doors; he almost expected to stumble into Cockatu, into cigarette-scrounging, joke-cracking Cockatu.

Next, he had overheard a conversation in a café; he hadn't meant to eavesdrop, but he was sitting directly behind the two men, a young Korean and a young American. They were talking in Korean, and seemed to have only just met, because they told each other their forenames. The American had said his name was Peter, or Paul, and the Korean introduced himself as John. He, Yunho, had been sitting with his back to

John. When he heard the name, he turned round, tapped the stranger on the shoulder and asked if he was really called John. The stranger replied that it was a Protestant forename, but he preferred it to his Korean one, because he taught at the university, and the foreigners could never remember Asian names. Peter or Paul had nodded fervently, and Yunho quickly headed off.

John hadn't resembled Johnny in the slightest, but he was wearing a black beret, and Yunho had remembered packing its double in Ikaino, so that his friend would have a piece of the certain past in his uncertain future.

He encountered Eve again fifteen years after their collective escape from Seoul; he had left the leper colony in 1975, after people had started to ask questions even there, especially about his time in the 'communists' den', Osaka. A year before, Park Chung-hee's wife had been assassinated in an attack intended for the dictator; to this day, unofficial sources claim that Park staged it in order to get rid of his wife. There were violent demonstrations at the time, and Park condemned all the protesting students as communist assassins, imposed sanctions on all the universities involved and had anyone who so much as behaved in a 'suspicious' way arrested. Yunho saw himself with no choice but to seek shelter in the anonymity of the cities; he found it in Seoul's slums.

By night he hid himself away, by day he looked for work, often keeping his head above water with small-scale trickery. One day, in a quiet corner of Jongno, he found a brand-new bench. He took possession of it, feeling like its owner. Like a king. He opened the newspaper, which he had swiped from a stranger's coat pocket, and discovered from the article on the front page that the eight men who had supposedly tried to overthrow the South Korean president at the behest of Kim Il-sung had been found guilty, and would be executed that same day – their corpses, that is, for their souls had already died a miserable death by torture.

He prepared himself to fly into a rage, just like he always did when he found out about some outrageous injustice, whether from the newspaper or the radio, and was looking forward to cursing loudly, a habit he had adopted through all the years when he was unable to confide in anyone, because the suspicion that he could be a terrorist had grown and grown. Suddenly, someone sat down on the other end of the bench, and he turned round to the intruder, to drive them away, with force if necessary . . .

It was Eve. She hadn't changed, not at first glance, but by the second he could see she had aged; she used more make-up, and the first traces, the lines and shadows, could be seen around her eyes.

She smiled at him, Yunho told me. She reached for his hand and squeezed it. Then she said his name, as though wanting to prove that she remembered him. Slowly and clearly. 'Yunho Kang.' He had no alias, no nickname. His name was simply Yunho. And what about her, he asked, what was she calling herself now? Still Eve Moon? She shook her head. What was a name anyway, she said, nothing but a disguise. She was glad he remembered her. He retorted that he had almost forgotten her. But only almost, she replied.

At that moment, an American man came over to them. He was tall, gangly, with the beginnings of a bald patch, and grey temples. She let go of Yunho's hand and said that this was her husband, Henry Lewis. Yunho nodded to him. Henry Lewis straightened his sunglasses. Eve said they had to make a move, they were leaving Seoul that evening, but she would be glad to receive news from him, did he have a card?

She asked Henry to hand over a business card, and wrote her telephone number and address on the back. She was living in the United States, she said, in Richmond, Virginia. He didn't have an address he could give her, so he wrote down the address of the post office which still exists in this neighbourhood today. No telephone number. She took his piece of paper and he her card, then Eve and Henry said goodbye to him. At the crossing, she turned round and called out that he mustn't forget to write, she had to know how he had been all these years.

Yunho shifted forwards to the edge of the sofa. He looked different on the couch, changed; he was no longer a small, frail Korean, but a gentleman who knew 'These Foolish Things' off by heart, humming along with the words, tapping his foot to the beat. He had spent a lot of time in jazz bars, he told me with a roguish grin, they were the best hiding places you could imagine. There was no politics there, no communism, no capitalism, no dictators, only music, 'Jazz jazz jazz!'

He laughed, clapped along loudly and jumped to his feet; he took my hands, pulled me up and spun me around. Our dance didn't fit Billie's song, but what did it matter, we were in a dimly lit, smoke-filled bar, the saxophonist playing his solo, the piano still holding back, tinkling softly in the background, and the percussion waiting to be deployed; during the drum solo, we made our best attempt at a tap dance.

Yunho bowed deeply and thanked me for the dance.

The time had come to go, and yet –

'I have one more question.'

He looked at me curiously.

'Yes?'

'What happened to Eiko? Was she ever found?'

He breathed out deeply. His face was flushed.

'No, I don't think so.'

While he was waiting for Johnny's letters from North Korea, he had kept an ear out for news, he said, but never heard anything definite.

'Shortly before I left Japan, the body of a young woman was found near the docks in Kobe, not far from Osaka. It was heavily decomposed. The police made a public appeal in an attempt to identify the dead woman. They suspected she was Korean, because inside the handbag found with her remains there was a note written in the Korean language.'

He gave a brief, loud cough.

'They were only able to decipher one word. "Pyongyang".'

Yunho looked at me thoughtfully. Slowly, he said he hoped things had gone better for Johnny, better than for the countless Korean Japanese who disappeared in North Korea in the 1970s and 1980s. Many ended up in labour camps, some were executed on the spot. Apparently the regime hadn't trusted the newcomers, at least that was what he had often read, but could these words really be believed? Everything was biased, everything was propaganda. Of the ninety thousand people who had emigrated to the Democratic People's Republic, there were sure to be some who had found the home they were searching for.

He cleared his throat. He was convinced that Johnny had been fortunate: that upon his arrival, which was ten years before the persecutions, he no longer had a past, but in its place a future. That he had managed to build a life in the North together with Tomoko – as a worker, a communist, a family man. As Mino Kim.

417

Yunho smiled. He preferred to believe that Johnny, Tomoko, Eiko and Yunsu had found and helped one another through famines, droughts and floods; that they had led and were still leading a happy life.

'Until their black hair is as grey as an onion's roots.'

His eyes, which had been sparkling a moment before, were once again still and clear. I nodded, put my bag over my shoulder and turned towards the door.

He held me back.

'Wait.'

He disappeared into the kitchen. I heard him open a box and close it again. When he came back, he had in his hand three small silver packets, and a pear. It was a Korean pear, he informed me; it had a tough but thin skin, and was native to the Daegu region, an indigenous inhabitant. It was so big, sweet and juicy that I would want to eat it at least twice, and these, he added, shaking the packets, I couldn't forget these either, they were chocolate cakes, Choco Pies. He didn't eat sweet things himself, sugar gave him toothache, but he regularly sent a box of them to North Korea. He had heard they were very popular there, not only as a snack, but for trading on the black market. 'Who knows,' he said, 'how many Choco Pies it takes to make a border guard interrupt his rounds.'

He winked at me.

'They're currency of a very special kind.'

I could come back any time, he added, he always had some in the house. I nodded and promised to visit him when I had eaten them all up. And the pear, he urged me. And the pear, I repeated. He extended his hand to say goodbye.

'Any time. You're always welcome.'

★

As I stepped outside, the light was fading . . .

Perhaps, though, it was the other way around. Perhaps the hours in which Yunho had spoken about the past had felt more immediate to me than the present, and it was the present that seemed to have passed by before it had even begun.

Above the roofs in the East, the moon came up; behind the church tower in the West, the sun went down.

Acknowledgements

I would like to thank everyone who, in countless conversations and interviews, has explained historical events and idiosyncrasies of Korean culture and history to me, as well as portraying their own personal experiences. Without their kindness, patience and assistance, this novel would not exist. In particular I would like to thank my family in Vienna, Seoul and Daejeon. My gratitude also goes to Fabrizio Bensi from the International Committee of the Red Cross in Geneva, Hyomi Kang in Osaka, Ryu and Eva Itose in Tokyo and Emma Freisinger in Chilgok, as well as the Seoul Art Space Yŏnhui.

Work on this novel was, to my great gratitude, supported by the Robert Musil Stipend from the Austrian Federal Ministry for Education, Arts and Culture.